THE TWINS

THE TWINS

TESSA DE LOO

Translated from the Dutch by
RUTH LEVITT

First published in The Netherlands by Uitgeverij De Arbeiderspers
as *De tweeling*, copyright © 1993 by Tessa De Loo

Translation copyright © 2000 by Ruth Levitt

Published in the United States by arrangement with
Arcadia Books, London by

Soho Press, Inc.
853 Broadway
New York, N.Y. 10003

The financial support of the Foundation for the Production and Translation of
Dutch Literature is gratefully acknowledged.

The following quotations are reprinted by permission of their respective pub-
lishers:
Karl Marx, *Capital*, translated from the third German edition of *Das Kapital*
by Samuel Moore and Edward Aveling and edited by Frederick Engels, Swan
Sonnenschein & Co. Ltd, 1896.
Friedrich Rückert: 'Kindertotenlieder' in *Penguin Book of Lieder*, translated by
S.S. Prawer, 1964.
Goethe's *Faust*, Part II, Act V translated by Louis MacNeice, Faber & Faber, 1951.

Library of Congress Cataloging-in-Publication Data

Loo, Tessa de.
[Tweeling. English]
The twins / Tessa de Loo ; translated from the Dutch by Ruth Levitt.
p. cm.
ISBN 1-56947-200-9 (alk. paper)
I. Levitt, Ruth.

PT5881.22.O524 T8513 2000
839.3'1364—dc21
00-020009

10 9 8 7 6 5 4 3 2 1

For my mother and Maria Hesse

Die Welt ist weit, die Welt ist schön,
wer weiss ob wir uns wiedersehen.

The world is wide, the world is beautiful,
who knows if we shall see each other again.

The translator warmly thanks
Rosemary Mitchell-Schuitevoerder and Jake Schuitevoerder
for their generous help

THE TWINS

PART 1

INTERBELLUM

1

GOODNESS ME, WHAT is this, a morgue?'
Lotte Goudriaan woke with a start from a pleasant doze
with a sense of numbness: to be old and yet not to feel your
body. Through her eyelashes she followed the rotund figure, naked
like herself under a dressing gown of innocuous pale blue, closing the
door noisily behind her. The woman waddled with evident distaste
into the dim resting room, between two rows of empty beds, up to the
one where Lotte was lying—her body between the pristine sheets an
old, long-drawn-out history of ill-health. Instinctively, she slid deeper
into the bed. The language the woman had made her inappropriate
remark in was German. German! What was a German doing here, in
Spa, where every square, every public garden, had a monument with
lists of the fallen of two world wars carved in stone? Her own country
was swarming with health resorts. Why Spa? Lotte closed her eyes
and tried to ignore the woman by forcing herself to concentrate on the
cooing of the doves that gathered, out of sight behind wrinkled white
silk blinds, on the eaves and in the courtyards of the Thermal Institute. But the German's every movement was a provocation in sound.
Quite audibly she pulled back the sheets on a bed directly opposite
Lotte's. She stretched herself out on it, yawned and sighed pointedly;
even when she finally lay still and seemed to surrender to the prescribed quiet, the silence she produced was painful on the ears. Lotte
swallowed. A feeling of tension was crawling up from her stomach to
her throat; a mental queasiness that had also come over her the previous day when she sat, up to her chin, in a peat bath.

While she had succumbed to the heat of the sour peat that relaxed
her stiff joints, an old nursery rhyme, hummed in an elderly woman's
unsteady mezzo, floated into the room through a crack in the door
from a neighboring bathroom. This song, which penetrated her
awareness for the first time in seventy years, released a vague mixture
of anxiety and irritation—feelings an aged patient ought to guard

against in a peat bath at forty degrees Celsius. A heart attack was lurking in the brown sludge, between the lumps and granules and half-
decayed twigs that drifted about. All of a sudden she could not bear
the heat anymore. She heaved herself up laboriously until she was
standing shakily in the metal bathtub, her body covered in a film of
liquid chocolate that evened out all irregularities. As though I were
already dead and buried, she thought. When she realized that her state
would give the woman who was coming to rinse her down a foolish,
alarming impression, she sagged slowly at the knees, back into the
sludge, holding tightly onto the edge of the bath with both hands. The
song stopped at that very moment, as abruptly as it had started, as
though it were no more than the flicker of a memory presumed lost.

The German could not tolerate being in bed for long. After a few
minutes she shuffled across the worn parquet floor again, towards a
table with two bottles of mineral water beside a stack of plastic
beakers. Lotte followed her actions intently, despite herself, as though
she had to keep on her guard.

'*Excusez moi, madame . . .*' With a slight inflection, in ponderous
school French, the woman turned unexpectedly to Lotte. '*C'est permis . . .* for us . . . to drink this water?'

The story that follows probably would not have happened if Lotte
had also replied in French. But on a reckless impulse she said, 'Yes,
das Wasser können Sie trinken.'

'*Ach so!*' The woman forgot the water, retraced her steps to Lotte's
bed, exclaiming delightedly, 'You're German!'

'No, yes, no . . .' Lotte stammered. But she had already lit the fuse;
crackling softly, the woman was coming towards her. Everything
about her was broad, round and curved, an elderly Walküre who
would not go away. She stood at the foot of Lotte's bed, casting a
shadow over it. She looked candidly at her, 'Where are you from, if I
might ask?' Lotte tried to retract her impulsiveness, 'From Holland.'
'But your German is faultless!' the woman insisted, spreading her
plump hands. 'From Cologne originally,' Lotte conceded, in the flat
tone of a forced admission. 'Cologne! But that's where I'm from too!'

Cologne, Köln. As the name of the city continued to resonate in
the rest room that had never known anything other than absolute

silence inside its walls, it occurred to Lotte for a moment that Cologne was a cursed city, somewhere you were better off not to have come from, a city totally annihilated to punish the arrogance of a people.

The door opened. A preoccupied, middle-aged man shambled in; he selected a bed and slid noiselessly between the sheets. In the dim light, only his death mask remained vaguely visible. Everything was as it had been again, except for the German. She leaned over and whispered, 'I'll wait for you in the lobby.'

Lotte stayed behind, the victim of confusion and irritation. That sounded like an order: I'll wait for you! She decided to disobey it. But the longer she lay there the more restless she became. The pushy German had somehow succeeded in depriving her of her hard-won calm. There was no escaping her: there was only one door out of the rest room and it opened onto the lobby.

Finally she got out of bed brusquely, slid into her slippers, tied her belt tightly round her middle and walked to the door, resolved to shake the woman off as quickly as possible. Entering the lobby, which was bathed in light, was like setting foot inside a temple dedicated to the goddess of health. The floor, laid diagonally with large tiles of broken white marble, together with an open atrium that gave an uninterrupted view of the balustrade on the first floor, created an illusion of expansiveness. This was reinforced by a ceiling painting of a fondant-colored Venus ringed by plump cherubim driving out of the sea in a shell. And there was the constant sound of running water from two grey-brown-veined marble fountains on either side of the lobby, flanked by robust Greek pillars. A glittering spout emerged from a gilded female head, like a protruding tongue dribbling a thin trickle of water. One fountain, discolored brown from the iron-bearing water that in better days the rich aristocracy of Europe had sought as a cure for their anaemia, was directly connected to the Source de la Reine; the other, to the Source Marie-Henriette, a spring from which flowed velvet-soft water that drove all toxins out of the body.

The elderly German had appropriated an antique chair for herself in this sanctuary of eternal youth. She was waiting for Lotte, turning the pages of a magazine, sipping a glass of spring water. Lotte approached reluctantly with the excuse, 'I'm sorry, I'm pressed for time.' The woman squeezed herself out of the austerely carved Empire-style chair. A pained expression skimmed over her face. 'Listen, listen,' she said, 'you're from Cologne. So I must just ask you what street you lived in.' Lotte sought support from one of the pillars; the ridges pressed through the towelling into her back. 'I can't remember. I was six when they sent me to Holland.'

'Six,' the woman repeated excitedly, 'six!'

'All I remember,' said Lotte hesitantly, 'is that we lived in a casino . . . or in a building that had once been a casino.'

'It can't be true! It can't be true!' The German's voice broke, she brought her hands to her head and pushed her fingertips against her temples. 'It can't be true!' Her irreverent bellowing filled the empty space, it echoed off the marble floor, rose up to disturb the peaceful scene on the ceiling. She stared at Lotte with wide eyes. With horror? With joy? Had she gone mad? She opened her arms, came right up to Lotte and hugged her. 'Lottchen,' she moaned, 'don't you understand? Don't you understand?' Lotte was overcome by dizziness, crushed between the pillar and the German's body. She felt an intense desire to escape from this preposterous intimacy, to go up in steam, to evaporate. But she was caught between her origins and her selective memory, which had long ago entered into a hostile alliance. 'You. . . . *meine Liebe*,' the woman said in her ear, 'I am Anna, the very same!'

THE MAGIC LANTERN of the early twentieth century leaves a lot to the imagination. The gap between the projection of one slide and another has to be filled in by the observers themselves. They are shown a Jugendstil bay window on a first floor overlooking the street. Two noses press flat against the glass, two pairs of eyes anxiously scrutinize the passers-by down below. All women look the same from above, hats on their pinned-up hair, long fitted coats with small buttons, lace-up boots. But only one of them is clutching a small shiny aluminum cashbox under her arm. They see her at the end of each day on the opposite side of the street; she shuts the double doors of Hope behind her and crosses with the day's taking in the cashbox. As soon as she comes home the girls lose interest in the cashbox; they cling to their mother. First, she has to undo a million buttons before she can lift them onto her lap. On rare occasions they are allowed to go to the shop with her; its name tells the passer-by that it is a socialist co-operative. Their mother, enthroned like a queen behind the high brown cash desk, fetches a chocolate marshmallow out of a cardboard box for them; she is the linchpin of all money transactions. Takings have doubled since she has been at the cash desk. She is intelligent, hardworking and trustworthy. She is also ill. But no one knows that yet. The illness is slowly taking hold of her even though on the outside she continues to look like a plump, blond Westphalian.

Another slide is placed in the projector—carefully—they have to be kept in proper sequence. The girls only go inside one particular room in the house with their father. Its permanent twilight is saturated with a bittersweet smell. Their mother is lying in an oak bedstead—a stranger with sunken cheeks and blue shadows under her eyes—beneath a malevolent engraving of black rocks and spindly spruces. They recoil from the despairing, resigned smile that appears on her face as they approach. Their father, who gently pushes them towards the bedstead each time, himself one day lies on an improvised bed in the living room. He instructs them to be as quiet as mice because he is ill and must sleep. Dejected, they sit next to each other on the sofa in the bay with their chins on the windowsill and look down—expecting the cashbox to appear in spite of the woman lying beneath the rocky landscape, to put an end to the strained silence. It is gradually growing dark. They have no sense of time; for them its passing is the same as the failure of the cashbox to appear. Then the bell rings hesitantly. They rush to the door. Anna always has to be the first, driven instinctively since birth; she stands on tiptoe and slides the bolt open. 'Aunt Käthe, Aunt Käthe,' she clings to her, 'have you come to fetch us?' 'Have you come to fetch us?' Lotte echoes.

The next slide suggests the projector is going to saddle us with a maudlin tale. There is a rectangular coffin on the sofa and Anna and Lotte are sitting on top of it, with their backs to a room full of unfamiliar relatives. Thanks to the coffin they can put their feet on the windowsill. They have discovered that they can drown out the wail-

ing and muttering by tapping the soles of their shoes against the window—the eerie black polished shoes that Aunt Käthe got for them—
at the same time they are kicking out at this incomprehensible
impediment to their vital existence and trying to restore everything to
normal again. Initially those present are inclined to be tolerant. After
all, there are no rules of conduct for three-year-olds who have lost
their mother but when the tapping persists and the girls remain deaf
to friendly warnings, forbearance turns into annoyance. Doesn't the
foot tapping have something about it of the primitive drum-roll that
according to the illustrated magazines, accompanies the bushmen in
Africa on the last journey to their deaths? A modicum of Christian
piety might reasonably be expected of the children in these circumstances. They are ordered off the coffin but they refuse stubbornly,
lashing out at the hands of those who want to lift them from it. Only
when the undertaker's men arrive in their sinister outfits and begin to
haul the coffin away do they allow themselves be taken in hand by
Aunt Käthe. After that, they behave in an exemplary manner, apart
from a small incident, in the long procession that shuffles behind the
bier beneath an unseemly warm spring sun. Aunt Käthe realizes in the
nick of time that they should take off their black woolen coats, which
their mother had sewn, in bed, specially for this occasion. The condition of her body caused her to underestimate the season.

The principal absentee from the funeral is in the hospital. Every
evening at half past seven Aunt Käthe positions herself opposite
one of the walls at the side, holding hands with each child. Then a
face appears in one of the many windows, just clear enough to convince Anna and Lotte that he has not been swallowed up into nothingness in the same treacherous way their mother was. They wave
and he waves back with a large white hand that passes back and
forth in front of his face as though he wants to wipe himself out.
Afterwards they go to sleep reassured. He comes home one day,
thinner and drawn. When they climb up to hug him he puts them
back on the ground with an embarrassed, melancholy laugh. 'I
mustn't kiss you,' he says weakly, 'otherwise you'll also become
sick.'

The slides acquire a more cheerful character. He resumes his occupation as the manager of a socialist institute, located in the former casino, which serves workers who want to liberate themselves from their ignorance. 'Knowledge is power' it says in Gothic letters above the library entrance. There is hardly any demarcation line between their home on the first floor and the rest of the building. Anna and Lotte, growing up by a happy turn of fate just like the caretaker's children in this proletarian palace of culture, play tag in the wide marble corridors, hide behind sturdy pillars and in the wings of the stage, play leapfrog in the immense circular hall, where their shrieks rise up to a high stained-glass window that coats them with carmine red and peacock blue when the sun shines through it. Lotte has discovered the acoustics; she stands directly beneath the highest point in the arched ceiling, throws her head back and sings the Cologne slow-tram song. Anna, by nature too restless to be able to stand still, and urged on by the boy from next door, uses a satin-upholstered Biedermeier couch as a trampoline until the springs begin to squeak and, dizzy from jumping, she falls, grazing her mouth on the mahogany arm rest. The couch is in the foyer, which still shows off its worldly *fin de siècle* luxury. Chandeliers hang from a gilded, flaking ceiling above a richly ornamented refreshment bar with copper taps. Dozens of stained mirrors hang round about and still reflect the compulsive gambling in the eyes of the old-money elite and their parasites, as well as a girl's face with a bleeding lip staining it red. Her father has strictly forbidden access to this room. Contrite, she rushes to his office. With her wounded upper lip, she is at the mercy of his inquiring gaze. 'What happened?' he asks, his index finger under her chin. She invents a lie on the spur of the moment. Spontaneously she creates a different situation, so readily available to her that it already seems instantly more plausible than the truth. With downcast eyes she confesses: while she was playing in the garden she fell against the edge of the wooden table on the grass. After he has staunched the blood quite equably, he takes her to the garden with him. 'So,' he says, 'let's see how it happened.' The treachery of the lie now dawns on her: the garden table is so high that a girl of her stature would have to fall straight down from the sky in order to be able to strike her upper lip on its edge. '*Ach* soooo . . .' says her father in a melodious tone—a melody that makes her suspicious. Between thumb and forefinger, he pinches a piece of skin on her bare upper arm and it gives her a pins-and-needles feeling. It is the only punishment she still remembers years later, a punishment that condemns her all her life to a stubborn preference for the truth.

But her wildness does not submit to being reined in so easily. Soon after, she breaks her elbow in a romp on the marble stairs in the hall. She rants and raves like a hysterical countess who has gambled away all her possessions, backed up by Lotte, whose capacity to feel pain and panic extends symbiotically to her sister's body. A plaster cast is fitted and the arm is hung in a sling. Lotte bursts into tears again when Anna comes out of hospital thus adorned. No one knows whether it is from solidarity or jealousy. She only calms down when her own left arm is hung in an imitation sling improvised with a tea towel.

Now a Christmas slide. Once Aunt Käthe had taken pity on the children she never left them. Their father married her quietly, to avoid being forced to be separated from them after he was discharged from hospital because no medical intervention could alter the clinical picture of his prognosis: a man with an infectious disease that could only be influenced by time, for good or ill, was regarded as not suited to bringing up children. To Anna and Lotte it goes without saying. Aunt Käthe is there as usual and is decorating a snow-clad tree in the room; all the branches bend under an anarchy of witches, Father Christmases, chimney sweeps, snowmen, dwarves and angels. The pungent smell of evergreen branches mixed with resin gives them a foretaste of the natural world that begins where Cologne ends. Their father's youngest brother, Heinrich, a bony youth of seventeen, has come from his village on the edge of the Teutoburger Wald to celebrate the festival of the tree with them. He, too, has brought natural aromas into the house: hay and pig manure, spiced with a dash of rising damp. His image as a young, jovial uncle smashes to smithereens when, out of petulance, he garbles the words of the Christmas carols they are singing. His brother joins in with him, grinning. Suddenly they are competing with each to find meaningless rhymes. 'Don't, don't,' Anna screams, horrified, hammering on her father's chest, 'the

carol doesn't go like that!' But the men laugh at her for her ortho-
doxy and surpass themselves in inventiveness. Anna sings in a trembling voice in a vain attempt to get the proper version to triumph,
then runs despairingly into the kitchen, where Aunt Käthe is slicing
bread. 'They are ruining the Christmas carol,' she cries, 'Daddy and
Uncle Heini.' Aunt Käthe enters the room like a goddess of
vengeance. 'What have you done to that child?' Anna is picked up
and calmed: handkerchiefs, a glass of water. 'It was only a little joke,'
soothes her father, 'the Christmas child was born nineteen hundred
and twenty-one years ago, now that's a good reason to be happy.' He
sits her on his knee and straightens the large bow on her head which
had become crooked in the confusion. 'I'll teach you a proper song,'
he says, 'listen!' In a hoarse voice, now and then interrupted by a
cough, he sings the melancholy song 'Two Grenadiers marched to
France, they had been caught in Russia . . .'

The magic lantern projects a stage; the scenery is a forest of tall
tree trunks. The theatre director is in search of a short actress; she
must not be more than a metre tall. 'Listen, Herr Bamberg,' he says,
'I'm looking for a girl who can take the part of a poor child who has
gotten lost in the wood. Now I'm thinking of one of your daughters . . .' 'Which of the two did you have in mind?' 'Who is the eldest?' 'They're the same age!' 'Ah, twins . . . curious. . . .' 'Whom did
you have in mind?' the father repeats. 'Well, I'd thought . . . the one
with the darker hair. The blonde seems too plump to play a starving
child.' 'But Anna would never forget her lines.' Their father fingers
his moustache proudly. 'She is . . . remarkable in that respect.' Mindful of the exhortation above the library door, he usually dedicates his
free evenings to classical writers and poets. In between times, as a
playful experiment, he has taught her a poem. 'Our Anna,' he
explains, 'has the memory of a parrot. She can recite Schiller's "The
Song of the Bell" without missing a line.' 'Good,' the director capitu-
lates, 'you're the father, you can judge better than I.'

'I don't approve,' demurs Aunt Käthe, 'the child is still too young
for such a performance.' But there is no gainsaying this father's ambi-
tion. So there Käthe sits on the day of the performance, flanked by
her seven sisters, with Lotte and her father beaming in the front row.

In the wings, the wardrobe mistress hides Anna's dress under a grey, worm-eaten winter coat and ties her white hair ribbon loosely to the belt. Without suspecting that it is a dress rehearsal for reality, that she is going to interpret this role for ten years without an audience, without applause, Anna presents such a believable, pitiful child on-stage that tears prick the step-aunts' eyes. After two men in hunting suits have carried Anna off between them out of the imaginary forest, she peeps inquisitively into the hall from the wings. The audience, no more than a collection of heads, does not interest her. She sees but one face in the semi-darkness, raised up towards the stage, that of the smallest person in the hall, insignificant and nondescript between the adults. Anna stares at her, overcome by an unfamiliar, terrifying sensation. For the first time she and Lotte exist as two individuals, separate from each other, due to the play and her role in it. Each with a particular point of view—Lotte from the hall, herself from the stage. This awareness of separation, of unwanted duality, suddenly upsets her and she storms diagonally across the stage, through the two lovers' reconciliation scene—the unbuttoned pauper's coat flaps round her and the belt with her hair ribbon slips backwards and onto the floor. Aunt Käthe's youngest sister cries excitedly in Cologne dialect, 'Ach, look at the little one!' A roar of laughter breaks out in the hall. There is applause, as though it is the director's stroke of genius. Unperturbed, Anna jumps down from the stage. She goes straight over to Lotte and only calms down when she has wormed herself in next to her on the same seat.

The projector, like a moonbeam, illuminates a bed with pale blue sheets. Beneath them, Anna and Lotte fall asleep at night, their limbs firmly intertwined like mating octopuses. The night tactfully unties this knot without their noticing so that, by morning, each wakes up on her side of the bed, their backs touching.

The magic lantern has access everywhere—it shows us a classroom. It is as though we can hear the scratching of the dip pens. Anna's passionate temperament does not lend itself to calligraphy. Whereas Lotte appropriates the alphabet with a steady hand, the letters will not obey Anna. After school, Anna sits next to her father in the office and scratches letters on her slate, which he keeps wiping off saying, 'Once again, no good,' until she comes up to his standard. From time to time, he goes over to spit into a blue bottle that is then closed tight so that the angry spirits can't escape. Afterwards, as a reward for her efforts, she is allowed to help with the cash. She deals tattered inflation notes into piles of ten with swift fingers—the balance runs into billions—until a fiery rash on her fingertips brings this pastime to a close.

Every Monday morning before lessons begin, the teacher pierces the pupils with her gaze and asks in an insinuating tone, 'Which of you was not in church yesterday?' Silence prevails, nobody stirs, until Anna raises her finger. 'Me.' Immediately Lotte's higher, brighter voice follows, 'Me too.' 'Then you are the devil's children,' decrees the mistress knowingly. The sisters see their excommunication reflected in the other children's eyes. 'But you are still far too young,' their father protests when they inform him of their obligation to attend children's mass on Sunday mornings, 'you wouldn't understand a word of it.' They have never seen either him or Aunt Käthe inside a church. Each Sunday they implore him; they can no longer bear the annihilating look of the teacher nor their classmates' teasing. Finally he puts his mug of beaten egg down on the table and rests his hands on their shoulders. 'Tomorrow,' he promises, 'I'll go to school with you.'

But when they are on the way, one on each side, it seems more as though they have to protect their father, so feverish and fragile does he look in the black coat that sways roomily about his thin figure. Leaning heavily on his stick, he has to pause every ten steps to catch his breath. The tap of the stick on the cobbles echoes behind him—a chain of echoes that prevents him from falling. They go inside the school building; he gestures to them to wait for him in the corridor and knocks on the classroom door. The mistress, thoroughly unsettled by the unusual interruption, invites him in with forced courtesy. Leaning side by side against the wall, Anna and Lotte fix their gazes on the door and listen. Suddenly their father's hoarse voice lashes out above that of the mistress, who is struggling to maintain self-control. 'How dare you! To children who are weaker than you.' Anna and Lotte look at each other dumbfounded. They straighten their backs; they no longer need to lean against the wall. A delightful, defiant strength flows through them. Proud, triumphant, self-assured—they cannot put a name to it but it is there. Thanks to him.

The door swings open. 'Come in,' he says, suppressing his coughing. Anna crosses the threshold first, quickly followed by Lotte. They stand by the blackboard. The mistress is not lying on the floor in small pieces. Yet it looks as though her spine has snapped in several places. With bowed head and sagging shoulders, she grips her desk. The pupils, motionless on the benches, look up at their father shyly and respectfully, his stage management is faultless. 'Right,' he pushes Anna and Lotte gently towards the teacher, 'and now apologize to my daughters, and that goes for the whole class.' The mistress eyes them obliquely. Her gaze immediately slides away again, as though it has come into contact with something unclean. 'I am sorry for what I said to you,' she says without feeling. 'It won't happen again.' A silence falls. What now? Could anything be added to the mistress's humiliation? 'And now I'm taking them home with me,' they hear their father's voice above them, 'but they will be here again tomorrow. If I hear of anything like this ever again I shall be back.'

Fortunately the mistress kept the promise that had been exacted from her, because he would not have been able to carry out his threat. He is already much less able to cope with the trench warfare raging in his lungs. A new slide: he deals with his administrative work stretched out on the sofa like a romantic poet, wheezing. In between, he receives friends who carefully hide their concern behind cheery chatter—his promising daughters in checked dresses with white starched collars are a welcome distraction with their poems and songs. That Lotte's song is interrupted as many as three times by a dry cough alarms no one except Aunt Käthe. Experience having taught her to be suspicious, she has Lotte examined by the family doctor. For several minutes he taps her thin chest, simultaneously bringing the stethoscope and his moustache close to her pale skin. He asks her to cough, which she does very easily, as though she has practised the cough like a song. 'I'm not happy about it,' he murmurs behind her, 'I hear a weak sound in the right lung.' Lotte stands in front of an anatomical dummy and fingers the pink heart with a slight shiver. With a bottle of cough syrup and an appointment for X-rays, he lets them go.

In the next dusky gold-yellow slide, we see not only the father's declining days but also the family's. From the casino the same influence emanates as when gambling was still going on there: all or nothing, to the death. It was a building one entered full of expectations and left ruined, an alchemical trick whose secret recipe was kept safe within its four walls. He beckons his daughters over to him with his long, thin index finger. He sits on the edge of the sofa breathing heavily. 'Listen,' he says slowly, as though speaking with a thick tongue, 'how long do you think I've got to live?' Anna and Lotte frown—this is a sum of astronomical numbers. 'Twenty years!' Anna bets. 'Thirty!' Lotte adds a little extra. 'So, that's what you think,' he says indulgently. He looks at them, his mouth open, with feverish, glancing eyes, as though he wants to say something else, but then he is overcome by a rasping coughing fit and drives them away with a fluttering hand.

A few days later, as soon as they come back from school, they are led to the bedroom by Aunt Käthe. The house smells of red cabbage with apples and cinnamon. The company in a circle round their father's bed contrasts unpleasantly with this spicy-sweet smell. Uncle Heinrich, a crumpled cap in his hands which are crossed in front of his belly, stares at his sleeping brother with a farmer's distrust. Is this such a special spectacle that they must stand there, with all of them, to look? Aunt Käthe pushes Anna and Lotte towards the bed. 'Johann,' she says, bringing her mouth close to his ear, 'here are the children.' When he discovers his daughters, his eyes begin to shine as though he is surreptitiously amused by the ridiculous play-acting around his bed. He will get up immediately, Lotte thinks, and send them all home. But then his mood changes. His gaze goes agitatedly from one to the other; he raises his perspiring head—from his secret inner world he seems to want to say something to them that cannot be delayed. 'Anneliese . . .' he utters. Immediately his head falls back onto the pillow and he sinks away again. On the sunken cheeks there is the dark bloom of stubble. 'Why does he say Anneliese to us?' asks Anna offended. 'He's thinking of your mother,' says Aunt Käthe.

After supper, one of the seven sisters takes them away from the celebration that is not really a celebration. They are put into an unfamiliar bed, a raft on a strange ocean, which they can only prevent from sinking by hugging each other fervently and lying without budging exactly in the middle of the bed. In the night, they dream that Aunt Käthe wakes them up and kisses them with a wet face, but when they do wake in the morning she is nowhere to be seen. Seven pairs of hands get Anna and Lotte out of bed and lift them onto a chair, to make it easier to dress them. 'Your father,' remarks one of the seven women, pulling on an underslip, 'died in the night.' At first the communication does not produce any reaction, but during the laborious lacing-up of the boots Anna sighs, 'Then he won't have to cough anymore.' 'And won't have any more pain in his chest,' Lotte backs her up.

The last slide shows the farewell. The funeral is invisible, as is the constant dreadful 'curtseying' that is expected of the girls on this occasion. Also invisible are the rows, Aunt Käthe's tears, her threat of legal action, and the packed suitcases. The last Lotte sees of Anna: she is standing halfway down the staircase in the hall, surrounded by the members of the family who have come from afar. To one side, already cast off, stands Aunt Käthe, the traces of futile lamentations on her face. Anna is full of self-confidence, in her mourning dress, with a large black bow settled like a crow in her blonde hair. Next to her stands the uncle who made fun of the Christmas carols; on the other side an aunt with a bust of intriguing dimensions, on which a golden cross rests, glittering. Several unclear figures without distinctive features complete the row. Behind Anna, his bony hands on her shoulders as though he has already appropriated her, stands a stiff old man in a worsted suit with a ragged moustache and a rampant growth of tufts of withered grass sticking out of his ears. The last Anna sees of Lotte: she is already by the door, right under the stained-glass window. Only from her face can you tell who it is, the rest of her is thickly wrapped up as though she is going on a polar expedition. Next to her is a stylish old lady leaning on an umbrella, thin leather gloves loose between her fingers, wearing an elegant hat with a veil. All day she has addressed the old man, whose hands press heavily on Anna's shoulders, in a superior, teasing tone of voice, as *'Lieber Bulli'*.

Neither Anna nor Lotte are worried. They do not throw themselves into each other's arms, they do not cry, they do not say goodbye in any way whatsoever—how could they; they have no notion of the phenomenon of distance in space and time. The only one who takes care to make the slightest gesture towards showing the appropriate pathos of farewell is Aunt Käthe, who dashes across the hall at the last moment and, in a torrent of tears, presses Lotte to her breast.

2

'*J'AI RETROUVÉE MA soeur, madame!*' Anna accosted a passing Spa guest who shrank back horrified. Lotte recognized with distaste the impetuosity and clamorousness of long, long ago.

'It's unbelievable!' Anna grasped her by her shoulders and stroked her arms. 'Let me look at you.'

Every muscle in Lotte's body braced itself. To have to be inspected now as well! Such familiarity provoked her repugnance—but she was being sucked in and lacked the strength to resist. To have been born virtually simultaneously from the same mother seventy-four years ago was not something she could walk away from, however sophisticated the mechanism of repression she had developed over half a century. Two shrewd, light blue eyes were looking her over curiously and somewhat ironically.

'You've turned into a real lady,' Anna decreed. 'Still so slim with that pinned-up hair . . . *sehr schön*, I must say.'

Lotte regarded Anna's opulent form and short hair with reserve; it suggested something youthful and self-willed about her.

'I never managed that,' said Anna with a laugh that resounded with self-deprecation as well as pride. She squeezed Lotte's arm, brought her face close, a shining, determined look in her eye. 'And you have Daddy's nose, *wunderbar!*'

'How . . . did you come to be here?' Cornered, Lotte deflected her. Anna let go of her, thank God.

'I've got arthritis. The body's entire locomotion system is worn out, you see.' She pointed to her knees, her hips. 'Someone told me about the peat baths at Spa—it's not far from Cologne. And you?'

Lotte hesitated, anticipating that what she was going to say would please her sister. 'Arthritis, too,' she mumbled.

'It must be a family complaint!' Anna cried enthusiastically. 'Listen, let's go and sit somewhere. I can't stand up for so long.'

There was nothing to be done. Something inevitable had commenced; resistance was of no avail.

'*Meine Schwester*, just imagine it!' Anna rejoiced, halfway along the corridor. An old man dozing on a bench by the wall jolted upright, his bony hands clasping his stick.

Carrying cups of coffee from a machine, they went into the lounge, which was dominated by a bold painting of a young woman in the company of a swan. By the time Lotte was comfortably seated and had drunk a few mouthfuls of coffee she regained some of her former equanimity.

'Who would have thought we'd ever see each other again . . .' Anna shook her head. 'And in such an extraordinary spot too . . . that must have a deeper meaning.'

Lotte squeezed the plastic beaker. She did not believe in deeper meanings, only in dumb coincidence—and this one considerably embarrassed her.

Anna did not know where to start. 'Are the peat baths doing you any good?'

'I've only been here three days,' Lotte vacillated. 'The only effect so far is a leaden tiredness.'

'That's the toxins coming out.' Anna assumed an annoyingly professional tone. Suddenly she bounced up. 'Do you still remember our bathtub in Cologne? With lion's feet? In the kitchen?'

Lotte frowned. Another bath was what came to her mind. She gazed outside contemplatively, where a wintry sun gave the buildings a naked look. 'Every Saturday evening my father washed us one by one in a washtub.'

'Your father?'

'My Dutch father.' Lotte smiled uneasily.

'What was he like . . . I mean, what sort of people . . . As a child I imagined all kinds of . . .' Anna groped in the air with her hands. 'Because I knew absolutely nothing, I made it up in my own fashion . . . I dreamed of calling on you . . . You have no idea how hard it was not to hear anything from you . . . Everyone behaved as though you didn't exist . . . So, anyway, what kind of people were they?'

Lotte pursued her lips. The idea of raking up old memories emitted a dubious attraction. They were lying deeply stashed away in a corner of her mind, under a thick layer of cobwebs. Wasn't it better to let them be than to go poking about there? Yet they were a part of herself; there was something tempting about bringing them to life in such improbable surroundings as the Thermal Institute, going after them at Anna's request. Challenged by the absurdity of it, even the immorality, she half closed her eyes and began to murmur softly to herself.

ON SATURDAY EVENING he scrubbed his four daughters clean in a washtub filled with warm soapsuds, growling, 'Sit still!' while his wife was taking advantage of the late shopping hours. The ritual was rounded off with a glass of warm milk; he whistled as he brought it to the boil. Four nighties, eight naked feet—sipping as slowly as possible to spin out the time. After he had accepted four goodnight kisses he resolutely sent them to bed. In summer the scenario worked differently. Then a group of older girls from the village gathered on the grass in front of the house in the rising mist to do rhythmic gymnastics on the overgrown football pitch. The silhouette of a delivery van was outlined against the red sky, churning up clouds of dust along the sandy path as it approached. It came to a halt at the entrance to the field, the back door was opened, and then the miracle was performed that took Lotte's breath away every Saturday evening: muscular arms hauled a piano out and placed it in a strategic position in the field amid buttercups and sorrel. Then a young man in an off-white summer suit sat down at the piano and launched classical melodies at marching pace into the evening sky.

The girls from the gymnastics club kicked their legs high and bent backwards; they stood on their toes with their arms stretched over their heads as though they had landed on the ground all together with invisible parachutes. All to the pianist's inexorable quadruple time. Mies, Maria, Jet and Lotte, still warm from the bath, observed the spectacle from the edge of the fence until they saw their mother looming up in the distance, erect on her Gazelle bicycle, its handlebars seeming to sag under the weight of bulging shopping bags.

No bath for Anna. Soon after her arrival at the ancestral farm on the Lippe, it turned out that baths were regarded as an exceptional, generally mistrusted activity. Immediately after the journey her grandfather sank into his usual chair, resting his socks on the edge of the cast-iron stove—an acrid smell of mould filled the small, cluttered living room—he was to die without his pale chest ever having been defiled by a piece of soap. 'I want a bath,' Anna whined. Softened by the stubbornness with which her niece stuck to her principles, Aunt Liesl put a large kettle of water on the fire and filled a washtub set on the flagstone floor. Thus was the tone set for a long-lasting habit, which Anna maintained singlehandedly after Aunt Liesl had left the house. Years later, when she began to lock the door for the process, Uncle Heinrich rattled the handle and called with a titillated laugh, 'You must be absolutely filthy if you have to make such a fuss.'

The village children were thoroughly suspicious of her town manners and cultured accent. They pinned a note to the back of her coat: Go away! She was outstanding at school—her classmates observed her triumphs with a mixture of fear and envy, and shunned her company. She gradually realized that to be dead meant that someone would always be absent from now on and could not be brought back, even by your fervent longing, to make short work of your tormentors with his powerful presence. According to this definition, Lotte was dead too. Anna kept hammering away, asking to rejoin Lotte, circling around her grandfather until he said viciously, 'Don't be so impatient! If she doesn't recover properly she'll die too. Is that what you want by any chance?' Desperately she turned to Aunt Liesl, who was spinning and said in a thin high voice '*Ich weiss nicht*, what's sup-

posed to happen . . . . ' Her sagging bosom rocked in time to the
wheel's movement. Above her head hung a print that the family had
received as a gift during the war when a son had been killed in action.
'There is no greater love than to lay down your life for your country'
was written in decorative letters beneath a dying soldier and an angel
who held out to him the palm of victory. Anna slunk off outside in
the vague hope that Uncle Heinrich could shed some light on the
question. But he was sitting on the WC in the back garden, in a
wooden hut painted dark green, tall and narrow, and lopsided. The
door had a heart shape sawn out of it; it stood wide open. He was sitting sprawled out, involved in conversation with a neighbour, who
was engaged in the same activity on the other side of a field of man-
gel wurzels, also with the door open. The tête-à-tête concerned the
shooting match and girls—Anna did not hazard this rifle range.

She trudged despondently to the river, crossed the bridge and stood
with shoulders drooping in front of a shrine to the Virgin, in the
shadow of an overhanging elderberry. Someone had put a bunch of
dark red peonies at the base of the statue. The mother was looking
down devotedly on her child, a mysterious, hidden intimacy suggesting that the stares of the curious were being ignored. Anna had the
impulse to upset this introspection and to damage that pious face.
Instead, she tugged the flowers out of the vase, ran onto the bridge
with them and with an angry toss of the wrist threw them into the
Lippe. She looked at them as they slowly floated away towards Holland. One peony behaved deviantly: after circling wildly in an eddy it
was sucked into the depths. Anna stared enviously at the spot where
the flower had disappeared. To vanish, from one moment to the next,
she wanted that for herself too—to join her beloved absent ones.
There was a stiff breeze carrying the smell of damp grass and straw.
She did not resist as it took hold of her and raised her up, her clothes
flapping. She soared aloft, with a deafening rustle, straight into the
cloudless sky. Far below her she saw her grandfather's farm, half hidden beneath the crown of a lime tree. She saw the fields, the grassy
alluvial sand banks where cattle grazed, the school, the church, the
Landolinus chapel—the whole settlement on both sides of the Lippe,
which tried to transcend its insignificance through desperate contor-

tions, its inhabitants inflating the village's status with fabrications about Widukind who, with his Saxon hordes, had offered bloody resistance to the king of the Frankish empire there. Anna, hovering far above, had nothing to do with those below.

Lotte lay in the garden in a pine summerhouse that was set on a rotating axle so that it could be turned towards the sun or away from it, as preferred. Stretched out in bed, she turned with the weather, her narrow face on a white lace-trimmed pillow. Her Dutch mother drew a kitchen chair up to the bed and taught her Dutch; she also gave her a book of fairy tales by the Brothers Grimm, with romantic illustrations. In German, 'So that you don't forget your mother tongue,' she said. She herself looked as though she had stepped out of the book of fairy tales. She was tall, erect and proud; she laughed easily—her teeth were as white as the doves that flew to and fro to the dovecote at the edge of the wood. Everything about her shone: her complexion, her blue eyes, her long brown hair held in place by a few strategically placed tortoiseshell combs. An abundance of the joy of living poured forth over everyone who came within her orbit. But the most fairy-tale thing about her was her unfeminine strength. If she saw her husband lugging a sack of coal she rushed over to him to take the burden lovingly from him—she carried it to the fireplace as though it were a sack of feathers.

Lotte soon realized that she had ended up with relatives: those of the long noses. The head of the line looked strikingly like her own father. The same acutely melancholy gaze, the thin arched nose, the dark hair combed back, even the same moustache. In fact he was a first cousin of her father and had passed his genetic characteristics undiluted onto his daughters; the same proud and sensitive organ of smell was already latent in them, within the round children's nose. Years later, when it had become dangerous to have such a long nose in the middle of your face, this simple biological fact would almost cost one of them her life.

Depending on the position of the sun, Lotte was always able to see another part of the universe from her home. There was the wood, on the other side of a wide ditch that bordered the garden on two sides. A group of conifers formed a natural gate by the dovecote, a dark niche that drew her gaze—across a mossy bridge straight into the twilight between the trees. From another sightline she saw the orchards and kitchen garden where the pumpkins expanded so fast that Lotte, who had become susceptible to fairy tales in which apples and bread rolls could speak, thought she could hear them groaning from their growing pains. Then there was the view of the house and a sturdy octagonal crenellated water tower—all in masonry with decorative arches in green glazed brick over the windows and doors. One day she saw her Dutch father climb up there to hoist a large flag. Her breath caught when she saw the diminutive figure at the top beside a flag that flapped in the wind like a sail—was it not the fate of fathers suddenly to be blown away out of the world?

At night she slept inside the house in a separate room. Then the nighttime landscape unfolded: strange hills and rocks, fir trees and alpine meadows, mountain streams. Her grandfather hovered above them in his mourning coat with tails; Anna was hanging from his claws, screaming silently. Lotte dashed over hills, up high, down low, to escape from the shadow he was casting over her. The ground rolled away beneath her, she was stumbling over cobbles—she woke up screaming and coughing. She was lifted up and put into another bed, where she slept in the crook of her Dutch mother's arm without further upset.

'THEN WHY DID they rush off with us, like thieves in the night,' Lotte asked herself, 'straight after the funeral?'

Anna laughed wryly. 'Because it was a disaster, with the useful bonus of an extra labourer on the farm. It was a village of conservative, Catholic farmers—that's what it was like then. Father fled from that milieu when he was nineteen. He went to Cologne and became a socialist. That short-sighted old man had never been able to stomach it, *verstehst du*. And then, as soon as the son who had defected was dead, he came to rescue us from that hotbed of heathendom and socialism. A hit-and-run operation, to prevent Aunt Käthe keeping us.'

Lotte had a light-headed feeling. It was unbelievable that this grotesque family history concerned her too. All of a sudden, just like that, the seal was being broken on a bitter mystery that she had closed an infinitely long time ago: shhh, don't think about it any more, it never happened.

'But,' she objected weakly, 'why did he . . . me . . . let me go to Holland then?' It seemed as though she was hearing only the echo of her own voice, or someone else was speaking for her.

Anna leaned forward and laid a plump hand on Lotte's. 'It didn't suit him that you were ill. A healthy child was a good investment, but a sick child . . . doctors, medicines, a sanatorium, a funeral: that could only cost money. It suited him that his sister Elisabeth offered to take you—although he entirely disapproved of her and was deeply suspicious of her fashionable mourning outfit. Her son, she said, lived not far from Amsterdam in a dry, wooded region, which was therapeutic for TB sufferers; there was even a sanatorium in the district. *Na ja*, you know all that much better than I do. This aunt herself had escaped from life on the farm in the previous century—imagine it, about a hundred years ago—to go to Holland as a maidservant and to marry there. I heard all that from Aunt Liesl, years after the war. Grandfather never showed the slightest interest in you anymore, not even after you were cured. A cat that was sickly in its youth never grew into a healthy, strong animal, was his attitude.'

'I wonder'—Lotte forced a smile—'if he would have let me go if he'd known that I had been entrusted to a Stalinist who brought me up on torrents of abuse against the Pope and the Church.'

'*Mein Gott*, really?' Bewildered, Anna shook her head. 'What an irony . . . because I would not have survived for long without that same Church.'

BREAD AND HOBNAILS, sausage and safety pins, nothing was unobtainable in the richly stocked shop and adjoining café where Anna read out her shopping list in a clear voice. 'Do you want to earn ten pfennigs, child?' lisped the woman behind the counter; the missing front tooth did not restrain her from smiling with a grocer's cunning. Anna nodded. 'Then come and read to my mother twice a week.' The mother, blind from cataracts, sat in a back room by the window, crumpled up in a worn-out tub chair. On the table in front of her were the mystical reflections of

Catharina van Emmerik. Each session of reading aloud had to close with the old woman's favourite passage: the one concerning the flagellation of Jesus before the crucifixion. The saint of Emmerik sketched the various stages of the flagellation without reticence: first he was whipped for a while with an ordinary whip, then a new, well-equipped soldier took the former's place, with a split whip, and as his strength diminished he in turn was replaced by a soldier with a flagellum, the barbs of which penetrated deeply into the skin. At each blow the woman hit the arm of the chair with her bony fingers, her mouth uttered moans that were somewhere between shrieks of pain and encouragement. Anna also reached a climax every time: the fusing together of her compassion for Jesus and her rage at the Roman soldiers and the actual instigators, the Jews. After she had closed the book with trembling fingers, the feeling of indignation slowly ebbed away. 'Come over here . . .' the old woman beckoned. Reluctantly Anna approached her chair. The old fingers that had drummed rhythmically on the armrest just before, groped at her plump limbs. Coolly Anna noted the signs of decay—liver spots on the white face, bags under the pale staring eyes, thin hair where the scalp shone through. 'Ach, stroke me on my head . . .' said the woman softly, squeezing Anna's hand. Anna did not obey. '*Bitte, bitte*, stroke my head.' Was this part of the reading aloud, like an encore? Eventually she did what she had been asked, quickly and mechanically. 'Our Anna prays for money,' Uncle Heinrich chuckled to everyone who would hear him, 'till she foams at the mouth.'

Anna did not ignore the flagellation of Jesus, who had gradually been taking the place of her father. Each Sunday she sat between her grandfather and her aunt in a Catholic church that dated back to the mass conversions of the Teutonic peoples. Looking round, her eyes had soon discovered a bas relief depicting the event on one of the whitewashed walls. One day Alois Jacobsmeyer, the pastor, who was reciting his breviary in a side chapel, saw her walking down the aisle with a wooden stool in her hand. Intently, she turned to the right, towards a series of age-old bas reliefs depicting the crucifixion of Christ. She climbed onto the stool and began to give Jesus's tormentors a tremendous beating with her fists. 'So!' It resounded vengefully through the church. 'So!' Worried, scratching his head, Jacobsmeyer asked himself whether the relief would be able to withstand such iconoclasm.

3

THE GET TOGETHER was threatening to take on a slightly more caustic character. Lotte had been uncomfortably nettled by the scene in the church as Anna, not without tenderness, described it. Suddenly a razor-sharp, hideous feeling flamed up in her that had lain smouldering all that time.

'And in that way the Church gave all of you a nice little alibi for murdering six million people,' she said. Red blotches appeared on her cheeks.

'Exactly,' said Anna, 'that's it exactly! That's why I am telling you, so that you'll understand that its foundations were already laid when we were young.'

Lotte slowly rose from her chair, 'I do not believe I need to understand. First, all of you people set fire to the world and on top of that you want us to go deeply into your motives.'

'You people? You are talking about your own people.'

'I have nothing to do with that people,' Lotte cried, full of abhorrence. Urging herself to be calm, she permitted herself to continue condescendingly, 'I am Dutch, in heart and soul.'

Did any compassion seep into the glance Anna cast her? 'Meine Liebe,' she said soothingly, 'for six years we sat on the same father's lap, you on one knee, me on the other. You can't actually rub that out just like that. Just look at us now, old and naked beneath our bathrobes, in our plastic slippers. Older and a bit wiser, I hope. Let's not accuse one another, but celebrate our reunion. I suggest we get dressed and go to a *patisserie* in the street named after Queen Astrid. They have'—she kissed her fingertips—'delicious cakes there.'

Lotte's rage ebbed. She nodded, ashamed that she had let go like that. They walked along the imposing passage together to the lockers. *Together*—what a word.

A quarter of an hour later they descended the steps of the monumental bathhouse, involuntarily holding on to each other because it was snowing and the steps were slippery.

It was not far. They entered a nondescript shop, walked through to the back past a display cabinet of delicacies gratifying to the eyes, to a refurbished living room where elderly ladies in fur hats were succumbing in complete silence to the matriarchal rite of coffee and cakes. A wagon wheel chandelier hung from the ceiling and cast a flattering light onto the clientele; on the walls paintings of imaginary landscapes in gaudy colours confirmed the atmosphere of reassuring kitsch.

They ordered *merveilleux*, an artful variant on a mouthful of air, held together with meringue, whipped cream and flaked almonds.

'Now I understand whom I heard singing yesterday.' The piece of meringue that Lotte was bringing to her mouth came to a pensive standstill mid-way.

'Who?'

'Yesterday, in one of the peat baths, someone was singing the Cologne slow-tram song.'

Anna laughed. 'I am guilty of bathroom coloratura if I think no one can hear. But . . . originally you were the one who liked singing.'

Lotte frowned. Round about them was the sound of civilized chatter; the shop bell rang now and then and a snowy customer came inside. 'I only began to sing properly,' she corrected her sister, 'after I had fallen through the ice.'

LOTTE WAS STANDING on the frosty grass at the side of the ditch. Her sisters were gliding by, swaying on Friesian wooden skates, making a long chain with the gardener's daughters from a neighboring property and a Brabant cousin who was staying there. The cousin's mother also appeared on the ice, a sturdy woman in a brown felt hat with a weather vane of duck feathers that indicated the wind's direction. She distributed sea-green and red striped peppermints to the children from a large paper cone. 'Just going to visit your mom for a minute,' she said, holding on to Lotte's hand, 'want to come with me, lass?' She took a run-up and slithered screaming exuberantly over the ditch, dragging Lotte along with her in her glacial pleasures. Thus they pelted and slid towards the house, the woman chatting non-stop in an incomprehensible dialect. They reached a dark green, half-submerged rowboat that marked the start of the danger zone where overflow water drained into the ditch; the children had been warned about this. 'No farther, no farther!' called Lotte, but the Brabant woman was chattering on as mechanically as the little wind-up locomotive at home that permitted no one to divert it from its idiosyncratic route between the table legs.

Lotte instinctively pulled herself free as the ice began to crack. She was not frightened. The firmness beneath her feet disappeared and the crystal floor opened to admit her into the territory of a sweet, premature death, ornamented with ferns and algae that moved together in a stream of air bubbles. The ice closed over her head. As the variety of forms slowly coalesced in light green, turquoise and silver, she thought with regret of the miniature sewing box that she had been carrying since Christmas in a pocket of her underslip . . . A shame too about her new red pullover and the newborn baby. Her Dutch mother, her father, her sisters were strung out one after the other like links in a chain—Anna came a long way behind them, vaguely visible in a burst of filtered light. No more, she thought. No more aniseed rusks.

A dying scream rose out of the Brabant woman, alerting the skating children. They scurried over to the woman; she was standing in the water up to her heavy breasts, rigid with terror. Not another sound came out of her wide-open mouth. The hat was still straight on her head; only the feather moved. 'Lotte . . . where is Lotte?' cried Jet, the youngest, shrilly. She got her skates off, ran home and returned at a gallop with her mother, who slid over the ice on her front to the unfortunate woman whose lower body had already drowned. With her hands under the woman's armpits she tried to drag her heavy body out of the water. But that petrified colossus would not move, stuck firmly in the mud. The gardener's wife came running, scream-

ing. She observed the rescue from the bank, in no state to do anything, tearing the hair out of her head. Because of her wailing, eventually her husband appeared. He had been a military hospital orderly
before turning to the cultivation of oleanders and orange trees. He
stamped on the ice from the bank and, by fragmenting the ice, cleared
a path to the drowning woman. At that moment Jet's high-pitched
voice pierced the freezing air. 'Mister, mister . . . Lotte's here . . . My
sister Lotte's here!' With a trembling finger she pointed to a spot in
the ice where a triangle of Lotte's imitation fur coat was shimmering
through the ice. The gardener cast an expert glance at his sister-in-
law, left her upright where she was, and dived beneath the ice. An
eternity later he returned to the world of the living with Lotte's dripping body. 'Stop' he said, spitting water, to her mother, who was tugging at his sister-in-law's body ever more desperately, but had not
managed to rescue more than the packet of sticky sweets. 'She's been
dead a long time.' With his free hand he pointed to a trickle of blood
dripping from the left corner of the woman's mouth.

One glance at Lotte's slack body was enough to make everyone
abandon hope for her, too. But the gardener, who had not hauled her
out of the Lethe for nothing, refused to give in. She was laid naked on
the dining table. It was reckoned that her sojourn beneath the ice had
lasted for half an hour. He tried mouth-to-mouth resuscitation, slapping her body all over, and rubbing her with a towel her mother had
warmed on the stove. He persisted desperately until a growling sound
signalled the start of breathing. Thus was Lotte slowly rubbed and
slapped back to life, through the stubborn perseverance of someone
whose actual speciality was keeping plants and trees alive.

She only properly regained consciousness in her mother's bed,
ringed by interested parties who came to inspect the medical miracle.
She was not surprised. Years ago Aunt Käthe had taken over caring for
her, then someone unfamiliar took her by the hand to Holland, and
now a wild stranger had taken her to the world on the other side of the
ice. What else could she be but sanguine about a pattern that kept
repeating itself with almost aesthetically well-founded insistence?

The other drowning victim was now lying on the table downstairs.
They had placed her hat on her belly with her hands over it, so that it

looked as if she was reporting bashfully at the gates of heaven. 'It's my fault she's dead,' cried the gardener's wife, rocking tormentedly back and forth on a kitchen chair. 'God has punished me! I saw Lotte lying there all that time and I said nothing. I thought: if I tell, you'll let go of my sister and she'll drown.' Lotte's mother corrected her, 'Don't deceive yourself. Your sister's heart gave out because she had just had a hot meal, your husband said, and Lotte was saved because she hadn't eaten yet.' 'And I had cooked such tasty chicken livers with sauerkraut and fried bacon,' lamented the other, 'that couldn't kill a person, surely . . .'

Back at school, the girl who had drowned was allowed to sit by the stove. She was her old self again except for one small flaw: her speech had not entirely thawed. She stammered so badly that her privileged position by the stove was nullified; she was passed over when it was her turn to speak in class. It took too long to let her express herself. A little monster sat between her thoughts and their utterance, pulling back the syllables just before they left her mouth. A superhuman effort was required to speak aloud through this opposing force: her head was put under great pressure, her heart went wild, her paralysed tongue twisted powerlessly. A cruel censor stood in the way and permitted almost nothing through.

Her mother discovered that she did not stutter when she sang with others. Her clear voice could be heard above the rest, she knew all the verses and effortlessly improvised a second part without stumbling over a word. The sandy path beside the football pitch led on to an avenue lined by beech trees that passed through a district of old villas to the radio station's studios. Lotte's mother cycled there on her Gazelle and persuaded the conductor of the children's choir, which sang on the radio each week, to give Lotte a chance. The fact that she was the smallest was amply compensated for by her voice, which lost none of its purity even in the straitjacket of a simple nursery rhyme. Each week the conductor selected someone to make a debut singing a solo of his or her choice. Lotte was placed on an orange box to reach the microphone. The artificial situation did not trouble her; the diffuse anxiety about stuttering that always lay dozing on the threshold of her unconscious—one eye open, one eye closed—disappeared instantly as soon as she started her song. Focusing on the conductor, whose grey mane waved in time with his baton, she broadcast "In Holland there is a house," her favorite song, into living rooms without a hitch. A couple of days later a picture postcard was delivered for her. 'You have a lovely voice,' was written in ornate handwriting, 'I hope your parents take pains with it.'

'ACH JA,' LOTTE sighed, 'the conductor was deported in the war. He was Jewish.'

There was an uncomfortable silence. How can there ever be talk of forgetting, Lotte asked herself, looking furtively at Anna; you have to be vigilant with every representative of this people.

'I don't really know if it is wise'—she hesitated—'to be sitting here with you eating cakes and behaving as though nothing was the matter.'

Anna sprang up. 'Who says we have to behave as though nothing is the matter? I was brought up in a culture you detest. You escaped from it just in time. Let me tell you now how your life would have turned out if you had stayed. Let me . . .'

'We know that past history of yours,' Lotte interrupted her wearily. 'The insult of Versailles. The Depression.'

Anna shook her head. 'Let me tell you something about the place the Jews occupied in our lives, in my life, before the war. In the countryside. We'll order another cup of coffee. Listen.'

IT TOOK YEARS for grandfather to die. He hardly came out from behind the stove—only in warmth did his bones stop rattling against each other. He hobbled outside once more on an oppressively hot day and stationed himself on a small bench in front of the house. Anna went to sit next to him. A black barouche came driving by; an old woman in widow's clothes was sitting on the box—wisps of grey hair clung to her sweaty face. She turned out to be a sister of his who lived six kilometres further on, on a large farm. They had not seen each other in twenty years. 'But Trude, what are you doing here?' his voice cracked. 'Well, if you won't visit me,' she snapped, baring three solitary teeth, 'then I will have to come to you.'

Uncle Heinrich, who preferred reading to milking cows, just like his dead brother, carried the full burden of the destitute farm on his shoulders. Above the stable doors of the Saxon half-timbered house built in 1779 it said: 'Grant, O greatest God—what thou command from us—we will dutifully accomplish this—in the utmost devotion.' A prophetic motto, with the emphasis on 'dutifully.' While Aunt Liesl hurried back and forth between housekeeping, chickens and kitchen garden, Uncle Heinrich had the greatest difficulty allocating his attention between the seduction of the printed word and fifty pigs, four cows with calves, a cart horse, fifty acres of their own land and twelve rented.

Even when doing business he scarcely put aside his reading matter. Uncle Heinrich would sit dourly in the kitchen with a book when the cattle dealer, Papa Rosenbaum, turned up, having scented that a cow was for sale, and would continue reading during the traditional game of bid and counter-bid. 'What do you want for it?' Papa Rosenbaum clapped his fat hands together. His hat was set back on his head as though he were a Chicago gangster, an antique watch-chain hung on his square chest. 'Six hundred,' Uncle Heinrich mumbled without looking up. 'Six hundred? I'm sorry, Bamberg, but that's laughable! I'm laughing my head off!' He burst out in an epic laugh; Uncle Heinrich was just becoming engrossed in an intriguing passage; Anna made herself invisible in a corner of the kitchen. When he had stopped laughing, Rosenbaum made a case about the price of cattle in the context of the wretched economic condition that the country found itself in. Where was he heading? He could offer four hundred, not a penny more. Uncle Heinrich did not flinch. 'Four hundred and fifty.' Nothing. 'Do you want to ruin me! I really can't do business like that.' Papa Rosenbaum stalked out of the kitchen and closed the door behind him with a bang. The tail of his coat had stuck in the door, obliging him to open it again to jerk it out. Hissing, he pulled his coat back. Then they could hear him pacing up and down in the yard, complaining loudly. 'I'll go bankrupt! My family will starve.' He got into his Wanderer and started the engine, got out, came inside again. 'My soul, my poor soul is dying!' The whole arsenal of threats and self-pity bounced off the invisible wall surrounding the impassive reader. After the ritual had been repeated three times, Rosenbaum took his watch out of his waistcoat pocket. 'I've been at it for an hour already, that's how my business goes down the drain. Very well, you get your six hundred.' Later, after she had witnessed this ceremony many more times, Anna understood that the outcome of the cattle trading had been settled by the antagonists beforehand and that it was gone through for their amusement.

A CLASS PHOTO was taken. Anna was ninth from the left in the third row, among fifty-four children's heads. She was looking straight into the camera, still wearing a black dress with a loose, drooping black bow on her head. Though the other children were standing close together there was a space around Anna as though they were instinctively afraid that homesickness might be infectious. Yet she had survived the village children's ostracism and, thanks to her inborn fearlessness, had won her classmates' trust. When she grew out of the mourning dress she received a collarless garment of season-proof dove-grey material made with room to grow. The number of permanent tasks imposed upon her on the farm rose in proportion to the centimetres she gained in height. There was one day of holiday in the year: the expedition to Wewelsburg, a medieval castle not far from the village. The hay carts were decorated with birch bark and coloured paper and pulled by cart horses, and everyone fought for a place on the cart of Lampen-Heini, a rich farmer who had light, swift horses. On the way they forgot everyday life, which was becoming increasingly meagre, and exuberantly sang walking songs.

They had a whole lot to forget. The millions of unemployed in the towns, for example, who had no money to buy anything, so the farm butter, potatoes and pork kept being sent back. Because of the rent, they could not afford artificial fertilizers or to pay taxes; they could only dream of a pair of new shoes or a skein of wool with which to mend stockings. There was a state of emergency in the Ruhr area. The unemployed were sent out to the countryside to work for farmers in return for bed and board. Children came next: the Church doled them out to every willing farmer's wife. The mysterious arrival of the pale, listless children and the almost metaphysical mediating role of the Church so moved the imaginations of Anna and her

friends that they invented a game: 'The Ruhr children arrive.' With a
stick they drew an imaginary village in the compressed earth, with a
church and the farms scattered around. They took turns playing the
mother. She fetched a Ruhr child from the church, walked through
the village with it and brought it into a house they had designed.
What happened after that did not bother them—it was about accepting a poor child; it touched their awakening maternal instinct. Anna
played passionately, identifying with the displaced children, until the
game became unexpectedly real in the person of Nettchen, who was
brought home by Aunt Liesl.

This was a flesh-and-blood Ruhr child. She came into the house
with Aunt Liesl, spindly and grimy, in worn-out shoes. Two long
brown plaits were pinned on top of her head; there were scabs on her
lips which she could not leave alone. She laughed mysteriously at
everything they said to her but said nothing in reply. Initially they
imagined that Nettchen could not speak, but eventually, once she
opened up falteringly, it appeared that she simply did not have many
thoughts. She could not keep up at school. She came home with corrected homework—underneath on the slate the teacher had written:
'Dear Anna, aren't you ashamed to let Nettchen go to school with
such exercises? Is there no time for you to help her?' Anna could not
ignore this challenge. Evening after evening she dedicated herself
with iron discipline to the renovation of Nettchen's neglected intellect. She was baffled that her efforts bore no fruit at all. Nettchen's
mysterious laugh at every question she persisted in answering incor-
rectly drove Anna to despair. 'Why give yourself all that trouble?'
Uncle Heinrich said laconically. 'Isn't Nettchen much better off as she
is than you or I?'

Nettchen was certainly interested in love. The handsomest of all
the boys living on the banks of the Lippe for miles around was in love
with Aunt Liesl. Each Sunday Leon Rosenbaum came to the farm
with a bunch of flowers. Their impossible love hastened to an
untimely end on a rusty garden bench overlooking a bed of young
cabbages. They were mute about what they had to say to each other.
Instead they held each other's hand and mumbled generalities that
instantly evaporated. Anna and Nettchen lay behind the gooseberry

bushes, expecting greater boldness. Sometimes Leon gave Aunt Liesl a chaste kiss. Her bosom rose and fell languorously, her golden cross heaved with it and Nettchen pinched Anna's arm.

During the Friday liturgy Anna grasped a vague sense of the connection between the half-heartedness of the courtship and the ending of the ever-recurring passage 'Flectamus genua' uttered in kneeling position: 'Let us pray for the Church, the Pope, the bishops, the government, the sick, travellers, the shipwrecked . . .' No single category was missed out, not even the Jews. When it came to their turn, at the very end, the faithful rose as one to their feet from their kneeling position—after all, the Jews had knelt mockingly before Jesus with the words: 'King of the Jews!' The prayer was rounded off: 'May our Lord God lift the veil from their hearts so that they too acknowledge our Lord Jesus Christ.'

Leon ceased his visits when he realized that all his efforts foundered on the golden cross. Aunt Liesl relapsed into dull taciturnity. For weeks she seemed to do her work blindly, until she made a decision that was more fitting to a threepenny opera: she took herself off into a Carmelite nunnery. At her departure she clasped Anna passionately to her and kissed her tenderly on the forehead. Nervously she fished a curled photograph of Leon out of the black handbag that she would have to relinquish at the convent gate and pushed it into Anna's hand.

Her departure fired the starting shot in a series of radical changes. Nettchen was returned to the church. The grandfather, whose all-seeing eye had maintained symbolic control to his final days, exchanged his earthly existence for immortality. He was buried in a snowy churchyard next to his wife, who had departed fifteen years earlier.

Back on the farm Uncle Heinrich rested a hand on Anna's shoulder. 'So Anna, now there's only the two of us and the stock. And you and I are no farmers at all. Come, let's get down to work.' This heroic acceptance of one's lot reminded Anna of her father, who had reconciled himself to his illness in the same way. She clutched her uncle by his funeral coat futilely. When he dies too, she thought, I'll really be alone.

4

I WROTE YOU dozens of letters.' Lotte sighed. 'I lay in my garden house and wrote. My mother had bought special writing paper for me with violets in the top left corner. All my letters ended with, "Dear Anna, why don't you write back? When will we see each other again?" '

'They must have intercepted all those letters and thrown them away—after they had read them out of their farmers' curiosity. And there I was, thinking you had forgotten me.'

Their eyes strayed to the other tables. Both were silent. Here they sat, almost seventy years later, and they still felt taken in and deceived; they did not know what they ought to do with these feelings. Had the lives of all the ladies here, with their silk blouses, their gold earrings, their carefully painted lips, also gone awry through such misunderstandings? Anna began to laugh sarcastically.

'Why are you laughing?' said Lotte suspiciously.

'Because my indignation has lost nothing of its strength, after all these years.' Anna drummed her fingers on the table. She remembered that she had decided one day that Lotte had died from the illness she was meant to have recovered from in Holland. Nobody had thought to send her an announcement of the death. Perhaps her grandfather had indeed received it, but kept quiet about it so as not to upset her. She had imagined Lotte dead like that because a dead Lotte was more bearable than one who had simply forgotten her. Moreover, dying ran in the family.

'It's like a book,' said Lotte. Time was rustling past her. Still, she could hear her mother, talking about Anna and saying compassionately, 'The poor child, ending up with such barbarians.' This description, which she had taken over gratuitously from her German mother-in-law, made Anna's fate more and more puzzling. Did this make Anna a barbarian too now? Didn't barbarians have any writing paper? She invented all sorts of excuses for Anna in this way, in order not to have to live with the thought that Anna was simply not replying to her letters.

BETWEEN UNCLE HEINRICH and the delicate, blond daughter of a gentleman farmer, strict unwritten laws that were best expressed as statistics barred the way: the quantity of livestock, the number of servants, acres of land. With Martha Höhnekop, who was his beloved's opposite in every way, he tried to free himself of her. He met Martha at a shooting match. In mutiny against the terror of rank, position and capital, he allowed his eyes to fall on someone who had nothing to lose. She was the eldest of a family of fourteen children. Her father ran a café that everyone with a dash of self-respect avoided. But Uncle Heinrich was drunk and Martha Höhnekop was available.

One day she walked into Anna's life. With long, rough strides that contrasted coarsely with the cream-coloured lace on her wedding dress, she entered the stuffy living room, threw her bouquet of roses and phlox onto the table and dropped, panting, into grandfather's chair. She could breathe again: the town hall, the church, the celebration meal—it exhausted her to try to be civilized and charming. Anna observed her closely. A sturdy woman with a large, flat face, narrow lips and broad jawbones; her eyes were crooked, mysterious, unfathomable, sunken. Her shiny black hair was pinned up, the rose that had been stuck there that morning and had stayed in place the whole day now slid out slowly. Her cheeks looked unnaturally red. Anna thought that was because of the wedding, but later on it seemed that the blush in her cheeks had been tattooed, as though she were suffering from a permanent excitement that could find no outlet. 'Send that child to bed,' she said to Uncle Heinrich, waving her hand at Anna. 'We've only just got married and yet we've such a big girl already,' replied the bridegroom with a false laugh. 'Not many could match us.' But the bride, who had had enough of Anna's candid, staring gaze, did not see what there was to laugh about.

The one thing about Martha Höhnekop that worked was her womb: a child was born every year. Beyond that she did not make the grade at all. When she got up at nine o'clock, yawning and scratching her head, Uncle Heinrich's day was already four hours old. From then

on, she knew how, in her pigheaded manner, to give the impression
that she was kept busy by the housekeeping, but in fact, like an ele-
mental force she swaggered about the small dwelling with her gross
body without lifting a finger. Much work would have been left
undone had an orphaned eleven-year-old girl not gone round seeing
to it. A girl who actually belonged to no one, although she ate with
them and slept under the same roof. Lazy, but clever enough, Aunt
Martha understood that an indispensable labourer had fallen into her
lap in the form of this so-called niece.

With every baby that was born, a piece of the child in Anna shrivelled up and the beast of burden increased in size in its place. Seven
days of her week began with milking the cows—the cans had to be
standing by the road by six o'clock. Then she had to feed the pigs,
horses, cows, calves and chickens, pump drinking water for them,
clean out the cowshed and cook the pigfeed, rub down the cows. This
chain of activities was called morning work, the pendant of which
was evening work. It began all over again in the afternoons at four
o'clock—after school. If the pendants had been figurines on the man-
telpiece, they would have shown two slaves sagging at the knees with
their backs bent—the clock ticking inexorably between them.

The existence she had been dreaming of, that of a grammar school
pupil, was becoming progressively more tenuous. In that dream her
life proceeded according to the original plan, in which her father set
high demands on her intellect—which fitted in badly between the
cows and pigs. Two teachers and a pastor had naively come to the
house to persuade Uncle Heinrich to permit her to go to the grammar
school. But their hymn of praise to her talents was dismissed by that
single primitive argument: 'No, we need her on the farm.'

He was never to surface from the shock of his impulsive marriage.
Apart from being an escape, his lightning raid had perhaps also been
a juvenile attempt to repair his shattered family life. That he had
brought a much greater woe on himself as a result was clear. He
armed himself against his disillusion by throwing himself into his
work with grim doggedness. He acquired the harsh, fixed expression
of a farmer who already knows that, however hard he drives himself,
his fate is immutable, so out of pure masochism he adds a little extra

to it. If Anna had not been there, his little companion in misfortune and sorrow, then he would have had to do battle with the primal force calling herself his wife, in order to get her to work too—a battle in which the loser would have been certain from the outset.

High mass on Sundays freed the house from Aunt Martha's presence for a few hours. This presented Papa Rosenbaum's youngest son with the opportunity to take Anna by surprise one hot summer's day. She had just put the potatoes and carrots in the soup to simmer with a piece of bacon. All of a sudden, through the steam, she saw a boy standing in the doorway. He took a few steps into the kitchen. She recognized Daniel Rosenbaum, who had sat near her in class. 'I'm going swimming in the Lippe,' he said casually. 'Can I undress here?' Anna looked at him absentmindedly. 'I suppose so,' she said, vaguely pointing, 'you can go into that room.' Swimming in the river, she thought with surprise, nobody ever does that. She did not know anyone who could swim. Peering at the bubbles and swirls on the surface of the simmering soup, she saw before her the life-threatening whirlpools of the Lippe. When she heard a sound behind her she turned round automatically. Young Rosenbaum was standing naked on the doormat, his erect member swathed in a beam of sunlight that entered through the window. He stared at her with defiant seriousness. The cooking spoon fell out of her hand. The thing with the eye at the top, standing out there darkly, independent of his thin boy's body, seemed to be aiming straight for her, like a rising cobra poised on the point of attack. She did not know anything like it existed, she refused it, she would have nothing to do with it and fled from the kitchen, past the "salute" that he had given her, outside behind the privet hedge. She was trembling. In the far distance the severe spire of the Landolinus church stuck up above the trees. That was pointing upwards too. She stooped to pick a bundle of grass, and pulled the blades apart one by one. How was it possible that while high mass was being celebrated there, something like this could manifest itself here—that both could exist in the same world?

Jesus had said, 'Be perfect, as Our Father in heaven is perfect.' Anna tried to keep this commandment scrupulously, although her efforts were put to the test severely on All Souls' Day. All prayers for the salvation of the souls of the dead were heard on this day in November. Those who had the opportunity to do so went to church six times to make the most of the chance. But the prayers were not only for dead loved ones. The greatest sacrifice was a prayer on behalf of the godless: 'Do something good for the sinner too.' She had already prayed for her father, for her mother, grandfather and for Lotte, too, to be on the safe side. For whom else can I pray now, she brooded, what is the very greatest penance I should do? Then Rosenbaum, naked, appeared unbidden before her, on the doormat, swathed in a sunbeam. In a flash the sacrifice being demanded of her was clear: why shouldn't she pray for one—arbitrarily chosen—dead Jew?

LOTTE SIPPED A glass of Grand Marnier that accompanied the third cup of coffee. 'It could just as well have been a non-Jewish boy.'

'Of course! I am only telling you to show you how ambivalent my attitude towards the Jews was and how that was fed by the Church. Now comes the worst.' Anna tossed back the final dregs. 'At some point they had disappeared, there were no more Jews in our village. No Rosenbaum came to buy cattle any more; a Christian cattle dealer took his place, without ceremony. Yet I never asked: Where has the Rosenbaum family gone? Never, you understand. Nobody ever asked anything, not even my uncle.'

'What did happen to that family?'

'I don't know! It's true when people say "we did not know." But why didn't we know? Because it didn't interest us at all! I reproach myself, now, that I didn't ask: Where have they gone?'

Lotte had been getting hot, she was feeling dizzy. Anna's self-reproach sounded hollow in her ears—what could you do with it? All the fur hats around them had disappeared. The lights in the wagon wheel overhead were still on, but at half strength. 'I believe they want us to be on our way,' she mumbled.

Anna stood up to pay, Lotte would not hear of it. But Anna beat her to it. She had already paid when Lotte was still searching for the lost sleeve of her coat. The Germans were too quick for everybody, with their strong Deutschemarks.

They had just been roaming about in the 1930s; now they stepped outside into a white, timeless world—now the compelling silence that prevailed evoked the sensation of entering a great void. Anna took Lotte's arm. Under the impression that their ways would part here, they stopped by the Lancers monument in the Place Royale—a heroic rider going to war wearing a helmet of snow.

'Until tomorrow.' Anna looked at Lotte solemnly and kissed her on both cheeks.

'Until tomorrow . . .' said Lotte weakly.

'Who would have thought it . . .' said Anna again.

Then they both crossed the road in the same direction.

'Where are you heading?' Anna asked.

'To my hotel.'

'Me too!'

They each turned out to be staying at a hotel on the other side of the railway line. 'That can't just be chance,' Anna laughed, holding onto Lotte's arm again. Thus they walked on, the snow crunching pleasantly under their feet. On the railway bridge they stopped to look out over the snow-covered roofs.

'Just think,' mused Anna, 'of all the famous celebrities who have come here to take the cure over the centuries. Even Tsar Peter the Great.'

'The town still has something distinguished about it,' Lotte agreed, brushing a strip of snow off the balustrade with a gloved finger. She loved the atmosphere of aristocratic élan and faded glory emanating from the buildings below. The nineteenth century was still tangibly present and evoked a longing for a more harmonious and better organized way of living, which had been lost forever. At the Thermal Baths, whenever anyone on the staff held out a hand to her to help her out of the bath and into a ready-warmed bathrobe, she imagined that she was a dowager or a marchioness who had brought her own lady's maid with her.

They shuffled on, from one lamp post to the next, from one pool of light to the next, until they were standing in front of a villa with two round towers. 'I'm there,' said Lotte. The building of white fondant sprinkled with icing sugar created an unreal, dreamy impression. This day, with all its implausibilities had been a dream and Anna, beside her, was not real.

'A palace,' Anna assessed soberly. 'I am lodging further on, it's altogether a simpler place.'

Lotte sensed criticism but was not inclined to explain that a sober family hotel was hiding behind the luxurious façade. 'I wish you . . . a pleasant evening,' she stammered.

'I can hardly wait until tomorrow,' Anna sighed, pulling Lotte firmly to her.

It took a long time before Lotte fell asleep. It was difficult to find a pain-free position. And whether she lay on her side or her back, she continued to replay the meeting and the unburdenings that had taken place. Conflicting emotions prevented sleep from overtaking her. How shall I tell my children? was her last thought as she dropped off, towards morning.

5

FULL OF SOMBRE forebodings, Lotte woke. The hotel room appeared strange and hostile; the snow-covered branches seen through the window evoked no poetic sentiments. Everything was painful. Her body evoked her aversion, not only because she could feel it with her every movement but because its origin could not be denied. A Dutch person, in a German body. In Belgium. She would have liked to have gone away silently, but the cure was a present from her children, so how could she take flight from her own birthday present? Allowing herself to be led astray by Anna was a form of disloyalty: the pain in her limbs was a warning that she had already gone too far. Those first years that Anna referred to—what did they really represent in a human life? They had been put into the world together, halfway through the First World War, while there had been wholesale death not even a hundred kilometres away. There was something improper about being born at such a moment, and twins at that. A curse must lie upon them. A great estrangement deservedly existed between them; it needed to remain so. Perhaps an impersonal, historical debt of guilt lay upon them and, in the course of their lives, independent of one another, they had had to repay it by enduring an amount of misfortune brought about by circumstances.

As Lotte was waiting in the basement for the preparation of her peat bath, Anna appeared in the doorway. There was already something familiar about her—hopefully this was not the precursor of some sort of family feeling! Anna slid down next to her on the white bench.

'How did you sleep, *meine Liebe*?'

'All right,' said Lotte superciliously.

'I slept wonderfully.' Anna massaged her thighs.

A woman in a white overall beckoned to Lotte. Anna grasped her by her shoulder. 'There's a lovely café next door, Relais de la Poste, let's meet there. This afternoon!'

Nodding vaguely, Lotte glided into the bathroom. How was it possible: once again Anna succeeded in taking her by surprise, presenting a *fait accompli*!

In the Relais de la Poste time had stood still since the beginning of the thirties. Dark brown wooden chairs, white tablecloths beneath plate glass, copper lamps with glass bulbs, everything originated from that period. The owner had seen no reason to change anything in accordance with the post-war fancies for steel, plastic or pseudo-rustic. It was quiet there, a few regulars chatting softly at the buffet. Passers-by with turned-up collars walked through the snow; across the street, the walls of the Thermal Institute made a grubby contrast. The woman behind the bar recommended a regional drink to the ladies to warm them up: Ratafia de Pommes. This apple liqueur, with its sweet-sour refinement vitiated Lotte's resistance. After the second glass she spotted a primitive radio with a lovely wooden case in a dark corner. Delighted, she walked over to it and let her fingers slide lovingly over the polished wood. 'Look at this,' she called. 'That crazy father of mine had one like it too!'

*   *   *

THE PURCHASE OF a gramophone from the firm Grammophon and
Polyphon in Amsterdam brought a reason for quarrels and sleeplessness to their home, as well as a source of pleasure. Hours of musical
gastronomy had preceded the definitive choice. Lotte's father listened
with eyes closed to Caruso's divine voice; his 'Hosannah' and 'Pagli-
acci,' almost caused Polyphon's luxurious auditorium in Leidsestraat
to come apart at the seams. The turntable was set beneath a flap in
the top of the new piece of furniture. It acquired a prominent position
in the living room; from then on the house was permeated with the
symphonies of Schubert and Beethoven, with the voice of the famous
tenor Jacques Urlus—who sang 'Murmelndes Lüftchen'—but also
with the serene voice of Aaltje Noordewier in Bach's *Passions*. He
played the machine until deep into the night; it enabled his love of
music to enter into a perfect symbiosis with the very newest achieve-
ments of electrical technology. His wife kept him company to the very
end of his nightly sessions since she had discovered that in his intoxi-
cated state he forgot to put out the lamps and stoves before going to
bed. He liked it loud. The children were developing sleep problems
from an excess of heavenly sounds. They dozed over their arithmetic
books at school; Lotte could hear the melting songs of *Orfeo* in surg-
ing waves right through reading lessons.

Polyphon's warehouse contained a stock of four thousand five
hundred different gramophone records. Lotte's mother was regularly
surprised by a representative from the firm holding a bill under her
nose. A quarrel about money then flared up during the music in the
evenings. 'I've already paid it.' 'You haven't paid it; they were at the
door again, that's no way to behave.' Jet and Lotte slid out of bed and
sat on the top step, their arms round each other's shoulders. What
had merely sounded like a threat from the bedroom grew into danger
out here. The music continued mercilessly, their parents' anger raised
above it. Sometimes an object hit the floor with a bang. Eventually
they descended the stairs crying, and entered the scene of battle in
bare feet, preparing themselves for the very worst. 'We had a bad
dream,' was their alibi. Lotte held on tightly to the sleeve of Jet's
nightdress. An instant cease-fire was declared. Their father went to

the miraculous object to put another record on; their mother hugged them guiltily to her bosom.

Their father's hunger for new music was, however, surpassed by his addiction to sound machines. Soon the reproduction quality of the gramophone no longer satisfied his demands. The Concertgebouw in Amsterdam was his standard; that was how it had to sound in his living room too. He installed all kinds of experimental advances in his workshop, amid a chaos of transformers, distributors, switchboards, loudspeakers and earth electrodes—the tips of his moustache were singed from soldering. He already had a series of successful attempts as a radio builder to his name, his home-made Chrystalphone surpassed those from the Edison works. He introduced so many ingenious alterations to the gramophone that the original machine could hardly be recognized anymore. When an Ultraphone was unexpectedly launched on the market, he adapted it immediately. This machine, which delighted even the most reserved of critics, had two sound arms and two needles at its disposal, so that the sound was transmitted twice with a short pause in between—a stereo effect ahead of its time. The gramophone with the human voice, wrote the press. Lotte's father took this as a personal declaration of war. Once more he stationed himself in his workshop; he did not rest until he had built a unit with two conical loudspeakers. Not only did the sound come from different sides, as in the concert hall, but he was the front-runner in the race to conquer surface noise. The two polished beech cases that dominated the room brought him a fame that extended beyond the Maas and the Waal rivers. Engineers from the light bulb industry drove north in a company car to hear the acoustic phenomenon with their own ears. Sound technicians from the broadcasting company, musicians, hobbyists, vague acquaintances followed—evening after evening new interested parties enjoyed the brilliant sound reproduction and the ever-expanding record collection. The instigator of all these technical and musical triumphs, completely self-taught in the world of sound, found himself in a permanent state of spiritual inebriation as a result of this overdose of interest and recognition. He put his records on the turntable with just as much vanity as a violinist tucks his violin under his chin. His moustache, once again restored to its former glory, shone as never before.

The local community's power and water supply was at risk as a result of these exciting evenings. These were his responsibility—a job he had attained through years of self-study of electrical theory. He now slept late into the day. On dark winter mornings his wife got out of bed, where she had spent no more than four hours, putting a housecoat over her nightdress, to turn on the pressure pumps in the ice-cold water tower, because there was no one else to do it. Sometimes it got to be too much for her. 'You think only of yourself,' she flung at his head when he eventually stumbled downstairs, his eyes still thick with sleep, 'get up only when it suits you. Egoist. Salon socialist.' He protested, weakly, looking in vain for arguments with which to defend himself. Driven to despair by his sudden irresponsibility, she punched him. The children saw him stagger; they fled over the bridge into the wood to build a hut as an alternative to the parental home. The building activities were drawn out as long as possible in the hope that the war would have subsided by the time they crossed the bridge in the reverse direction. Hours later, hungry and worried, they walked gingerly back to the house. From the wood they could already see their parents sitting on the garden bench under the climbing pear tree, arms wound around each other and blissful smiles on their lips—equilibrium had been restored.

The children did their homework in the back room; the gramophone was silent whenever their father was out on a tour of inspection. A company Harley Davidson took him round the outskirts of the district. He raced along majestic avenues in his long leather coat, leggings on his calves, his eyes protected by huge goggles, the flaps of his cap fluttering against his head like the wings of a drunken bird. After he got home and discarded his outfit, he took a volume of the collected works of Marx or Lenin from the bookshelf and flopped into an armchair with it.

Suddenly the sliding doors would open. 'What are you doing?' he would say sternly. 'Homework.' 'Which subject?' 'Dutch history.' 'Close those books, you can learn much more from this. Listen: ". . . Wherever a part of society possesses the monopoly of the means of production, the labourer, free or not free, must add to the working time necessary for his own maintenance and extra working time in order to produce the means of subsistence for the owner of the means of production, whether this proprietor be the Athenian perfect gentleman, Etruscan theocrat, civis Romanus, Norman Baron, American slave owner, Wallachian Boyard, modern landlord or capitalist." ' He cast a meaningful glance at them over the cover of *Das Kapital*, decorated with floral stems. 'Understand, the worker labors by the sweat of his brow so that the rich can dedicate themselves entirely to doing nothing, that's how the world works, get that into your heads.' And he continued his lecture, which could last for hours when he got into his stride, until they were released by their mother, who would assign them imaginary tasks. When they complained about having to weed the kitchen garden he rubbed their noses in the fate of people of their age from the previous century. 'At two, three, four o'clock in the morning nine and ten-year-old children were dragged out of their unhealthy dormitory towns and forced to work for their mere subsistence until eleven or twelve at night, while their limbs wasted away, their bodies bent, their features were dulled and their human countenances stiffened into expressionless masks, just one glimpse of which was terrifying.'

He treated guests with more subtlety. First he tempted them with heavenly music. When he had entirely hooked them and their souls were enfeebled by emotion, he turned the volume knob low and, as though in spontaneous inspiration, opened a book which just happened to be lying there ready all the while. Some politely managed to escape in time, others got into strenuous disputes that lasted deep into the night. He only provoked genuine resistance when, in the early hours, with the imposing loudspeakers in the background as proof of his resourceful intellect, he made known his opposition to the monarchy. Spurred on by the gin, they were prepared to go a long way with him in his arguments about historical materialism, they were even prepared to turn a blind eye to his philippics against Christendom, but as soon as the royal family was mentioned he had stepped over the line: This was implacably opposed. His music, alcohol and powers of persuasion were no match for their love of the

House of Orange. He did his best to conceal his contempt, stroking
his moustache with a pointed index finger. One of the guests, Professor Koning, lecturer in colonial history at the University of Amsterdam, became so addicted to the debates that he came back to
philosophize every Saturday evening until the bottom of the gin bottle was visible. Lotte's father, who had a child-like, unsocialist respect
for authority in the province of learning, was very proud of this
friendship, which went so far that the professor bought a thatched
house on the other side of the wood.

On the Queen's birthday her father refused to hang the flag from
the water tower. But a prominent member of the provincial council,
who lived in the neighborhood and took a stroll in the wood every
day, reported his negligence. 'Come on,' said his wife the following
year, 'hang up the flag, otherwise we'll get into trouble. 'Preposterous,' he protested, 'to display the flag for a perfectly ordinary
woman.' 'You're talking about the Queen.' She looked like a queen
herself, in her cream-coloured shantung dress, proud, charming and
unrelenting. The children supported her, they had decorated their
bicycles with conifer branches and orange lanterns: 'Everyone hangs
out the flag, Dad.' He sniffed: 'The masses!' 'If you won't do it I will.'
His wife marched off with long strides; he followed behind angrily.
At the door of the water tower he grabbed her and turned her round.
He went in, jaws clenched.

An inspector came to the school to compile a register of the pupils.
He stood in front of the class with a list: they had to stand up one by
one and say their names. In a flat, dull voice he added: 'And what
does your father do?' They answered without faltering. Lotte owned
to the surname of her Dutch parents absentmindedly: Rockanje. But
she stared at him open-mouthed without saying anything when it
came to her father's profession. 'Lotte,' said the mistress affably, 'you
do know what your father does?' It took a great effort of strength to
emit the words: 'I d-don't k-know yet.' Her head was ready to burst.
Did she have to list everything her father did? Where ought she to
begin? The inspector by-passed this hitch in the machinery and continued his checking with a neutral expression. Suddenly Lotte had an

inspiration. She raised her finger 'I k-know it now.' 'Well,' said the mistress and inspector in unison, 'what is your father then?' 'Tower watchman for the Queen!' she cried without stuttering.

'IF GRANDFATHER HAD known that you had gone straight into a Communist nest . . .' cried Anna with hilarity, 'what a joke!'

'But my mother was against it. "Don't think," she said to him, "that the workers will be more humane if they seize power." She would sometimes petulantly pull him down from his pink cloud when he wouldn't stop his glorification of Marx and persisted in harping on righteously about money and work. "Try to live like that yourself, dear; only fine words come out of your mouth." '

An old man came in, stamping his boots, snow on his bushy eyebrows. His watery blue eyes timidly assessed the clientele. He left a track of melting snow behind him on the way to the counter. Lotte had red blotches on her cheeks from the Ratafia de Pommes. Anna's eyes were shining. Lotte's old-fashioned, precise German sounded like music to her ears, interspersed now and then with a Cologne word that had gone out of fashion long ago.

'That *Schicki-Micki* type,' she said, 'who fetched you from Cologne, what kind of a person was she?'

Lotte stared out the window. 'I went to stay with her in Amsterdam from time to time. If you looked from the living room into the mirror by the window you could see the Albert Cuyp market. In the mornings, we went to the market together while Grandpa went to the barber to be shaved. First she bought meat and vegetables. But her real aim was to touch the things on a stall full of beads, buttons, velvets, laces, silks. There she stood, endlessly dreaming, everything passing through her hands. After deliberating for a long time she bought something minuscule, a pair of mother-of-pearl buttons or something. She was still very elegant. "Look," she said once, "this is what I was like when I was young." She pulled her sagging skin taut with the tips of her fingers. I was shocked. I didn't recognize her like that. "Can't I go to see Anna?" I asked her one day. "*Ach du, Schätzchen,* you have no idea how stubborn and narrow-minded our

family is. We have absolutely no contact with them. Later, when
you're grown up, you can look for Anna on your own account. Then
the two of you together won't give a damn about that whole tribe.'

Anna laughed. 'A photograph of her hung above grandfather's
chair when he was still alive—as a young girl in a white dress, her
face shaded by a straw hat. *Ein wunderschönes* picture. That photo
would be a hundred years old now. Think of it, Lotte, a hundred
years! The world has never changed as radically as it has in the last
hundred years. No wonder you and I are a bit confused. Let's drink
something more!'

The layers of time were grating over each. Before the war, after the
war, the Depression years, a century ago . . . diverse landscapes that
Anna hurtled through tipsily, as though in a runaway train. One
moment she was in a steam-driven train and wisps of smoke were
drifting past the window, the next moment she was sitting on bright
green leatherette in a modern express train. Figures from the past
stood in the stations they whizzed past. They did not wave but
looked at the phantom express with screwed-up eyes and frowns. The
station in Berlin was on fire, the platforms were full of smoke and
dust. Where did this journey end? At the edge of time? It left her cold.
She clinked her glass against Lotte's and toasted her health.

'I also asked her . . .' said Lotte.

'Who?'

'Grandma . . . Aunt Elisabeth . . . I asked her: Did you know my
father when he was young? I mean, my real father. "Your father," she
said, "was a nice, intelligent boy, the revolutionary of the family. I
was very taken with him. That's why I was at his funeral and you are
here now, *du Kleine. Ach ja,* sensitive types die young and those
Schweinehunde grow ancient—that is how the world is . . ."' Lotte
added tenderly, 'Grandma loved swear-words.'

'If only such a fairy godmother had appeared for me then,' said Anna
not without bitterness, 'I would have been spared a lot of suffering.'

THIRTY-FIVE MARKS PER month orphan's allowance was paid for
Anna. That was a lot of money yet Aunt Martha carried on as though
she were a parasite, a bloodsucker who had clamped onto the young

family. She projected onto Anna the chronic displeasure that she had brought into the marriage as a dowry; Anna was broken in spirit and numb from the work and defenceless against her deviousness. Whenever Anna looked in Uncle Heinrich's cracked shaving mirror, she said scornfully, 'Why look in the mirror, you're going to die anyway. Your father had tuberculosis, your mother breast cancer, you'll get one of the two as well. Don't fancy your chances.' Anna, who had read many fairy tales, recognized in her the cliché of the wicked stepmother but the justice that always triumphed in the stories was a long time coming in reality. 'Why do you need a new dress, why should you drink milk, you are going to die anyway.'

Now that all worldly needs were being strangled at birth and ridiculed, the old longing to disappear forever seeped into her again. But to die, how did you do that? If you got a disease, it happened by itself. Intentionally instigating the change from being-there to not-being-there was more difficult. Uncertainty drove her to the Church—time stolen from the pigs and cows that had to be made up later. By praying as faultlessly as possible she hoped for a miraculous admission to heaven. But God, her second inaccessible father, did not make the effort to descend to the modest Landolinus church. At the very most He allowed Alois Jacobsmeyer to appear out of the semi-darkness; he had had a soft spot for Anna since she had given the Romans what for. He was the one who had implored her uncle: 'Send her to the grammar school! There isn't a better pupil in the village. We'll pay for it all.' Anna seized his soutane and authoritatively asked him to give her a means of disappearing from the world that would not cause inconvenience. Shocked, he whispered: 'Don't do anything stupid! God has only given you this one life, it is all you have. He wants you to live it until it ends naturally. Have patience, you will be free when you are twenty-one.' But twenty-one was unbearably far off. 'I'll never keep going,' she said angrily. 'Yes you will.' He took her head in his hands and rocked it gently to and fro. 'You must!'

Not long after that, her body seemed to have made a decision, weakened by the daily battle of attrition and the frugal food. She caught a cold that would not clear up. Jacobsmeyer urged her to go to the doctor but Aunt Martha waved his advice aside—that sort of cold would wear off by itself. Then he thought up a trick to combat the cough without being accused of interfering in other people's business. He wandered over to the farm after mass. Anna was in the cowshed when Aunt Martha stuck her head round the corner, her cheekbones red with suppressed anger. 'The pastor is here for you.' Jacobsmeyer was sitting in the kitchen with a gurgling baby on his lap. He drew a narrow brown bottle out of his soutane. 'It can't go on any longer,' he said to Anna. 'You cough all the way through the mass, I can't understand my own words.' With a combination of triumph and indignation Aunt Martha cried: 'That one there? But she has no manners, we know that already!' 'I have brought a medicine for her with me,' Jacobsmeyer continued imperturbably. 'Frau Bamberg, will you see to it that she takes it regularly?' Aunt Martha nodded, taken by surprise. 'And if her clothes are wet from sweat,' he went on, 'she must change, so that she doesn't catch a new cold.' 'Oh yes,' scoffed Aunt Martha, 'then she'd have to go into the field to hang her shirt up on the willows and wait naked until it was dry. The men here would certainly appreciate that.' He admonished her, piqued because he had unwittingly nurtured her squalid fantasy, 'You ought to buy her some extra shirts, Frau Bamberg.' He stood up with dignity and passed the baby to her. 'You must think about this little one of yours but also of Anna . . . they are all God's children.' He turned round at the door: 'And she must drink a lot of milk, with cream.' 'If he pays for it himself,' snarled Aunt Martha when the door had closed behind him.

'And?' enquired Jacobsmeyer. Anna looked at the floor, leaning on one of the pillars in the nave. 'Aunt Martha has given me one of her worn-out old shirts. But I am not allowed to drink milk, that has to go for sale.' 'God forgive me,' he sighed, 'when you centrifuge milk, Anna, put your mouth under the spout now and then. But do look round regularly, otherwise she'll see what's going on.'

Uncle Heinrich erected between himself and his wife a screen of work activities, card games with villagers, newspapers and library books, which were read by Anna, too, in stolen quarters of an hour. He did not object, except when she wanted to read *All Quiet on the Western Front*. He forbade it not because of the war horrors but because of an indecent scene, which she was quite unable to discover when she nevertheless read the book in secret, because she lacked the antennae for that sort of wavelength. The fate of four nineteen-year-old boys in the trench warfare of 1914–18 strengthened her in the belief that a man's life was not valued. The life of a soldier was something like a candle in front of the statue of Mary—when it had burnt down a new one was put in the holder.

They discussed the books they had read—in the mornings while Aunt Martha was still in bed, in the afternoons when she was having a nap and in the evenings when she was in bed again. Although the conversations were fleeting, fitted in as they went along, they created a secret bond between two who were like-minded, the last descendants of one family, against the ominous background of the wife upstairs who was still a stranger to them both. Only much later on did Anna understand that Aunt Martha must have felt this alliance, through the walls—perhaps in her morbid suspicion she had even seen an unspoken love in it. Her aunt bided her time until a chance arose to drive a wedge between them. Bernd Möller unintentionally became her tool.

Anna went to find him in his workshop to inquire whether the problem with the haycart's axle had been fixed yet. He did not look up from the threshing cart he was repairing; she had to repeat her question before an intelligible reply came from his mouth. No, he had not yet got round to it. A newspaper was open among the nuts and bolts on his workbench. Anna bent inquisitively over the columns, avid for anything that appeared in print. Quiet returned to the workshop except for the prosaic sounds of repair work. 'Are you still here?' said Bernd Möller, surprised. 'What are you doing?' 'Reading.' 'What are you reading?' Anna turned back to the front page. '*The Völkischer Beobachter.*' That's not for you, all politics.' Anna folded open the paper and held it up to his nose. 'Who is this?' With a black fingernail, under which chicken and pig muck had collected, she pointed to the portrait of a man with a clenched fist and a provoked, irate look, who was screaming inaudibly, a flag with black spiders' legs in a white circle in the background. 'Adolf Hitler,' said Bernd Möller, wiping his nose on his sleeve. She turned up her nose. 'It looks as though he wants to go and fight.' 'That is what he wants to do.' The mechanic put his monkey wrench on the floor and slowly stood up from his crouch. 'For me, for you, for all of us. Against unemployment and poverty.'

He forgot all about the job he had been engrossed in just before and sat on the workbench to explain to her the plans the man in the photograph had for the German people. Long-awaited work, a New Order—even for the ordinary man who was driving himself into the ground every day for a plate of pea soup. Look, here it was in writing. Bernd Möller had an aura of optimism about him. Someone had appeared on the horizon who was preparing great changes, who was going to put an end to the poverty and chaos in the country. Stirred by his enthusiasm, Anna had the feeling that something might then improve for her too—even if it were perhaps only something small. A long-awaited father figure who would take up the cudgels for her and who would break through the chains of drudgery, fatigue and hunger. She looked intently at the photograph. What he was giving expression to and what had initially aroused her distaste was, on further inspection, precisely what she felt beneath her veneer of slavish obedience: rage and mutiny.

That evening she said to her uncle in a conspiratorial tone, 'There's someone who is going to put an end to poverty.' He was sitting in the chair his father had died in; she was on the sofa beneath the soldier killed in action. 'That's good news,' he said, looking ironically at her over his book, 'how do you make that out?' 'It's in the *Völkischer Beobachter*. Adolf Hitler has said . . .' 'What?' he cried. The book slid out of his hands. 'That fool? You don't know what you're saying. Only dumb, desperate people trail after that ridiculous figure. Who did you learn that nonsense from?' 'From Bernd Möller,' she said, offended and confused. 'Oh, I get it, that's his way of rebelling. The *Völkischer Beobachter*! One doesn't read it! No one here reads that paper. Every right-thinking person, every right-minded Catholic votes for the Centre Party. Pope Pius X's encyclical describes exactly how poverty can be overcome from the Christian point of view. Listen, girl—this Hitler wants just one thing with his bragging: war.' He bent over to pick up his book and looked at her as though he were listen-

ing acutely for something. 'I won't have you associating with Bernd
Möller, understand that.'

But Anna could not allow herself to give up this ray of hope so easily. The following day she scurried over to the workshop. Bernd
Möller shook his head at her uncle's reaction. 'I'll explain to you
exactly why he said that—so that you don't look shocked at me any
longer with your lovely blue eyes. I can't stand that.' He smiled. 'You
simply have to let them talk, those brave farmers, those obedient
Catholics. They don't know any better. They are just animals who
have lived in a cage for too long: If you throw the door open they
simply stay in there. If we had to wait until the Centre Party settled
our problems we'd all starve.' His self-confidence aroused trust. She
needed to believe in a chance of change, there was no alternative.
And Bernd Möller kept this belief alive with cheerful hymns. She did
her work at a faster pace purely to be able to steal over to his workshop in between times and talk with him, or to watch him while he
fiddled inside the motor of a farm machine. They did not only talk
politics. The pitfalls of everyday life, the attitude that you should take
towards it, the books Anna had been reading, her cough—no subject
was taboo in the intimacy of the old, draughty shed, as she sat with
one buttock on the open newspaper and the other on the scored
wood of the workbench.

'Although you're only sixteen, you're an exceptional girl,' said
Bernd. He heaped praise on her; in his eyes she was a little, philo-
sophical Virgin with a big heart that was beating for all the outcasts
and unfortunates in the world. The new Germany would get off the
ground more easily if there were more such young women. She had a
great future before her, he assured her, squeezing her hands with their
split and broken nails in his fists smeared with engine oil. Over time
that future increasingly took on the form of a house he was going to
build for her. A rustic, old-fashioned house with a gabled roof, shutters, a Bavarian veranda along the full width of the façade and a massive oak door, which he would push open to carry her across the
threshold when she was eighteen. Anna allowed these fantasies to
glance off her indifferently. Marriage she had never thought about,
the very idea of it was ridiculous to her. Whenever he conjured up

these dream pictures to her she looked intently at the floor strewn
with tools and machine parts—apparently this was a sacrifice that
had to be made now and then for friendship.

When the rye was being harvested she had no time for these inter-
ludes. A little boy from the village pushed a letter into her hand: 'This
evening at half past eight behind the Lady Chapel by the bridge.' It
was already twilight by that time and it smelled intoxicatingly of
damp hay. She did not recognize him at first. He crossed the bridge in
a brown uniform that was rather a tight fit and he had a parting in his
hair. There was an officious expression on his face that did not
become him. He grasped her by her wrists. 'Your house is going to be
built, Anna! An architect in Paderborn has done a design. It's waiting
for you, you must approve the drawing!' She gazed at him impassively. All of a sudden she no longer knew what she had been seeking
at the Lady Chapel with a wild stranger with whom she had no affinity who was badgering her about a house that ought to remain a fantasy instead of turning up on paper and, even worse, being built stone
by stone on this sandy ground. Aroused by his own excitement, he
threw his muscular mechanic's arms around her, demanding too
much of his sleeves. She heard the threads snap and over his shoulder
saw the neighbour passing by with a young goat on a rope. Ashamed,
she hid her face in his chest; he took it for affection and increased the
pressure of his arms. When he eventually let her go she dashed across
the bridge towards the farm, stumbling over her own feet as though
she had narrowly escaped from a great danger.

The neighbour did not neglect her citizen's duty and the next day
reported Anna's wooing to Aunt Martha, who understood instantly
that this was what she had been waiting for all that time. Concealing
her triumph behind an exemplary display of moral indignation, she
disclosed the report of the rendezvous to her husband, embellishing it
with shocking details that unerringly hit him below the belt. Anna,
still suspecting nothing, was fetching water for the pigs. When she
turned round, Uncle Heinrich was standing on the threshold.
Although he was not heavily built, he looked as though he filled the
whole doorway. Why was something so threatening emanating from
him? The figure, cramped by suppressed tension, approached her and

came within a metre of her. She felt suddenly that an unknown misunderstanding was festering between them, which had to be cleared
up as fast as possible.

'What would your father say' he began, in a gruesomely controlled
voice, 'if he caught you with that womanizer, that agitator? Eh?
Would you have dared if he had still been alive?' Anna stiffened, she
could see the whole chain of cause and effect in one second. 'Would
you have dared?' he repeated, lending force to his question with a
slap on her face. 'Well?' As she brought a hand up to her cheek in disbelief he hit her on the other cheek. She turned away and ducked to
escape his hands; this evasive reflex only provoked his frenzy further.
His fists landed wherever he could reach her. When she fell over on
the slippery ground he pulled her up by her hair and punched her in
the stomach. The rage he dealt out to her was greater than himself
and greater than the cause. It was concentrated from all his resentment against a world in which he was powerless, but also from the
like-mindedness between Anna and him, and their solidarity—perhaps even his defencelessness against the young woman she had
become without having any inkling of it. Of all that impenetrable,
murky motivation, Anna had not the slightest suspicion—for her all
that existed were the blows and punches, and the cries he uttered, as
though he was suffering more than she in this thrashing. At one
moment one side of the cowshed flashed by, next the other again, and
the pigs' snouts moving by on either side like amazed witnesses. She
lost all sense of time until, beneath the raised arm with which she was
protecting her head, she saw Aunt Martha positioned on the threshold in order to enjoy the full measure of her punishment. His wife's
appearance brought Uncle Heinrich out of his fury. He stopped
abruptly, looking down at Anna with surprise, glassily. Without deign-
ing to look at his wife, he pushed her aside and disappeared outside.

Anna got up laboriously—a searing pain dragged through her
whole body. Aunt Martha was a black blob heavily outlined against
the daylight behind her. 'What must the neighbours think,' she
growled, 'you've made a hell of a noise.' 'What noise?' moaned Anna.
Who had yelled with each blow? Not her, she had clamped her lips
tight. The record had to be set straight, even in the midst of chaos.

Collecting the last of her strength, she crawled towards her aunt, her broken nails reaching for the skin of the weak, naked arms. The woman who was so large and looked so strong, crossed her arms anxiously across her breasts; the deepset eyes above the wide cheekbones sunk even further into their sockets. She fled backwards out of the cowshed, Anna stumbled after her and, splaying out her arms, fell over on the grass.

No more clatter of combat, but absolute silence. Guilty Uncle Heinrich put food and drink on the floor by her bed; like a wild animal she only touched the plates when he had gone. For the first days she lay on her stomach because the pain in her back was so bad, then she exchanged the monotonous panorama of wood grain and knots in the floor for that of the wall, and turned half on her side, because the contractions and stabbing pains in her belly were now drowning out all other forms of pain. It was becoming worse instead of diminishing. An unbearable paradox; she could not endure it any more and yet she was enduring it. With each wave of pain she lapsed into a soft wail that penetrated to the kitchen down the chimney hung with hams and sausages. Eventually Uncle Heinrich stumbled upstairs to ask her what could be done to put an end to the moaning. In a rasping voice Anna complained of stabbing in her belly. That frightened him, the reproductive organs were sacred: Go forth and multiply. What had never been considered necessary for her cough was to happen now; an appointment was made with a doctor. She had to promise her aunt dutifully to keep quiet about the injuries and bruises. New tortures were announced. The law required an adult woman to be present as a chaperone at an internal examination. Lying on her black and blue back, beneath Aunt Martha's vulture glare, Anna felt his cool rubber finger penetrate a region she had not suspected of existing until then. A piercing pain split her down the middle. 'It's a bit uncomfortable,' said the voice of her benefactor. Uncomfortable! Had *he* ever been cleaved in half? Tears slid dully down her cheeks without her permission, a triumph she did not concede to her aunt. 'Come, come,' said the doctor, 'let's not make a drama of it. Your womb is twisted, I'm trying to get it back in position.'

The pain subsided. Aunt Martha's lust for power was stronger

than ever before, as though she had been present at an initiation ritual that henceforth gave her new power over Anna. During mass,
behind the stocky straight back of her aunt, she crumpled a letter for
Jacobsmeyer into the hand of an old school friend, containing a simple but urgent message: 'Help! Anna.' During the Gregorian hymns
her eyes strayed involuntarily to the bas relief where Jesus was being
flogged. Her breath caught. She quickly directed her gaze up to the
vaulted roof decorated with tendrils, where the singing voices joined
the echo of the prayers. The note reached the pastor wonderfully fast;
he took her aside as she was leaving the church. She rolled up the
sleeves of her Sunday dress and said, 'My back also looks like my
arms.' Although Jacobsmeyer was, from his profession, on familiar
terms with violence in the Bible and with the Christian idea that suffering was the shortest route to God, he was put off his stride when
confronted by it in reality. He lifted his glasses from his nose, put
them back and raised them again before he laid a trembling hand on
her head.

6

6 NON . . . JE NE *regrette rien* . . .
'Ha!' Anna cried. Startled roughly out of his reverie,
the old man in the bar blinked his watery eyes, there
was a puddle of melted snow under his bar stool. 'Ha! *Je ne regrette
rien* . . . the queen of love never has regrets. She took a young lover
when she had one foot in the grave—her musical heir, her nightingale
who sang like a crow . . .' She laughed mockingly. 'Little Sparrow,
picked out of the gutter . . . I was also a little sparrow in the gutter—
now I'm an old woman teased by memories. An old woman who'll
have another.' She snapped her fingers towards the bar.

'*Ach ja,*' Lotte said quietly, in an attempt to neutralize Anna's emo-
tionality, 'the older you become the more you live in the past. You
forget things that happened yesterday.'

Anna raised her eyebrows at this clichéd remark. But to Lotte it was the practical and ever successful opening for a lament about old age, a conversational ploy for keeping the discussion in safe waters. Full glasses were set before them, with a smile from the proprietess. Perhaps she had been on the wrong side in the war, as had many Belgians? It was difficult for her to imagine Anna, that well-fed, quick-witted woman sitting opposite her, as an ill-treated, sickly girl of sixteen in her Sunday dress, gagged by her step-aunt, who had been allocated so many bad qualities that it was a caricature. Wasn't Anna exaggerating? Had time distorted her memories? She was instantly ashamed of her persistent scepticism. Barbarians, her mother had said. She could really see why now. It was all so extreme. Lotte regarded malicious, violent behaviour as a sickness, to be cordoned off safely and kept at a distance. In that light she diagnosed Aunt Martha as dangerously mentally deranged—no wonder Uncle Heinrich slowly went mad under her influence.

'That aunt of yours was a pathological case.' She took a reckless sip.

Anna laughed dryly. 'Not necessarily. She was merely a woman who was good for nothing. There are people like that. According to Christian morality they are evil, according to psychiatry they are sick. What difference does it make when you're the victim of it? But let's have something more cheerful. About you.'

Lotte did not miss the insinuation: compared with Anna's youth, hers was, in Anna's eyes, a model of freedom from trouble. Of the two of them, Anna was the one entitled to sympathy. Although ostensibly she spoke with distance and irony about the past, in ways she was making a subtle call for compassion. The compassion that had always been withheld from her and was now expected from her sister—no, demanded. But that role did not appeal to her.

'About your singing,' Anna coaxed, 'your lovely voice.'

'God, I'm hot,' said Lotte. She stood up lopsidedly to take her jacket off, fumbling with the sleeves—defects had appeared in the coordination of her movements as a result of the apple liqueur. There were two possibilities: to give Anna what she requested or to remain silent. The latter felt hard to her, she enjoyed talking about her life. Who was still interested in it? Not her children. And if she kept quiet it would all be lost, as though it had never happened.

SINGING GRADUALLY ELBOWED out the stuttering: the pleasure of singing was greater than the anxiety preceding the first sound. Her body grew and her voice grew with it—actually her voice was always rather older than herself. When she was accepted into a famous teenage choir, only her voice properly belonged there. The choir was directed by Catharina Metz, a dark, melancholy woman with a fluffy moustache that she sometimes shaved off but more often left, from indifference—the delicate hairs trembled with her vibrato. There were still yellowed newspaper cuttings about her singing career, which had come to an abrupt end with her father's illness. They never got to see the mysterious invalid; he lived his abstract existence in a wing of the house overgrown with Virginia creeper and wisteria, and it only manifested itself in the dark rings under his daughter's eyes. Sometimes she suddenly stopped the rehearsal with a raised finger to listen with concentration to something that was inaudible to the pupils. She guided them with a gentle hand via unfamiliar French and Italian composers into the territory of the great classics.

Whenever the choir performed for the radio, Lotte's mother urged everyone to take a place in a circle around the Chrystalphone, in an imposing amphitheatre of kitchen chairs. On one Sunday morning Lotte's voice came into the living room unexpectedly, separate from the choir, in a Bach cantata. Uncertain of the results, she came home—she could not hear her own voice in the studio. There a celebration was in progress, alcohol was on the table, her mother hugged her, moved, and presented her with a bouquet of flowers that tickled her nostrils. She had a sneezing fit. 'Mind your voice!' cried Mies sarcastically; she liked to be the centre of attention herself. Her father was looking feverishly in his record collection for that particular cantata—his way of indicating his appreciation. Lotte fell into an armchair, bewildered, and pensively downed a brimming glass of advocaat that Marie had held out to her with a respectful laugh. It gave her a scandalously pleasurable feeling that she was earning suc-

cess with something that she herself enjoyed to the roots of her hair.
(The reward was already there in the singing itself). Two days later
she received a perfumed letter: 'Your timbre is unique, it is a rare gift.
I will still remember your voice in twenty years, and that is something
others would give everything for.' Catharina Metz recognized the
sender as a famous music critic. Blushing, Lotte packed the letter in
the suitcase she had come with from Germany. Along with her
mourning dress and Anna's embroidered handkerchief that had been
in one of the pockets, here was where she kept the sewing case that
had drowned with her and a newspaper cutting about Amelita Galli-
Curci. Later she moved the letter to a drawer in her dressing table
where a scent of violets still lingered after sixty years.

She had first heard Amelita Galli-Curci in a duet with Caruso. It
was a hot afternoon in September. She was walking home through the
wood after school with Jet. The water tower shimmered through the
trees when suddenly she stopped. Like a force of nature, a voice was
coming from an open window which was so enchanting that Lotte
was all attention—a gigantic, immobile ear. Jet pulled impatiently on
her sleeve and then walked on, shrugging her shoulders. Lotte wanted
to delay as long as possible the banal moment of coming home and
discovering that the voice emanated from a groove in an ebony disc.
So she stood there with eyes closed until the last sounds had died
away between the tree trunks.

The queen of coloratura singing, Galli-Curci, married to a marquis
from the foot of the boot of Italy, scored triumphs in the United
States immediately after the First World War 'as a lyric soprano of
unusual beauty, pure and crystal clear from low A flat to high C',
according to *Opera World* of the day. In the cutting that Lotte kept,
there was a photograph of a majestic, dark-haired woman who defied
the camera with a raised chin—a Rembrandtesque hat on her head at
an angle, a shawl with large flowers and birds draped over her shoulders, and two showy rings on her right hand, which rested militarily
on her breast, just above the heart. A Napoleonic stance. Thus
inspired, Lotte slipped into the water tower, ignoring the strict prohi-
bition—long hair or ribbons could get caught in one of the machines.
She positioned herself—chin up, hand on chest, directed her gaze

upwards and brought about a change of scenery: the metal stairs no longer led to a reservoir filled with sand, gravel and coal, but spiralled endlessly upwards on their own axis, into a firmament full of stars—they might also have been theatre lights. As yet unhampered by excessive self-criticism, she sang 'Caro Nome' or 'Veranno a te' in her own Italian version as she had managed to learn it from the record. Her voice filled the whole tower from the low A flat to the high E, ascending the stairs to the place where the steps became fainter and fainter, in never-ending Escherian revolutions. Her chest expanded. Drunk from the melody and the sound of her own voice, she floated away to another phase in her life—the reservoir arched high above her, a stained-glass window separated the light into coloured fragments, somewhere behind her the sound reverberated through the marble corridors of a labyrinthine building. It was an indefinable feeling that nevertheless half penetrated her consciousness and was immediately forgotten, as soon as she stopped singing.

A walnut piano of obscure East European make was acquired so that she could accompany herself. The money for it and for lessons was scraped together by her mother, to her father's bloodthirsty delight: now it was his turn to make a row about irresponsible expenditure. He readily over-indulged himself in idolizing such famous figures as Marx and Stalin, Beethoven and Caruso, but he could not imagine that something exceptional, for which sacrifices had to be made, could be developing within reach in his own surroundings, where trifles made him bad tempered increasingly often.

The piano brought a tuner to the house every three months. He was long and thin with a gypsy's bird-of-prey nose. His black, curly hair was shaved on the sides but stuck up on top so that from a distance he looked as though he had a beret on his head. He always wore the same close-fitting black suit that elicited all kinds of speculation. Was it a wedding outfit from before the war, the dress coat of an undertaker, a morning coat with the tails cut off, or a theatrical costume worn by the Devil or Death? Below his tight trousers he wore modern American shoes, which he kept in impeccable condition. He was a man of contrasts. The leanness of his body was compensated for by the visible dimensions of his genitalia, which, because of the shortage of space, he made room for in his right trouser leg, or on another occasion in his left. The whispering modesty of his voice was cancelled out by the honky-tonk sounds he elicited from the piano. The sisters fled to the kitchen, united in their aversion to his *thing*, but also amazed that his face remained so neutral in the presence of that which made itself so evident below his belt. They were commissioned to take him coffee, but no one dared. They clung to each other, giggling. Eventually Lotte took the cup in—he was her tuner. He accepted it with a smile, unaware of the consternation he was arousing with his controversial body. After his visit the cup was washed up with extra soap.

He was also a serviceable amateur photographer. Lotte's mother persuaded him to take a family portrait on the occasion of Eefje's birth. She had invited him for a Sunday afternoon in May; above the white garden bench that was selected to be the central ornament, a swallow's nest hung beneath the roof gable—the parental couple were doing overtime flying back and forth. Nervous activity prevailed before the photographer's arrival; up to the last moment dresses were being adjusted and straightened. Lotte's father refused to put on another suit. He was not planning to pose, he said, only the Tsar and Tsarina had themselves commemorated *en famille*. 'What have I got to do with that man?' he added scornfully. 'You don't have to do anything with that man,' said his wife, 'he's coming here to take photographs, I shall offer him a cup of coffee convivially and you will present him with a cigar.' But he was in the mood for sabotage, enjoying the power tossed into his lap by the occasion.

He was nowhere to be found when the photographer arrived lugging a heavy telescopic camera and stand. Irresistible in a dress with poppies on a cream background, Lotte's mother steered him into the garden. Her offspring trickled outside while he was positioning himself and his equipment where she indicated, directly opposite the bench. Mies, who worked in a millinery, wore a cognac-coloured suit with an inverted bird's nest of raffia on her head. Marie wanted to establish for posterity that she was the ugly duckling of the family; she had on a high-necked grey dress and refused to remove her glasses for the photograph. Jet and Lotte walked about stiffly, like fallen angels, in white organdie dresses with flounces and ruches. Koen, still a baby when Lotte had fallen through the ice, refused to wear long trousers to hide the grazes on his knees.

At the photographer's request, their mother, with the newborn in her arms, seated herself in the middle of the bench and in the interest of the composition, she was flanked by the organdie dresses. The others stood behind, a climbing rose pricking them in the back. 'Lovely . . .' he murmured, studying the tableau vivant in his lens, 'er . . . isn't Sir to be part of it?' 'Sir is in a bad mood,' said Lotte's mother, 'so we don't want him in the photograph.' 'Could there be a little smile perhaps?' They did their best to forget the big spoilsport and troublemaker and stared straight at the camera; the young swallows piped, a light breeze wafted the scent of lilacs, the photographer bent behind his magic box—the whole situation could have been agreeable if that lacuna had not existed there in the middle behind the bench, a missing figure resting his hands on their mother's shoulders. The photographer implored them to laugh. Forced attempts—only Mies smiled attractively, like a film star, eyeing the lens with a sensuous expression; Koen was scratching open the scabs on his knees.

At that moment Beethoven's Ninth, booming and massive, began through the open window. The volume was turned up as far as the loudspeakers could manage. The photographer held his temples in his hands and shut his eyes pathetically. I cannot concentrate like this, he gestured. For the first time Lotte experienced a piercing-sweet, poisonous emotion that she could not yet define as hate. She looked over the photographer's head to the tops of the conifers that were moving gently in the breeze and wished furiously that her thoughts had the power to kill. 'Laugh!' cried their mother, prodding and pinching them, 'Laugh, kids!' She showed her radiant smile, all teeth bared (didn't she want to tear him to pieces?). Her eyes joined in too, she was beside herself with pleasure. 'We've got one more child,' she shouted above the scherzo, 'a big, stubborn child, in there.' She gestured towards the window with her head, laughing sideways. A cloud passed in front of the sun, the photographer raised his long black arm to the sky and pushed it away. He held his breath and pushed the shutter in.

Lotte's father did not always opt out. He put up fierce resistance
when she was sent to a Christian school because the state schools
were not accepting any more pupils. He looked at his wife with utter
disgust as though she had enrolled Lotte at an institution for the mentally handicapped. 'You'll see,' she said laconically, 'that in her case
religious stuff will go in one ear and out the other.' She was proved
right, though not in the way she meant.

The Bible had the appeal of the forbidden. Just as some girls
sneaked into a bioscope with painted lips to watch an adult film
breathlessly, Lotte was secretly thrilled by the Bible, which certainly
also carried the 'over eighteen' warning label with all that death and
killing, adultery and fornication it poured over the innocent reader.
What tame reading matter her father's favourite book was in comparison. Diligently she studied the stories of blood and miracles.
Attempts to exchange ideas with her classmates ran straight into a
wall of indifference. They had absolutely no thoughts about it; they
were brought up on religion like a daily dose of cod liver oil. Similarly, with the minister's daughter with whom she shared her bench,
the Bible was not a subject for contemplation but a duty, a soporific
aspect of Sundays—weekly imprisonment in the gloomy confirmation
classroom next door to the church. Their blind, uninterested acceptance of it as a ragbag of stories presented as 'what happened' shocked
her. With her outstanding marks in biblical history, she was the only
one taking religion seriously!

The director of the school, a man with a face etched from ice by a
razor-sharp pen, spied at the pane in the door as the pupils ended the
lessons with a prayer, and saw that one of them was looking out of
the window waiting resignedly for the ritual to end. He hurried into
the classroom and with pursed lips said to the religious instruction
teacher: 'She must stay behind.' A bony finger was pointed at her. The
chosen one or the doomed? The class emptied. 'You were not praying,' declared the director. 'No sir.' 'How is it that you do not pray?'
'Sir, I never pray.' 'You never pray?' The narrow top lip was raised in
an involuntary biting movement. 'No.' 'And what about at home?'
'They don't pray there either.' 'Then do you never go to church?' 'No,
I never go to church.' The religious instruction teacher stroked his

apostolic beard in amazement. 'But how did you end up at this school then?' 'There was no place anywhere else. My mother enrolled me, she wasn't asked whether I was a Christian.' The director stared at her with a suspicious frown, as though she were withholding from him the principal point at issue. It was clear that she was guilty of something, though he could not decide what it was. 'But you get the highest marks in the class in religious instruction,' exclaimed her teacher. 'I am hearing it all for the first time,' said Lotte, 'I have been listening very carefully.' 'And what do you make of it?' he asked, suddenly curious. 'I assume you have perceived that it is all profound truth,' said the director, supporting him. Lotte swallowed. She cast him a nervous glance—if she told him the truth that had been burning on the tip of her tongue all these months, he would expel her from the school immediately. 'Devil's children!' echoed a voice from an immense distance. 'Devil's children!' An apparition she vaguely recognized urged her on. Something black, something flapping about, the mournful tapping of a stick . . . It was no more than a diffuse feeling. 'No,' she said, suddenly seizing courage. 'Why not?' asked the director sharply. She looked over his bony shoulder to the outside, where shining black branches moved to and fro against a dark grey sky. 'It doesn't make sense,' she said. 'According to the story of creation, God is almighty and He is love. Then how is it possible that He has let the Devil loose among the people . . . if He can do everything?' 'That is . . . a mystery of faith,' stammered her teacher. What a bromide! She looked from one to the other, overcome with contempt and pity at their boundless naiveté. 'Adam and Eve lived in Paradise and ate from that forbidden fruit . . .' She sighed. 'I think of it like Snow White.' The teacher took his glasses from his nose, fished a handkerchief out of his jacket pocket with thumb and forefinger and began to clean them thoroughly. The director's pronounced Adam's apple went up and down, he emitted a dry, cynical laugh. 'You cannot prove these things,' he announced, 'you must simply believe them.' Lotte scratched the back of her head. Her skull itched, she understood that it would be impolite, at this moment, to scratch vigorously all over with the nails of both hands. 'At one time you believed in Santa Claus,' she mumbled, 'but then one day no more.' Oh dear, she was

on cracking ice, she had already gone too far. All she could do was
walk boldly onwards, continuously shifting her weight. The director
looked at her as though he wanted to tear her heathen's tongue out of
her mouth. 'She doesn't understand at all,' sounded the deep voice of
the religious instruction teacher, which gave a warm, bronzy dimension to the Bible stories. He put his glasses on and looked laconically
at the director, who let his hands drop, the right one clenched into a
fist; it was pointed at Lotte with the index finger sticking out like the
barrel of a pistol. 'You are obliged to obey the rules of this school,
think it over, from now on you will pray with the others as is normal.'
He turned his high, crooked back with its drooping shoulders on her.
Stooped beneath three centuries of Calvinism, he walked out of the
classroom with something sharp in his step, as though he was put in
the right by this command.

'AND . . .' ANNA ASKED, her arm linked in Lotte's, 'did you pray
with them from then on?'

They had left the café, whose interior harmonized perfectly with
the period that haunted them, and were walking step by step through
the snow. It had already grown dark again. Nineteenth-century
façades rose on either side—balconies, towers, bays, *oeils-de-boeuf*,
dormer windows. In the shop window of a neighborhood stationer's,
between calendars, desk diaries and dip pens, was a book in which
the Russian President set out his vision for the future; a dog was cautiously lifting its paws as it embarked on an untrodden piece of snow,
the trees of the Athenée Royale stood motionless in their spot, the
Christmas decorations were still twinkling in a greengrocer's.

'Of course not,' Lotte said, out of breath. The street kept ascending, and the alcohol too, it made her dizzy. They rested on the railway
bridge. A red signal burned in the distance in the snow, a white spire
stood out sharply in the dark sky. 'The director took every opportunity to thwart me. One day'—she giggled—'I was wearing a dress
with a V-neck. He stopped me in the corridor. "Now then, you must
ask your mother for another dress you can wear. This one really is
too naked." ' A wave of Ratafia de Pommes ascended; she swallowed
and began to laugh again. 'One time I rode to school on my father's

bicycle. I got off in the playground and put it in the bicycle rack. As I turned around I almost bumped right into the director. "Don't do that ever again," he cried, "here, in public, in full view of everyone, getting off a man's bicycle! Shame on you!" I looked at him, baffled. What did he mean, I asked myself, why does it bother him?'

Their laughter sounded dryly over the cotton-wool snow. They plodded onwards. When they reached Lotte's hotel, Anna invited herself for dinner. They were seated opposite each other beneath a salmon-pink ceiling with white ornamental borders and crystal chandeliers. At the next table was a young woman who was taking a postnatal rehabilitation treatment at the Thermal Institute. They agreed they would be better off ordering a carafe of water than a carafe of wine. For hors d'oeuvre they had *crudités* with Ardennes ham and strips of smoked pork; they cut the fat off the ham and left the smoked pork. The mother of the newborn folded her hands and closed her eyes before picking up her knife and fork.

'Wouldn't you like to . . . to . . .' Lotte whispered with an ironic laugh in the woman's direction, 'I mean . . . before the meal . . .'

'I? Say grace before the meal?' Anna draped the salmon-pink napkin on her lap. 'Understand me correctly, I do still believe, in my own way, but I renounced the institution of the Church long ago. Yet I have not forgotten what the Church did for me then. Don't underestimate how far Church and Society were caught up in one another. Those were quite different times—quite different.'

JACOBSMEYER SUMMONED HELP from the child welfare agency. They sent a social worker to the farm. Aunt Martha started on about Anna, who was eavesdropping behind the door. All that time her poor aunt had been harbouring a viper; the child did not want to be good for anything, she associated with older men—she was a whore, young as she was. To Anna's amazement, the social worker encouraged her aunt uncritically in her litany of complaints. Her last hope was flying away. The woman had come to help Aunt Martha, not her. When she had finished letting off steam, the woman said calmly, 'Now I'd like to talk to the child alone.' Anna fled back to the kitchen. With a satisfied laugh around her mouth, Aunt Martha came

to fetch her. Anna went into the living room fatalistically—Aunt
Martha went outside, confident of her case. The social worker closed
the door behind Anna, stood there with her back against it, opened
her arms and said, 'Trust me, I will help you.'

Beneath her gaze, which signalled that she could see through Aunt
Martha, Anna's resistance melted. She understood that someone was
throwing her a lifeline, someone for whom a nod was as good as a
wink. A representative from another world who was objective and
reasonable and perhaps (she hesitated) also more loving. Outside, she
saw her aunt picking pears, right under the window, in the hope of
catching something of the tirade that would be meted out to the
young cuckoo. Anna relaxed. Was her serfdom really over? Would
she no longer be at the mercy of the capriciousness and mistrust of a
mentally deranged pear-picker?

She was plucked out of the house as she was, in her farming
clothes. She had a nourishing meal at Jacobsmeyer's. He gave her his
blessing and money for clothes and waved to her as she rode in a car
(for the first time in her life) out of the village on the Lippe. Up and
down hills, through forests that flamed yellow and orange, until a village appeared, its houses ascending high up the slope, to come as
close as possible to the ambit of the church towering over everything,
and a half-timbered castle with dozens of tiny windows and slate
roofs. Leaning against the church was a convent of the Poor Clares. A
nun in a black habit hurried through the gate to meet them with open
arms.

Compresses of crushed comfrey on the blue bruises, ointment on
the cuts in her hands, age-old Franciscan calm, carefully conserved
within the thick walls, foaming milk in large mugs, the unselfish
devotion of the nuns, who fluttered along the lofty corridors like
black butterflies. From her bed she could see the castle of Baron von
Zitsewitz—a name from a fairy tale, like the Marquis of Carabas. She
had literally come straight into the lap of the Mother Church, together
with a group of fellow sufferers, chosen ones, emergencies. They were
silent about their pasts as though by tacit agreement. From the nuns
they learned the skills with which they would cope in the world later
on: sewing, cooking, looking after children and even serving at table.

There was a room specially for them where people from outside came to eat at lunchtime, well-fed guinea pigs (*Mittagstischgäste*), who consumed their experiments with relish.

That even greater preparations were being made beyond the convent wall did not get through to them. There was no radio, no newspaper, only a gramophone with a stock of fashionable popular songs, to which they danced with the younger nuns—beneath the disapproving gaze of a cardinal in purple formal robes whose portrait hung over the fireplace. The tango, '*Was machst du mit dem Knie, lieber Hans,*' made Anna most breathless; she circled the dance floor at a wild pace, her stockings sagging, her partner's habit clutched against her calves. It was the top hit of the convent until one day Anna listened carefully to the words and discovered that Hans was using the tango as an alibi to drive his knee like a wedge between the thighs of his partner on each upbeat. She warned Sister Clementine, who was swirling round in the arms of a sturdily built orphan girl, a blissful smile on her lips as though she were in the arms of her heavenly bridegroom. The record was put on again; still breathing hard, the nun listened to the words with her eyes closed. She swayed her head gently in time. Blushes slowly appeared on her cheeks, her mouth dropped open. The last sounds left a hideous silence behind. With raised head, Sister Clementine walked to the gramophone and lifted the record off the turntable with two outstretched fingers. Following Hans's example she raised her knee. Without scruple she brought the record down on it and broke it in two.

Anna's stained honour had been avenged, but she soon discovered that far greater humiliations threatened it. One of the *Mittagstischgäste* was a forester, a middle-aged man, with a jagged purple scar precisely in the middle of his bald head, as though a drunken surgeon had unsuccessfully attempted a lobotomy. Whenever anyone's eyes fell on it he declared casually that it had been caused by a piece of shrapnel during a night-time patrol. Anna served him with scrupulous respect, *All Quiet on the Western Front* still in the back of her mind. That pleased him, familiarity would have offended him. One day, with an authoritative nod, he beckoned her over. He seized her by one wrist. 'And . . .' his eyes shone suggestively, 'have the nuns let their hair grow?' 'What do you mean?' With vicarious shame Anna thought of Sister Clementine's cropped head. She had once seen it and been moved by its vulnerable nakedness. 'Because soon, when the convents are shut down, they'll all have to get out of their habits,' he said with a greasy laugh, 'then we'll really see what they've got for legs!' Her wrist was released. Her serving tray of filled dishes trembled in her hands; she crashed it down on one of the tables to be rid of it and ran blindly out of the dining room without bothering about the other guests. The blood was throbbing at her temples, the clumping of her feet resounded through the lofty corridors. She knocked sharply on Mother Superior's door. Once inside she forgot all the rules of politeness and, out of breath, blurted out her evident expectation that the filthy *Mittagstischgäste* would immediately be dragged out by his pig ears from behind his piled-up plate, through the corridor of the convent, and deposited on the granite pavement, after which the bang of the closing door would resound in his ears for days to come.

'Gently, shhh, quiet now . . . !' The abbess raised her hands beseechingly, 'Now what exactly did he say?' 'That all the sisters must take off their habits because the convents are being closed. How can he say such a thing?' panted Anna. Mother Superior walked softly to the door, which Anna had left open, and shut it carefully. 'Let us pray,' she said, turning round. 'How did he get that idea?' Anna insisted stubbornly. The abbess sighed. 'That doesn't concern us, it is all politics. They have chosen that Antichrist all together—he wants to close the convents and churches, let us pray that it will never happen.' 'Antichrist?' Anna stammered. The forester acquired horns on either side of his scar. Mother Superior put an arm round her shoulders. 'Adolf Hitler,' she said gently.

A short circuit in Anna's head. A photograph, Bernd Möller, Uncle Heinrich, whizzed past each other, contradictory, evil. The champion of the poor and the unemployed turned out to be a destroyer of churches and convents. Her uncle was still being proved right—but did that justify the assault? How could she have been so mistaken? She was ashamed—at the same time she felt contempt for this titanic idealist's arrogance: How could he do anything to Christendom, or the Church, which had already held out for nineteen centuries? God would intercede personally, she was sure. That's why Mother Superior said 'Let us pray.' A strong faith, no attacker would be a match for it. The abbess went to the window and looked outside, a halo of yellow lime leaves around her wimple. 'What we have discussed here,' she said calmly, 'stays within the four walls of my room. Never talk about it with the others, you will get yourself into trouble.' Anna nodded, although she was not afraid of anyone.

The first month of the year 1933 was almost over when Anna looked down below out of a window on the first floor, and saw a gigantic flag flying where two roads crossed at the centre of the village. She recognized the spiders' legs with the points bent to the right; they rotated before your eyes if you looked at them for long. She hurried irreverently down the broad oak stairs, her footsteps rattling through the staircase. 'A flag!' she cried, storming into the refectory where two nuns were laying plates on the table with the precision of draughts pieces. 'They have hung out that flag, in the middle of the village, and no one is taking it down!' Mother Superior came in because of the racket, a soothing expression on her face. 'If I were a boy,' Anna raised her hands, 'it wouldn't be up there anymore!' 'But you are a girl,' the abbess reminded her, 'so behave like one.' 'But that flag—' Anna spluttered, pointing through the walls at the thing that taunted the sky. Mother Superior shook her head. 'Anna, you lack moderation. There are two possibilities for you: either you will become something formidable or you will end up in the gutter—there is nothing in between.' 'But the Nazarene said . . .' she stammered, gasping for breath, '. . . because thou art lukewarm, and neither cold nor hot, I will spew thee out of my mouth . . .' The abbess laughed indulgently. '*Ach* Anna, we could take that flag down, but what it stands for . . . we are powerless against that. Hitler became Chancellor of the Reich today.'

Annoyed, Anna ran outside. The word *powerless* coming from the mouth of the Mother Superior was an insult addressed to the Almighty. The gate of the convent closed behind her with a crash. The road led straight down to the crossroads. She stopped beneath the flagpole. She threw her head back. It was no more than a piece of cloth. If it rained it would get wet, in the wind it would flap. There wasn't much left of the provocative symbol she'd seen from the window on the first floor. From close up, as an object, it was disappointing. She turned around in order to see the convent better for once. But it paled into insignificance, together with the church, the naked treetops, the January greyness of walls and roofs, in comparison with the red-white-black decoration on the spires of the fairy-tale castle. Von Zitsewitz had also hung out the flag.

7

'THEY WERE SO good to me.' Anna took her leave from the nuns. Her education in the convent had been completed, the tuberculous cold treated, she had gained fifteen kilos, a callus had grown over her inner injuries. It gave her an unprecedented self-assurance to have been brought back from absolute rock bottom. She returned home, down from the mountain to the river. She would not allow herself to be taken advantage of again. Uncle Heinrich— joy at her return gleamed through his reticence. Aunt Martha—her jealousy at Anna's rosy appearance, the frustration that she was alive at all, gleamed through her forced self-control. But she kept quiet: the eyes of the world (pastor, child welfare) were directed at her from now on.

During Anna's voluntary exile a change had crept into the village. Ever since farmers' sons with their own horses had been able to enlist in Hitler's elite corps, the Reiter SA, its image had risen to staggering heights. Moreover, he had upgraded the farming classes to the honorary first rank of providers in the Third Reich, the pivot on which the society turned, the Reichsnährstand. Former school comrades, brothers and lovers of Anna's former friends—almost everyone joined the SA. No longer did anyone say: You don't do a thing like that. Only in the Catholic Congregation of Virgins, to which she had belonged since her confirmation at fourteen, were there some girls who shared Anna's distaste. The leader of the congregation, Frau Thiele, a teacher in whose class they had all been, had hastily set up a singing group, a dance group and a theatre group, to prevent her pupils going over to the Nazi youth organization, the Bund Deutscher Mädel, BDM, which had beaten her to it. Nevertheless her days as leader were numbered. A decree obliged her to join the National Socialist teachers' union. A subsequent decree forbade members of this union from being active in church organizations.

Jacobsmeyer took Anna to one side after mass. 'Listen, Anna,' he looked at her conspiratorially, 'this time I want to ask something of you. Will you replace Frau Thiele as leader of the congregation?' 'I?' Anna's voice caught. 'I'm just eighteen, they won't take me seriously!' 'Shhh,' he calmed her. 'I haven't finished yet. At the same time you and a group of trustworthy girls will join the BDM.' Anna's mouth dropped open. He unfolded his plan, smiling slightly. To infiltrate the girls' section of the Hitler Youth, to bring him reports of everything that went on there and, finally, with God's help, to undermine the local section from within. 'You can do it, Anna, I've known you a long time.' Anna stared at him with bewilderment. This representative of God, so trusted and reliable in the incense-scented robe in which he had just conducted the mass, would shrink from nothing! It filled her with pride that he had selected her for this mission. At last she could do something instead of remaining stuck in the fatalism that Mother Superior had preached. 'Will you do it or won't you?' Jacobsmeyer asked.

One Sunday she sang and danced for the Catholic Church, the next for the Hitler Youth—in a dark blue skirt with white blouse and brown jacket, the neckscarf through a ring-shaped toggle of plaited leather links. Jacobsmeyer was well rewarded. They received political training and learned how to write press reports. Anna was praised for her ability with the pen. Uncle Heinrich looked the other way, having been put in the picture by Jacobsmeyer. One sunny day in April the headmaster, who remembered Anna as an exceptional pupil, cycled out to the farm. 'I've brought you something.' He took a thin book out of his briefcase. 'Will you learn this by heart? The fact of the matter is a big celebration is being organized, on the first of May a play is being staged.' Anna wiped her muddy hands on her overall and leafed through it quickly. Uncle Heinrich came over suspiciously. 'The Kreisleiter, the political chief of the district, is looking for a Germania . . .' The teacher picked nervously at the lock on his case. 'She has to be sturdily built and blond.' 'Why our Anna, of all people?' said Uncle Heinrich. 'There are plenty more blond girls in the village'. 'Because she's the only one who speaks decent German and can recite poetry.' 'Yes, that she can,' boomed Uncle Heinrich. 'But listen here . . . Germania! That's really going too far!' 'We've got no one else,' the headmaster pleaded. 'I am a public servant, I have a family, I must see that it happens.'

There were rehearsals all month long. At the dress rehearsal Anna wore an elaborate wig of long blond curls. She had to recite the most melodramatic verses that ever flowed from a German pen with a straight face. A soldier from the war with a bloody bandage around his head lay at her feet; he had to be visible from the back of the hall. Anna positioned herself facing an imaginary horizon; 'All around I see distress in German provinces, no rays of hope, no sunlight . . . poor, unhappy Germania, all her sons are dying here . . . the people are laid low there . . .' The only acting talent required of the soldier was to be dead in a convincing manner, but the artery in his neck ignored the stage directions and pulsed so firmly that Anna burst out laughing halfway through the elegy. Shaking all over—the curls joining in subversively—Germania stumbled from the stage, her hand over her mouth, as though she might pass out at any moment. 'What's going on now,' shouted the director, at the end of his tether because failure was forbidden. 'I can't go on,' Anna hiccuped from the wings, 'if I've got to be serious! In God's name put a bandage around his neck, too.'

But on the first of May Germania did not desert her role for a moment. She acted with so much dedication that she convinced herself, too, not just her audience. Afterwards the Kreisleiter opened the ball. Without giving her a chance to change, he invited her to dance with an authoritative nod of the head. They waltzed over the empty dance floor, her chin on his epaulette, the goddess costume billowing out, the curls describing a circle around her head. Around them, boys in uniform and girls with garlands in their hair watched in admiration. The Kreisleiter was dancing with her! She was the tangible symbol of something they believed in, unsuspecting that the symbol in question had sneaked inside from the enemy camp. The triumph went to her head. The Kreisleiter held on to her firmly, as though from then on he was going energetically to take good care of sorrowful Germania's fate. Anna felt herself submitting to temptation, allowing herself to be led with her eyes closed, and thoroughly enjoying her new status. Her former one, that of the poor maltreated orphan, was now quite hopelessly outdated. After the celebration she floated home on a pink cloud with golden edges. Uncle Heinrich tore the cloud to shreds with his scepticism. 'That's how they get young people to do their dirty work, the seducers,' he said disdainfully. 'Now even you see how they do it.'

The district section of the BDM sent a young woman with expertly pinned-up hair to the village to introduce morning gymnastics to the local section. From then on they had to gather on the square by the church at the crack of dawn, she announced, not to start the day with Our Father, but to hoist the flag, sing the national hymn and the Horst Wessel song. After that they would do morning gymnastics for a healthy and supple body, pushing up, swinging around, bending the knees, arms raised, bending over. She lectured them in a high-pitched, urban accent. The charitable farmers' daughters observed her silently and full of inner resistance. How could they combine all these rituals with their work on the farm, which had already begun while it was still dark? Anna's eyes narrowed. When the woman had finished she stepped forwards out of the circle. 'I invite you,' she said, 'to start the gymnastics with me at five in the morning on the farm. You can pump water, feed the chickens and fifty pigs, give the calves water, and during the milking you can raise your arms up high and bend your knees, while the animals stay contentedly beside you.' The circle burst into relieved laughter. The leader laughed along with them, shocked; she rearranged something in her hairdo and hastily disappeared. Nearby yet unseen, Jacobsmeyer recorded her first success. There was no more mention of morning gymnastics.

In the autumn Hitler called the farmers together at Bückeberg near

Hamelen to celebrate the harvest festival. Uncle Heinrich went along, curious despite himself. After he got back he fell into a gruesome week-long silence. Trustworthy people had become scarce in the village; the only person he could ultimately disclose his news to was Anna. Millions of farmers from the whole country had flocked together on that day, he recounted. In Lower Saxony, the Teutonic heartland full of holy oaks where the spirit of Widukind roamed about, they had waited on both sides of the road where the march would take place. Uncle Heinrich stood among them. He had read *Mein Kampf*, he knew that the author wanted to put its contents into practice word for word, he knew who would be coming past on parade. But what actually happened was beyond his wildest fantasies. The Führer's appearance, perfectly stage-managed from beginning to end by carefully chosen artists, exceeded those of Nero, Augustus and Caesar put together. The crowds began to cheer, songs flowed through the ranks, a frenzied passion caught hold of the masses, red-white-black banners fluttered against a purple sky. Unanimous adoration went out to the single magical figure in whose hands lay the fate of the whole nation. Uncle Heinrich fought against the pull of the seduction as though he had fallen straight into a whirlpool in the Lippe. Gasping for breath, he wrested himself free from the gigantic, heaving, clamouring body and fled. 'They will follow him blindly,' he predicted, 'this Pied Piper of Hamelen. To the abyss.'

The Pied Piper's lust for power was tangible everywhere, not even the Archbishop of Paderborn was spared. He was arranging a pilgrimage to a shrine of the Virgin Mary on a Sunday; the BDM promptly organized a gathering on the same Sunday. 'Fine,' said the archbishop, 'then we'll arrange the pilgrimage for the following Sunday.' The BDM followed his example. The archbishop was not dismayed, and once more rearranged the event, his footsteps again followed by the BDM. Eventually the pilgrimage was postponed indefinitely. Anna's patience was exhausted. 'Why are you doing that' she asked at the next opportunity, 'sabotaging the pilgrimage?' 'What do you mean?' the leader of the BDM looked at her inanely. 'We're not doing anything.' Anna said severely, 'We are Catholics, we really do want to go there.' The others nodded in agreement. The leader shrugged her shoulders. 'I know nothing about it.' 'You're lying! You've thwarted the Archbishop of Paderborn intentionally. You are an underhanded mob. I don't go along with it. I am a Catholic first and only after that a member of the BDM.' The leader's mock innocence was driving Anna into a blind rage. 'You're lying!' She pushed her chair back—the feet slid across the floor—and walked up to the woman, who hid her uncertainty behind a sheepish smile. 'I'll have nothing to do with someone who lies,' cried Anna. 'Good-bye.' She went out without the Hitler salute, the door closed behind her with a bang. All chairs were immediately pushed back, the entire complement of the local section of the BDM stood up and left the room; the leader remained, her hands raised in astonishment, deserted. Jacobsmeyer's assignment had been completed: the BDM had disbanded itself in this village.

Anna was just cleaning the pig shed, putting straw down, taking the muck out, when a large black Mercedes drove into the yard, a small flag with a swastika on the bonnet. Who have we here, she thought, and walked into the yard inquisitively. A sturdy woman got out, in a uniform richly decorated with badges. A real high-up, Anna could see, a *Gauführerin*. The driver stayed inside the car and stared glassily ahead. After a haughty glance at the farming things, and looking past Anna, the woman stuck her arm out towards Uncle Heinrich. 'Heil Hitler, I am looking for Anna Bamberg.' Uncle Heinrich looked at her with weary suspicion and said nothing. Crossly, as though she had accidentally addressed a deaf mute, she turned to Anna. 'Heil Hitler, are you Anna Bamberg?' 'Yes.' Anna's figure was assessed from on high, from head to toe—her muddy overall, her unpainted clogs. 'Are you the one who excelled at writing press reports?' she asked sceptically. 'Yes.' Anna wiped her nose on her sleeve, 'Did you by any chance think I couldn't read or write because I can clean out the pig shed?' The woman ignored her remark. The way her body had been crammed into the uniform was almost pathetic—the tension of the compressed flesh transferred itself to her fixed, controlled expression. She had come to call Anna to order, how could Anna break up the BDM just like that? 'Just like that?' said Anna. 'You are liars, that's what, just like that. I will have nothing

more to do with it, leave me in peace, I've got work to do.' She
turned, picked up her muck cart and called over her shoulder: 'The
Reichsnährstand is the first rank in the Third Reich.' She heard the
Mercedes door slam sharply behind her.

'ÇA VOUS A *plu?*' asked the waitress, bending towards them with a
smile.

'Non, non, je ne veux plus,' Lotte said hurriedly.

Anna began to laugh. 'She was asking if you liked it.'

Yes, of course Lotte liked it. She blushed. What in heaven's name
had she eaten? She had been chewing and swallowing automatically,
absorbed by Anna's account. The enemy image that she had been fostering for years was coming increasingly under revision. Everything
was upside down—the alcohol had not yet worn off, the plentiful
meal was taking a toll, inviolable certainties were crumbling. Two
pairs of eyes looked at her expectantly—what dessert would she like?
A list of sweets was rattled off; she could not understand another
word of French. Coffee, she just wanted coffee.

Anna picked up the thread again, indefatigably. 'So you see how
Hitler caused a furor among us in the village. I'll tell you something
else. A couple of years ago on a trip, by chance I went back to the
Wewelsburg, you know, where we used to go for picnics with farm
carts. In the war Himmler selected that castle for the establishment of
a cultural centre for the Third Reich. He had a tower built, of gigantic dimensions, of diabolical beauty, a symbol of power. They could
do that, the Nazis. More than four hundred people died in the construction of that monument. The cemetery where they are buried was
obliterated later on. The irony is that people flock there now from all
over the world—everyone is overawed by its beauty. Himmler's
scheme still works, that's the gruesome thing. They should paint that
tower bright red; they should paint the Jews' martyrdom on it.'

Lotte looked around startled. Anna was becoming louder as she
got more excited. The last sentences resounded provocatively
through the sedate, salmon-pink space. She gave Anna hand signals
to turn the volume down a little.

Anna took the hint. 'Oh well,' she continued more softly, 'since political relationships have changed they have set up a little war museum there. I looked around it a bit, there were all sorts of things on display. Right away I discovered two paper ballots from our village, neatly framed. One from the thirtieth of January, when Hitler came to power, and one from March in the same year, on the occasion of a constitutional amendment that empowered him to make regulations by-passing the parliament. My heart stood still. Uncle Heinrich seems to have been badly mistaken—at that time he thought there were only a few idiots in the village with National Socialist sympathies. From those ballots it was evident that on the thirtieth of January one-quarter of our fellow villagers had already voted for Hitler; two months later—already, two-thirds. The farmers, the baker, the greengrocer, Uncle Heinrich's card-playing chums—suddenly they appeared in a different light. I was shocked, after all those years. It was lurking there all that time but he didn't know it.'

She rested her hand on Lotte's and looked at her with concern. 'Sometimes I worry that it is repeating itself. That ridiculous "One Nation" clamour for reunification, the rising nationalism. I never thought people would still be susceptible to that idiocy, in a Europe where you can fly from Cologne to Paris in an hour, to Rome in two hours. It bothers me, I don't want to be a Cassandra, but . . .'

'It's different for us,' Lotte interrupted her.

'The Dutch, yes . . . damned spice traders!' Anna retorted. 'You have a different attitude towards foreigners because you were involved in world trade from early on. But the Germans—have you ever really thought about what kind of people we are? The ordinary man was never anything, never possessed anything. He never had any possibility of a decent existence. And if by chance he ever did have something, then there would be a war and everything of his would be lost again. And so it went on, for ages.'

'But where did the Prussians get their pride from then?' Lotte forced herself to stay alert despite her fatigue.

'If you've got nothing and are nobody you need something else to be proud of. That's what Hitler cleverly took advantage of. The little

man acquired a function, got a rank, a title: block warden, group
leader, provincial commander. In that way they could command, they
could act out their assertiveness.'

The coffee arrived. Lotte was relieved. She raised the cup eagerly
to her lips. Anna observed her wryly. 'The Dutch and their cup of coffee. Their lives and happiness have depended on it ever since they
shipped the first coffee beans from the colonies.'

Lotte counter-attacked. 'Did you never have the slightest sympathy
for Hitler again?'

'Sympathy? *Meine Liebe!* I found him loathsome. That general's
voice. *"Vórrr Vierrrzehn Jáhrrren! Die Schande von Verrrsáilles!"* I
felt nothing for him. I was an obedient child of the Catholic Church
and believed what the pastor said to me because he was good to me.
Very simple. Yet many obedient Catholics eventually allowed themselves to be tempted. Goebbels, who himself was brought up by the
Jesuits, craftily introduced the traditional Catholic values that lay
deeply embedded in people into Nazi propaganda. The purity, the
chastity of the German people, was glorified. The German man didn't
meddle with sex, except when he had chosen a wife: a proper German woman, of course, who didn't smoke, didn't drink, didn't make
herself up and had no illegitimate children. They married and had
twelve children whom they donated to the Führer. Those ideals were
hammered into them.'

Lotte sighed, staring at her empty cup.

'Why do you sigh?' Anna asked.

'It's all too much for me right now, Anna.'

Anna opened her mouth and closed it again. She realized that she
preferred doing the talking, that she wanted to explain everything,
everything, endlessly setting out justifications. About the fate of the
populations in the areas they had occupied, of which the Germans
meanwhile had been fully informed. But they were obliged to keep
quiet about what they themselves had experienced during twelve
years of tyranny: what reason did the aggressor have to complain—
had he not brought it on himself?

She controlled herself. 'If I blather on too much you must tell me to call a halt, Lotte. Father did that too, long ago, do you remember? He stuck his fingers in his ears and cried, "Quiet, Anna. Please be quiet!"

Lotte did not remember it at all. Every time she tried to bring her original father to mind, the screen of her Dutch father slid over his image precisely because of the outward likeness—dominant, indelible. The coffee was beginning to work, she was reviving. But Anna would have to restrain herself for once. Enough politics, it was her turn now.

8

THEY WERE SITTING on the raked gravel, the scent of a dark red climbing rose became more profound in the summer evening heat. Lotte was staring at the edge of the wood that was becoming progressively blacker. Her mother was swaying gently in time with Bruch's Violin Concerto in G, which lost none of its strength as it emerged through the open window. Opposite them sat two music lovers who came to admire the sound reproduction. Sammy Goldschmidt, flautist in the Radio Philharmonic Orchestra, listened with his eyes closed; Ernst Goudriaan, a student violin maker from Utrecht, rested his chin on the tips of his fingers. The host himself was operating the equipment, out of sight behind the scenes. After the concert was over he came outside to refill his glass and to decline their praises with charming modesty. At that instant a nightingale began to sing in the wood, which had now turned into an impenetrable immensity.

'He means to complete with Bruch,' suggested Ernst Goudriaan. They listened with amazement to the mysterious solo—a clear nocturnal jubilation, not intended for an imagined audience but purely for its own enjoyment. Lotte's father sat on the edge of his chair. Struck by the record being played on a perfect machine in the depths of the wood, he knocked back two glasses of gin one after the other

and shook his head: exceptional, what a sound! The following
evening he stole into the wood like a thief, lugging his recording
equipment, to find a strategic position, but the nightingale cancelled
the performance. Much patience was dedicated to this. Evening after
evening he hunted for its voice with stubborn perseverance until one
night the miracle was repeated right over his head and he could
secure it on a lacquered disc for ever. He went to the radio station
with this hunting trophy. 'We have a surprise for the listener': the
broadcast was interrupted in order to transmit the nightingale,
almost live, into the ether.

Why doesn't he record my voice, thought Lotte. The more meticu-
lously her mother followed her performances—she never failed to turn
up whenever the choir was appearing somewhere, she was instantly
recognizable among a thousand strange heads by the glow of her
chestnut-hued upswept hairdo—the more absent-minded he became
when Lotte sang on the radio. To everyone's great irritation he would
begin to twiddle the knobs distractedly, as though there was something
interfering with the sound reproduction. Could he not tolerate the fact
that he was not the only one in the family who brought music into the
house? Or was it because she had not inherited that musicality from
him? Her own father was sometimes vaguely visible in the form of an
imprecise longing, as though she was looking at him through a clouded
pane. She wanted to clean the condensation off the glass in order to see
him as he had been, to smash the cocoon of silence, to hear his voice as
it had sounded. All those years he had slumbered in her—now his utter
absence was infiltrating her, a negative, a total nothing. It was different
with Anna. Lotte remembered her chiefly in a busy succession of movements, swift feet on a stone floor, jumping up and down, a powerful
voice, a plump body that joined up precisely with her own in the middle of an enormous mattress. Anna. An illegal thought, a secret feeling.
Not only did a border separate her from Anna, not only the distance,
but above all the time period that had lengthened meanwhile, and
opaque family relationships.

But Anna was kept alive. Even if it was via Bram Frinkel, eight
years old, who had come to The Netherlands from Berlin halfway
through the school year. Koen brought him home after school—foot-

ball did not trouble itself with language barriers. Lotte got chatting to him in his own language; the words presented themselves as though they had never been out of use. For him she was an enclave of his home country—and he for her. Airily he told her why his parents had left it: There was no room for Jews in Germany anymore. His father, a violinist, could pursue his profession in The Netherlands. Lotte taught him to say Dutch tongue twisters, he grimaced at the impossible *g* sound and the meticulous *ij*. Koen reacted to his sister's fluent German with surprise and distaste. He played alone with the ball a few metres away, offended, during her private chats with Bram.

Something happened that no one had thought possible. Lotte's mother, the radiant, the indestructible, caught an ailment that could not be dismissed with a reassuring diagnosis as flu or a cold. The first symptom was that she drove her husband out of the bedroom. From then on he slept on an improvised bed in his workshop, in a smell of solder and blown fuses, and during the day he moved about the house in a grim state—his worst moods of the past paled in comparison with this. Straight through the floor, from her bed by the three-bayed window with the view onto the rhododendrons, the meadow, the ditch and the edge of the wood, the children heard a torrent of enraged accusations directed at their father. The family doctor climbed the stairs with bowed head. It looked as though even he was threatening to succumb beneath the forces that were let loose on him on the first floor. Leaning on the dining table, defeated, her daughters speculated on the nature of the strange illness, not suspecting that they would only get to the bottom of what was possessing their mother only after all taboos had been gradually lifted years later.

The disease had begun with mistrust of her husband, who came home ever later from his trips to Amsterdam. One evening she had followed him with a friend—heavily made-up, dressed in fashionable coats with turned-up collars and Pola Negri hats. They spoke to him in disguised voices in Amsterdam slang. He did not recognize them beneath the street lamp in the shade of their hats. When, like a regular, he indicated his readiness to go along with their advances, they had linked their arms tightly and run off in shock and left him there puzzled. The next phase of the disease was brought home with him from the capital city and passed on to her. This was the most tangible symptom, which the doctor could combat with injections. Afterwards she lapsed into a state of great moroseness, which was followed by eruptions of rage—seen in retrospect it was the phase that preceded the cure, a cure that she herself would adopt in an unorthodox way.

Of all these things her daughters had not the slightest notion as they deliberated at the dining table like foolish geese. They had been equipped with a minimum of sexual information, which could be summed up in their mother's breezy motto: Nature must be left to its own devices. But that nature, which drove her back into the arms of the great troublemaker again after each row, aroused their fundamental suspicion. The idea of being stuck with such a man as their father for their whole lives was such a hundred-percent-safe contraceptive that none of them 'had ever been kissed.' Not even Mies, with her close-fitting suits and her wide, greedy mouth. This was simultaneously tangled up with the fact that their mother seemed unconsciously to rebel against this fate imposed by nature, by allowing her daughters to read social-conscience literature. About desperate servant girls who got pregnant by the master of the house, about mothers of twelve children in damp basements who had to defend themselves evening after evening from the roving hands of their drunken spouses, about black female slaves abused by those who had bought them for a few pieces of silver. Women out of Emile Zola, Dostoevsky, Harriet Beecher Stowe. If that was the 'full life' where nature was left to its own devices, for the time being as they sat there around the table her daughters wanted nothing to do with it. So they bowed their heads timidly during the outbursts of rage that came from upstairs like a thunderstorm, which they, too, were powerless against.

Suddenly it went quiet up above. Without further explanation their mother got up, dressed herself carefully and left the house in silence with an absent-minded expression on her face. She was stared after by her bewildered daughters, who watched her disappear in the drizzle on her Gazelle in her familiar upright posture. That afternoon a painting one and a half metres wide was delivered, an impressionist representation of the marshlands their mother had a soft spot for: heavy, threatening clouds in a silver sky, reflected in a ripple-free lake edged by reeds and weeping willows. Shortly afterwards, she (who had bought it from a very promising painter, and would have to bleed financially for it at home), returned—completely cured, her cheeks flushed with revenge. It was given a prominent place in the living room, above her husband's sound system, and in silent competition with it. In safer times he certainly would have started a war on account of her extravagant purchase. Now, with badly faked enthusiasm, he seized the chance to make the unexpected cure permanent. Less than a year later an afterthought was born—Bart—the outcome of the restored peace.

From the inscrutability of all those emotions Lotte sought compensation in music. There was structure in it: the way the notes were arranged, carried by the beat, each fulfilling its function in the great totality, arousing the spirit by the artful ensemble. After the matriculation examinations were over she applied herself with redoubled industry to studying singing and to harmony theory lessons. An annoying factor was that her piano was in the same room as the gramophone. A symbolic arrangement: while she was practising, her father would come in and quite innocently put a record on or take a book out of the bookcase, gesturing to her to be quiet because he wanted to concentrate. She sat paralysed at the piano, cold sweat running down her back. She could no longer breathe when they were in the same room—he used up all the oxygen. She closed her eyes and submitted to his show of strength. Onto the inner surface of her eyelids she projected an Arcadian world in which the whole family, to the accompaniment of a nightingale's song, was walking in sober black behind his coffin.

On the day that her youngest sister was four, it looked as though her dream picture was actually going to come true. On his way home from work in the afternoon, her father was accustomed to collect an order at the confectioner's shop. As his Harley was being repaired, he had asked for a lift home from a colleague who was just as enthusiastic a motorcyclist as he. He left the shop with a cake box in his right hand and a bag of butter biscuits in his left. He mounted carefully behind his colleague. In the interests of the cake they approached the junction they had to cross at a snail's pace. From the left at top speed, bent low over the handlebars, came a man on a motorbike, who only realized that he had to give way after Lotte's father was already lying motionless on the ground in a strangely contorted position, his head on the edge of the kerb between a bag of crumbled biscuits and a crushed cake box, a trickle of blood coming out of the corner of his mouth.

He came around in the ambulance. 'Where are you taking me?' he inquired suspiciously. 'To the hospital.' 'No, no,' he protested, sitting up, 'I want you to take me home, there is no better nurse than my own wife.' His wishes were respected. He was carried inside on a stretcher. 'Mind your head,' he warned at a bend in the stairs, 'it's very low here.' His wife opened the bedroom door with a trembling hand. While the family doctor was ringing the doorbell downstairs they put him carefully into the bed. He thanked them politely as they left, but when the doctor was examining him and asked under what circumstances the accident had happened, he mumbled in surprise: 'An accident? Was there an accident' 'You have had an accident,' said the doctor solemnly, 'they brought you home just now.' 'Who? Me?' He frowned wearily. 'Where is my wife?' 'She is standing here next to me.'

While the children waited tensely downstairs beneath coloured festoons, and the cake stand remained ostentatiously empty in the centre of the table, the doctor hesitantly diagnosed serious concussion and broken ribs. To be certain, he called in a specialist whose cool suggestion of a serious fracture at the base of the skull brought a threat into the house that was to extinguish all signs of life for six months. 'Wait,' he said, 'we cannot do anything but wait.' Marie and Jet took the festoons down, in the unspoken conviction that every minute they remained hanging up would work to their father's detriment. Eefje picked listlessly at her new doll in a corner of the denuded room.

Their father had to lie flat. Grey, motionless, with eyes closed, he lay in the darkened room that smelled of disinfectants and eau de cologne—as though he were already lying in state. He was not dead, but neither was this living. Day and night his wife moistened his fore-head, temples, and wrists with a wet facecloth and manoeuvred tea-spoonfuls of lukewarm water between his cracked lips. His breath rasped past his broken ribs, now and then he moaned from the murky no-man's-land where he was floating on the silver wings of morphine. The youngest children were taken to a sister of their mother: absolute quiet was a condition of his recovery. Every activity in the house was performed with kid gloves on—they tiptoed, they whispered, they shrank from the sound of their own breath. It seemed as though they were all unintentionally bringing death into the house, and this radical absence of sound and the emphatic silencing of Beethoven and Bach, of sopranos and baritones, altos and basses, cre-ated an atmosphere in which it could prosper. They could hear it rustling behind closed doors.

When it was Lotte's turn to take over the vigil and she looked at the stubble adorning the sunken cheeks like mould, she had the sneaking fear that the strength of her powers of imagination had landed him in this condition. She regretted the vengeful fantasies he had provoked in her. Had there really been covert angry intent in his behaviour or had it been his usual, familiar egoism? She fervently hoped he would sur-vive, otherwise from then on she would have to practise strict censor-ship over her thoughts. More than that, the picture of her own father as he had awaited death, surrounded by members of the family, per-meated her with a sense of guilt. All those years she had successfully repressed it, but as a result of the striking likeness, it returned together with the anxiety-producing feeling of alienation that it had caused. In this way the watch was a continually recurring form of self-torment because, every time, it evoked this gamut of feelings.

After a few hours she was relieved again by her mother, who kept watch like a sphinx for the rest of the twenty-four hours. Sometimes she leaned over him to listen that he was still breathing. 'You will not slip away from me,' she whispered, 'my old rascal.' She did not neg-lect herself. Regularly she changed her dress so that, on the rare occa-sions he opened his eyes, he would find an attractive woman by his bed. Through a chink in the curtains she saw the sun come up and go down, she saw the mist over the meadow, she heard the cooing of the wood pigeons. At night she saw the stars; she could not put a light on to read a book—perhaps that was her greatest sacrifice.

Yet even with her stubborn presence, she could not prevent his getting double pneumonia with pleurisy after three weeks. The doctor was a bad actor: it was obviously difficult for him to conceal that it could all end at any moment. He arranged for a night nurse, who treated the peaks of the fever with cold compresses. At night the patient's delirium was the only sound in the house. The nurse attached bags of ice cubes to his head. 'No,' he protested, shooting upright out of his dream with staring eyes; he flailed at them with spastic arm movements: 'I don't want that crown! I don't want to be king of England, I won't, I won't!' The nurse grabbed the bags from the pillow and pushed him back with gentle insistence. 'You must remain lying flat,' she exhorted him. 'I don't want that crown,' he whined, 'I want Mrs. Simpson!' Rebelliously he sank back into his deep, feverish sleep.

When the crisis had abated, he opened his eyes and in chastened calm saw the strange woman's face wreathed in a shock of stiff hair that stood on end. She looked back fiercely from beneath her bristly eyebrows—her normal facial expression, not meant to convey anything in particular. 'You look strikingly like Beethoven,' he said with amazement. 'You are very observant,' she admitted, 'in fact he was a relation.' They were just about to heave a sigh of relief when a blood clot in his leg reintroduced the possibility of death. The doctor became entangled in conflicting treatments: the patient had to sit up on account of the thrombosis, while it was vital that he lie flat because of the skull fracture.

Because visits to the patient had been forbidden, the house had been cut off from the world, an island, with the poor, afflicted body at its centre. To escape from this vacuum, this interruption of her usual life, Lotte strolled in the garden and ended up at the back in the orchard. She stroked her hand over the peeling paint of the TB house, she picked off a piece of moss, broke a twig from the walnut tree whose robust crown embodied the fourteen intervening years. The swivel mechanism of the house had rusted completely so that the open side pointed permanently to the east. The east. She sat down on the rickety kitchen chair and imagined an unfamiliar Anna in the year 1936. Not in a clearly defined physical form, but as an accumulation of energy, lit up, vital; Anna alive. She was full of remorse and shame for having thought so little about her for so long, as though Anna had become a lost cause. She tried to put herself in the place of the child with a lung infection who had lain looking about her in fevered amazement. What she had been too young, too sick, too dependent for then, now seemed ridiculously simple: Get on a train back to Cologne. She fantasized about seeing Anna again—just thinking about her was a mild antidote to her father's continuing flirtation with death.

On Sunday he suddenly became short of breath. Like a fish on dry land he gasped for air with a gaping mouth. His wife propped him up against the pillows, gave him water, unbuttoned his pyjama jacket— he clutched at his heart. The doctor was alerted. An unfamiliar locum doctor gave him a large injection straight into his heart. 'A last rescue bid,' he whispered, putting the syringe away in his bag, 'prepare yourself for the worst, Madam.' Hours of waiting. It was a miracle that her resilience had not yet been exhausted after all those months. The question, Will he pull through or won't he?, so permeated the atmosphere in the house that Lotte walked in the wood because she feared that, at such close quarters, an involuntary thought escaping censorship might be fatal to him at the critical moment. By evening his breathing was regular. He took a drink of water and asked his wife to put Mozart's *Requiem* on downstairs, full volume with all the doors open. She let the needle descend onto the record with a trembling hand. Melancholy sounds floated up the stairs. Jet burst into tears. 'Be happy,' said her mother, 'that you aren't hearing the music at his funeral, but that he can enjoy it himself now.'

After this apotheosis the healing process went ahead slowly: he returned to life in style. Bit by bit he was allowed visits. 'But what's happened to Hans Koning?' he complained, still translucent with weakness. 'He's sure to come,' his wife pacified him. 'But does he really know what's going on?' 'Of course.' But the professor did not get in touch at all. As dependable as the weekly visits with which he had honoured the house before the accident had been, so was his absence now obstinate. Lotte's mother telephoned. He turned up on the doorstep with a dejected face, in polite response to her summons. He stumped upstairs, bumped his head at the turn in the stairs, and stood embarrassed at the end of the bed without shaking the patient's hand. 'How are you?' he inquired, coughing dryly behind the enormous fleshy hand with which he used to wave objections away. The patient did not conceal his joy. The mere presence of his bosom friend and fellow spirit brought more colour to his cheeks than all his other visitors put together. 'I'm lying here but . . .' he sighed, 'would you believe that I crave an old-fashioned Saturday evening.' Hans Koning looked at him tensely. 'Listen, my dear fellow, I'm no good in sick rooms . . .' To demonstrate this he looked around him tormentedly, as though he were trying in vain to survive in a poisonous atmosphere. 'I mean it, I simply cannot stand it for a minute!' 'But . . .' the patient sputtered in disbelief. The professor proceeded towards the door. 'Give me a ring when you are your old self again.' He turned around, holding the doorknob. 'Get well soon.'

Faithful to his allergy, he did not show up again during the months of slow recovery. The patient had to struggle with bouts of depression. Why was his best friend staying away, just now when he had a crying need for his company to heal his shattered mind, and stimulate his fantasies, so that he could regain his former opinions with bravura? The professor's absence was a personal defeat. 'What do I matter to anyone actually,' he asked himself, propped up against the pillows, 'I am nobody, what have I achieved, nothing, I haven't any standing in the world, why didn't I simply die?' His wife hastened to convince him of his excellence, enlarging expansively on his merits, spiriting away his unpleasant characteristics. She sincerely believed it, so fervently did she hope that he would become his old self again. His resistance to so many flattering words collapsed at once. 'You are a tremendous woman,' he whispered, falling asleep consoled.

The day he came downstairs, shuffling step by step into the living room, dizzy from the effort, to drink a cup of coffee in an armchair that was hastily pushed by the fireplace was an impressive crossing of boundaries, which they would not forget. The bench in the garden was the next milestone. He won territory bit by bit in this way until, one day when he was alone at home, he grew too ambitious in his urge to conquer. Perhaps the absence of his wife made him anxious, perhaps he could no longer resist after months of suppressing the longing for a spirited exchange of views. Giving in to a light-hearted impulse, he waddled over the plank across the ditch, into the wood, slowly and with concentration—one leg limping a bit as a result of the thrombosis, his heart beating excitedly. When he reached the Koning family's house on the other side of the wood, in pure exhaustion he hugged one of the two dark green pillars supporting the porch over the door. He did not know how long he hung there like that, fighting against breathlessness and palpitations, and the fear that the professor would find him in that state. He only pressed the bell when he had recovered a little. His friend opened the door himself, in a three-piece suit, a silver watch chain like a festoon on his breast. His beard bobbed up with fright. 'Heavens, what are you doing here? You're the last person I expected here. I regret . . .' He lowered his voice as though he were on the point of letting the other in on a secret. 'We're just expecting visitors, they'll be here at any moment. How could you have timed it so wretchedly. You had better come in, then you can leave via the kitchen door.' Lotte's father stumbled along the passage and sank into a kitchen chair. 'One moment,' he panted, 'I must just . . . may I . . . might I have a glass of water?' 'I'll have a look for you . . .' The professor threw open all the kitchen cupboards and slammed the doors closed with a bang. 'God, where does she keep the glasses . . . a cup will do.' The unwelcome visitor drank his water. The professor opened the kitchen door with a wave. 'Better luck next time. Jesus, you look lousy.'

Lotte's mother looked up when she heard crunching on the gravel. She saw her husband, whom she had thought to be in bed, stumbling along the garden path, seeking support from a pear tree halfway along and staring at the house with a dazed, hollow gaze as though he had sensed something dreadful there. When she looked more closely she saw that he was crying. That same evening she told the professor by letter she was terminating their friendship. Her dip pen, scratching over the writing paper, called him an arch-egoist whose humanity disappeared on the threshold of sickrooms and on the doorstep of his own house.

'YET IT IS striking,' said Anna, 'that you had a fantasy about travelling to Cologne at just that time.'

'Why?'

'Because at that time I also had an urge to go to Cologne which became stronger and stronger.'

Anna had reached the age at which her own father had become oppressed in the symbiotic world between church and river: no more than a collection of farms and their inhabitants who watched each other being born and dying. Similarly in her case that mental tedium did not convert into fatalistic acceptance of destiny, but into rebelliousness. She tugged Jacobsmeyer by the sleeve of his soutane. 'How am I ever going to get out of this village?' Her voice disturbed the calm in the Landolinus church. 'Surely it isn't my vocation to lug pig muck for the rest of my life?' Jacobsmeyer nodded pensively. 'Perhaps I do know of something for you . . .' He stroked his chin contemplatively. 'The Archbishop of Paderborn is looking for a young woman to replace his elderly housekeeper in the long run. He wants to have her trained at an institute in Cologne where the daughters of well-to-do families learn about managing maids and servants. A school for ladies . . .' He laughed ironically.

Uncle Heinrich was not against it. Aunt Martha had more difficulty gracefully accepting the departure of an unpaid worker. 'You don't know what you're embarking on,' she said scornfully, recoiling at the thought of all that work she would now have to shoulder. 'It will come to nothing, I can tell you that.' Anna stirred the soup in silence; she had little inclination to get involved in another scene at this eleventh hour. 'Why don't you say anything? Do you feel you're already too good for us? I'll tell you something: it will work out badly for you there. I can already see the day that you'—her voice broke—'come crawling back here on your knees, begging for a piece of bread. Don't think . . .' Anna sighed wearily, 'Why excite yourself?' she said coolly, without looking up from the pan, 'I'm going to die anyway; you've always said so. Surely I won't reach twenty-one?'

She was enrolled for the new semester. Uncle Heinrich contacted a cousin in Cologne for lodgings and ordered a tailor to make a coat of indestructible material to last a lifetime. In the same way that a bride in her wedding dress and veil is initiated into being a married woman, Anna predicted that this coat would usher in a totally new existence. Some days before her departure she was summoned to Jacobsmeyer. 'I have something awful to tell you, Anna, this job isn't going to happen.' 'You can't mean that.' She slumped down in one of the gleaming polished pews and looked at the statue of the Virgin Mary, which suddenly seemed self-satisfied to her. She couldn't go back anymore—she had already discarded her former existence—that was all she knew. Jacobsmeyer paced up and down in front of the altar, rubbing his jaw. 'You know what,' he turned abruptly, 'we won't say anything to your uncle and aunt. I'll pay for the school. You say nothing, pack your suitcase, travel to Cologne and attend your lessons.'

On the first day of November Anna caught the train at Paderborn. She wore a trench coat made with room to grow, and to go with it a grey felt hat with a brown feather from the summer plumage of a pink-footed goose. Her possessions were in a cardboard margarine box. The train rode through pine forests and towards yellow deciduous forests, through meadows and ploughed fields. She closed her eyes and opened them again, hoping to see something she recognized. The landscape slid by neutrally. Yet she felt that she was coming steadily closer to her birthplace, that the thread which had held her tight for fourteen years had slackened, but it was being gathered in now—in the puff-puffing tempo of the train. But when the train roared into the station the feeling of being on the way home deserted her. The massive presence of the cathedral right next to the station, with its serrated silhouette of pointed spires protruding against the anthracite-coloured sky like a sombre warning, intimidated her. How futile her pleas would be in this outsized place of worship, since it had already been hard enough to be heard up above from the Landolinus church. She clutched the cardboard box to her belly. And now for Uncle Franz, she said to herself. She dug a carefully folded

piece of paper out of her coat pocket. In Gothic letters of almost cal-
ligraphic beauty, Uncle Heinrich had written the name of a hospital
where his cousin was chief maintenance technician. A passer-by told
her in Cologne slang which tram she had to take. She suppressed the
inclination to greet everyone when she got on, and passed down the
aisle between all these fellow citizens—yes, fellow citizens. But no
one noticed her. They were staring outside with a certain resignation,
as though they had not personally chosen to ride in this tram through
this city at this point in time. The high façades, the bustle of people,
the traffic; the density of life in the city of her youth overwhelmed her.
In the village she had always been the daughter of old Bamberg's
renegade son who died young; here, in the overcrowded anonymity,
she was absolutely nobody.

As she pushed open the heavy door of the hospital, she had the distressing sense that she was stepping into a city within a city. There
were births and deaths in both, in greater concentration here. She
waited for her uncle in the foyer on the edge of a leather armchair.
The glances of passers-by rested on her just a little too long. Suspiciously she tried to see herself through others' eyes. She saw someone
in a medieval coat, with a hunting hat and a droll feather and a
shabby box on her lap—a rare example of a type that had become
extinct in the city long ago. I look ridiculous, she judged. A man in a
white coat came up to her. A look of horror slid fleetingly across his
face, but he subdued it immediately and shook her jovially by the
hand. She tried to remember him from the funeral, hoping to find
something from the past in his face, since she had not yet succeeded
with Cologne in that respect. But she recognized nothing—he did not
look like her father or Uncle Heinrich or her grandfather. His cheerfulness was definitely not a family trait either. 'Is that all your luggage?'
he asked, taking the cardboard box from her. Anna nodded silently.
She took off the ridiculous hat, so as to have something in her hand,
and followed him, ashamedly stroking the feather with her finger.

His house was in the hospital grounds. He left her there in the care
of his wife, who welcomed her with a baby in her arms. Aunt Vicki
showed her around, chatting airily. She was plump, her reddish-blond
frizzy hair held in check by combs. There was a little dimple in the

middle of her chin, which sometimes made her expression look bashful, as though someone were unexpectedly deceiving her, but then an unrestrained laugh brushed her face clean again. Anna walked through the middle-class house in a daze. A room with polished furniture—just for sitting in! The enormous horn of a gramophone gaped boldly at her. A real WC with washbasin. Hot running water. A bedroom to herself: wallpaper with a medallion motif, a dressing table with a marble top and washstand, a hanging cupboard—for the clothes she did not possess. The wooden privy at the back on the farm, the pump she washed under, the attic with the worm-eaten floor where she slept—these were abruptly banished to the hazy region of unwelcome memories.

Dizzily she slid between starched sheets that evening. Although she had tumbled into a different existence in a single day, she had the feeling of being farther than ever from the city that had survived inside her for all these years: The microcosm of a six-year-old, a covered-in city, where life was intact and round and where trusted voices sounded. Aunt Vicki put her head round the door 'Schlaf wohl, Anna.' 'Gute Nacht . . .' she replied hesitantly. Her aunt and uncle's good nature confused her, accustomed as she was to surliness and suspicion.

At the school for ladies she was the only one who came from the country. No one noticed. She wore her aunt's dresses; she had always retained her High German—her father's vehicle for distancing himself from his family. Yet she could only half follow the pupils' conversations; their language referred to an unknown world with its own jargon: an impending engagement, a thé dansant on Sunday afternoon. No thés dansants for Anna, but in the nearby bioscope the magical darkness recalled those vague memories of the theatre in the Casino. Heinrich George and Zarah Leander with curls plastered on her temples and a rose behind her ear. Die grosse Liebe. Heimat, La Habañera. The UFA films were preceded by a newsreel, images of reality acquired the allure of dream pictures. Across the white screen marched lively soldiers. Germany had an army again, it was busy at high speed pulling itself together, out of the malaise. Healthy, athletically built boys were sent out by the Reichsarbeitsdienst to drain the marshes or to bring in the harvest. Beaming girls not wearing make-up helped on the farms, they cleaned and polished and looked after the children, they worked as health visitors. They smiled indefatigably, lived in camps and began the day by hoisting flags and singing the Horst Wessel song lustily: '*Die Strassen frei, die Reihen fest gescholossen.*' It was going well in Germany, everyone was helping enthusiastically with reconstruction, it was the end of chaos, poverty, unemployment. There was structure again, a structure that had the colour of ripe corn and a summery sky, of blond hair and blue eyes. Despite her mistrust of flags and marching songs, her dislike of the screaming Austrian and the warnings that came out of Uncle Heinrich's Bückeberg adventure, she was at the same time swept along by optimism, together with the others sitting close together there in the intimacy of the warm bioscope. The pictures gave one a comfortable feeling of confidence. Everything in the world outside was under control, and on top of that they also got a film into the bargain. The total improvement was no surprise to Anna—it coincided naturally with the progressive line that her own life was taking. Germany was climbing up out of the pit; so was she. This was not a sober observation but an impression of the senses, a rising awareness of simultaneous ascent. The bar of chocolate Aunt Vicki shared with her during the performance was the best proof of it: Who would have been able to eat chocolate previously?

Yet Cologne, with its history going back to Roman times, continued to intimidate and disillusion her. The sturdy round towers with battlements that she often passed subtly indicated to her that fourteen years' exile on the edge of the Teutoburger Wald amounted to nothing compared with being a Roman tower in Teutonic Germany for nineteen centuries. And the Lippe was no more than a ditch compared with the Rhine. One Sunday afternoon she was walking in a park with her aunt and the pram; a wintry sun cast long white strips between the tree trunks. She still had a problem with simply not having to do anything on one day of the week: walking about without a purpose, bending over the glittering surface of a pond, lifting the baby out of the pram and holding it up against the blue sky with outstretched arms so that it could waggle its limbs about. On impulse she said, 'Let's walk past the Casino, where I . . . where we used to live.' That 'we,' said out loud, legitimized the idea: she ought to go to the Casino on behalf of her father and Lotte too; they would accompany her and be looking over her shoulder. Aunt Vicki shrugged her shoulders, fine, it was all the same to her. In her innocence, chatting peacefully about trifles, she served as a lightning conductor for the sudden anxiety that clamped Anna's throat shut. As though she were an indifferent passer-by, she was strolling along the street from which, as a child, she had gone, carried off in the opposite direction by hasty family members. The street was inextricably linked with the figure of her father walking over the cobblestones in a black coat, leaning heavily on his stick and from time to time bringing out his spit bottle and quickly hiding it away again. By then the dark cloud on which he would float away—out of the city, the country, the world—was already hanging over the street, above the Casino, the church and the school.

They passed the school—the windows began high above the ground, it was impossible to see outside through them; past the church built in a merciless nineteenth-century style that inspired fear of the Supreme Being. She stopped a little further on. Her gaze ascended the façade up to the stained-glass windows, it slid sideways down towards the varnished double door with copper bell and small, latticed windows. Wherever she directed her gaze it ricocheted back. The building shut her out, denied that she had breathed inside it, that her thoughts and feelings had filled its spaces, that her father and Lotte had been alive there. These walls had once enclosed family life, now they formed an immovable obstacle between her and the others. 'They have asphalted the street,' she said disdainfully, 'there used to be cobblestones'. They walked on, as though it were any street. Everything was normal, the sun was shining, it was winter, 1936 was coming to an end, 1922 was unimaginably long ago. Her first six years, and those who had had a part in them, had left no trace, there was nothing to recall their existence.

The village on the Lippe did not exist any more either. Uncle Heinrich did not get in touch with her nor she with him. Only Jacobsmeyer had a letter from her now and then. When she was twenty-one years

old the Court of Justice summoned her to sign the guardianship declaration so that her uncle could be released officially from his responsibilities. It was a long screed. She started reading it cursorily; she
understood that her signature indicated her approval of the manner in
which he had exercised his guardianship in the past. Did what it said in
the declaration concur with reality? She felt hot, she felt cold. She simply could not read any further. This text referred to somebody else,
from another life. She looked up from the document in confusion.
Opposite her, in a sterile office behind a metal desk, the duty official
nodded impatiently at her. She wrote her signature with an angry
stroke. This Anna, smelling of soap, clothed in clean city clothes, put
the pen down, pushed the document brusquely towards the official,
stood up and left the building. She went down the stone front steps and
walked in the city, a city that would have to be reconstructed anew on
the sunken foundations of her memory.

The ink on the certificate from the school for ladies was hardly dry
before she had a job, as a live-in servant girl with one free Sunday
every fortnight. She went into service with the Stolz family, who lived
in the eastern part of the city in a neighborhood of small villas, not
far from the Bayer industrial complex where Stolz worked as a
chemist. She had no notion at all about what it meant to be the servant girl, an organic component of your employer's household. Her
expectation that she would be in charge of the Stolz family's housekeeping was already belied on the first day, when it became evident
that the legislative and executive powers were divided. The first lay
with Frau Stolz who had devised a factory system to enable the
household activities to proceed as fast and efficiently as possible.
Since her marriage, nine years ago, the skirting boards in her villa
were dusted each morning at ten o'clock, on Thursday afternoons the
shirts were ironed at two-thirty, on Saturday mornings the windows
were cleaned at nine o'clock. She had worked out to the decimal
point how long each task required. The elements of the programme
slotted so tightly into one another that the executive power hardly
had time to breathe in between. As though in a silent film, Anna sped
from one task to the next. With a hog's hair brush she dusted the

skirting boards—halfway through this the doorbell rang, she put her brush in her coverall pocket and answered the door. After the interruption, which had not been included in the programme, she resumed her work feverishly. On her daily checkup, Frau Stolz ran her index finger over the half metre that Anna had overlooked because of the delay. 'You have not dusted here today.'

That her insistence on total obedience crushed all forms of personal initiative not only escaped Frau Stolz but she also blamed her subordinate for it. One afternoon she went out visiting. Anna had to iron all the shirts before she returned. It began to rain. Anna looked up, saw the drops on the window, was caught in a dilemma: if she went upstairs to close the bedroom windows she might not finish the ironing in time. She did not dare take the risk. A little later on Frau Stolz stormed into the room, out of breath. 'I wouldn't have thought it,' she cried triumphantly. 'I say to my friend: I must go, the windows are open at home, it will rain in. She says, Isn't there anyone at home? Oh yes, I say, our servant-girl—but don't think that the idea will occur to her!'

Frau Stolz was convinced that, apart from laying down requirements, which she saw as a form of upbringing, she also had a major responsibility for Anna's welfare. She could not tolerate Anna being alone in her attic room on free evenings, but invited her down for a cup of chocolate milk in the sitting room. She taught her openwork and embroidery, cross-stitch and petit point. Skills that a young woman had to master, she explained, magnanimously providing Anna with the materials that were needed. They sat there as a threesome like that, Herr Stolz with his newspaper, his wife and the servant-girl united by a piece of needlework. Their daughter, Gitte, a girl of eight with long plaits, was already in bed.

Whenever a speech was expected from the Führer, Herr Stolz switched on the *Volksempfänger*—the standard-issue utility radio set. Anna listened and did not listen. It was the same as the embroidery that she was working on: She did it but her mind was not involved. Goebbels spoke first, about issues that fell far outside her field of vision. 'The plutocracy—the Wall Street Jews want to ruin us . . .' *ta ta ta*, so it went on. This was only the prelude. Marching music, military commands, *Sieg Heil, Sieg Heil.* Then he himself spoke, directly to his people, too loud as usual, and he kept that up throughout the broadcast. 'I must first of all reassure Mr. Minister Eden that we Germans do not in the least want to be isolated and also that we do not feel isolated at all . . .' Herr Stolz nodded in agreement. He folded his hands over the curve of his belly and listened attentively. Anna impassively allowed the bragging to drift over her, she waited until it was over, just as you wait for a rainbow to end—meanwhile she continued to breathe quietly. The Führer had become an institution. Everything was being decided and organized at an abstract level, over her head, she had not the slightest influence. So she felt entirely indifferent about it, the silent struggle against Frau Stolz's authority was already exhausting enough.

Over the edge of her embroidery she had already peeked dozens of times at the walnut bookcase where the books were kept behind glass as though they were jewels. She could not resist the temptation any longer. 'Herr Stolz, excuse me, may I . . . ?' She pointed towards the sanctuary with her embroidery needle, '. . . may I read a book one day?' 'Of course.' He nodded to her with surprise. 'Choose one.' Avoiding Frau Stolz's amazed look, Anna stood up and went to the bookcase hesitantly. She pushed open the squeaking doors; a delightful smell arose from the bound volumes, many with gilt-lettered spines; a smell of thousands and yet more thousands of printed pages, of cardboard covers, of stories that begged to be woken out of hibernation, of escaping from the foolish, unreal here and now—the promise of infinitely more fascinating worlds than that of cross-stitch and openwork. She read the titles giddily, Frau Stolz's eyes burning holes in her back. She dared not hesitate too long, took out *The Sorrows of Young Werther.* 'That is much too difficult,' sputtered Frau Stolz. 'Have you read it?' said her husband. 'No, but . . .' 'Well then, let her, culture is for everyone nowadays. It wouldn't do you any harm if you read a book sometimes, too.' Frau Stolz fell silent, and then laughed at Anna, to smooth things over. It was not clear whether the smoothing over referred to the humiliating remark from her husband or to the painful fact that she did not read. Anna opened the book and buried herself in it.

From this it seemed that the balding, wayward chemist was the weak spot in Frau Stolz's armour. Perhaps her domineering and perfectionism were purely means of preserving her self-respect. She recovered her strength whenever they were women together. The day after Anna had given evidence of her appetite for reading, she asked, holding the lid of the laundry basket in front of her like a shield, 'Don't you take any washing to your aunt on Sundays?' 'No,' Anna said, surprised. 'How is it that you hardly ever have any washing, a dress now and then . . .' 'I've only got two dresses.' '. . . And now and then some underclothes . . . never a sanitary towel . . .' 'Sanitary towel? What's that?' Frau Stolz's eyes popped. She towered over Anna, who grew smaller and smaller. She possessed nothing, two dresses, some underclothes, she was nobody. 'You're not really telling me that you don't know what sanitary towels are?' 'No,' said Anna, 'never heard of them.' 'But you menstruate?' 'Menstr—? No.' 'But every woman menstruates, each month.' Anna was silent for a moment, bewildered. 'I am not aware that I am lacking anything,' she said defiantly. 'Listen . . .' Frau Stolz laid her impeccably well-cared-for hand on Anna's shoulder with maternal concern. In a lowered voice, creating an atmosphere of familiarity that aroused great distrust in Anna, she initiated her into the secrets of the female cycle. Frau Stolz's 'we,' which referred to all women in the world, met with violent aversion in Anna. If it was womanly to lose blood every month, just as Frau Stolz lost blood every month, then she was proud that her body was having nothing to do with it.

But Frau Stolz made an appointment for her with her gynaecologist. During the examination he asked her how it could be that the hymen was broken. 'Have you ever been with a man?' It did not strike Anna that a reply was expected. She scanned the ceiling stubbornly—she had discovered cracks and colours, shapes and figures that were unintentionally expressing something, the significance of which she strenuously tried to comprehend, as diversionary tactics against the penetration by fingers, by metal, in an area that truly belonged to her but that she could in no way make her own. He posed the question more forcefully. She shook her head indignantly. 'Shhh,' he soothed, nodding calmingly at her, 'relax. Have you been examined before?' 'Yes,' she whispered, 'it was when . . . they tried to turn my womb.' The memory of the previous examination pressed itself forward, the atmosphere of secrecy in which it had taken place, the presence of the phantom Aunt Martha who guarded her virginity from a corner of the consulting room. 'You have indeed got a crooked womb,' said the doctor, 'something can only be done about it operatively. Moreover the ovaries are undeveloped, but we've got a solution for that.' The animal word 'ovary' made her think of the births of piglets and calves in an odour of hay and muck, of sweat and effort.

While she was getting dressed behind a curtain, the doctor telephoned Frau Stolz to inform her of his findings. He employed lovely, poetic phraseology about her: the hymen, the uterus, ovaria, follicles. Anna had the uneasy feeling, just as she had had years before, that an entirely strange woman was involved in an obscure fight with her to appropriate her female organs. 'One every day,' said the doctor smiling. He handed her a prescription. 'Such a good-looking blond girl ought to be able to have a whole lot of children!'

Every day Frau Stolz checked that Anna took her pill. She had assumed total responsibility for her fertility, as precisely as she had regarded it as her duty to teach her embroidery. Anna's exterior and interior had to be orderly and flawless, like the skirting boards when they had just been dusted. Only Anna's thoughts escaped her all-seeing eye. She did not see that a rebel was biding her time beneath an increasingly thinner veneer of servitude, provoked to the extreme. Months later, when the treatment first showed a dubious effect, she regarded this as a personal victory over chaos; with the proper organization of Anna's belly, order was also being restored to the world.

There were further secret watchers over her fertility—equally concerned with order. That summer the Stolzs went travelling for a week, leaving Gitte behind in Anna's care. They went to the swimming baths together in the afternoon, beach bags dangling over their shoulders. Each day there was a clear blue sky above the roofs and the motionless treetops. When they came home on one of these languid afternoons, there was a strange car in front of the house. Two men were leaning on the doors, their hands in their pockets, their eyes screwed up against the sun. They hurried after Anna up the garden path as she put the key in the lock. 'Good afternoon, *gnädige Frau*, may we have a word with you?' Anna pushed the front door open, Gitte shot into the house under her arm, upstairs to her room. In the hall they remained standing, Anna with raised eyebrows, the two men—although somewhat embarrassed—assertive. 'You see, we have come from the *Erbgesundheitsamt*, the genetic investigation branch of the health ministry. You have a servant, a certain . . .' Documents were consulted. 'Anna Bamberg? 'Yes indeed,' said Anna haughtily, 'what about her? 'Well, you see . . .' they both began together. They laughed apologetically to one another, after which one of the two did the talking and the other confined himself to nodding supportively. 'We don't know exactly, we're still investigating, but this Anna Bamberg is a bit feeble-minded?' 'Oh really?' said Anna icily, 'Is that what she is? She looks quite normal, this employee.' 'Yes, yes,' he breathed, 'that could well be so, *gnädige Frau*, but . . . you must understand . . . this woman has to be sterilized.' Once again she was hearing a word for the first time; Frau Stolz would certainly know what it meant. She kept her options open: 'Why?' 'Well, you see, we cannot . . . feeble-mindedness is inherited. If she has children, they will be feeble-minded children, too.' A ticklish laugh rose up from her chest. 'How do you make out that Anna . . .' 'Haven't you noticed anything about her then?' 'No.' 'Listen . . .' The one who had done the talking held up the documents like a trophy. 'It's all in the guardianship declaration.'

As she was listening to what he had to say, she was conscious that they represented a sort of bizarre unreality, standing together in the hall—as long as she was the lady of the house to them, regarding herself as feeling at her ease in her own hall, and at the same time referring to herself as though she were an absent third—an abstract—person.

The men had been to the court and read the guardianship declaration that she herself had signed. The part she had left unread concerned the obligatory annual reports by Uncle Heinrich, in which he had to account for the fact that he was keeping Anna Bamberg, daughter of so and so, on the farm. He had filled it in conscientiously every year, saying that since the death of her grandfather he was exercising the guardianship, that she was feeble-minded and too delicate in health to be educated or look for a job. It was so matter-of-fact there, so unadorned, in the same phraseology every year, that no one from the guardianship board had ever contemplated going to look at the problem child with their own eyes.

There it stood in black and white, in the familiar calligraphy: Anna Bamberg is feeble-minded and in delicate health. A single sentence erased her, destroyed the only thing—except for two dresses and some underclothes—she possessed: that she, the daughter of Johann Bamberg, was equipped with a good brain and a parrot's memory. The hall was too small for the explosion in her head—of rage with retroactive strength, which could not be expressed anywhere in the absence of a target. The beach bag, still hanging from her shoulder, slid to the ground. She succeeded in channeling her rage and directing it at the functionaries in an ice cold way. 'Gentlemen, she is standing here before you, Anna Bamberg. I am the delicate, feeble-minded girl you are looking for. What would you like to know? How much six times twelve is? From when to when the Thirty Years War lasted? Should I take a dictation for you? Just say!' They backed off in shock. One of the documents fell to the floor. They did not have the courage to bend down and pick it up. 'Just say! I've had enough of it now. More than enough. When my uncle wrote that in the guardianship declaration he did so because he had kept me at home to work for him for nothing all those years—in the sheds, on the land, day in day out, year in year out, without end. Because he beat me up, because he allowed me to be terrorized by his wife and because your dear Board of Supervision believed him all those years! That judge of yours, the one who's mentioned here at the top of the declaration—why did it never enter his head to find out if everything really tallied with the facts? And now on top of that you want to sterilize me. I have had enough, I really have had absolutely enough!'

One of the two glanced over his shoulder timidly to see the height of the doorknob. The other snatched the document off the floor, laughing nervously. '*Entschuldigung, Entschuldigung . . .*' they mumbled, going backwards out of the hall towards the door. 'We did not realize that . . .' Suddenly they had disappeared. She stood there in the hall, left to the mercy of her bewilderment, which was much too great and violent for her alone. She heard the car start and drive away. She was nauseated, she was disgusted by the two gullible innocents who had come to convey the disastrous tidings to her, the whole story was so sickening that she felt the need to do something violent, to shatter something that was totally respected and valued, to destroy something. But it was too hot; now she just felt that it was altogether too hot for anything. Her dress was clinging to her body; it was too hot to think about anything. Yet they were within reach, the things it would be nice to destroy: all the objects around her, the interior with its compulsive Prussian order would be a lovely target. Dropping lengthwise into a chair in the spotless room she looked around with weary eyes. She felt no urgency at all, the stolid neatness left her cold, everything left her cold, it did not matter to her. The rage imploded beneath her skull, the emotions ebbed away; empty and exhausted she looked around the room that was utterly strange to her, even though she had dusted, polished and washed all the components a thousand times.

Eventually the word *sterilize* got her moving again. She stood up listlessly, went to the bookcase and took out the dictionary blindly. 'Make infertile.' Therefore her ovaries, which thanks to Frau Stolz's tenacity were developing very slightly, would be returned to their former condition by order of the county authorities, or even removed from her body, to be absolutely certain. So the court wanted to organize things in order that no feeble-minded children would ever be born again. But surely that was idiocy, she said to herself, it is just as feeble-minded as not tolerating, for any reason, any dust anywhere along half a metre of skirting board.

9

THE DAY BEGAN with an absolutely clear sky and harsh sun-light—the snow hurt the eyes. Their lives were becoming active. On the Place Royale it was busy opposite the Thermal Institute—an attempt to make up for lost sunshine? When they came across one another at the changing rooms Anna proposed going for a walk after lunch. To one of the springs perhaps, provided that was acceptable at their age, with their rickety joints, in the snow, on the hills, and so on. Lotte yielded to Anna's self-mockery.

Each equipped with a stick, they passed the Pouhon Pierre-le-Grand. Just for a second they looked right through the building. Their gaze travelled through high bow windows above the door and emerged via stained-glass windows in pastel colours illuminated by the low sun. They had decided to begin with the Sauvenière spring, the oldest spring in Spa, and not to go there through the wood—over difficult, impassable footpaths bearing such idyllic names as Promenade des Artistes and Promenade des Hêtres—but simply along the road to Francorchamps; then they couldn't get lost. In the discussion that preceded this decision, they secretly noticed the same fastidiousness in one another, the same profusion of fantasies when they considered what could go wrong on the way. Was that old age or a family trait?

There was no snow left on the branches of the trees. They plod-ded up a constantly rising incline. Anna was panting prodigiously. Lotte was not troubled by breathlessness—she registered this small difference, not without satisfaction: she had often felt weak and weary in contrast to Anna's indefatigable vitality. She was instantly ashamed of her thoughts. Surely she wasn't engaged in a competi-tion with this woman who was her sister? 'Let's catch our breath.' Anna laid a hand on her arm. They stopped on the verge, a car struggled past now and then in the melting snow. They stood there side by side and looked at the landscape of white hills stretched out in front of them, quiet and still, as though it had originated in their own fantasies.

'There's a legend connected with the Sauvenière spring,' said Anna. 'The patron saint of Spa, Saint Remaclus, fell asleep while praying by the spring. As a reprimand God saw to it that his foot sank into the ground and left an impression in the rock. Newly married men have taken their wives to the spring since the Middle Ages; it had a reputation for encouraging fertility. If the bride placed her foot in the impression left by Saint Remaclus and drank water from the spring, the newlyweds could be confident they would be blessed with heirs. A lovely story, no?' She laughed. 'Perhaps there were hormones in the spring water!'

'It was a medieval sales talk of course, to entice people to the spring,' said Lotte.

They continued their walk. The road ascended even farther.

'We seem to be climbing Mount Golgotha.' Anna sighed.

The road now went through a beech wood, smooth dark trunks rose up on either side. A hollow opened on the left of the road, with a brook flowing in it twisting blackly through the snow. After a single passing car they were entirely alone for the first time. Far more than the public places where they had already met, this desolation emphasized their being together. Only the two of them, in the Ardennes— somewhere in these woods, these hills, East and West had come to blows, twice.

'*Ach*, my poor feet,' said Anna.

A small hexagonal pitched roof appeared in their field of view, somewhat lower than the road. There was a small opening in the ground filled with brown water. A little house had been built around it to protect the sanctuary. The impression of the foot was there, too, in the hard stone floor, close to a tap from which they did not dare drink. They had imagined something bubbling up out of the ground spontaneously, but here everything seemed to be concealed deep below the pathetic little construction, which would not have looked out of place in a Catholic cemetery.

'Saint Remaclus would be embarrassed,' said Anna with disappointment.

'The café is closed.' Lotte nodded her head towards a tea garden, which looked dark and abandoned.

'There's no money to be made from two old women,' said Anna. 'Oh well, they have constructed a little brick wall for us, let's give our poor feet a bit of a rest.'

So this was the object of the pilgrimage, which had set their joints on fire: a spot by the roadside, lacking any romance, adapted to the demands of tourism.

'If there had been such a fertility spring in our neighbourhood,' Anna laughed to herself, 'I certainly would have drunk litres and litres once.'

'Those pills you took helped, didn't they?'

'*Ach,*' she waved the idea away as though chasing off a fly, 'that whole women's story never got sorted out in me. I've never had a normal cycle. Nor did my womb get back into position: years after the war X-rays showed that during my growing years because of labouring on the farm, my spine had set too deeply into my pelvis. Otherwise I certainly might have been ten centimetres taller, like you.'

Lotte could see before her the group photo of her children and grandchildren taken on the occasion of her seventieth birthday, a photo brimming to the edges with offspring. She felt guilty, just for a while—it was an uneasy feeling when the roles were reversed. In a certain sense then, Anna had worked for two. If her own lungs had been healthy she, too, would have grown up in her grandfather's house and been put to work. A staggering thought. An incomprehensible arbitrariness; if Anna had been afflicted with TB instead of her, everything would have been the other way around. Would she have made the same choices then? She looked with confusion at the profile beside her. A dangerous potential emanated from the reversal of her ideas. It would clearly be better to keep the relationships as they were. 'Never trust a Kraut—once a Kraut always a Kraut,' said her Dutch father, who could not be trusted an inch himself. In the war, those who could be trusted had been carefully distinguished from those who could not. It had to be so, without that firm division they would not have managed. Either you were a collaborator with the

Nazis or you weren't. This division did not suddenly cease to exist after the war, only a past participle was added.

'Let's go,' she shivered. 'I'm getting cold.'

They strolled on despite the pain in their joints which protested at the resumption of the walk. The sun had disappeared behind the trees: the reflection on the clouds cast a pink glow over the snow-covered fields. As they were approaching the built-up centre of Spa the silhouette of an old chalet towered above the trees to the right of the road. Lotte stopped.

'Look,' she exclaimed, 'what a lovely house.'

'A ruin,' Anna said coolly.

'That woodcarving . . .' Lotte walked to the edge of the bank. The house, dark and mysterious in the twilight, seemed to be built of dream fragments. It was lofty and square, with balconies of dark brown stained wood on each floor along the full extent of the façade, connected to each level by wooden stairs. Doors with shutters of delicate lattice-work opened out onto the balconies. The broad protruding eaves were decorated with lacy carving. It must once have been a pleasure to wake up in this house, she imagined, to throw open the shutters, walk out onto the balcony in bare feet and look down onto the garden in the early morning sun. The house seemed to have been punished for that good life. Black holes gaped behind the broken windows, shutters hung crookedly off their hinges, parts of the sagging stairs seemed to have been hacked off for firewood.

'A house out of a Chekhov story,' Lotte sighed.

'A house of rich people, who never touched a duster themselves,' Anna corrected. 'Pity the servant girl, who had to keep such a barn clean.'

'They've simply let it collapse,' said Lotte indignantly.

'Who could afford such a house now—the heating bills, the maintenance, the staff . . .'

Anna's pragmatism annoyed Lotte. It sounded like: justice at last. 'Everything of beauty is disappearing,' she complained.

'Komm, meine Liebe.' Anna walked on decisively. This lament for an old house that was about to collapse. She, Anna, was also old; her shutters were also hanging crookedly off their hinges.

They walked on without saying any more. Anna, disapproving, was resolute in her silence, Lotte felt it with each step. The surroundings were becoming more densely built up, here and there the pavements had been cleared. Spa accepted them again—there was something reassuring about the lit-up shops, the bustle of people and of traffic. They came to rest at a patisserie in Place Albert, over a light tart of pears with whisked egg white. A potpourri of familiar melodies was playing in the background.

Lotte looked up with an expression of recognition. 'Isn't that "Lili Marlene"?

'The number-one hit of the war,' said Anna scornfully.

'Yes . . . I still remember what a stir she caused, Marlene Dietrich. She saw it all coming and left Germany in time.'

'So she could have a career in Hollywood, you mean.'

That scepticism again. Not anticipating the fire she would be stoking, she said with irritation, 'I still don't understand how all of you didn't see it coming. Hitler would not have got a foothold with you, despite the Depression . . .'

'But you hadn't had your confidence taken away as we had. He, this buffoon, gave it back to us. With his marches, party rallies, his speeches. With the most impressive Olympic Games of all time. The foreigners stood cheering, and Herr Hitler was host to the world. No one was saying, You're no good. They all came. And then the newspapers, periodicals, the radio, the bioscope magazine, they all carried that one message—there wasn't anything else. You took it in, every day, there was only one version. . . . You swallowed it the way you swallow advertising. It ground its way into our heads, slowly but surely. *Ach,* you can't imagine it.'

Anna sighed, she stuck her fork abruptly into the tart.

'Industry was flourishing. The young didn't hang around on the streets. They were in the Hitler Youth and came to school fresh and happy. They were training for military service so that they would make good soldiers later on. When the war broke out they were already used to camps and discipline . . . It was all planned but no one realized it. The girls automatically became *Blitzmädel,* task force squads of young women in the Wehrmacht. And there was the Ideology and Aesthetics division for the educated youth—where they learnt rhythmics, dancing, singing, making music: that's how they also won over the higher echelon. It was an orderly, beautiful, fantastic world.'

It was being said in an ironic voice, it's true, but so loud that Lotte made beseeching gestures and looked around nervously.

'I can sense only opposition in you. You must understand this once and for all,' Anna continued just as loudly. 'The mothers were relieved of the care of their children, there was no boredom, no drug addicts, you didn't have the shambles we have now. Most people of my age who were involved still dream about it all the time. You should talk to a former BDM leader or an *Arbeitsführerin*, your hair would stand on end. It was their youth, the time of their lives, *wunderschön!*'

Lotte stared at her. It was as though Anna had become larger and larger during this hymn of praise, as though—with her cake fork in her hand—she had acquired vast dimensions. This bumptiousness, this *wunderschöne*, fatal enthusiasm from before the war, filled the whole *patisserie*.

'Yet there were exceptions, people who didn't lose their reason!' Lotte was speaking into the wind; her words were blown back into her face—so weak did she feel in her defence. 'Even when a whole people loses its head like that, there are exceptions.'

'Of course. But the political opposition had been waved aside at once, you know that, they had neatly removed them. The rest of them, the intellectuals, the clever ones, like those who had contacts with foreigners so they could also get hold of other information, or people like Uncle Heinrich, who understood it intuitively: all those people would have been in great danger if they had opened their mouths. That's why you didn't hear voices of dissent. All hands were raised in the same direction, the one direction . . .'

'But you, Anna . . . Why did you do nothing?

'I was a servant girl, "the maid of," a non-person. I had to be there all the time, for the *gnädige Frau,* I had to do what she wanted me to, like lightning. I didn't take kindly to Hitler, but beyond that I didn't care; it was all the same to me.'

The blood rose to Lotte's head. One way or another Anna was becoming increasingly elusive—she was putting up a smoke screen under the guise of candour. But Lotte would not permit herself to be misled.

'And the Jews,' she said fiercely, 'the disappearances, Kristall-nacht . . . ?'

'The official answer to that was: We have taken them in for pro-tection because otherwise the wrath of the people would kill them. Because the Jews had brought about all the miseries: the First World War, the scandalous Treaty of Versailles, the Depression, degeneracy in art . . . that even persists now in some German heads, it was so hammered in. Listen . . . Lotte . . .'

Anna leaned close to Lotte across the table. There was a fleck of egg-white foam on her top lip. Lotte felt that the last opponents of the Nazi regime were represented by this trivial bit of foam—and at once a thick, shiny tongue came out to lick it away from its insecure position on her top lip.

'Listen, you can pose all these questions because you know about everything that happened. We didn't yet know where it was all lead-ing so we didn't pose the questions. Why are you looking at me like that?'

'*Wir haben es nicht gewusst* . . . We did not know . . . We've all heard that one for so long.'

Anna started pricking the base of her tart with her fork, she really seemed angry. That pricking was getting on Lotte's nerves, she was very close to becoming angry herself.

'You all point with your accusing fingers,' Anna snapped. 'You've been doing that for forty-five years already, but that's the easy way. Why did the German people let it happen, you cry. But I turn that around and ask: Why did you in the West let it happen? You allowed us to re-arm quietly—when you could have intervened under the Treaty of Versailles. You allowed us to march into the Rhineland without let or hindrance, and then Austria. And then you bargained away Czechoslovakia to us. The German emigrants in France, in Eng-land, in America, warned you. No one listened. Why didn't they stop that idiot while it was still possible? Why did you leave us to our fate, turned over to a dictator?'

'So *we* did it, finally!'

'Why? That's what I ask.'

Lotte's eyes sparkled. 'You twist things beautifully, Anna,' she said with a hostile laugh. 'This really is the prettiest argument I've ever heard to exonerate the Germans.' She stood up angrily. 'Allow me to pay,' she said haughtily. She lifted her coat from the back of the chair and veered off towards the young woman at the cash till. *Ouch*, the walk had severely affected her calves.

Anna stood up in a panic. Why was Lotte so cross all of a sudden? She had set out her ideas in all sincerity. They had not been formed unthinkingly, just like that: you could not see past the piles of books she had read in order to discern those lurid patterns. It was doubtful whether Lotte had taken so much trouble to read up about it.

'Lotte,' she called, 'wait a moment.'

'I'm tired,' said her sister over her shoulder. Suddenly she looked very old and fragile. 'I think I really am very tired.'

10

AS THE DOOR of the *patisserie* closed behind Lotte, Anna snatched her winter coat from the chair. She found it stuffy among all those women—it was smoky and her hard-won insights had evoked nothing but unwillingness and a lack of comprehension in the only person in the world she wanted to convince. It was one big misunderstanding. She wormed her way between two chairs to the cash till. Lotte had paid for her, too—was she trying to justify her over-hasty departure in that way? Anna went out into the snow; she tried to breathe deeply but it seemed as though her lungs had shrunk. Her heart was beating fast and unevenly. Here, now, it could happen, just like that, suddenly; the breach with Lotte would never be mended. Walking slowly, she tried to get her breathing under control; perhaps it was the sudden feeling of futility that was making her short of breath.

Lotte was relieved. The act of defiance that she had committed just now uplifted her, she felt liberated—she had allowed herself to be taken in too far by Anna, the limits of her empathy had been reached. It was as though they had been involved in a mock battle. They tossed worn-out arguments that had been heard a thousand times at each other's heads, ostensibly going right to the heart of their direct opposition to one another while, actually, something much larger was going on beyond them. Something that withdrew as soon as you tried to bring it closer to you by observing it through a telescope.

They arrived at the Thermal Institute at the same time the next morning, except that Lotte was standing at the foot of the stairs while, for unknown reasons, Anna was on the opposite side of the road, waiting for a military procession to pass. Surely she hadn't been on the lookout? Lotte would not have noticed her if she hadn't waved and called out. Lotte waited. She had slept wonderfully well that night after she had made up her mind not to allow herself to become so upset by Anna anymore. And now there she was, waving; then she disappeared for a moment behind a jeep, a tank, a military ambulance. There was no end to the procession creeping by her according to its own logic. Helmeted heads, looking ahead with martial bearing, as though they had just taken Spa by force purely to enable them to drive through it. Lotte began to laugh. She saw that Anna was laughing too, on the other side. Were they both discovering at the same moment that nothing more than a mock performance separated them? When the last camouflage-painted tank had passed, Anna crossed the street shaking her head.

As though nothing special had occurred the day before, they ascended the steps of the Thermal Institute, supporting each other. It seemed that the previous day had cleared out something thorny—you could not tell what twists the human spirit would take. Later in the day they met up again in one of the corridors. On a long white bench they discussed the effects of the different baths on their muscles and joints like seasoned visitors at a health resort. Now the most intensive treatment was over, the curative results would have to reveal themselves gradually. They decided to have dinner that evening in a restaurant opposite the Pouhon Pierre-le-Grand. According to Anna, whose scrutiny did not miss much, it looked convivial and affordable.

LOTTE'S FATHER DID not emerge unscathed from his illness. The thrombosed leg limped a bit with every step. His heart sometimes began to beat faster for no reason. Then he would clutch his chest as though the moment he was going to die had actually arrived. The gesture immediately revived the old anxiety in everyone. Conversation stopped, music was turned off, a window was opened—although they knew that he exploited his palpitations and feigned them at times when other methods for attracting attention failed. He had been the focal point at all times during his long period of illness, his wife had been completely devoted to him as she had been in the springtime of their marriage before she became distracted by the children. After his recovery the youngest returned home and he fell into the old habit, worse than ever, of provoking the children (her children) with unreasonable demands and punishments. It was the simplest way of getting into a row with her; during the reconciliations he regained exclusive rights to her for a while. Instead of being grateful for the fact that he had survived three different causes of death, he was embittered, as though the regained life in no way fulfilled his expectations. He also developed the habit of sniffing repeatedly, first through one nostril, then the other—even the smell of his second life did not please him.

The sniffing got on Lotte's nerves; she could hear it everywhere. Behind closed doors, at the end of the passage, just around the corner, at night through the bedroom walls. She dreamed of escaping from this father and from the disharmony that he constantly induced in the family in different ways on account of his inexhaustible inventiveness. She also wished to be released from his permanent grousing. About the impotence of Minister-President Colijn, who intended to combat the Depression by cutting payments to the unemployed and loans to civil servants. Her father noticed it especially in the slower growth of his record collection. He grumbled about the Communist Party, which had called on all political parties to sink their underlying

differences in a collective fight against the National Socialist movement—now he could no longer draw his sword against the popes and
Calvinists. He groused about Hitler, who had merely been a half-wit
at first, but had gradually come to enjoy the status of a dangerous
lunatic. He complained about the German people who marched
behind the dangerous lunatic, whereby he conveniently overlooked
that his own mother was German as well as his grandparents on her
side—and also his musical niece. Sniffing violently, he took possession of the newspaper as soon as it dropped through the letter box,
like a dog grips a bone between its teeth, and would not surrender it
to anyone. The more Lotte heard his carrying on against the German
people, the more that people filled her with affection. Each negative
remark on his part aroused her longing for a reunion with Anna. If
her father thought that the Germans were good for nothing, she
wanted to be one of them.

Theo de Zwaan, Marie's fiancé, set out for Germany with two
friends on the rumor that there was abundant work there. After two
weeks he was back again. Instead of having earned something he had
spent all his savings on a Leica that hung on his chest like a war trophy. 'How will you get it into your head!' said Lotte's mother, 'We
don't buy German goods on principle and you come home flaunting
a pricey Leica.' But he was not elated in the slightest about his purchase, rather it seemed like a sort of plaster over a wound. He was
depressed and sparing with information. Yes, there was work
enough there, but he had no business being in that country. Half the
people were in uniform, even children, there was a revolting general
enthusiasm about the Anschluss with Austria, there were posters,
banners everywhere, placards with '*Ein Volk—Ein Reich—Ein
Führer*.' He had seen it with his own eyes and wanted nothing more
to do with it. 'I could have told you that already,' said his future
father-in-law, 'then you could have saved yourself the whole trip.'
Lotte mistrusted the bearer of these bad tidings. Probably no one
had wanted to take him on, you could see from afar that he was a
drip. The way he had experienced Germany had been coloured by
frustration of course, it spoke well for the country that it did not
take on anyone just like that.

To compensate, Theo longed for the camera to provide him with glittering photographs. He asked Jet and Lotte to be guinea pigs. As neither of them could take him seriously, they put on men's trousers and jackets and homburg hats, for a joke. With their lips made up to excess, they permitted themselves to be immortalized beside the water tower in masculine poses, leaning on each other's shoulders, cigars in their mouths; staring into the camera with sphinx's eyes like Greta Garbo; in an imitation of Marlene Dietrich— 'I'm ready for love from head to toe.' Eventually they burst out in uncontrollable laughter. Theo took his photos, phlegmatic as always, setting the diaphragm and deciding the angle of view. When the minuscule pictures with zigzag edges had been developed, the worldly, sultry, negligent, independent women they perceived aroused their curiosity. Was this them? Their mother passed the photos around among visitors with a proud laugh: just see what good-looking daughters I have!

A Mahler symphony was on the turntable. Lotte attached herself to the group that sat in a circle listening as though at a religious confession—a waterfall was gushing down at the foot of a rock in a clearing in a wood, threatening rumblings sounded from behind the mountaintops, deer were on the run. Sammy Goldschmidt was listening with pursed lips, mentally he was performing along with it. For Ernst Goudriaan, who was gazing ahead darkly, the music seemed to arouse more sombre visions. 'Who was the conductor?' he asked when the last note had died away and they seemed rather dejected because the spell had broken. 'Wilhelm Furtwängler,' said Lotte's father, sniffing left and right. 'Furtwängler!' said Goudriaan. 'He plays for the Nazis now!' 'Furtwängler?' Lotte's mother repeated shocked. 'Oh well,' her husband muttered, 'that symphony was recorded years ago, we've already enjoyed it many times.'

Goudriaan looked round uneasily. He was just back from Germany, he explained. It sounded like an apology. He had been serving an apprenticeship with a famous violin maker. During that time he had lodged with a Jewish family, and had more or less become a member of the household. A few days ago the violin maker had come up to him. 'I have heard that you are staying with Jewish people. If you want to complete your training here you must leave there as quickly as possible.' 'But I have nothing to do with those regulations,' Goudriaan retorted. 'I am Dutch.' 'You are here in Germany, you have to go along with it. Either you leave that family or you do not remain here any longer.' 'Then I'll leave,' said Goudriaan.

Disbelief and indignation filled the room, Goudriaan submitted to it with a dejected laugh. Hesitating between sympathy and suspicion, Lotte looked at the slender student. It was difficult for her to imagine him as a violin maker—woodshavings on his impeccable suit, endlessly scraping with a plane—a craft that evoked associations of muscular arms and workmen's overalls. Her father put Beethoven's Ninth on, in a more kosher performance. Would they never again be able to listen to music open-mindedly from then on? The '*Alle Menschen werden Brüder*' resounded magisterially; why wasn't it '*Alle Menschen werden Schwester*'?

As the year progressed it became increasingly difficult to find excuses for her native country. Never before had the radio been listened to as much as it was in the September days, when Chamberlain flew to Germany three times to prevent war and, finally, with Daladier, sacrificed Czechoslovakia for peace. Everyone was relieved, only Lotte's father was agitated that France as well as England had reneged on their treaty with the Czechs in such a cowardly way. 'Out of pure fear of Bolshevism,' he sniffed contemptuously. 'In their hearts they admire the way Hitler has cleansed his country of Communists.' 'That fear isn't so crazy,' said his wife, with her predictable arguments again, 'when the workers seize power on a large scale, those people who come to the top also terrorize the people.' 'Do you know who you're talking about?' He was offended. 'You're talking about Stalin; he has to keep a whole continent in harness.' Then he became sentimental; everyone knew how the ancient discussion would go. Lotte hid behind her music theory. The division of roles had already been fixed in advance. Her mother appointed herself defender of democracy, made a plea for a natural equilibrium between the parties; her father jeered the democratic principle away, 'Do you by any chance want to claim that we have a democracy here;

the poor are getting even poorer!' He allowed himself to be swept along by his feelings, took a sip of gin, the war that had been averted at the last minute was pushed into the background. Another much older war was being fought out here under the pretext of a difference in political opinions—a battle that always remained unresolved. 'Don't make me laugh,' her mother had the last word. 'You know best of all that you yourself would be a dictator here in the house if you had the chance.'

Lotte had had funds saved up for a trip to Germany for a long time—the closer the threat of war grew, the harder it was to speak about her plan out loud. They listened masochistically to the radio all together, to a summary of a belligerent speech by Reichsminister Hess. They reassured each other: The Netherlands would never get involved, we have always been neutral. Anyway, half of The Netherlands is related to the Germans: our prince, the former queen Emma, grandmother in Amsterdam, you name them. Louis Davids' death was a greater tragedy than the annexation of Lithuania and the Italian invasion of Albania—Lotte's mother walked about the house wailing and slapping her forehead with the flat of her hands as though she blamed herself; she sang his songs melancholically sitting on the bench under the pear tree.

'Now your Papa Stalin has made a poor showing,' she said when Hitler and Stalin signed a non-aggression pact. 'It's Stalin's trick.' Her husband laughed at such short-sightedness. 'There's something behind it. It suits him well to make a pact at this moment.' The queen made a calm radio broadcast: there is no reason at all for concern. Mobilization was being proclaimed in order to preserve the country's neutrality; Theo de Zwaan left on one of the hundreds of extra trains, not discontented; at last he had something to do.

'Holland with its tin soldiers,' sniffed Lotte's mother, slipping a bag of apples and sandwiches into his hands. Two days later the Germans invaded Poland and another two days later England and France declared themselves at war with Germany: there was nothing more to discuss with Hitler. Yet faith in the safety of the negligible little kingdom by the sea, which no side had chosen, was still intact.

* * *

'SO YOU SEE, you were just as naive as we were,' said Anna.

Lotte nodded.

They continued eating, lost in thought. To Lotte's dismay, Anna mashed her potato croquettes; she cut hers into pieces of equal size, which Anna thought petty.

'Are they real?' Anna stroked her finger over a red flower that was blossoming with suspect luxuriance in a slender pot by their table.

'It's all plastic,' said Lotte, who had already seen this when she came in.

'You're right,' Anna withdrew her finger, 'it's much too dark for plants here. *Ach* . . . that makes me think of Frau Stolz's cactuses . . .' She grinned. 'They were fatal to me, you might say.'

THE CONTENTS OF the bookcase had prevented Anna's disguised serfdom from being unbearable. The embroidery was hardly progressing, it lay on her lap for the sake of form, being creased by the book open on it. Herr Stolz divided his attention between the newspaper and the radio, which exclusively reported successes. 'Ten years ago we were the pariahs of Europe, and now Chamberlain takes the trouble to visit us three times—who would have thought it,' said Stolz with satisfaction. 'We have our Führer's genius to thank for that entirely.' On New Year's Day Hitler totted up the balance on the radio. 'The year 1938 was the richest in terms of events in the whole history of our people.' The Third Reich had grown to ten million souls by restoring the German minorities in the surrounding territories to the German community—*Heim ins Reich*. Frau Stolz said with satisfaction that at last she dared again to be proud that she was a German. With a glass of Sekt they toasted the astonishing dynamism of the Führer and the big things he intended for them.

This euphoria left Anna unmoved. She had never been struck by the idea of being a German. When she heard Hitler and Beneš, the Czech president, blustering about each other on the radio she thought: Give them each a club and they can fight it out between them. What is it to do with us? Tired of the villa district next to the enthusiastically smoking factory chimneys, broken in spirit by the suppression of her rebelliousness, she did her work in a deadly routine. But one weekday during the same winter, just like that, she suddenly reached saturation point. From a small, innocent incident that single inevitable spark sprang up.

She had to clean the dining room on Thursday morning at half past five. Everyone was still asleep; it was silent and cold in the house. Beneath a large window overlooking the back garden was a window seat made of black marble on which there were cactus plants. An exotic desert flower never appeared between the spines—it was unthinkable that anything could come into flower under Frau Stolz's regime. She had to take the cactuses off the window seat one by one, then she polished it with wax until the gleaming black surface reflected her own face. Later that day Frau Stolz called Anna to her. 'Anna, you forgot the window seat this morning.' Anna denied it. 'You are lying, look, here and here.' Copying her employer, she sank to her knees. In two places the polish had not been totally wiped away. There were a few clouds left behind, which could not be seen against the background of the dark garden at half past six in the morning. They stood up. Merciless winter light shone inside. Frau Stolz's face was flat and chilly, an icy shield against Anna's accumulated rage.

She started to take her overall off. 'Don't worry, Frau Stolz, about your window seat, your cactuses, your skirting boards, I won't touch them with another finger, I promise you.' 'You need to be able to accept a bit of criticism,' said Frau Stolz. Anna looked at the cactuses, took stock of the whole room, all the objects that had been through her hands and, now that it came to it, sided with Frau Stolz. 'I can't work like this,' she said flatly, 'this small-minded order, the Prussian sense of duty, there is no place for me here. Put me in the middle of the desert and I'll lay out a lovely garden for you, but in my own way.' 'Ah . . .' it dawned on Frau Stolz, 'you want to sort out the linen here!' Anna looked at her; suddenly it was from a dizzying distance. She looked at her properly, for the first time and the last time, Frau Stolz, as she stood there, a sturdy, rectangular woman. There she stood, exactly as she was, with her shocking limitations. The woman was thinking feverishly; it was very difficult for her to consider an appropriate *coup de grâce* that would enable her to maintain her dignity. 'Do you know what it is with you? You have got too

many big ideas . . .'—she snatched the coverall out of Anna's hands—
'you won't rest until you are in the banqueting hall at Bayer being
waited on by two servants.'

Gitte would not let Anna go. On the day of her departure she had
locked all the doors in the villa. She sat on the dark red velvet-cov-
ered sofa with her legs apart and arms folded, her bony knees sticking
out apologetically: You can't leave me behind here alone. 'Where are
the keys!' Her mother gave her a good shaking; Gitte did not move a
muscle. Anna went rigid between her suitcases; she recognized, in
painful comparison, the girl's feelings. 'I threw them in the WC and
pulled the chain,' said Gitte arrogantly. She was registering her
absolute opposition to Anna's desertion. Formidably calm, Frau Stolz
went to telephone a locksmith. Anna embraced Gitte in farewell but
she turned away, aggrieved. Finally Anna went to the kitchen with
her suitcases, opened a high narrow window above the draining
board, threw her baggage out and threw herself after it, off the sinking ship into the depths, which crunched pleasantly under her feet as
she landed.

She returned to her uncle's house, to the bedroom with the medallion wallpaper, the living room with the easy chairs and the gramophone and Uncle Franz's operetta music, but she was oblivious to it.
Furniture and practical objects still came under the heading of compulsion—the compulsion of cleaning, every week, the eternally recurring tasks. Uninspired, she wrote off applications in answer to
advertisements. She had a bath, got out and stood politely before her
dripping reflection in the mirror. 'How do you do, I am Anna Bamberg, my mother has been dead for years, my father, too, then I also
had a sister, Lotte, but to be honest she has not been around for a
long time either. I, Anna, on the other hand, am alive and kicking,
that is obvious . . .'

A reply came to one of the letters, an envelope of marbled paper
with the sender's name in unadorned, businesslike handwriting.
Charlotte von Garlitz Dublow, Countess von Falkenau. Instead of
inviting Anna for an interview she announced her arrival, on the very
same day. A countess! Aunt Vicki excitedly ran to her clothes cupboard to find a dress for Anna. Anna stared at the upright, sober let-

ters, overcome with misgivings—a countess, that recalled associations with serfdom, there went her tender, hard-won freedom.
Through a chink in the net curtains she watched the countess getting
out of her Kaiser-Freser; beneath her open fur coat she was wearing a
cream silk blouse. Aunt Vicki pinched Anna in the palm of her hand.

The sitting room, which not long ago had struck Anna as the high
point of luxury and comfort, became conventional and bourgeois
with this lady in it. She kept hold of Anna's hand as she scrutinized
her without embarrassment. 'I would like to ask you something,' she
said. 'Are you related to Johannes Bamberg?' In a reflex Anna withdrew her hand, in no condition to reply to a direct question, innocently posed. No one had ever spoken this name again: The family
had buried his memory along with his material remains. She looked
at the woman without seeing her. The tick of the pendulum in this
room affected her for the first time—the tap of a stick on a cobbled
street. Aunt Vicki looked from one to the other, wringing her hands,
and when the silence had persisted too long said, 'Johannes Bamberg,
yes, that was her father, a cousin of my husband . . . I never knew him
because he died young.' 'Her father then,' the woman interrupted her,
satisfied, turning her swan's neck towards Anna. 'Yes indeed, her
father,' breathed Aunt Vicki obligingly. 'Then everything is in order.'
A gloved hand descended on Anna's shoulder. 'Will you come with
me? My car is outside.' 'But her things,' cried Aunt Vicki, breathless
at the speed with which the transaction was being concluded. 'I'll
send my chauffeur later on.' The countess with the unpronounceable
name guided Anna out in front of her, out of the bourgeois living
room, along the passage; Aunt Vicki had no opportunity to open the
front door for her, she did everything herself with great determina-
tion. As she gracefully swept one hand through her short brown hair,
she held the car door open for Anna with her other. Anna stepped in
blankly, as though hypnotized.

Cologne slipped past on either side, a mobile stage set. Time and
place lost their normal proportions. Her father's name had set something going that still seemed mainly like a film rolling at accelerated
speed. It was a blatant abduction; had he taken responsibility for her
again after all this time, and was the woman behind the wheel an

emissary fulfilling his commission in style? She steered the car with one hand, lit a cigarette with the other. An angel who smoked. They left the built-up area behind; did the inhabited world stop here? The car turned off the road, a manicured finger pressed the klaxon, wrought iron gates opened. A broad drive, flanked by old trees whose crowns were enmeshed in each other. In the park landscape that flickered past between the trees, Anna recognized the Elysian Fields from Herr Stolz's Greek mythology. Lawns sloping to the horizon, evergreen hedges, groups of trees and shrubs—all maintained with care and trimmed into shape like the driver's fingernails. They penetrated deeper into the tunnel beneath an arch of black branches, which ended in a circle of light. A motionless figure in a dark suit stood at the top of the steps of a majestic, blindingly white house; only his eyes followed the semicircle the car described before it came to a halt at the foot of the steps. The woman got out. Anna, who was expected to do the same, remained seated, disoriented. 'Come, we're here.' The door opened, she squirmed out, blinking. Dizziness overcame her as she went up the wide stairs. She could see no more of the dark figure than a long arm with a hand on it that held the door open for them, thereafter he seemed to command two arms with which he helped them out of their coats, in the centre of an enormous hall with passageways, doors and stairs leading off it.

She was assigned a room on the first floor with a view onto a turquoise swimming pool—an unreal, poisonous element amid the natural green lawns. The governess, cook, servants, chauffeur, washerwoman, cleaning women, maids and gardeners seemed to live in contented symbiosis; each had his or her own territory. It was a centuries-old collaboration, a stylized form of servitude to the former Prussian nobility, which had proved its effectiveness in the centuries-long governance of castles and country houses. Anna was entrusted with the care of Frau von Garlitz's wardrobe, replacing the previous chambermaid who had been dismissed. Whenever a seam was loose she had to repair it, she took the clothes to the washerwoman, picked up the evening dress that lay crumpled on the parquet floor and hung it in the cupboard. This luxurious life stood in such stark contrast to the daily battle of attrition in her previous job that she was ashamed of the size of the wages: double what she had earned with Frau Stolz, not counting the tips and gifts that Frau von Garlitz regularly slipped the staff with an intimate laugh.

In hours of idleness she floated through the house. *En passant* she learned how the table had to be laid when a general, a big industrialist, a baron came to dine; which dinner service was sufficiently respectful without overdoing it; she learned to arrange a seasonal bouquet on a half-moon table beneath an eighteenth-century still life with grapes and pheasants. Frau von Garlitz slept separately from her husband—their bedrooms, in a private wing of the house, were joined by a pink marble bathroom. A search for her nightdress, which had to be hung up in the morning, brought Anna into Herr von Garlitz's bedroom, as a smirking maid had advised, where to her disillusionment the sought item lay carelessly on the floor by his bed—the countess had gone to him!

Anna won the trust of the cook, who generously provided her with background information, legitimized by a devout attachment to her employer. The *gnädige Frau* was born a von Falkenau, related to the oldest Prussian nobility. Her husband, on the other hand, Wilhelm von Garlitz Dublow, merely came from the coal-scuttle. Anna raised her eyebrows. The Ruhr area, the cook explained. His father, captain of a ship that had brought the Kaiser to Norway, had fallen in love with one of the Kaiserin's ladies in waiting, Countess Dublow. He was ennobled in great haste in order to be able to marry her. Thus Garlitz came into his 'von' and Dublow was added on at the end. In recognition of Kaiser Wilhelm, their firstborn was named after him.

The respect and affection with which the cook spoke about the *gnädige Frau* was diametrically opposed to the disdain with which she disclosed Herr von Garlitz's curriculum vitae. 'He is a weakling, a Casanova,' she said, 'but she is crazy about him, the poor woman.' The management of the factory, Die Basilwerke, where vitamin preparations and herbal remedies were manufactured as restoratives for the Wehrmacht troops, he left to subordinates. 'Horses, he is always messing around with horses,' the woman sighed defeatedly, as though all the misery in the world resulted from it. Invisible behind a medieval rampart, the factory grounds bordered the park. Sometimes he spurred his horse and galloped around the nineteenth-century complex of buildings to remind the workers that the chimneys were smoking at his expense.

'Have you met my husband yet?' said Frau von Garlitz. 'Come, then I'll introduce you.' She rushed down the entrance steps to meet him. Anna followed awkwardly. She saw a snippet from a UFA film: the godchild of the Kaiser, in a white uniform, bolt upright on his Lippizaner, trotting between the black shiny pillars of the drive. At the foot of the steps the Rider on the White Horse came to a halt; he dismounted and allowed himself to be embraced with self-indulgent absent-mindedness. 'Anna, my new chambermaid.' Frau von Garlitz pushed her gently towards him. He gave her a hand fleetingly while his eyes looked for a baluster to tie the reins around. To him, Anna understood, I am less than a horse.

The discovery of the library put an end to her parasitic feeling. It was a spacious room, the walls clothed in books, apart from three windows where bare vine tendrils tapped in the breeze—a treasury that was carefully maintained, supplied with fresh flowers and where even the fire was kept burning in the hearth. Everything for the satisfaction of an imaginary reader: she never found anyone there. *La Divina Commedia*, the *Petit Larousse, Der abenteuerliche Simplicissimus, Don Quixote*, the *Prophesies* of Nostradamus, Goethe's *Faust* and *Farbenlehre* . . . were next to each other in no order. There were first editions. The books cracked peevishly when they were opened, the accusing smell of neglect rose up—a book that is unread does not exist, was being whispered. Anna saw that an immense task awaited her here.

One day she posed the question that had been burning on her lips since the start. '*Ach ja . . .*' Pensively Frau von Garlitz pursed her heart-shaped dark-red-painted mouth. 'My father was staying here when I was working through all those letters of application. Bamberg, I mumbled out loud, your letter in my hand, Anna Bamberg . . . My father looked up from his newspaper. "Didn't I know a Bamberg . . . wait a moment . . . one Johannes Bamberg, a splendid chap, a first-rate employee, I have special memories of him, my God it must be thirty years ago." I said to myself, if Anna Bamberg is related to him I'll accept her and regard it as a sign from above that my choice is correct.' Giggling, she continued: 'I don't believe in God or Jesus Christ but I do in signs from above, it's fun!' 'What sort of special memories were they?' Anna asked. 'You'll have to ask him that yourself, in due course. My father used to run the factory here. Your father must have worked for him—and made an impression!'

The house was an island in the effervescing twentieth century, and the library was another island within that house, where the seventeenth, eighteenth and nineteenth centuries were better represented than the twentieth. Anna rummaged at her leisure, reassured about the legitimacy of her privileged position as chambermaid to Frau von Garlitz. She knew now that it was her rightful inheritance, her father's reputation was his legacy (how much more valuable than money and possessions). Long before her birth with unconscious foresightedness he had already bequeathed her something. This same form of parental love, which extended from before birth to long after death, gave her the feeling that he was still concerned about her with retrospective strength.

Thus she came effortlessly through the winter, spring and summer. Sometimes she walked about the house with an evening dress or a nightdress in her fingers, but mostly she read, with everyone's assent. She did not know that it was merely an interlude—a long held breath.

THE DRIPPING CANDLE that stood between the plates was reflected in Anna's eyes.

'The rigid discipline,' said Lotte, 'that the chemist's wife expected from you, that really was typically German.'

'Ach, it was her view of household order.' Anna moderated her observation, 'Simply: I could not function in such a system of total availability.' She began to laugh. 'Suddenly it reminds me of something.' She pinched Lotte's hand from sheer pleasure. 'Somewhere in the fifties I met the Stolzs again. I was working in child welfare and was on a delegation visiting Bayer—I believe it was about an unemployment relief project for displaced children. We were grandly received in the banqueting hall, with two liveried attendants to each guest. Halfway through the meal I suddenly heard Frau Stolz's reproach again: You won't be satisfied until you . . . at Bayer . . . and so on. And now there I was! I choked, my neighbour anxiously clapped me on the back. After it was over I drove off, in my first Volkswagen—a thousand metres up to the house. They still lived there, only the bell was no longer polished spick and span with Sidol and the stairs at the front were no longer spotless. I rang the bell. An old woman stuck her head out of the window: "Anna!" Of course I must come inside. There were photographs of Gitte with husband and children on the sideboard—its doors had panes of glass that had to be cleaned one by one with a chamois leather. Just then Herr Doctor came home from work, he was amazed: "Do tell us, what's brought you here by chance." I repeated his wife's prophetic remark. "And today I was sitting there, with two servants!" He burst out in uncontrollable laughter. His wife joined in, in embarrassment. I felt sorry for her. "You see," he prodded his wife, "didn't I always say to you: You won't make a housemaid out of that girl in a hundred years!"'

PART 2

WAR

1

O N SUNDAY MORNING there was a flea market in the nineteenth-century covered promenade that extended deep into
the Parc de Sept Heures from the Place Royale. It was
sunny, but there was a bleak wind from the east. The traders stamped
to keep warm beneath elegant, curly flying buttresses, others paced
up and down between the wrought iron pillars. Anna and Lotte
strolled past the goods on display: vases, ornaments, old gramophone
records, picture postcards. They stopped in front of an unpainted
rocking horse that was staring inertly at the statue of a saint.

'You still remember the rocking horse we always fought over!'
cried Anna, so loudly that the market-goers looked in their direction.
Lotte thought she could see distaste in their expressions for having
disturbed the Sunday quiet. In German, what's more! Firmly she said,
'No, I don't remember.'

'Yes . . . yes . . . it was painted blue and white with proper reins
and a brown saddle; we pushed each other off until Papa intervened
with a tactical proposition: Today, Sunday, is Lotte's day for horse
riding, Monday for Anna, Tuesday for Lotte again, and so on. What
do you two say about that? I had completely forgotten,' she clapped
her hands. 'How lovely that it's suddenly there again.'

The horse had no effect on Lotte; it just severed the gentle feeling
of solidarity that there had been among all those objects from the
past. How was it that her memory only functioned properly from
after the sickbed in the garden, in the care of her Dutch mother? It
was handicapping her for the first time; it made her incomplete.

'The war is in fashion,' Anna observed. 'There's still money to be
made.' Military helmets and belts were laid out on a piece of velvet
cloth. Yes, the war was peacefully present everywhere: a soldier's
water flask lay next to an ancient coffee grinder, beneath crumpled
romantic novels and detective stories there was a richly illustrated
treatise on military insignias and uniforms in the Third Reich; on a

stall with old portraits of married couples, certificates of baptism and confirmation, there was a framed photograph of a young soldier who looked defiantly into the lens.

'He did not yet know that a monument would be erected for him here,' said Lotte.

'Look how he puffs out his chest, the poor boy, he solemnly believed in his mission.'

'Not really . . . He wasn't fighting for an ideal, he had to defend his country.'

Her sister took her arm and pulled her away. I won't be provoked, thought Anna. Behind in the park, the Chalet du Parc had stood for at least a century by a steep rock wall. Here they came to a halt. The sun shone inside horizontally, the vapor from the coffee curled upwards, blue in a beam of light.

We always get together in public places, thought Lotte, as though there was still something improper about our meeting.

THE SKY DID not take on the colour of fate, the cook did not break off kneading the dough for a second, the chauffeur did not let his newspaper drop, the servant walked through with a fully laden tray as usual, Anna's darning needle did not stray off course for a moment, no one anticipated that in the margin of innocent, everyday activity a fracture had occurred that morning, when a familiar voice which they had already heard so often that for a long time they had no longer been listening to it resounded in the kitchen on the *Volksempfänger*: 'At dawn on the firrrst of Septemberrr Gerrrman trrroops crrrossed the Polish borrrderrr . . . Frrrom today bomb will be rrrepaid with bomb . . .'

A few hours later too, when Anna was just standing in the middle of the lawn to enjoy the unreal beauty of the house and grounds, she did not realize that there, beneath the same sky, in the same daylight, something had been set in motion that was far more unreal—a process of total alienation that they would be dragged into all together. Something indefinable glistened high up in the air. She narrowed her eyes into slits. Simultaneously with an exploding sound in the far distance, white clouds appeared from nowhere and removed the thing from view. At that same moment the house began to speak;

it shouted at her from all its openings: 'Are you mad? Get away from there, come inside, it's war!' 'What?' called Anna, walking towards the house, cupping her ears in her hands. 'It's war!' Frau von Garlitz, gesticulating wildly, hung out of one of the windows. She sent her husband outside to prevent Anna's act of hara-kiri; they bumped into each other at the doorway. 'It's a British reconnaissance aircraft,' he said curtly, 'our anti-aircraft guns are bringing it down. You had better stay inside.' His Clark Gable moustache moved up and down emotionally, despite his masculine composure. Ridiculous, Anna thought, all that fuss. War—it was no more than a word, she almost wished that something really would happen, something that was more than a dot in the air, so that the word would acquire meaning.

Three days later, after England and France had declared war on Germany, Frau von Garlitz gathered her children, her staff and her most essential possessions and breathlessly handed the premises over to Anna. 'Put the upper floor in order for the Saarland refugees.' She laid her hands on Anna's shoulders, a gesture symbolizing the transfer of goods and chattels. 'We are going to the east.' She departed for the family estate in East Brandenburg, on her head an asymmetrical cloche hat like a crooked helmet, on either side a child, and in her wake the obedient, giant household.

Anna, in her new role as the housekeeper, opened her book and continued where she was, in calm expectation of the Saarlanders. No fear was aroused in her at being alone on the ship after the rats had deserted—her nervous system was not sensitized to vague threats. During the eighteen days that the Polish campaign lasted her body benefited, uninhibitedly, from the enormous amount of provisions in the cellar, her mind from those in the library. One day, instead of a group of dispossessed refugees, the whole troop was there at the main door again and daily activities were resumed as though they had not been away—except for Herr von Garlitz, who had marched off to Poland as an officer, and at the Tucheler Heide had had the good fortune to dislocate his kneecap; thereafter the expensive godchild was immediately removed from the front line.

The war became a farce. The troops at the Westwall and Maginot Line lay in wait opposite each other in their ambushes like Boy Scouts;

they grew cabbages and potatoes between the fortifications and toasted each other's health with beer mugs raised high. After his recovery, Herr von Garlitz, who was stationed somewhere in the district with his regiment, came home every Sunday with a company of officers who fell upon the supplies of drink in their reckless boredom. Despite rationing, all through the week his wife was busy obtaining the ingredients for a celebration meal. But Anna was only half aware of it. Shortly after the Polish campaign she had received a letter from Holland.

DISTURBED BY THE political developments, Grandmother travelled from Amsterdam to Cologne to find an old bosom friend, in case the borders were about to be closed. She returned, mortified to the depths of her soul, and swore that she would never set foot over the border again. One rainy day in October she came to give an account of her stay. She kept on her black hat—with the frilly bits and pieces and the purple velvet violets, which undoubtedly came from the Albert Cuyp market stall—the whole afternoon. She had caught a streaming cold in Germany, she said, from emotion. Lotte did not move from her side. In the shade of the hat brim Grandmother sighed. 'It was a very unpleasant situation.' Her German accent had deteriorated. Continually interrupting herself to wipe her nose with a lace handkerchief, she related that whenever they spoke about the war her Cologne friend put a tea cosy on the telephone, fearful of being overheard. When a daughter-in-law came to visit with a child in Hitler Youth uniform, the friend nervously changed the subject to an insignificant topic. 'German women adore the Führer,' she explained afterwards. 'I am ashamed.' Grandmother coughed. 'I am ashamed for all those crazy German women.'

Grandmother had also been to her second cousin Franz, 'a sympathetic chap.' She had heard a few things about Anna from him. She looked fleetingly at Lotte's mother as though seeking support. She nodded indulgently. Blood rose to Lotte's head, she did know where to look. 'And . . . ?' she said with a pinched voice. Grandmother applied her handkerchief again, it seemed interminable. Anna had ended up well, according to Franz, with an aristocratic family on the outskirts of Cologne.

Lotte stared at the network of broken veins on the ruddy cheeks and tried to locate the eyes above them, which hid behind the slits of heavily drooping eyelids. Grandmother was somewhat impenetrable, despite her readiness to communicate; one day she would suddenly not be there anymore and would take away with her forever, irretrievably, a wealth of images, sounds, secrets, pieces of information, smells from another period. A sudden anxiety came over Lotte: the old woman was the only umbilical cord that joined her to the formative past. 'Do you have her address?' she asked agitatedly. 'Why?' said her mother. 'Then I can write to her.' The two women exchanged a knowing glance across her, the rain came over the field in waves, lashing against the windows. 'Yes, I have her address,' Grandmother said softly. 'I want to go and find her,' Lotte explained. 'Now?' her mother cried shrilly. 'In this situation?' 'It will have to happen sooner or later, of course,' said Grandmother pensively. 'We can't prevent her.' 'It's war there!' Lotte's mother argued. With both hands Grandmother lifted the hat from her head—to supply herself with air or to acknowledge her powerlessness against the force of attraction between two halves of twins? She placed the hat in her lap and stared wearily and dejectedly at the violets as her fingers mechanically fingered the brim. 'If an old person like me can come back unscathed,' she said, shrugging her shoulders, 'then a healthy young woman will certainly manage it, too.'

Lotte wrote a letter in which courtesy and romantic yearning created a peculiar friction against one another, and ended with the statement of her readiness to come to Germany. In reply she received a formal letter, elegantly signed by Anna Bamberg, with the invitation to spend New Year's Eve at the estate of the von Garlitz family. Up to the last minute Lotte was worried about whether she would get a travel permit. Eventually she was able to travel on the 30th of December. In her coat pocket was the embroidered handkerchief that she had kept in her suitcase all those years, being returned by her to its original owner.

When they crossed the border and the customs officials asked for her papers in German, she said to herself: my country. She tried to see the image of her father before her, but that other father kept pushing himself into the foreground. It suited her better to think of 'the country of my birth' or: the country of composers and conductors, of symphonies and songs—how much easier it would be to sing a song such as 'The shepherd on the rocks' in a country with mountains instead of meadows. That each second was bringing her closer to Anna was almost incomprehensible. She had depicted the reunion in numerous versions in her fantasies, and still it remained a blank. The nearer it came the more her longing was further thwarted by anxiety—an irrational anxiety without any logic. To distract herself she looked outside with exaggerated attention. She bit into one of the apples that her mother had put in the bag. Just for a moment a slight feeling of guilt flared up, or treason, but it changed into pity immediately: from Germany her mother looked insignificant, puny.

At last the train slowed down and pulled into the station. Anxiety won. She wanted to stay inside the intimacy of the compartment forever, but the train stopped and began to unload its passengers, who thronged outside, mesmerized by the journey. The cold hit her in the face; she swayed back, put her suitcase down on the platform and loathed the pressing throng around her, the winter, the strange station, herself in her sudden cowardice. Shivering, she fished the handkerchief out of her winter coat. Instead of waving it, as had been arranged, she held it up awkwardly between thumb and forefinger. The reunion was suddenly so unavoidable that she observed the passing faces without attempting to look for anything familiar in them. Somewhere a conductor blew his whistle. The sound skimmed over the travellers' heads like a bird's shriek. Then behind her she heard her name being spoken softly, hesitantly. It sounded like a quiet sigh from the mouth of the crowd. She turned slowly, a pale face lit up between the winter coats . . . a round and yet pointed face where the contrasts seemed to balance each other. Lotte thrust the handkerchief forwards in a reflex, the other accepted it cautiously. 'Anna?' The woman opposite her closed her eyes in acknowledgement. In the poetic picture in Lotte's head the two sisters fell into each other's arms; on the platform in Cologne they shook hands formally and their smiles made little clouds in the frozen air. Then the woman picked up Lotte's suitcase and began to walk towards the exit, exhorting Lotte to follow her with a nod.

Everything was enormous and overwhelming: the lofty, sooty roof of the station, the immense hall dominated by an advertisement for 4711 in colored glass, the monumental presence of the cathedral, the towers like two guards watching over Cologne, twins, in fact—a double warning from above. Everything was enormous and overwhelming except the reunion, which proceeded with great aloofness and efficiency, as though they were both operating on behalf of someone else and it was not about each of them. At a dry fountain at the foot of the cathedral Anna shifted the suitcase to her other hand to get money out of her pocket for tram tickets. It occurred to Lotte that there was a greater degree of intimacy between the numerals of Route 11, which was taking them through the narrow streets of the inner city, than between Anna and herself. In vain she looked for family features in the pale face. 'So this is Cologne,' she remarked with a stiff laugh, to break the silence. 'Yes, one can indeed say so,' said Anna ironically. She leaned towards Lotte. 'And . . . do you still remember this song?

With a teasing expression on her face she sang softly:

Ding ding ding
comes the tram
with the conductor
and if you don't have fifteen pence
you have to run behind it . . .

Nothing in the children's song, which could have been the key to their mutual recognition, the renewal of the old bond, aroused anything in Lotte—perhaps too many arias and cantatas had slipped in between. Anna looked at her expectantly. Lotte replied to the test of authenticity with an embarrassed shrug of her shoulders. Silently Anna turned away from her and transferred her attention to the dark grey surface of the Rhine. The tram rumbled over the bridge. It seems as though she rather reproaches me, thought Lotte, perhaps she has seen me as a deserter for eighteen years.

'Eighteen years . . .' she now said aloud, 'it's eighteen years ago . . .'

Suddenly the spell seemed to be broken. The tram reached the other side. 'Why did you never write to me . . . at the time?' Lotte asked, like a tentative defence and attack combined. 'Because I heard nothing from you,' Anna snapped. 'That can't be so,' Lotte lashed out, 'I wrote dozens of letters to you and each letter ended with: Anna, why don't you write back?' Anna's composure seemed disturbed just for a moment. But it was no more than a ripple—she shrugged and said flatly: 'Then they intercepted those letters. I never received them.' Lotte looked at her with bewilderment. 'Why would they do a thing like that?' Anna stared outside ostentatiously, as though it did not concern her. 'You don't know them,' she said disinterestedly. Disconcerted by excitement and indignant at Anna's detachment—this was a crucial point—Lotte cried: 'They couldn't do that, just like that?' Impassive, Anna turned her face to her. 'That's how they are.' Irritably she added, 'It's best to get the bad things said straight away . . . You have come here full of expectations but I . . . I'm telling you honestly . . . I really do not know what that is . . . family . . . or special family feeling. I'm sorry, but now that you've suddenly returned like a female Lazarus I don't know what to do with you. Long ago I had already reconciled myself to my fate of being alone on this earth. I belong to no one, no one belongs to me, those are the facts. I have nothing to offer you.'

'But yet we're . . . we have the same parents . . . ,' Lotte repudiated weakly, 'that must count for something surely? In order to know who we are we must surely know . . . how it all began?' 'I know precisely who I am: nobody. That suits me very well!' Bitterness shimmered through her provocative statement making her voice loud and rough. Some passengers looked around. Lotte remained silent, intimidated, she was in a cold sweat. Again she had the feeling that Anna was blaming her. But for what? For still being alive? For wanting to give the term *sister* meaning? Was this her punishment for the long-cherished fantasy of two orphans who would finally plunge into each other's arms, pure and unsullied by time, distance and family matters? Grandmother's description of the small-minded Catholic milieu of primitive farmers was now really taking shape.

Later she would reproach herself for not deciding at that moment to come straight back on the same tram. There was no more doubt that the reunion was a failure and that remaining could only make everything worse. It would still be possible to spend New Year's Eve at home, with mulled wine, lardy cake and music. But a misplaced sort of stubbornness compelled her not to be daunted. In the German fairy tales that she had been over-fed on as a child, many-headed monsters and dragons had to be slain to free the enchanted princess. Perhaps she was refusing to admit failure already at this stage, perhaps she wanted to put off the moment when she would return home without illusions, perhaps she hoped to break through the armour and learn what was hiding beneath it.

The tram stopped; Anna indicated that they had to get off. This was her last chance: I'm sorry, Anna, I believe it would be better if I went back—but she stood up and snatched her suitcase. All of a sudden she could not bear the thought of Anna appropriating it again. They got off, it had become dark and icy cold, the suitcase knocked against her leg with every step. 'All cars have been requisitioned,' Anna explained coolly. 'Now we do everything on foot.' Iron gates opened, a drive lined with dark tree trunks stretched out before them, the moon performed a sinister shadow play with the branches above her head. We are going the same way for the first time, she and I, thought Lotte, and a misplaced sentimental feeling flowed through her. She still had the inclination to embrace her sister, who walked next to her in fierce silence . . . let's stop this charade, for God's sake. But they walked along the endless drive a metre apart from one another, together and yet separate. A white house fluoresced in the dark, with blind, black windows. Wide stairs describing an elegant arc, first curving away from each other and then coming together, led to a baroque entrance.

Preparations for New Year's Eve were under way within the darkened house. Herr von Garlitz was expected home; his wife was trying to estimate how much food and drink his companions would get through. Helped by her status, money and charm, she knew how to get hold of a variety of products that had been unobtainable for ordinary people for a long time. Anna displayed feverish industry from Lotte's arrival to her departure. In between activities she introduced her sister to the countess, the cook, the butler, the governess and the other members of the staff, all exactly as was proper but without any kind of enthusiasm. The two sisters were compared. You could see it in the eyes, pronounced the cook, the same blue, but beyond that the differences were greater than the similarities. Frau von Garlitz complimented Lotte on her German. Eighteen years and still quite without accent! The work was hectic. You could already smell New Year's Eve in the kitchen, its arrival was tangible in the staff's tense activity. Lotte stood at the window of her guest room in pyjamas and looked out through a chink in the blackout at the reflection of the moon in the swimming pool; Anna had said a curt 'gute Nacht' and not exchanged another word with her. The day ended in greater mystery than it had begun. Instead of 'How will Anna be?' it was 'Who is Anna?'

The following day was also about staff busily walking back and forth, involved in dim preparations, until an invasion of officers forced them back to the wings. Lotte fled into the grounds. If at first she had felt only unwelcome, the uniforms and caps, loud voices— some with drawling eastern sounds or an ugly rolled 'r'—made her into a confirmed outsider. Shivering, she walked in the park. German ground. German grass. German trees. . . . Country of her birth? The kitchen garden at home and the neglected fruit trees struck her as a paradise compared with this emphatic wealth per linear metre of lawn, per square metre of swimming pool, per cubic metre of German air. The rest of the day she wasted in the staff sitting-room, leafing through the *Illustrierte Beobachter*, already contemplating the return journey and the way she would disguise her disillusionment at home. The evening meal in the kitchen was bolted hurriedly, Anna appeared at table in a black dress with a white, starched collar and a cap on her head. 'Here you see what a chambermaid's life is like,' she said, again managing to make it sound like an accusation. 'Can I help anywhere?' Lotte stammered. 'Why not?' said Anna sarcastically. 'I have another uniform like this, that will be a splendid metamorphosis.'

Lotte let the waitress's dress slide over her shoulders—a desperate attempt to creep into Anna's skin, or at any rate to be twins on the outside for once. She entered the dining room with a soup tureen in

her hands, her gaze straight ahead on the bow of Anna's apron ribbons, which were tied with mathematical precision. The officers, who
had exchanged their uniforms for dinner jackets, were seated on
either side of a long table decorated with evergreen sprigs. The reflection of candles in branching candlelabrum glittered in the table silver
and in the dark red sequins on the countess's low-cut dress. She sat at
the head of the table, twinkling; her husband sat opposite her in his
dual role as host and officer. Anna and Lotte were unnoticed as they
put the dishes down—as though they were transparent. Anna's
phrase 'I am nobody' acquired an additional dimension. They went
back noiselessly, serving was the waiters' job.

That is how the festive evening slipped through their fingers in dull
servility. Dirty plates, glasses, spoons, empty dishes. The guests
became increasingly boisterous; it was hard to keep up with the pace
at which wine and Sekt had to be fetched. One of them, a well-fed
officer with a shining red face, performed an improvised sword dance
with one of the weapons taken off the wall around his half-empty
glass which had been displaced onto the parquet floor. Anna's arrival
with a strawberry bavarois disturbed the acrobat's concentration—
losing his unsteady equilibrium he thudded backwards onto the solitary piece of family crystal. With bloodshot eyes he crawled upright,
the fragments sticking out of his backside like crows' feet. Enthusiastic applause rang out. One guest roared, 'The first victim has fallen at
the Westwall!'

At that moment Lotte, also carrying a dish of bavarois in her
hands, became convinced of her sister's fearlessness. Anna set the dish
of gently wobbling pudding on the table, bent over the affected area
and picked out the pieces of glass with a neutral expression, as
though she were gleaning corn. Then she supported the wounded one
towards the bandage cupboard. Just before leaving the room, he laid
his hand on her bottom, to indicate that his spirit was unbroken—
Anna coolly pushed the hand away.

Around midnight the staff crowded together in the communal sitting room and at twelve they hugged each other with foaming glasses
in hand. The sisters kissed each other like ice queens. Something
external immediately provided them with a magnificent excuse to dis-

tance themselves again: a rifle shot, and then another, made everyone rush over to the windows. 'Lights out,' someone roared. They rolled up the blackout curtains and pressed their noses to the glass. 'Dear heaven,' groaned the cook, 'they've gone mad!' Some officers, laughing and hawking, were aiming at a white bath towel hung over a low branch. They shot again, the material moved a little and fell back, slack. The cook went to the door. 'It's a scandal,' she cried angrily. 'I'm going to do something about it!' The governess stopped her. 'Calm down, Frau Lenzmeyer, it's not up to you to call senior officers to order.' The cook knocked back a few glasses of Sekt in frustration. The shooting continued; Lotte slipped away to her room unseen, where she let herself drop onto the guest bed.

The shots in the night and the image of the riddled towel brought to mind the disquieting stories of Theo de Zwaan and Ernst Goudriaan on their return from Germany—stories that had only increased her longing. It was only now that they took on meaning. She felt the threat that emanated from each shot, fired out of boredom and the lack of a more suitable target. Up to now *enemy* had been an empty word—here it was acquiring significance. A significance that replenished itself with Anna's cold New Year's kiss, with a gloomy walk in the grounds, with the failure to retrieve a feeling for anything as vague as "country of birth." The shooting stopped, a song started up instead. In utter loathing she screwed her eyes shut. She took the cap off her head, untied the apron and looked at herself in the mirror. The black dress exactly suited the funeral of her illusions.

She had already put her suitcase in the hall when she went into the kitchen for breakfast. It looked as though they had worked the whole night through—not a dirty glass or scrap of pudding recalled the previous evening. Everything was focused on a hearty breakfast, on no account could the guests return to the Westwall on half-empty stomachs. Anna hurried to and fro, composed, without a trace of weariness, her blonde hair correctly waved around her cap. Lotte approached her about the tram departure times. She would inquire, she called over her shoulder, disappearing down the passage with a silver dish full of rolls. Ignoring Lotte's objections, Frau von Garlitz decided that one of the officers would take her to the station.

The guests automatically allowed Anna to help them into their heavy coats, embroiled in their conversations right up to leaving. Lotte stood by stiffly, holding her suitcase. The acrobat grumbled noisily to his neighbour about the tenants on his property in Brandenburg. 'They are so stupid, so dirty, indolent—actually they're not people, but somewhere between human and animal . . .' Anna froze, his coat in her hands. 'It is easy for you to talk,' she said sullenly. 'I'd like to see you if you had to drudge like a farmer.' All heads turned towards her, the countess looked on open-mouthed. In pure astonishment at such impudence, the officer permitted her to help him into his coat as willingly as a baby. His face went the same colour as the previous evening after his fall. It was probably the recollection of her efficient management of him that restrained him from demanding her immediate dismissal. At that moment the signal for departure sounded on the other side of the vestibule. Lotte grasped her suitcase. Anna came up to her to shake hands. She smiled again for the first time since Lotte's arrival—perhaps less from friendliness than out of satisfaction at the way she had cut an arrogant landowner down to size. 'We'll write sometime . . .' she said, looking over her shoulder—Frau von Garlitz was calling. The last thing Lotte heard was her cultured, enraged voice, 'Who do you think you are, offending our guests! If I ever see anything like that again . . .' A short, stocky officer seized Lotte's suitcase and hurriedly pushed her outside. She climbed into a military car. She let herself be driven away without turning around, down the drive, into a suburb swathed in profound quiet. Anna kept reappearing with raised chin, a coat in her hands, and each time she heard her angry retort, which had to be a justification for her own past. The designation 'barbarians' resonated in a remote corner of Lotte's mind. Curiosity overcame her: Anna's unflinching honesty had admirable aspects. But it was too late, they were crossing the Rhine—inaccessibility through distance would be less chafing than inaccessibility in proximity. She stared at the cathedral. The two towers soared upwards—already centuries ago they must have found a method for remaining joyful beside each other at their point of origin.

Throughout the journey the officers kept silent in the presence of the parcel from Holland that had to be delivered to the station.

2

IN A GUST of cold air a boy came in, followed by his father who had bought one of the helmets at the market. He put it on his son's head, grinning, after he had ordered two Cokes. Even from the table where Lotte and Anna were sitting it was evident that the father-son romance was revived by the purchase of the helmet. As long as the glow lasted they were participants in the same adventure, a war that neither of them had experienced. If there had been a feather headdress in the market, then the battle of Winnetou against the whites would as easily have had this effect.

'American Coke and a German helmet . . .' Anna shook her head, 'I'm getting old.'

Lotte's thoughts had not disengaged from that unfortunate New Year's Eve. 'I'll never forget it,' she murmured, 'all those drunken officers, shooting. I had the feeling I was among fanatic Hitler supporters.'

'Are you mad?' Anna sat up straight; something needed putting right. 'The von Garlitz family, they were old nobility, they were industrialists! Of course they had helped that buffoon into the saddle, in return he polished off the communists and got them their Greater German Reich. But you don't really think they thought much of the son of a customs official? They were able to use him well, for a while; only when it was their turn to die on the battlefield did they realize that that parvenu had used them too.'

She burst out laughing.

'What is there to laugh about?' said Lotte edgily.

'I can still see myself running through that house in cap and apron.

What a misery. All the time I was trying frenetically to forget that the visit was for me—think about it; for the first time in my life I was being visited. You have no idea what difficulty it caused me. Those officers were a lovely alibi. How I worked!'

Lotte was silently building a pyramid of sugar lumps. 'It has stayed with me like a decadent image,' she murmured, 'those officers in the night . . . an enemy you can expect anything from if he is capable of shooting at towels.'

'They were dancing on top of a volcano,' Anna interrupted her, 'why do you think they drank so much?'

ANNA PACED ABOUT in her bedroom. Her body hurt with every step, as though someone had given her a beating. She struck her palm with her fist. The recurring silence was unbearable. It was a silence with a double foundation, left behind by someone who had now gone away for good. Not because others had arranged it so, but through her own guilt. She was besieged by images she had seen fleetingly in between work duties: her sister's figure—in the grounds with coat flapping about, alone at the long kitchen table by an empty plate after the meal, seen from behind as she went upstairs despondently. Piece by piece, silent indictments. Rewinding and playing the film again—differently. Too late, too late, too late. Why, that was what she wanted to know. The answer would not be found in the best-equipped library but was hidden within herself. The only thing she knew was that, from the moment Lotte had turned to her on the platform, she had come face to face with her father. His long curved nose, his narrow face and dark wavy hair, his melancholy, stubborn gaze. There was something improper—as though Lotte had stolen him or engaged in unfair competition. In Lotte she did not encounter the thickly swathed six-year-old sister who had been abducted by a woman in a veil. Now there was someone else who could exert rights over her father, someone who was perhaps more entitled than herself because she looked so staggeringly like him. So this was Lotte. Why now?

Restless and self-reproaching, she wrestled on that double trail all through the winter that pushed drifts of snow against the house and deposited a crow at the top of the steps, frozen to death, so that Hannelore, one of the maids, on finding it in the morning, said it was a bad omen after which the washerwoman warned her that superstition brought bad luck, and Anna, forgetting everything for a while, had to laugh at this rare recursive form of superstition. The past revisited Anna for the second time without her intention. Hannelore, eighteen years old, recently extracted from Lower Saxony by the countess, had been placed under Anna's care since her arrival. The girl boldly announced that she was going dancing at the casino on Sunday afternoon. 'You can't permit her to go,' said Frau von Garlitz, 'unless you go, too.'

The casino seemed to be flirting with the new socialism. The walls no longer shut her out, the doors with the copper handles stood wide open. She wore a Marian blue dress; red silk shimmered through the skirt, her employer's perfume still wafted out from the material. Anna handed the tickets in with a chaperone's characteristic lack of enthusiasm. Thus she gained entrance to her own hall. The field of marble, the leapfrog square, the hide-and-seek pillars, the high dome where the songs collected . . . the marble staircase where she had fallen over . . . everything was still there. Somewhere she must, they must still be there . . . behind the pillars, in the passages . . . clouds of condensed breath rose up into the dome. Hannelore disappeared in the foyer. There were the sofas—Anna's trampolines. She heard a deep, rushing silence through the hum of voices, through the dance music, through the clapping and tapping of heels on the dance floor inside. Hannelore had saved places, wine was ordered, and Hannelore vanished. Anna caught a glimpse of her now and then, waltzing around in the arms of a soldier whose shaved, thick-set neck kept coming back into view. The Westwall seemed to have been emptied; the cat-and-mouse war had transferred to the casino foyer on this Sunday afternoon in April.

She drank her wine without tasting it and looked ahead of her fixedly—all of a sudden somebody placed himself between her and her memories. 'May I have the pleasure?' She stood up dejectedly and allowed herself to be led to the dance floor. '*Was machst du mit dem Knie, lieber Hans*' seemed like something from a former life. The soldier carried himself impeccably. She stared at the silver V on his sleeve with a vacant gaze. After the dance ended he returned her to her seat. Just as she was going to sit down a new number started up; he nodded briefly and invited her again. The images slowly ebbed away during the second dance, which was more compelling than the previous one. She now perceived this soldier clearly. His face seemed remarkably trustworthy to her—it was more the face of a person than a soldier, she reasoned without interest.

She moved her gaze away and discovered a large framed photograph of the Norwegian fjords on the wall. Were conquests already being flaunted? 'They are suitably topical with their wall decorations here,' she said gruffly. 'It might also have been the bridges over the Moldau,' he added. His accent surprised her. 'You are an Ostmarker . . .' 'Austrian,' he corrected her with a courteous nod. 'But they are all soldiers out of operettas with red roses in their rifles instead of bullets.' His face set. 'Not much to laugh or sing about in Czechoslovakia.' 'Being a soldier is not your vocation, so it sounds.' 'I was called up,' he smiled, 'I'd a thousand times rather be at home in Vienna . . . with roses in my rifle.' He spoke so melodiously that it seemed as though everything he said was in jest. Holding her more tightly, he began to describe passionate circles over the dance floor. When the number was over he brought her back ceremoniously—a pattern that kept repeating itself, as soon as the orchestra started on a new number he raced across the parquet floor again and stood before her. At about half past eleven he excused himself. He had to be back in the barracks by twelve. 'May I see you again?' he asked. 'Excuse me, I haven't introduced myself: Martin Grosalie.' 'You can telephone me,' she said flatly, 'number fifty two thousand.' 'Are you serious?' He looked uncertainly at her. 'Why?' 'It is such an improbable number.' 'You don't really think I'm imagining it,' she said, annoyed. Blushing, he leant forward to kiss her hand. '*Ich küsse Ihre Hand, Madame*,' said Anna ironically, pulling her hand away from beneath his lips.

The soldier was not deterred. He telephoned two days later. No argument instantly occurred to her for refusing the request for a meeting. They met in a café on the Alter Markt; it rained incessantly. A feeling of alienation, shame, overcame her as they sat opposite one another without the dance's option of escaping. But with the bravura of a schoolboy he took upon himself full responsibility for the meeting. He described Vienna to her, Schönbrunn, the Nashmarkt, the Prater, the house where Schubert was born, the house where Mozart lived, the house where Haydn died. The survey reviewed all the sights, he recreated his city and strolled through it with her, pointing everything out on the way, lively, enthusiastic—not in order to win her over but to put something else at a distance, something that was increasingly present in the background and was biding its time. Anna, too, who thought she had nothing to do with it, felt it was there. Yet it still broke through unexpectedly. 'And now we're here,' he sighed, 'opposite the French, with all that equipment, and they are opposite us. Why? I hope that the joke is over soon, then we can all go home again.'

Other meetings followed: he collected her from the house, every-one called him a nice, polite boy, which needled her. She harassed the nice polite boy with teasing, which he openly enjoyed—she poked fun at his accent, his courtesy, at Austria. One evening there was a danc-ing party at the Stadthalle. When it was drawing to a close Anna dragged him towards the exit. 'Come, it's over.' 'No, no, they're play-ing a couple more numbers,' he implored her. 'Shall we have a bet? If I win I can say '*du*' instead of '*Sie*'. He won. They sauntered silently through the deserted avenues in the suburb, the moon curved behind the clouds, there was a sweet smell of young foliage. I can't start say-ing *du* just like that yet, thought Anna. At the bottom step in front of the house he kissed her, abruptly, as though he were settling a score with a voice that had forbidden him to do so all the way there. 'You're crying.' Anna was shocked. 'Not *Sie, du,*' he corrected her hoarsely. Under these circumstances she did not dare to take her leave; she could not abandon a weeping soldier at the foot of the steps. Although she would have preferred to run inside to think about it behind a locked door, she pulled him into the grounds towards a stone bench surrounded on three sides by a shining, clipped yew hedge that seemed to be pointed out by the moonlight. They sat down. Fragments of films and books shot though her head, in which the characters turned out all right in the next phase; embraces, official declarations ... but a weeping admirer was not included among those. Although she regarded crying as a sign of weakness in herself,

it occurred to her that on the contrary, for a man it demanded
courage. The last time she had cried—an eternity ago—it was in rage,
humiliation and pain. In the soldier's case it had to be something else;
she did not dare to venture further. He pressed her hand and looked
serenely ahead towards the sleeping house. Something in her that had
been waiting all that time fluttered away; an agreeable lethargy overcame her. 'I'm so sleepy all of a sudden,' she yawned. 'Lie down,' he
whispered, 'put your head in my lap.' Without hesitating she
stretched out, dozed off, stupefied by his soldier's aura.

During her sleep the sickle of the moon moved to another place in
the sky. She woke relaxed, in a condition of complete submission
such as she had not known since her childhood. Unnoticed, she
observed him. Sitting there, motionless, he reminded her of her
grandfather's dying soldier who lifted his face to a descending angel.
It looked as though he were communicating wordlessly in an intimate
way with something that was invisible to her. He swallowed. His
Adam's apple rose and fell, which gave him back his earthliness.
Ashamed of her clandestine observation she said his name. He bent
over her. 'I had never thought . . .' he laid a finger on her lips, 'that
anything so beautiful could exist as when a girl falls asleep on your
lap.' 'Didn't I say so,' she remained sober, 'you are a Rosenkavalier.'

In the following days her thoughts went on circling round the soldier like a cloud of summer flies. How could he be simultaneously
trustworthy and mysterious?—paradox held her in pleasant confusion. There did not seem to be a way back; they arranged to go to the
Drachenfels at Whitsun. A picnic basket was packed. But that epony-
mous dragon did not wait for their arrival. It had been woken from a
sleep that had lasted about two decades, it stretched, yawned, looked
in the mirror to see if its eyes were in place and its scales were shining,
sharpened its claws on the rock face, opened its mouth wide to check
the fire and sulphurous fumes mechanism and descended from the
mountain, thrashing about with puffed-out chest and sweeping tail,
in a westerly direction.

The telephone rang on the ninth of May. 'For you,' said Hannelore. Anna picked it up. The soldier was out of breath on the other
end of the line. 'All leave has been cancelled.' Alarm, quick march.

He had climbed over the barracks wall to telephone her. He had to go back immediately. If they found him he would be shot dead, without mercy. She was still standing there with the receiver in her hand long after he had put the phone down. There it was again, no longer in the background. It cast its entire shadow over her, settling itself in her diaphragm, tears slid down her cheeks entirely of their own accord. '*Ja ja,*' said Frau von Garlitz, 'that's war, eh?' The laconic observation made Anna furious. Tears that had been conserved for years now flowed out. She had read enough to know that crying for a soldier who was departing for the front joined her to the company of millions of women throughout the ages. It had been written and sung about over and over again, but even so her grief was the only one, the worst one of all. Again she was powerless against the things that were happening; this time it was a powerlessness for two.

His first Feldpost letter came from Bad Godesberg. 'I am here in a gymnasium, I have a candle, pencil and paper, and I am writing to you because I care about you. Please let me hear something.' So began a correspondence that would last for years. It would survive the campaigns in Belgium, France, Russia, up to the last letter, which was not written by him. Their love really developed on paper, with all the self-denial that was associated with it: All's well with me . . .

'The French are coming!' Frau von Garlitz fled to the east with her retinue again. Anna and Hannelore were left behind to take care of the house. The door of the air-raid shelter, which had foresightedly been built in 1934, would not close anymore. The swimming pool had been plentifully filled with water for extinguishing fires as required by ordinance. Everything was well organized.

THEY WERE DRIFTING like the sole survivors of a shipwreck in an ocean of coffee, tea, wine, Ratafia de Pommes—bad for the arthritis, good for the soul. A warm Gulf Stream repeatedly brought them in sight of new, unfamiliar coasts but they didn't land anywhere. It was still Sunday. They ordered lunch. Instead of exploring the environs of Spa on painful feet they preferred to go down the paths and avenues of the past, even though the risk of land mines was gradually increasing.

* * *

YEARS LATER LOTTE'S children were taught that the war began on the tenth of May 1940. But for the Germans it had already begun earlier, in September, or before that—a matter of perspective—in 1933, when the frustrated Sunday painter came to power. On that tenth of May the family did not leave the radio for a moment. Lotte looked outside through the tall windows. The unreal events that the broadcaster reported in a neutral voice were counteracted by the cloudless sky. Parachutists? Bombing raids on airfields? German troops crossing the border, as German housemaids had done all those years ago?

But the German army made swift progress. Rumours and facts jostled each other: the German parachutists were disguised as postmen and country policemen, the country was teeming with spies, the royal family had fled, Rotterdam was in flames. The Germans were threatening to bomb other towns as well. Dutch soldiers defended themselves with the courage of despair. The Netherlands was small, but not small enough to be able to hide itself—from a bomber you could see it in its entirely.

The capitulation was frustrating but it also removed anxiety. Threatened towns were spared, the occupier knew how to behave: no plundering, rape or slaughter as had been described in the books. Nevertheless, from then on marching columns constituted part of the street scene and the echoes of stamping boots and battle songs could be heard there. On the way to her singing teacher, Lotte chanced upon a group of Germans walking abreast, blocking the cycle path. Ringing her bell emphatically but in vain, she turned onto the road in order to pass. One of the soldiers ran after her, insulted that she had dared to ring a warning, and tried to grab her luggage rack. She stood up on the pedals to go faster, the blood *whooshed* in her ears, his swearing pursued her. She could hear the roaring and shooting in the night again. The soldier expanded, he swelled up behind her into something of monstrous dimensions that wanted to overtake her, pull her back, punish her. But she gradually gained ground. She did not dare look around until she was three roads farther on and it had become quite quiet behind her.

Music was a good chaser-out of devils. For some time the choir's accompanist for radio broadcasts had been a well-reputed student from the conservatory, David de Vries. Lotte asked him to accompany her study of Mahler's *Kindertotenlieder* at home, so she could concentrate fully on the singing part, which was hard enough. Thus together twice a week they submitted to the magic spell of pain transformed into beauty: I often think they have only gone out/and will soon be coming home again./It is a beautiful day—do not worry,/they have gone for a long walk./Yes, they have only gone out and will presently be home again.

The songs suffused her with an indefinable homesickness—her voice, unhampered by shortness of breath, no longer came from her chest but from her whole body. She became a single accumulation of music, of diffuse longing; in between she saw the profile of her accompanist, in heart-rending abandonment as though he were effortlessly identifying with the grieving father. When they stopped, the feeling continued to float, it was difficult to part, they turned around to one another with the music still in their ears, full of reluctance to break the spell and dissolve into ordinary life separate from one another. He lingered increasingly before putting the music in his case—at such moments he was easy prey for Lotte's father, who permitted him to hear his newest acquisitions.

He was also a diligent sailor, so as not to turn into an anaemic and languid musician like Chopin. On a fine day in summer he hired a boat and invited her out for a trip on the Loosdrecht Lakes. He praised her father as he initiated her into sailing: so sympathetic, and what an impressive apparatus he had built! It would be blasphemy to say anything against him. Blasphemous of the fine day, of the water lapping against the boat in syncopation, of the wind that gave her goose bumps that were smoothed out again by the sun, blasphemous of the sight of his sun-tanned body and long fingers, which were not now dancing over the keys but were involved in an active game with ropes, boom and rudder.

The compliment seemed to be a way in for him to complain about his own father. Originally a cantor in a synagogue, he had been unable to resist the attractions of popular song. He enjoyed a reputation among a large public, in The Netherlands as well as Germany: gramophone records of his were in circulation. Fame brought him pleasures and sorrows. Young women crowded outside his hotel room, he waited in a shiny dressing gown, champagne in an ice bucket, until the very loveliest of them forced her way in to him. He bought his way out of his guilt about his sick wife with gaudy jewellery, but his sentimental songs remained innocent and cheerful in tone. After his performances the audiences went home emboldened—they were prepared for life again. David, who accompanied his father on tour, sat in an adjoining compartment in the train the next morning: He could not bear his father's presence. He closed his eyes in disgust and mentally escaped to Palestine, musing about studying medicine there after the conservatory—you would get more out of being a pioneer there. The trip always ended with his father's remorse. Moved to tears by his only son's rejection, he begged him for understanding and affection in exchange for laying the whole world at his feet. 'You'll get a sailboat from me, boy,' he implored him, 'but let's wait until the war is over.'

Lotte, who was letting the water flow over her feet, did not yet know that the imaginary sailboat mentioned here for the first time would become the symbol of something that would cast a shadow over the rest of her life. Something, too, that would not be compatible with a cloudless sky, billowing white sails, and a joint dive into the lake—where they stealthily touched each other for the first time; the water was a good alibi.

The early days of the war shambled along on the level of concern about groceries. More and more necessities were rationed; Lotte's mother encountered few problems with it at first—because of their living out of the way she always kept large supplies in the house. She got chests of tea from China from a former colonial who lived on one of the country estates, milk was fetched warm and foaming from the farmer, she baked bread herself. She did not condone hoarding, but only stocked up on green soap. To comply with the blackout no extra measures had to be taken, drawing the horsehair curtains completely closed was sufficient. Theo de Zwaan was released from captivity in June. He had noticed no warlike activities, he had been stationed in Limburg at a place where nothing happened. 'He hid himself in a haystack of course,' said his mother-in-law, 'and waited quietly until the smoke of battle lifted.'

3

THE HEAVY LUNCH had driven them out into the fresh air. Shivering, Lotte sheltered behind her collar: it seemed that the east wind had become even more vicious. Anna, who commanded a robust layer of natural protection and was anyway less inclined to allow herself to be influenced by weather conditions, walked cheerfully into the Parc de Sept Heures. It was deserted now that the flea market had packed up. A clump of man-sized yellowed bamboo was rustling in the wind. Anna wondered whether the bamboo would recover in the spring; Lotte thought it certainly would and added the intelligence that once in a hundred years bamboo bushes all over the world flowered at the same time. This struck Anna as a myth, although she granted that there were plants that bloomed for just one night, though no one had witnessed it.

Suddenly they were standing in front of a small natural stone monument that leaned against a steep rock, seeming to close Spa off on the north side like a wall against the rest of the world. The monument had been erected to the designers of the footpaths around Spa. They were listed: from the Comte de Lynden-Aspremont in 1718 up to Joseph Servais in 1846. At the bottom there was a basin filled with frozen water; two copper frogs crouched on the edge with their heads thrown back; in summer, water probably spewed out of their open mouths. Anna had the bizarre sensation that they themselves were the two frogs, shut out by the ice and holding themselves in equilibrium on the edge, in expectation of the thaw.

They turned right in unison, walked along Avenue Reine Astrid and a little later found themselves in front of an iron gate that was the entrance to a building housing the Musée de la Ville d'Eau. They nodded to each other and went inside. An old woman, huddled behind a table with picture postcards, sold entrance tickets. Her face, round and red, like a shrivelled star fruit, was marked by an intricate network of wrinkles that got in each other's way. But somewhere between the creases her eyes shone as she handed them their tickets with a gnarled hand. Anna asked for a guidebook—something faltered in the mechanism; the head began to nod fiercely and a pale mimeographed sheet of paper appeared.

'Scandalous,' Anna whispered, 'a woman of a hundred still put to work.'

Suddenly they felt very young. With a certain bravura they went into the first room. The illuminated glass cases contained a large collection of 'Jolitées,' objects that had been used by the visitors over the centuries: snuff and tobacco pouches, water bottles, walking sticks with the head of Napoleon or a wild animal, watch cases, quadrille boxes, delicate pieces of furniture—all painted and carved out of the celebrated wood proudly called 'Bois de Spa'—as though it were a kind of marble. The arcadian images of elegant strollers with or without wig and crinoline on the routes laid out by Lynden-Aspremont and Servais elicited cries of wonder from Lotte. Anna felt annoyed at the frivolous baubles and saw the exploitation of underpaid crafts people in the painted miniatures. She held the mimeographed page up, a long way from her eyes, and began to read out loud with a shaky accent.

'Long before Spa became Spa, Pliny the Roman had already praised the curative action of the waters that bubbled up in that area. Henry VIII's physician had ordered his patient to drink the water from these springs. Spa became known throughout Europe and the water, in flat bottles packed in plaited willow baskets, found its way along all points of the compass. In 1717 Tsar Peter the Great honoured the town with a visit. The European aristocracy followed his example, surrounded by adventurers and hangers-on—statesmen, famous scientists, artists and ladies of royal blood strolled from foun-

tain to fountain, a stick in one hand and a bottle in the other, and
drank eagerly of the miraculous water that even enjoyed a reputation
for curing the pangs of love. They were called 'Bobelins' by the
inhabitants of the town. There was one firm rule of behaviour that
the Bobelins had to stick to: All serious matters were absolutely prohibited. Quiet, harmony and relaxation were ingredients of the cure.
Famous names followed: Descartes, Christina of Sweden, Bollandius,
the Margrave of Brandenburg, the Count of Orléans, Pauline Bonaparte. . . .' Anna fanned herself with a hand. '*Pfff*—yes of course,
only the rich people could afford such a cure, they had all the time in
the world while the staff worked themselves into the ground. It was a
miracle that they managed to become ill on top of that; from their
earliest youth they had eaten well, played sports, had not had to lug
muck carts. . . .

Deaf to Anna's ranting, Lotte leaned over a trinket case displaying
a picture of two corseted ladies wearing wide plumed hats and drinking glasses of water. 'Look at this,' she pulled on Anna's sleeve, 'what
an elegant fashion that was, a really feminine silhouette, they were
women with style.'

'Of course they had style.' Anna retorted, 'they were brought up
like that. I worked for them for years, I know exactly what they're
like. It is all a façade—they were not a whisker better than us, these
people who were nobility on the outside. I feel I am on a decidedly
higher level than that so-called elite.'

Lotte pulled her along from one display case to the next. She
refused to allow her pleasure to be spoilt by carping at the aristocracy. She simply wanted to enjoy the curious paraphernalia with
which that class had surrounded itself—life in that period seemed so
much more intense and richly coloured than life now. All at once they
were in the hall again, the old woman had fallen asleep or, perhaps,
even died. They left the museum—the wind pursued them two blocks
farther into the, by now, trustworthy *patisserie*, where they once
again took seats beneath the hideous wrought-iron lamp fitting and
ordered *merveilleux*, this time with coconut.

*   *   *

AFTER THE FRENCH campaign the family returned from the east; the
Führer had done it again! The Sekt flowed in torrents, the flush of victory lasted until the first English bombing raids over Cologne. Anna
made attempts to learn to swim—she floated on her back in the water
for extinguishing fires and looked at the blue sky through her eyelashes. Weightlessness—to be there and not there—to forget for a
while that Martin was in Poland with his division. After their first
meetings, which subsequently seemed to have taken place in a dream
rather than in reality, he began to be an ordinary person in the Feldpost letters, in his choice of words, his observations: a tree in Odrzy-
wót that was a thousand years old, a richly gilded baroque church in
a village where there were more pigs than people, a weathered old
man who lisped three words of German in which he bragged because
his forefathers had been with Garibaldi on the barricades, a locality
with hundreds of lakes that reflected the sky, so that you ended up
not knowing what was above and what was below. Warlike matters
were not mentioned at all though marriage was—a proposal full of
Viennese flourish and elegance. From the moment he had seen her on
the other side of the dance floor, in her blue dress, lacking any form of
coquetry, even sending out a mildly aggressive 'don't come too near
me,' he had known it. On his next leave he wanted to ask her father
for her hand. But he is dead, she retorted. Her guardian then? She
had declared him dead. He had to ask someone for her hand surely?
She found his obstinacy on this point old-fashioned but endearing
and suggested that Uncle Franz should take that role upon himself.
The idea of a marriage was so extravagant that she burst out laughing from time to time. I'm going to get married, she said to herself. It
sounded as though it concerned somebody else—something like marriage could not possibly have anything to do with her. But at the same
time the seriousness of it did permeate her, as expressed in the stereo-
types: one body, one soul—'til death us do part . . . Never to be alone
again—her fate would be coupled to his forever in the practical and
metaphysical sense. She would no longer be 'the chambermaid of' but
'the wife of' . . . Yet stronger than all these considerations was a feeling of tranquility—events overtook her in any case.

One afternoon in the autumn Martin got off the train safe and sound. The smoke from the locomotive hung under the roof; coughing, she allowed herself to be embraced. Then he held her away with outstretched arms to look at her. She was shocked. During his absence he had become transparent in the physical sense. On paper he was as familiar to her as someone whom she had known since her youth, someone to whom no detail was too irrelevant. Now everything switched around at high speed. The old friend from the letters evaporated; in his stead was a soldier with a tanned face and shining eyes. To conceal her shyness she forced a way to the exit for him through the throng.

The cook, housemaids, governess, washerwoman, he won them all over again with his courtesy, the flawlessness of his appearance and a rare combination of natural authority and boyishness. After the news of the imminent engagement they treated Anna with a new respect. Frau von Garlitz arranged two rooms for them in a small hotel in the Eifel; they deserved some undisturbed time together after all those months of separation and uncertainty, she thought.

Through a landscape that the autumn had set on fire, the train puffed southwards, with interruptions. A cousin of the hotel owner, who was himself at the front, fetched them from the station in a rickety jalopy that, preserved as a museum piece for years, was standing in for the requisitioned car. Wheels rattling on the road, forest air and an unfamiliar destination. At any moment Anna expected to see a convent appearing on the crest of a hill next to the von Zitsewitz castle at a bend in the road. One glance at Martin's profile brought her back to 1940—times had moved on, don't look back. Under his care she would be able to go on anywhere. Although up to now in spirit she had withdrawn as much as possible from reality as it presented itself to her, and in compensation had been in league with the world of literary imagination, now, as each bump in the unmade road threw her against Martin, she felt reconciled to everyday reality—she even loved the bumps in the road that were throwing her against him.

There was an atmosphere of charming, dilapidated chic at the hotel. The only guests, they dined in the faded dining room in the company of an invisible elite who ate in a whisper at the tables scattered between dusty palms. Via the radio the owner's wife was in permanent contact with the nocturnal threat that was flying over the sea towards Germany. Instead of calm music from a string band, during the evening the meal was repeatedly graced by the familiar tick-tock, followed by a report of approaching danger. Determined not to let this one evening that was meant for them be disturbed by any calamities, they let the woman show them to their rooms, which were pointedly at the opposite ends of a long passage, as though an extremely sensitive pair of scales had to be kept in balance.

But a little later on there was a knock at her door and he surprised her with a bottle of Sekt. On the edge of the bed, they drank it all at a frivolous pace. The war disappeared from their consciousness— they were seized by a sense of freedom, separated from the external world, separated from time, in a room that belonged to someone else, among objects that had been seen by thousands of others. They touched each other, raised up out of themselves by the tingling Sekt and a dizzying lightness. He began to undress her with trembling fingers, draping her clothes carefully over a chair. They crept into the bed shivering and pulled the sheets over them. 'I have not been with a woman before,' he confided in her ear. His erect member seemed to want to bring something to her memory, a warning, a reflex that had nothing to do with the here and now. Veiled by the vague recollection of a recollection, she lay still while he explored her body with his lips. He could do what he wanted with it, it was worth little—others had always decided its fate.

'The sky, Martin, look, the sky!' Anna raised her head from his chest. They got out of bed and went to the window. In the north behind the hills a red glow fanned out in all directions. Dull roars sounded, like an approaching thunderstorm or drumroll. Anna felt a great disgust at the disturber of the peace on the horizon and at the unrelenting employer who could reclaim Martin at any moment. 'It's on fire in any case,' she said, 'come.' She closed the curtains with a brusque gesture and pulled him back to the bed with her; over the headboard hung a Lorelei swathed in clouds, brushing her blond hair on the fateful rock.

* * *

A METRE-HIGH MOUNTAIN of debris blocked the tram rails; the passengers got out and continued on their way, clambering over twisting
paths that had come into being in a few days. The route passed
between burnt-out blocks whose scorched façades were still standing
half upright. Anna thought of a line of verse by Schiller: 'Horror
dwells in the bleak window caverns . . .' In an intact window-frame
curtains flapped; farther on, like a doll's house, the blasted-away
front façade gave full view of completely furnished floors; the residents had not returned to rehang the chandelier that had taken wing.
They got lost in the disrupted layout of streets; a man with a sweating
face clearing rubble told them the way. Peculiarity was the norm; life
had resumed its course—the ordinary noises of the city prevailed
instead of the reverberations of explosions and collapsing buildings,
of crackling sheets of fire, of frightened screams and wailing. People
clambered with their shopping bags over the rubble beneath which,
perhaps, fellow citizens still lay.

Aunt Vicki seemed to have lost some of her talkativeness because
of the terror; Uncle Franz was quiet and controlled as always—if the
hospital also caught fire he would have to remain quiet and controlled. During the evening meal he tossed Anna an approving look:
Bravo *Mädchen*, you've brought an excellent chap with you. Aunt
Vicki was beaming, too: Martin was so polite and attentive—a man
who knew instinctively what was due a woman. Uncle Franz played
operetta songs in honour of the Austrian, until the siren sounded
right in the middle of '*Mein Liebeslied soll ein Walzer sein.*' Prepro-
grammed, Aunt Vicki went to the child's room, lifted her, sleeping,
out of bed and hurried with her to the shelter. They followed her
mechanically. The tumult of hasty footsteps and voices was everywhere. They settled on an empty spot in a corner. Anna looked up
anxiously at the gas pipes and sewers and imagined how they would
all go under in a porridge of sewage if one of the pipes burst. The
prospect was so disgusting that she prayed silently that if the pipes
did have to burst it should be the gas. This alternative calmed her.
Every time the thought of the sewer pipe threatened to gain the upper
hand she performed the praying ritual hoping for the gas. But for the

time being nothing happened. Aunt Vicki's child slept on—it was unthinkable that anyone would want to kill an angel with blond hair and gently fluttering eyelids. Perhaps she was a talisman that made everyone in the immediate vicinity unassailable. Anna herself felt sleepy at the sight. She leaned against Martin and slowly dozed off. She continued to sleep peacefully when the ground began to tremble. 'Wake her!' cried Aunt Vicki, upset at the idea of an adult woman meeting death asleep. From her slumber Anna heard Martin's calming voice: 'Let her sleep, what difference does it make?' The ground shook again. His arm was around her. Nothing could happen to her.

In the face of this permanent menace from the English squadrons, Frau von Garlitz finally fled for good to her parents' estate in Brandenburg. Although the house was far from the city centre, on the other side of the Rhine, the chemical factory immediately bordering the grounds seemed an attractive target. Martin returned to Poland once again; Anna stayed behind alone as housekeeper—a strange, vacant position, a lengthy, inert waiting—for what? An old feeling—to be deserted by everyone, remaining behind in hostile surroundings— drove her restlessly through the rooms of the house. Even the library offered no solace, her attention evaporated over the pages. Her powers of imagination failed, except on the point about the different deaths that a soldier could die. She exercised virtuoso indefatigability in creating threatening scenarios that took place in unfamiliar locations in Poland. A primitive country, they said. To pull herself together she cleaned the antique cupboards and polished them fanatically. After the cupboards she started on the beams—everything had to shine. When it got dark she descended to the luxuriously appointed air raid shelter where her bed was, resisting the feeling that she was entering a tomb, to stretch herself out in her quilted coffin, hands crossed, eyes closed, so.

At the end of the winter she was instructed to close the house and come to the east. In order not to leave it to the wolves just like that, she packed everything of value, table silver, crystal, dinner services, put it in the polished cupboards, locked them and stuck the large iron keys to the floor with plaster. She took the curtains down from the rods, folded them up and stored them away together with the expensive linen. Then she went into the garden to look at the house from a distance once more. Without curtains, it looked vulnerable and transparent in the pale March sun. She left it behind in no-man's-land, hollow, lifeless, all the rooms chilled. To the extent that the house was riveted to this spot, so she herself was being uprooted again. She was going away—the series of departures and arrivals, of attaching and detaching, was growing ever longer. With a suitcase in each hand she walked down the drive to the tram stop. In Cologne she boarded a train that would take her in an easterly direction to one terminus.

On first acquaintance with Berlin she was shocked by the inhabitants' rudeness. Dazed from the journey, encumbered by her suitcases, she accosted two passers-by on the platform. 'Excuse me please, could you tell me where the Schlesische Bahnhof is?' After a disapproving look, as though she had begged for alms, they hastily walked away to the stairs. She stopped another traveller, omitting the 'Excuse me please' this time, but she had not finished speaking before he, too, walked away shaking his head. Now she dropped all politeness. '*Schlesische Bahnhof!*' Her voice resounded beneath the roof. A man with a homburg hat like a gangster said sarcastically, 'It's staring you in the face, are you blind?' He jerked his head upwards to a sign on which it was written in block letters.

The ancestral castle was situated on the Oder in extensive estates with twisting paths, ponds, a family chapel and mossy gravestones in the shadow of conifers and yews. A central section topped with a tympanum, the porch hidden behind two tall white pillars, divided the façade into symmetrical halves. The neo-classical severity was compensated for by southern yellow plasterwork and by geese scratching about freely on the terraces. Her arrival had been badly needed. Rudolf, Frau von Garlitz's son, had contracted tuberculosis of the spleen. A guardian angel was needed day and night, who would watch over his strict diet and his rest periods and relieve the seven-year-old's boredom by reading aloud. Separated from his contemporaries, he was confined by his illness, which was threatening not only his own survival but also the expectations for the future of his grandfather, whose only male descendant he was. The old man came every day, twirling the tips of his white moustache, inquiring about his grandson's health. Every day Anna had to forbid him to bring sweets. Thus her status as guardian angel inclined more and more to that of jailer. Uncles, aunts and cousins who brought delicacies surreptitiously, as if smuggling a saw blade inside a cake, to release the poor patient from his rigid diet, were unwittingly smuggling his death to him. She read to him from his favorite books to make him forget about the sweets that had been thrown away, and to forget that the only thing she was waiting for was a letter from Poland. Waiting, you could assuredly say, was something which she had been adequately steeped in.

Meanwhile, however, she obtained an answer to the question of why her father's name had had such a magic effect on Frau von Garlitz. She had asked von Falkenau point blank. 'Johannes Bamberg . . . yes . . . wait a minute . . . I'll never forget him . . . an exceptional young person, very dedicated and ingenious, he thought up various improvements within the business to make things work more efficiently.' He looked at Anna thoughtfully. 'Outwardly you don't look like him but in you I detect the same effort and incorruptibility. Alas, we were not able to profit long from your father. I remember that he was offered another job. He was a socialist, well yes, that was his affair . . . An extraordinary person, that Bamberg . . .'

'YOU YOURSELVES HAD started it with the bombing of towns,' said Lotte, who was annoyed at the way Anna depicted the inhabitants of Cologne as victims. When she thought of the bombing of Rotterdam and London her sympathy froze.

'Yes, of course we'd started it,' said Anna.

'Then you shouldn't have been surprised that there was retaliation.'

'We weren't surprised, we were afraid—just like the Londoners when they were packed on top of each other in air raid shelters. That fear is actually universal!'

'With the difference that you had yourselves to thank for it. You yourselves had chosen a regime that would shrink from nothing, even bombing towns.'

Anna sighed. She rested her plump arms on the table, leaned forwards and looked wearily at Lotte. 'I have just explained to you how the poor stupid people let themselves be blinded. Why won't you accept that? We'll never get a step further this way.'

Lotte sipped from her empty cup. She felt the rage rising to her head— she was being lectured here, would you believe! What arrogance!

'I'll tell you now in exact detail why I can't accept it,' she said angrily, 'perhaps then, in your turn, you'll also understand something for once.'

THE WATER THAT had lapped against the keel of the boat was scraping beneath their Friesian skates six months later. They were gliding over the ice in a cadenza, hands criss-crossed in each other's. It looked as though, together, they made one skater. Frosted reed borders and willows shot past; above them the sun hung low and slowly turned red. Lotte stumbled over a crack in the ice; David caught her. Twisting on the narrow blades they stopped, facing each other; he kissed her frozen lips. 'Ice queen . . .' he said in her ear, 'what would you say if we were to get engaged.' 'But . . .' Lotte began. She looked at him in amazement. He laughed and kissed her on the end of her nose, which was numb from cold. 'Think about it.' he said. He grasped her hands and they zigzagged onwards. Mist formed; minuscule particles of water took on the colour of the setting sun. The cold penetrated through her clothes. A line of verse from the song cycle went round in her head: 'In such stormy weather, I never would have sent the children out . . .'

In the dark they cycled back. Outside her home he said goodbye. 'I wouldn't want to give you a fright,' he said, 'but I'm simply mad about you.' She blew on her hands, he took them in his and rubbed them warm. 'I'll come on Saturday,' he promised, and then we'll talk it over.' 'No, no . . .' she said in confusion, 'I mean . . . I can't on Saturday . . . Let's wait a little . . .' He kissed her cheerfully. 'Fine . . . fine . . . We're not in a rush.' He rode off humming, turning around to wave once more.

For days, absentmindedly, she did the things that had to be done. For her, the stage of an as-yet-unacknowledged love could last for ever, unspoken, even if painful; she loved the secrecy. A concept like 'getting engaged' made her nervous. Yet she knew that ultimately she would not say no. Before their relationship accelerated and everyone interfered with it she wanted to harbour her ambivalent feelings in solitude. Perhaps he felt it—she heard nothing from him.

The illusion that the war was turning out well came to an end. In Amsterdam's Jewish quarter there were clashes between WA men, stirring up trouble, and Jewish gangs; a WA man was killed. In reprisal, on the twenty-second of February, hundreds of young Jewish men were picked up arbitrarily. In the official report there was mention of 'a murder so horrible and bestial, as only Jews were capable of committing,' but the illegal newspaper *Het Parool* demythologized the affair: It was a question of manslaughter in an ordinary fight—the dead body had been found with a cosh around the wrist! Lotte's father brought home a manifesto from the underground Communist Party, exhorting resistance to the Jewish pogroms: Strike!!!Strike!!!Strike!!! the working people were urged. The strikes that broke out in various parts of the country thereafter were stopped by the Germans with executions. Calm apparently returned.

Just as Lotte was beginning to grow restless—it had been ages—she was telephoned by David's father. In a dull tone he asked if it would be convenient if he and his wife could come round the same evening, they had something to discuss with her. Blood rushed to her head. Why was David sending his parents instead of coming himself? After everything he had said about them? They were received solemnly (the famous singer!). Lotte's father shook their hands in silence; the singer smiled sadly, turning his seducer's moustache into a stripe. His glance slid over the four sisters. 'And who is Lotte?' Lotte nodded cautiously. David's mother hurried to seize both her hands and squeeze them delicately. Overcome with emotion she clicked open her crocodile-skin bag and took out a handkerchief. 'We did not know that he had a girlfriend,' she said, moved.

Her husband did the talking after they had sat down. The reason for their visit was a postcard from David from Buchenwald, in which

he asked his parents to convey his greetings to Lotte because he had
not been able to say goodbye to her. 'Buchen-wald . . . ?' Lotte stammered. De Vries swallowed and stroked his forehead in a gesture of
despairing resignation. Staring at the floor he explained that David
was arrested in Amsterdam's Jewish quarter on Saturday the twenty-
second of February, while he was making music with a group of
friends. The Grüne Polizei had burst in suddenly; they had to stand
with their backs to the wall. 'Which of you is Jewish?' was screamed
at them. Without thinking for a second, his head was probably still in
the music, David had taken a step forward. Two other Jews in the
group wisely kept their mouths shut. He was taken to the Jonas
Daniël Meierplein, where rows of companions in misfortune were
already waiting. Without a charge, without any form of trial, they
had been transported to a camp in Germany.

David's mother sobbed into her handkerchief. Desperately looking
around him, the father took heart. 'You'll see, after a few months of
labour camp, the boys will be sent home. The Germans wanted to
make an example: Think about it, no more disturbances. David is
well, he's done a lot of sport . . . He isn't having a bad time there . . .
Here, read it . . .' Lotte bent over a few miserable lines on the card
buried beneath rubber stamps: '. . . I am fine, we are working
heartily . . .' He had had this card in his hands. It was rather alarming, a card that could leave the camp freely and find the way home
while the sender was held in captivity. Yet the full extent of the situation's seriousness did not immediately get through to her. It was so
bizarre, so absurd, so senseless, that it could not be comprehended.
Automatically she looked at the piano—the sheet music still lay open
at the page they had been on. Everything in her resisted the thought
that he had disappeared just like that, just like that. Immediately she
also clung on to the idea of a labour camp, a sort of scout camp—
chopping wood in the open air, planting trees.

'We are sending him back a card', said his father, 'would you like to
write a line?' 'Dear David . . .' she squeezed into the little space under
the fully written card. Her pen stopped, floating above the paper. She
felt his father's eyes on her, driving her pen. She wanted to write in
code, something personal, something essential. A line from the song

cycle came to her—without thinking it over she wrote a variant of it: '. . . I hope you have only gone out and will presently be home again . . .' As she reread the line it suddenly evoked a strong fear in her. What in God's name had she written down? A quotation from a poem of mourning, an elegy. Too late, too late to change anything. She gave the card back with a trembling hand. She could not bear it any longer; in the room, the sight of his parents upset her, nor could she bear the sympathy of her parents . . . a world that could let someone disappear just like that took her breath away. She stood up abruptly and went out of the room without any polite excuses, out of the house, outside. She sat down on a step at the garden house with a throbbing heart. It penetrated her like a slow-acting poison, something that was almost as intolerable as David's disappearance: On the twenty-second of February he would have come to her . . . if she had wanted that.

For weeks she subjected herself to strenuous self-analysis, put herself on the rack: Why had she not gone along with his spontaneous suggestion? Why did she have such a need to keep her options open, for the sake of form? If she had wanted to put him to the test a bit, provoke . . . why all that reserve? She lashed herself with questions that she could not answer, questions that, bit by bit, gave her an increasingly monstrous picture of herself, which invariably brought her to the same merciless conclusion.

His father telephoned again. They had received a second card, this time from Mauthausen, with the cryptic text, 'If I do not get my sailboat quickly, then it will be too late.' He cried desperately, 'My boy is imploring us to help, but what can I do? I wish I could take his place—I am an old man, he has his whole life in front of him.' Lotte sought for words in vain—when she really needed to find them they seemed not to exist. If David did not survive then the whole idea of justice was an illusion—only arbitrariness ruled, chaos, in the midst of which one person, with all his plans, expectations, hopes, fantasies, signified nothing—nothing. At night the boat with the billowing sails drifted through her dreams. The Loosdrecht Lakes swelled into an ocean—now he sat beaming and tanned at the rudder, then he was in the water again and trying frenetically to haul himself into the boat, holding onto the edge with petrified fingers while she looked on.

She received a recent photograph from his father. Painfully innocent, David was laughing at the photographer. That naiveté had cost him his freedom, perhaps his life. He had been in the wrong place at the wrong time—she could not look at the photograph without that thought. Reverence prevented her from tearing it up, again and again she forced herself to look at it. David had cycled out of her life waving cheerfully; that movement of his arm, back and forth, stayed longest with her as though something more was being conveyed, which was of great significance. And what had he been humming as he disappeared in the darkness?

Music irritated her. All those melodies, measures, subtleties, struck her as ridiculous—useless frills, false sentiments. Her voice refused to work in the upper registers, in the lower it vibrated uncertainly. Catharina Metz sent her home: 'Pull yourself together a bit first.'

4

WHERE DID ALL the water come from and where did it go to? Anna lay in a shining copper bathtub; bubbles of air rose from her skin, a network of scales. Her body lay pale and fish-like in the water. There must be an ingenious system of pipes through which the water flowed from the springs to the Thermal Institute via the bathtubs, before it was conveyed away again— the body it lapped around for half an hour was merely a way station. All that water, invisible, flowing inaudibly, like blood in the arteries, the bathtubs a pumping heart. How many bottles of mineral water am I lying in, she thought.

Long ago this same body sat in a bathtub on the kitchen floor, Uncle Heinrich drummed mockingly at the closed kitchen door: You must be really filthy if you have a bath every week. It seemed that a loaded silence reigned in this bathroom, as though the guests of the past were invisibly present and anxiously ensuring that they did not reveal themselves. How many, which famous dead had been in this bathroom, in this bathtub? Were their thoughts left behind here, could the silence be top heavy from it? What they had thought wouldn't have been up to much, she chuckled.

From those unknown dead it was but a small step to Lotte's death. Shame, rage, sorrow had prevented Anna from sleeping the whole night. Yet we are sisters, she remonstrated stubbornly with herself. But didn't age go together with leniency, with wisdom? If the two of us can't surmount all these barriers how can others manage? Then the world will stay in the grip of irreconcilability for centuries, then you can multiply the duration of each war by at least four generations. Of course—Germany had been able to extort reconciliation with all its money, but one football competition was enough to reveal that the old enmity was still alive and kicking.

Something in the angle of the light, in the green reflection off the tiles, in the peaceful privacy, brought her back to the casino. Lotte was sitting opposite her in the bath with lion's feet, a dark woman (Aunt Käthe?) leaned over them and poured a thin trickle of cold water down their backs from a blue enamel jug. They took turns shivering, trembling with pleasure. She could see Lotte very sharply before her, with her damp dark hair, her eyes screwed tightly closed—the picture was clear, more lifelike than that of Lotte as she sat at the table opposite her the previous day. It is still all there, she said, full of surprise. Although the bombing had left no tile, no stone of the casino intact, it is still all there in my head; those years in between signify nothing.

What history has subjected us to we cannot weigh on scales, she thought. Suffering does not separate us, but connects us—as pleasure connected us then. This insight, however absurd it seemed, relieved her. At the same moment the woman in the overall came in to help her out of the bath. She offered Anna an inviting hand. Without strange antics, upright and dignified, she stepped over the edge of the bath and descended. Like Pauline Bonaparte, assisted by her chambermaid, she grinned inwardly.

They found each other in the coffee room at the end of the morning. Although the door was always invitingly open, they had never

come across anyone in there. Now and then a guest shuffled through
the labyrinth of passages but mostly it was quiet and empty—January
was the slack season.

'I slept so badly,' Anna confided. 'The whole night I saw the image
of that one young man who stepped forward unsuspectingly.'

Lotte nodded absentmindedly, sipping her coffee and a glass of
mineral water alternately. Anna had the feeling that she did not want
to go on with it.

'I don't want to give the impression that I am bidding against you
in terms of the distress that befell me,' she said carefully, 'but my husband was killed in the war, too—in the same bloody war—after I had
gone through years of worry . . .'

THE FIRST NOTES of Beethoven's Fifth Symphony sounded in the
dining room. '*Ta ta ta ta* . . . The Wehrmacht High Command
announces: The Twenty-eighth Infantry Division is advancing to Russia . . .' Anna was preparing a piece of bread for Rudolf. Slowly she
spread some butter on it mixed with tears. Old von Falkenau sitting
opposite eating breakfast watched her pityingly. 'You mustn't cry,
Fräulein,' he shook his head, 'after all, your fiancé isn't in the
infantry! He isn't in any danger with the signals corps. Anyway,
you'll see, the whole operation will be over in six weeks. Did you
think that that nation was going to defend itself? They are glad to be
being released from communism.' Anna laughed dejectedly. Although
von Falkenau, a war horse with connections in the highest military
circles, got his information firsthand, no reassurance from outside
was adequate to soothe her anxiety. What was one soldier among a
million soldiers—a bit of fluff in the wind over the tundra, in the
wastes of a country where the sun rose on one side as it set on the
other. It was a nonsensical war, chiefly expressed in huge numbers
that far exceeded the powers of imagination, '*Ta ta ta ta* . . . The
Wehrmacht High Command announces . . .': thirty thousand Russian
prisoners of war, forty thousand, fifty thousand. What happened to
them, where did they manage to live? Questions that the practical
spirit, at home, posed quite innocently to itself while the victory chatter zigzagged outside from the radio through the open garden doors

and whipped the roses up into more profuse bloom. When a letter eventually arrived it was already fourteen days old. Meanwhile, perhaps Martin had already been killed in action. She went to see the newsreel in the nearby town, she read the paper, but the more efforts she made to assess his chances of survival in relation to the advancing armies, the more she felt a powerless outsider. Sitting at home and unable to do anything—a front that nobody spoke about.

At the end of October, a telegram arrived. 'Please come to Vienna. Immediately. We will get married.' Her suitcase, containing a home-made wedding dress and an officially authenticated family tree, had been ready for months. She travelled to Vienna in great haste. As she got off she hesitated. For one moment it was as though a strong gust of air was pushing her back inside the train. There he stood in actuality, after having died a hundred deaths in her imagination. He was there, returned from an immensity in which an ordinary person would be lost. Time and space had brought him here as though it were the most ordinary thing in the world. He was flanked by his parents. She envied him slightly for having two parents to whom he could point her out: Look, that's her now. Father and son both wore suits and hats, Martin's was crooked, the other's was straight. The father was slim and youthful, but there was a troubled expression on his face in the shade of his hat brim, as though he were constantly looking into a strong sun. The mother also gave the impression that existence demanded a superhuman effort from her. She pursed her lips together stiffly as though she were blowing up a balloon; she wore her heavily permed black hair like a cap on her head. Between these two people, who seemed to be ignoring one another, Martin stood and beamed.

The father said goodbye in a wide, treeless shopping street where trams rumbled past, at the entrance to a massive six-storey building. The moment had now come for him to go back to his wife again, he explained courteously—but, by the way, she warmly invited them round. Anna looked from one to the other in amazement. Why hadn't Martin told her that his parents were divorced? The father raised his hat and walked to the tram stop. The three of them climbed the steps of the building where Martin had grown up, on the first floor, above a chemist's. Anna, having become used to large rooms with carpets, antique furniture, paintings and family portraits, recoiled when she entered the small rooms crammed with knickknacks.

After his mother had sent Martin out on an errand she led Anna to her guest room with exaggerated hospitality. 'So,' she said, glad to be closing the door behind them, 'now we can talk to each other as woman to woman. Listen. I want to warn you, for your own good. Don't get married. Abandon the wedding while you still can. Marriage is men's invention, they are the only ones to benefit from it. Through that one transaction they acquire a mother, a whore, a cook, a worker, entirely for themselves. Everything in one go, gratis. You never hear anything about the wife. She sits nicely locked up, in those few square metres, with her scanty housekeeping money. She has walked into a nasty trap, but by the time that dawns on her it is too late. Don't do it, dear, be wise, I am saying this to you in friendship.' Anna tried to release herself from the black, hypnotic eyes. 'I can assure you that I love Martin very much,' she declared to her. '*Ach, love . . .*!' said the woman condescendingly, 'all lies and deceit to drive a woman mad.' Anna began to open her suitcase with trembling hands, she took out a blouse at random. 'Would you excuse me,' she said weakly. 'I would like to change.' 'Think it over!' The woman left the room triumphantly. Anna sagged onto the edge of the bed. She finds me unsuitable, was her first thought. What kind of mother is this who tries to upset her son's plans behind his back? The plans of a soldier who has to return quickly, to the war! Staring at her wedding dress in a state of shock, she subsided into a tangle of thoughts and reflections until Martin knocked on her door, full of impatient happiness. 'May I come in . . . ?' Courageously she decided to hold her tongue.

After the evening meal the mother placed a porcelain plate with a flower pattern in front of her son. 'I have another surprise for you my boy, something you're absolutely crazy about.' With a mysterious laugh she conjured up a jar of apricot compote and began to fill the plate with it. 'Doesn't Anna get any?' said Martin. 'But I kept it specially for you . . .' A mischievous, warmongering glitter in her eye. Martin sighed. 'I would like you to lay another plate.' The mother stood there without moving. In the cluttered rooms she was queen,

whoever ventured into her territory was exposed to a strange specimen of deranged maternal love. Stirring up strife gave way to being
the injured party. 'Ach so . . . therefore I have to do it for her . . .'
'Yes, otherwise I won't eat a mouthful of it.'

Outside the four rooms she had no hold over them. Breathing
more freely, they went into the city that showed off stylishly with its
churches, palaces, symmetrical parks and ponds, botanical gardens
and orangeries, cake shops. This was his city, the preview of her
future. Here she would live as soon as the war was over. In a museum
they admired the Habsburg art treasures, they looked down over the
roofs from the Leopoldsberg. Tickets for the opera and theatre were
scarce, except for a soldier with a leave permit. To every performance
they went to he also invited his mother. She insisted each time that
her close friend should accompany them, an ample Viennese with
many frills and lace, quickly moved to emotion; during the performances she felt impelled to inform them of every whim that fluttered
through her head. 'Mother,' Martin said eventually, 'I am happy to
take you with us, but please . . . that friend doesn't always have to be
there?' 'So . . .' she raised her chin, offended, 'isn't my friend to your
liking? You didn't ask for my approval in the choice of your friend.'
Martin apologized for her in the bedroom, watching Anna wearily. 'I
am sorry, don't blame her . . . She has been like that since the day my
father left her. I was very small then. She has never been a normal
mother, as a mother ought to be. She has always wanted to possess
me, in a tyrannical way. To provoke him. Nothing can be done about
it, that is simply how it is now.'

The sense of expectancy that the city had aroused in Anna ebbed
slowly away. It seemed to her that her mother-in-law was floating over
it with outspread wings—no district, no building escaped her shadow,
wherever they went. One day when they came home, they encountered the atmosphere of a morgue. The curtains were closed, a sharp
smell of vinegar struck their throats. Cautiously they opened the bedroom door. His mother lay in bed with eyes shut; her close friend sat
next to her and reverently applied a heart compress soaked in vinegar.
'Shhh . . .' she whispered with a finger to her lips, 'your mother has
had an attack of nerves.' Martin clenched his jaw muscles. After a

cool look at the scene he turned around and left the room. Anna lingered at the foot of the bed, looking down uneasily at the ashen mother. My God, she thought, if he deals with his mother like this, how will he deal with me later if there's anything the matter with me? She found it stuffy; she tiptoed out of the room with her hand on her throat. Martin was sitting at the kitchen table, depressed. 'I know what you're thinking,' he said. 'But I tell you: it's all play-acting. There's nothing wrong with her.' 'How can you be sure of that now?' said Anna indignantly. 'Fine,' he sighed. 'You're being sympathetic in spite of everything. Go back there and feel her pulse, then you'll see how serious it is.' Anna returned to the bedroom timidly. She put a finger on the substantial wrist. The friend nodded blandly to her. The heartbeat was calm and regular, just as it should be. The eyes did not open a chink, she lay on the pillows like an enormous black dahlia.

'I have something to confess to you,' said Martin, 'I've already been walking around all day with it and didn't dare tell you. We cannot get married now.' Anna went rigid. 'Why not?' He put an arm round her. His leave was actually illegal, he explained, he had a forged his leave permit. After his company had been in action for weeks they were given three weeks to recuperate. In Russia, mind you. The company commander, a pleasant chap, had suggested, 'Before you all have to be in that hell again I advise you . . . go home for two weeks. On my authority.' Martin would betray them all by getting married, it was an official event; his superiors had to be notified. Anna nodded without saying anything. Suddenly the war was again hugely present. He laid his head on her shoulder contritely. Everything paled into insignificance beside the fact that he would soon be returning to the east. And she to the north. That they were no more than pawns on a world-sized chessboard. 'That hell,' Anna repeated thoughtfully. 'Just tell me honestly, Martin, what is it like there—don't protect me.' He put a finger on her lips. 'Shhh . . . don't talk about it,' he whispered. 'I'm here precisely to forget it.'

As the attack of hypochondria began to bore her, the mother rose from her apparent death. Pottering about the apartment, she took up her post again. Martin and Anna made plans for their last week. 'I think I'll go to the savings bank,' he mused. 'I don't want us to have to penny-pinch.' On the way to the hat stand they heard the front door slam shut. They left the house; the sky, which promised rain, was the colour of the façades in the tenth district. Martin gripped her arm. 'Well, just look . . .' A block ahead of them, on the opposite side of the street, his mother was dashing in the same direction as they were—head forward, a large leather bag in her hand like a weapon. 'What a hurry she's in,' he said astonished. They passed a shop window with dirndls. 'Can you see me in a thing like that?' Anna said jokingly. Martin turned up his nose. 'That's for gushing types who like an alpine glow and forest horns.'

'That's odd,' said the bank official, smiling slightly, 'two minutes ago your mother withdrew the last of the money in the account.' 'But there was a hefty sum in there,' Martin cried, 'years of savings.' He had to sit down. Dazed, staring ahead, he shook his head. 'Before I left I gave her a letter of authority,' he said flatly, 'for emergencies.' Anna pushed him outside gently. He threw his hat in the air. 'I'm broke,' he cried with a shrill laugh that echoed round the walls, '*Ach du liebe Augustin*, everything has gone . . .'

Gruesomely cheerful, he went inside the apartment. His mother was already in the kitchen as though she had never been away. Martin picked up a kitchen chair and stood on it. 'And what was left in my bank account?' he asked rhetorically. 'Nothing!' He picked up one of the carefully labelled jars of apricot compote from the shelf, let it slither out of his hands onto the floor and reached out to take a new jar. 'I've been taking care of him all those years,' his mother began to lament to herself, '. . . gone without food myself . . . not a shred of gratitude . . .' Martin looked down on his whining mother with a jar in his hands. Suddenly he put it back quietly on the shelf, turned it so the label faced outwards decoratively and got down from the chair. 'Come,' he said calmly, gripping Anna by one arm, 'we're going to pack.' In a cloud of self-pity, the mother traversed her paltry empire; she threw herself pathetically on her son's half-packed suitcase on the bed. Anna pushed her wedding dress, which she had hung up, into her suitcase and closed it. A dull, throbbing headache located itself between her and the outside world; she followed Martin mechanically out of the house, into the street, onto the tram.

They were received by Martin's father and his second wife with calm, silent understanding. Anna, who had thought her initiation as a member of the family was now behind her, was brought into the know about the latest mysteries. The father had recently renewed his paternal role after an involuntary interruption of twenty years. All that time Martin's mother denied him access to his son, and depicted him to his son as a frivolous womanizer and profiteer. When Martin was in the fourth grade at the grammar school she refused, for reasons perhaps only she knew the logic of, to accept the father's monthly school payment any longer. To the son, she said the father no longer wanted to pay; to the father, that the son had had enough of studying. She had found a place for him as a pupil in a first-class hairdressing salon just by the Opera in Kärntnerstrasse. Ever since then, instead of Homer's hexameters it was the heads of moody divas that he bent over. Her manoeuvres only came to light when Martin had sought to contact his father on the occasion of his imminent marriage.

With retrospective force Anna now understood the strange, three-headed reception at the station. The one did not want to yield to the other; the father would not allow himself to be by-passed anymore. All that involvement in family entanglements perplexed her; she was inclined to count herself lucky to be parentless— although in a certain sense Martin, too, had become an orphan years ago, with the absence of his father, under the domination of a hysterical mother.

They resumed their trips with desperate energy. They climbed from the Untere Belvedere, the seventeenth-century palace of Prince Eugen of Savoy, who liberated Vienna from the Turks, to the even larger Obere Belvedere, the symbol of his power. They visited the Karlskirche, where Martin wanted to be married. They got drunk at the Heuriger tavern. During the days that remained it was as though a reservoir had to be filled with joint pleasures and enjoyments that they would be able to draw from for the rest of their lives.

She and his father took him to the train. 'I'll manage fine . . .' he cried from the window of the departing train, 'Russia is large and the Tsar far away!'

* * *

'I STILL WELL remember how afraid we were,' said Lotte, 'that autumn, that the Russians would lose.'

'I only thought about the life of that one . . .' Anna stared at her nails. 'That was the only thing that interested me. Beyond that I didn't see, didn't hear. I hoped and prayed that he would come back. People totally forget that now, the continuous anxiety in which every one of us at home had to live—there were millions of boys like Martin.'

Lotte felt compelled to help her recall that millions of Russians had been slaughtered by those same boys.

Anna sprang up. 'We simply didn't think about that. With us all you heard was: Advance, advance, Bialystok, Leningrad, Ukraine. Hermann Goering delivered a major speech, "We have conquered the most fertile country in the world." He promised, "We will do some fine things there, from now on we will have enough butter, enough flour." Germany was being depopulated: anyone who had skills to contribute was sent there to give advice about farming, health services. Even the greatest fool was somebody there and could do something. The prisoners of war were brought back here to work in the factories. It became a crazy organizational machine, a huge achievement in a certain sense. People at home became ingenious too—you made a jacket out of an old tablecloth, you made your own shoes . . .'

'The Dutch did that, too,' Lotte snapped.

'Naturally . . . an emergency mobilizes all the forces that normally lie fallow. That's why people are so bored now—they have to go on creativity courses—that is the malaise of this age.'

Lotte cut Anna off vindictively, sensing that her defence was increasingly acquiring the character of a hymn of praise. '—And then the winter set in.'

'Yes, General Mud. Then the swift advance was over.'

'Napoleon had already got stuck in the mud and cold—we fervently hoped history would repeat itself and it did. Now Hitler has lost the war, we said straight away.'

'We thought: We must help the boys get through the winter. They wrote home that they were cold and everyone got going—even the

children and the patients in hospital. Everyone got on with knitting.
Sheets and tablecloths were sewn together, fur coats sent, all via the
Red Cross, behind the party leaders' backs. Everyone took care that
their husband, their son, their father wouldn't be cold. *Ach ja . . .*' she
stared outside, the air was the colour of the slate roofs, 'I still have his
Gefrierfleisch-Abzeichen at home—the decoration for that dreadful
winter in Russia when there were so many frozen toes, fingers, noses.
The Order of the Deep Freeze, the people dubbed it cynically.'

HERR VON GARLITZ'S mother, at one time a courtier of the empress,
decided to spend her last days in the inhabited world and moved to
Potsdam. The forty-five room castle she left behind was on the other
side of the Oder in a Frederickian ribbon-built village, of which there
were many in Brandenburg. At one time Frederick the Great had
reclaimed and populated this border province—he put a prince there:
in the middle of the fields a castle was built for him, a road was
paved, to the right and left of it houses for the farm workers were
built, there was a church, a small school. In exchange for their total
availability, the workers were given grain and a piece of land large
enough to keep a pig and a cow.

Because it was far away from where the bombs were falling, Herr
von Garlitz decided they should all move to the estate where he had
grown up. He travelled ahead with his wife in order to make the
arrangements, leaving the children behind in Anna's care in his par-
ents-in-law's house. Six weeks later she received a summons from
Frau von Garlitz: Come here. I need you. We have tracked down
Adelheid, Rudolf's former nanny, she will assume care of the children.' And once again Anna set off with her two suitcases, one with
the wedding dress and Martin's Feldpost letters, and one with her
other possessions. She was fetched from the station in a horse cart—
her employe, less soignée than before, sat, slightly dishevelled, on the
box. She had acquired a charming indifference, a laissez-faire that
surprised Anna, accustomed to her good manners and self-control in
all circumstances. 'You'll laugh to death,' said the countess at the top
of her voice, trundling over the unpaved country road, with the same
abandon as when she had carried Anna off in her Kaiser-Freser a cen-

tury ago. 'All you can do is laugh, the castle is so dreadfully run down, you can't imagine it, you'll have to see it with your own eyes.'

After a half-hour journey through an uninhabited world where even the succession of forests and fields conveyed a certain monotony, they drove into a village. All the ingredients were there: church, school, workers' houses on either side of the road. Only the castle was hidden from view on account of a wall, draped wearily with the branches of old chestnut trees and maples. The gate was opened by a man who had such a squint that it looked as though he was welcoming other people alongside Anna and the countess. The cart bumped inside; the gate was closed behind them. And there was the castle, massive, robust, light grey walls covered with creepers, white window frames and a forest of chimneys on the red roofs. It was turned in on itself, shy, as though it were an individual who would not readily divulge its secrets. Out of a Frederickian need for symmetry, a porch had been introduced in the middle of the front façade with a staircase that began broadly and invitingly but narrowed as it approached the double front door. Square pillars on either side of it supported a tympanum above which the family coat of arms had been sculpted in relief. They drove around the side to the service entrance. Various outbuildings and sheds enclosed a cobbled inner courtyard.

Frau von Garlitz led her into the house. Scarcely had Anna set foot on the landing when various craftsmen who were busy with restoration work on the second floor shook the dust and grit from their clothes—it fell down the staircase onto Anna's Viennese hat. Hilarious laughter filled the space. 'Now you know what it's like here,' said Frau von Garlitz.

A thorough inventory that same day proved that she had not been exaggerating. As well as the structural problems resulting from years of maintenance backlog, the interior was filthy and threadbare. In every room hung the penetrating smell of an obstinate old lady who for fifty years had demanded that everything should stay as it had been in her youth. Rickety suits of armour clanked in the draughty hall and passages—there were whimsical tree trunks with phosphorescent lights that, with spooky kitsch, woke the unsuspecting passerby who, half-asleep, had to go to the WC at night. Frau von Garlitz's bedroom was an urgent case. Since her arrival six weeks ago she had been sleeping in the same nightdress, the same sheets, in a bed whose satin canopy sagged low beneath the dust. Everything was so filthy that you were already infected just by looking at it. 'My heavens,' Anna whispered, 'what a pigsty.' Frau von Garlitz raised her hands helplessly. 'I don't know where anything is, by God, nothing, I mean sheets and so on.' 'But they must be somewhere,' said Anna huskily, throwing open the windows. It began to dawn on her that with that one candid, timid gesture the countess was transferring full responsibility for the decayed estate to her. 'How glad I am that you are here,' she sighed girlishly.

Thus the renovation began. For a year Anna went from room to room with a succession of Polish labourers and cleaning women from the village until all forty-five had undergone a transformation. The German tenants—sent off to war—had been replaced by Polish forced labourers and Russian prisoners of war, housed in the stables, permanently guarded by four armed soldiers. There were no tractors or petrol. At six o'clock in the morning eighty oxen teams manned by Russians, supervised by an agricultural inspector exempted from military service, went into the surrounding fields with rattling carts where they worked the whole day at an un-Russian pace to fetch in the quota of grain decreed by the Reich. Potatoes, grain, milk, butter, everything had to be handed over, apart from a small ration for individual use. For the castle inhabitants a wall cupboard had been constructed with compartments in which each kept his own store of butter—one hundred and twenty-five grams per week. They had to hand over half to the kitchen for cooking, the other half was for bread. Humanity seemed to be divided into two camps: the one spread everything on one piece and had dry bread for the rest of the week, the other carefully spread each piece with a puritanically wafer-thin layer.

Before the great refit could proceed like clockwork, Anna had to do battle with traditional ways. Unsure, because she had to direct a complicated, unfathomed household on the basis of her pathetic certificate from the School of Housekeeping for Young Ladies of the Better Circles, she roamed through the rooms in the hope of discovering a domestic structure. She ended up in the laundry room, where four jovial fat women from the village scrubbed sheets in oval washtubs, singing, laughing and chatting. The little procession traipsed from there to the cellar where the sheets were put through the mangle and smoothed with irons that contained a piece of glowing metal. They did not rush themselves, the wash was done in fourteen days, then a new lot arrived and they began all over again. Each day was punctuated by an ample lunchtime break. Mamselle made coffee and baked biscuits; it was really pleasant—it was beyond their range of interests that this social event might be taking place against a backdrop of forty-five rooms in a state of disintegration. Good Lord, thought Anna, this surely can't go on.

At the back of the laundry she discovered an enormous washing machine with a centrifuge under a thick layer of dust. 'Broken,' the women waved it aside fatalistically. Long elevated transmission belts crossed the courtyard and ended up at a generator in a distillery, where vodka was made from potatoes. 'What's wrong with this?' she asked the mechanic. 'Is it broken?' 'I don't know,' he rumbled, shrugging his shoulders. Anna had the feeling that she was swimming in treacle, in a river of listlessness and indifference. 'What sort of an answer is that: "I don't know,"' said Anna sharply. 'Perhaps you could just have a look at it.' Sighing, with a vacant gaze, the man bent over the machine. A few hours later he had repaired it in spite of himself. The next morning at six o'clock Anna put the washing in the machine; the enormous thing, about a metre across, started to move; a lively wood fire was burning beneath it; on their arrival the washerwomen were greeted with joyful sounds: *boom, boom, boom, tch, tch, tch, klop, klop, klop.* They blinked, nonplussed, and then they were furious. What did this Rhinelander imagine, did she think she could interfere in their lives just like that, they had washed by hand as long as they could remember, it suited them very well, there was no need at all for change now. 'Why should you wash and iron for fourteen days?' cried Anna above the din. One load was already spun; the sun was shining outside; she hung the washing on the line and hurried back to the laundry. She taught the women how the machines had to be used, ignoring their disapproving looks. 'You can go and sit next to it quietly.' Anna trudged back and forth to the line. At the end of the day the washing smelled delightful and had been folded neatly. Everything was ready—thirteen days remained to clean the house. A little revolution. When the women realized that, their rage turned to hate—which gradually melted in the winter when they and their children were ill and Anna brewed camomile tea for them and wrapped them up warmly and drove to town at night with them when they were about to have a child. In this way she compensated silently for Frau von Garlitz's negligence—it was the nobility's traditional duty to care for the welfare of the tenants.

Room after room was mucked out. Anna's amazement at the cobwebs, the dust, the mould and dead insects, which the old countess had collected over the years, soon turned into robust perseverance. There was one room that outdid all the rest: the Emperor's Room. It had remained a locked sanctuary since Kaiser Wilhelm had spent one night there as the guest of his wife's former courtier. As soon as they opened the door a musty sour air came at them. They took down the curtains and drapes, they pulled the sheets and pillows from the canopied bed in a cloud of dust and mites, but even when the whole room had been stripped, that penetrating imperial smell still hung there. Finally they unstitched the mattress: maggots teemed where his excellency's body had rested, gladly jumping out of the horsehair into sudden freedom. Anna was horrified. It is wartime, she thought feverishly, we can't throw expensive horsehair away just like that. Suddenly she remembered the still she had seen in the distillery. They crossed the courtyard with the mattress and toppled the contents into the boiler, beneath which a gentle fire burned. The maggots exploded like popcorn. When no further form of activity could be detected between the hairs, the horsehair was washed and dried in the sun. Finally she took the expensive load to a mattressmaker, armed with two litres of vodka.

The attic was full of objects that the age had vomited up years ago. The only valuables Anna discovered were a series of English engravings, old hunting scenes in mahogany frames, which found a place in the corridors and the hall. A staggering amount of kitsch was found under the filth, from a period that seemed to have a preference for curlicues. They brought everything into the courtyard for a public sale. The announcement went from mouth to mouth: 'Everything going for fifty pfennings.' Polish women from the nearby dwellings crowded forward in threadbare, shapeless clothes with scarves tied tightly around their pale, round faces. They brightened up at the sight of the luxury articles: they fingered the symbols of a rich and carefree existence with shining eyes. After they had hesitated endlessly over their purchases, eventually they rushed off as though someone might take them from them—a silk-covered tabouret or a tea cosy in the form of a rococo lady.

After the sugar beets had been harvested they were washed, sliced, and pressed in a nauseatingly sweet smoke by the Polish women. Then they were made into a syrup; everything became sticky and clinging. Each one got a sack of beets for themselves as payment. 'May we use the press . . . ?' they gestured, shyly demonstrating how hard pressing by hand in a cloth was. 'Of course,' said Anna, 'we've finished, we don't need it anymore.' Some hours later Herr von Garlitz came up to her in riding attire. 'Listen here,' he called her to order, 'now what have you done, you have given the Poles the press.' 'Yes, why not?' said Anna defiantly. She was irritated by this fashionable, indolent presence in the middle of the hum of activity. 'Do you think'—he raised his chin—'the Poles would give us a press if we were in Poland?' He looked challengingly at her and answered for her. 'They certainly would not do so, precisely because they hate us.' 'But after all, we don't hate them,' Anna retorted. 'Anyway, if the Poles are so much worse than us, as you say, and I am meant to follow their example and be like them, then that makes us not a whisker better and we have no right to behave as though they ought to obey us.' He shook his head at the paradoxical reasoning. 'They are *Untermenschen*,' he said with dignity. 'If they are *Untermenschen* and we are the *Herrenmenschen* as you say,' she tried to put it diplomatically 'then actually I can't be like the Poles, so shouldn't I be like us, namely a *Herrenmensch?*' The whole idea of *Untermensch, Herrenmensch, Ubermensch* struck her as ridiculous, but she had just enough political awareness to under-stand intuitively that she could not say that out loud to a lackey of the Führer. Von Garlitz frowned: this dialectic was going over his head.

Somewhere he sensed that he had been put in his place by a self-opin-
ionated—unfortunately indispensable—member of the staff who
impudently deployed her power against his, as employer, over his
household. It was all too much for him; shaking off the confusion he
walked away with short, measured steps, his head bent, thwacking a
tree here and there with his riding whip.

The excessive work shortened the time between Feldpost letters.
Martin wrote about the beauty of fields full of sunflowers; he had
found a case of books at a weekly market, a recipe for borscht followed. There was a strange contradiction between the tumultuous
triumphal processions of the Wehrmacht on the radio and the
peaceful calm in Martin's letters in which a rifle shot never
sounded, a house never burned. In the autumn he was stationed
near Tula. When it began to freeze and knitting needles were click-
ing everywhere to ward off the tundra cold, Anna sent him a parcel
in the blind hope that it would find its way into infinity. Rumours
of people who had died in action came ever closer, an anonymous
threat that was denied in the newsreels, where the soldiers smoked
cigarettes cheerfully in their snow caves. At first it was second
cousins, student friends, friends of friends, then it was brothers,
fiancés, fathers. But winter had a Chekhovian beauty in Martin's
letters. With his comrades he had come across a farm where there
was a grand piano. One grand piano amid endless fields of snow,
but badly out of tune from the cold. The family slept on a platform
built over the stove. The soldiers hauled the mattress off and combined their strength to lift the piano. It thawed quickly; there was
music night after night. Martin's courteous apologies were waved
off by the farmer: he thought it was more important to hear
Mozart and Bach than that they should be warm at night. The
more colourful the events being described the more suspicious
Anna became.

One of the Russian prisoners carried unusual responsibilities: he
had to light the stoves in the castle and keep them going. Day in,
day out, he went from room to room with a basket of wood. No
one said anything to him—it was punishable to regard Russians as
human beings. One day Anna found herself in a room with him.

Shy, almost invisible, he did his work as though he had realized that he had no right to exist except as the bringer of fire. She spoke to him, without preliminaries, simply because they were two individuals in one space. To her surprise, he replied in broken German—moreover he appeared to be called Wilhelm: after the German Kaiser had visited the Tsar, all newborn babies had been called Wilhelm. Another godchild of the emperor, Anna grinned to herself. His explanation was full of softly vibrating Russian consonants. After the first introduction, she could regularly be found in rooms where the stove was being lit. They were suffering from hunger in the stables, he whispered, there were shortages of everything. She stole food for him from the kitchen. In the evenings she cut discarded blue-checked quilt covers into pieces and made them into handkerchiefs for the prisoners. She collected discarded toothbrushes, remains of toothpaste, pocket combs with a few broken teeth and soap. Wilhelm smuggled the spoils to the stables where they were eagerly put to use. She did not ask herself why she did it; subversive intentions were strange to her—she simply could not tolerate the disharmony between the relative comfort in the castle and the hardship in the stables.

Between stoves, Wilhelm brought her up to date with the rumours doing the rounds among the Russians and the Poles, rumours that revealed a world in the shadow of the jubilant newsreels: The German offensive was stuck, precisely when they thought the Russian army had been exhausted by the millions of losses, one hundred living Soviet soldiers came forward for every dead one. And Tula? Anna asked with a shrinking heart. He apologized: the rumours were not that detailed. How did they reach them in fact? Well . . . he spread his hands with an eastern smile. Where the information came from remained a mystery to her. Had the news been brought by the last flock of birds who pierced the grey sky, or had they had the benefit of a well-trained marathon runner who covered the distance to the Polish border in Olympic time and on the way called in at all the estates where Poles were working?

*　　*　　*

'YOU REALLY ARE a proper German,' said Lotte shaking her head.

'How so?' Anna was on her guard.

'A proper, efficient German . . . as when you solved that washing machine problem . . . all thoroughly in the spirit of the economic miracle. But what I ask myself . . .'

'Yes . . .' Anna was nothing if not obliging, so as to explain everything, but also to dispel every misunderstanding.

'Were the washerwomen ultimately better off in that organized housekeeping of yours? Could they still laugh, sing, gossip?

'*Pfff* . . .' Anna shrugged her shoulders wearily. 'They still got their coffee and biscuits, you know. But you can't halt progress. In the days of the landlords the workers learned to read and write, more was not thought necessary. Then came the time when the workers refused to allow themselves to be kept in ignorance any longer—I was such a person—they got trained, television arrived, the computer. If you want to go back to laughing, singing and gossiping, you'll have to eliminate technology and the benefits we get from it.'

'But a lot has been lost.'

'You mustn't romanticize it.'

And so they were back again at their old point of difference. They stared outside past the woman with the swan, attempting to organize their thoughts, which were fluttering in the wind in all directions, like scraps of paper, as they retrieved memories.

'I can well understand that you did something for the Russian prisoners,' mused Lotte, 'somewhere you were hoping that the Russians themselves would do the same for Martin if he were taken prisoner.'

'No.' Anna pursed her lips, 'I did it to be helpful, without thinking further about it.'

'Other motives could nevertheless be hidden underneath. From the moment the first people in hiding came knocking at our door, at last I had the feeling of being able to do something—as though we were still doing something for David . . . with each person in hiding we could keep out of the occupier's hands.'

'So you had people hiding in your house.'

Lotte nodded.
'Jewish?'
'Mostly.'
Anna sighed, and all her curves sighed too.

5

THEY HAD LUNCHEON AT A restaurant on Place Albert, with a view of a colossal angel that had alighted on a tall plinth and was observing humanity from there with perplexity. Afterwards they made a small excursion around the town, their daily dose of therapeutic activity. They wandered into a grey granite church with three towers, whose steeples pointed firmly to the sky like schoolmasters' pencils. For once they were in agreement that it was an exceptionally ugly church. Uninspired, they strolled through the dim space, a leaflet about its history in hand. 'Built in 1885 in Romanic-Rhine style following the Cologne school,' Anna read. 'I didn't know we exported such hideous architecture then.' They dawdled by a sculpture that had come from a much older church on the same spot: a group of angels with swords and bishops' staves. Bored, they walked out of the church into a café directly opposite—a consolation for the disillusioned churchgoer. They were both in urgent need of coffee. A fighter jet crossed the sky diagonally, behind the misanthropic steeples, as though it wanted to erase them.

WHEN THE FRINKEL family, an elegantly dressed trio, came to the door one day in the summer, nobody realized that with this apparently innocent visit, a period in the lives of Lotte's mother and her family was coming to an end. Bram Frinkel, eighteen years old by then, had arranged the meeting; he had remained friends with Koen all those years. They drank something that had to pass for coffee. Lotte's father put on Bach's Double Concerto in honour of Max

Frinkel, who had acquired a certain fame as first violin in a radio orchestra since his emigration from Germany. The gathering listened attentively; it was as though the guests had come specially to hear the concert. But when the last sounds died the war immediately took its place—in the sudden silence, in the surrogate coffee, in the presence of the Frinkels. 'You luff muziek . . .' began Frinkel, stroking his chin uneasily. These circumstances emboldened him to ask Lotte's parents for hospitality, in return for payment of the costs, of course, and only for a short time, until a definite solution had been found. 'All ze Jews from Hilversum haff to assemble in Amsterdam,' he said meaning-fully. 'You live so splendidly out of the way here,' continued his wife Sara in faultless Dutch, 'Max could do his daily violin practice with-out anyone hearing.' She was small and vivacious, her lips and nails the same colour as her dress.

Bram's bed was put in Koen's room, and the Frinkels took up residence in the nursery, from where dizzy runs and flageolet har-monics made the walls tremble. When the father stopped, the son took over with gypsy music and Slav dances. They were looked up by a friend from Germany whom they had taken into their confi-dence, Leon Stein. He had left his country to fight Fascism in the Spanish Civil War. After that he worked in Haarlem for many years for his uncle, a manufacturer of barrels and crates, who was allowed by the Germans, for a lot of money, to get away to Amer-ica. He had been able to take his horses but not his nephew, who had become stateless after his Spanish adventure. The New World, on the other side of the ocean, open to all nationalities, closed its borders hermetically to anyone who had no nationality. Stein needed to go into hiding urgently. But it was only from time to time, he said. The old flair of the Spanish anti-Fascists had not been extinguished in him and had driven him to the Dutch resistance— for him it was a strong case of contempt for death because he looked thoroughly Jewish, even when he wore a German uniform during a surprise attack on a distribution office and gave orders in his mother tongue.

A bed was put up for him in Lotte's father's office; he slept there like a soldier on a narrow wooden plank, feverishly devising plans, always nervous—only when he was in the greatest danger would a mild calm come over him, he confessed. He was elusive, his life hung together on secrets—at one point he would shelter with them for three weeks, then he disappeared for a month without warning.

One morning at dawn they were awakened by rifle shots. People ran about the house in pyjamas, the Frinkel family desperately looking for a way to make themselves invisible. Koen went to see how the land lay—the allure of danger shone in his eyes. He wandered into the wood quasi-casually. There he came upon three Austrian soldiers, hardly older than himself, who were out hunting, to break the monotony of their daily rations. He was given a cigarette, they chatted about hares and rabbits. Later that day they would be starting a raid in the neighborhood, they said carelessly, sometimes it was easier to catch a Jew than a rabbit. Koen led them to a hill on the other side of the wood that was riddled with tunnels and holes. They departed with fraternal shoulder-slapping.

Breathlessly he reported back. 'They are only hunting hares and rabbits now but in a couple of hours they will be hunting for . . . for . . .' He could not get the word past his lips. Ashamed, he looked at his friend standing barefoot on the tiled floor, numb with cold. Shots sounded again in the distance. Max Frinkel massaged his fingers nervously. 'The Noteboom ladies!' he cried. His wife nodded emphatically. 'Two admirers,' she explained, 'they sat in the front row at each concert. If you get into difficulties, come to us, they once offered. However, they are a bit eccentric . . .' They were taken there at top speed. The ladies lived with forty-eight cats in a large ramshackle villa held upright by creepers and ivy. Although one was the mother of the other, there was great difficulty telling which of the captivating ladies was the elder, with their grey buns and Karl Marx glasses. They could take a hint, of course the famous violinist was welcome—they took in all strays, whether they walked on two feet or four.

After the Frinkels had gone, the raid was awaited calmly. Lotte's mother enjoyed the sudden peace of mind. Only now did she realize how much strain the Frinkels' presence had caused. The continual fear of an unexpected visit, that the youngest children would let their tongues run away with them, the anxiety lest a small, fatal slip, so insignificant that you overlooked it—the fear of reprisals that no one dared to imagine . . . a fear that went along with a sense of guilt: All that time she had been putting her children at risk. We won't start that again, she decided. They are fine there, with the Noteboom ladies.

There was more than enough to be anxious about. If only the Russians did not surrender, for example, because then everything would be lost. During the Stalingrad period, Jet sleepwalked through the house at night. Lotte woke up, discovered the bed next to her empty and found her sister bolt upright and pale as a statue in the living room, where she slowly and dreamily negotiated the tables and chairs without colliding with anything. To prevent her from falling down the stairs Lotte locked the bedroom door from then on, but the urge to walk had to find an outlet: One night Jet opened the balcony door and walked out into the rain in her nightdress. Lotte was awakened by the wind blowing across her forehead. Not just the bed, the balcony appeared to be empty. Disconcerted, she peered into the night, had Jet got wings? Only when she looked out over the balustrade, into the deep did she see her lying, soaking wet, in a bed of overblown asters that had been spoilt by the rain. For many weeks Jet lay in a darkened room with severe concussion; a persistent headache had taken the place of her somnambulism. Even so, she demanded to be kept up to date with the latest developments in the east—with nothing spared.

Rain in the Netherlands was snow in Russia. It seemed as if an unusually large amount of rain fell that autumn. One evening even Lotte's mother's good intentions were rained out. The bell rang; two men had braved the rotten weather. The face of one was hidden behind heavily framed glasses misted over from the rain. The other seemed to be Lotte's father's barber; he did not immediately recognize him as such—what was a barber without his customary entourage of knives, razors and mirrors. Authenticating themselves by dropping Leon Stein's name, the barber asked for temporary hiding for his companion, who was in great need. It would be only for a couple of days. No one said anything. Lotte held her breath. The silence was heavy with tension that was not so much the result of doubt as of inevitability. The possibility of a free choice was only apparent—in actuality it had already been decided, at a suprahuman or even essentially human level. It was impossible to say no, to say, Go back outside into the storm, the rain, make sure you find a roof for your head. 'We aren't taking people anymore,' she heard her father saying. 'It's too risky.' 'The Frinkels' bed is still there,' her mother proposed. Her hands began to fiddle with the unwelcome guest's coat; she took the wet thing from him and hung it on a clothes hanger next to the stove. She offered him a chair, took his glasses, dried them with a piece of her skirt and put them back on his nose. 'So, at least now you can see where you have ended up.'

Ruben Meyer discovered that there was a sleepwalker, bored stiff, in one of the rooms upstairs. He sat on her bed and began to read aloud to her; he brought her tea and improved on the news from the front for her. After six weeks, when still no other address had been found for him, he admitted that he was suffering from sleeplessness because of anxiety about his family. The baker in a Utrecht village with whom they had been hiding was being blackmailed by his sister-in-law, who had noticed that in the store behind the oven it smelled not only of bread and currant buns but also of cold sweat. Ruben had been smuggled to the Gooi region by a laundry in a basket of dirty washing, to search for a safe place for them. 'The barber was going to organize it . . .' His eyes darted back and forth behind the thick lenses. 'I don't understand . . .' 'We can't wait for that,' said Lotte's mother.

She sent Lotte out on the job. The train rode through a barren landscape beneath a drab, joyless sky. The woods, the hay were not themselves anymore, they had lost their innocence under the tread of strange boots, they had become hiding place and tragic scene simultaneously. That she could calmly ride through there, while Ruben could not, distorted the landscape into something that never again, just like that, could be called beautiful. Absurd, senseless movements were being made in it, she was on the way to his family, he had settled with her family—everything was an expenditure of energy, a fundamental disorder, no one could follow the rhythm of his own life.

In the bakery, squeezed together in a small oppressive room, she discovered his mother, ten-year-old brother, sister and brother-in-law, emaciated and beside themselves with fear. The mother clung to her 'Please take my boy with you, take him out of here!' 'We'll come and fetch you as soon as possible,'—Lotte tried to calm her—'but it has got to be properly organized.' 'My little boy, my *bubele*,' the mother pleaded, 'take him along with you.' A boy was standing somewhat to the side with an exercise book in his hand. It seemed as though he was consciously distancing himself from her, in masculine shame at his mother's pleas. He looked much too Jewish to be able to travel in the train. 'Sums?' she asked, buying time. 'I am writing a story,' he said with dignity, 'about shipwrecked people washed ashore on an island in the Pacific Ocean.' 'And what else?' she encouraged him, feverishly asking herself what she ought to do. She was not equipped for such a dilemma; she was no more than a pawn who had been pushed out to start exploring the situation. This was not a decision that she could just make on her own initiative. 'They think it is uninhabited and they will be able to live there safely, but there are cannibals who hunt them with spears and . . .' 'Here,' the mother ripped a diamond ring from her finger. Lotte shook her head, an unbearable heaviness pressed on her temples. 'It is not a question of money. The Germans will just pick him off the train, it would be irresponsible. But we'll come and fetch you . . . we'll come and fetch all of you as soon as possible . . .'

That same evening, contact was made again with the laundry boss via the barber. He could take no more than three people, at the end of the week. Because Mrs. Meyer looked the least Jewish of the four of them, Lotte's mother decided to fetch her straight away by train the following day. She took a broad-brimmed hat with her. They travelled back together like women friends, chatting. The nervous tics on the face of the one, because she had to leave her children behind for a few days, were camouflaged in the shadow cast by the hat. The laundry boss came punctually as arranged, so did fate: The Germans had been there just before him—all three had been picked up the night before.

'My little boy, my *bubele*, take him along with you . . .' Lotte had to hide her desperation; she felt she was being judged by an invisible tribunal. If she had known that the child would be seized she would certainly have taken the risk of the train journey. If he had been picked up on that occasion she would definitely have been guilty, but less so than now: Now she hadn't even tried. This was a lacerating, dead-end thought that went back and forth like a diabolo between guilt and guilt. She was being confronted with an intrinsic, subtle cruelty of an existence that offered her no possibility of a choice. She had not been prepared for life to become so serious. What made it even worse was that no one thought of blaming her at all and she was seemingly struggling with a luxuriously self-indulgent problem in comparison with Ruben Meyer's legitimate sorrow and loneliness. It was decided to be silent about it in front of his mother: What pretense could they come up with for a Jewish mother who was beside herself? They led her to believe that her children had been taken to another address that evening. Every day she complained, 'But couldn't they write a letter all the same?' 'That's still much too dangerous,' her son mollified her with a breaking heart. 'The post is also being intercepted. No one must know where they are.' He walked about the house with drooping shoulders; it exhausted him to lie to his mother every day.

David's father came over carrying a box. Although he had not received any more news from his son he had regained something of the old indestructibility that had characterized the mood of his songs. 'We are also going into hiding,' he said, 'I've got some knick-knacks here . . . some bits and pieces.' He tapped the box. 'We would be very sorry if they were lost. Would it be all right with you if we buried it here in your garden or in the wood?' 'It's fine with me,' said Lotte's father casually, 'but not in the garden, because every inch of it's in use now.' He was alluding to the tobacco plants that he had sown and for which he would also have sacrificed a large part of the kitchen garden if his wife had not set limits. Lotte leaned on the balcony and watched the two men walking into the wood with a shovel—it made her feel uneasy, although she did not know why.

* * *

'YOU ARE STILL as angry as ever,' Anna remarked, assessing Lotte accurately, 'you have been hoarding your rage for almost fifty years. Get it out! I am the obvious person, I offer myself, I've certainly stood in hotter fires before in my life. You have every reason to be angry!'

'I'm not angry at all.' Lotte's hand were clenched into fists on the table. She spread her fingers out hastily. 'I am merely telling you what happened.'

'Why deny you are angry? You have been projecting all that rage onto me for days now, *selbstveurständlich*.' Anna leaned back contentedly. 'I am offering myself, go on, blame me!'

'But I have been doing that continuously,' Lotte sighed, 'and you keep shooting back in defence.'

'I won't anymore, come on. You must first blow off steam . . .'

Lotte looked at her sceptically now that they were onto the therapeutic tack, in this coffee house with big-city allure, among business people and housewives who were calmly sipping their coffee.

'I'll help you a little bit. We'll order another cup of coffee and then I'll tell you something I'm still as deeply ashamed of as ever.'

MARTIN'S LETTERS WERE coming from deeper and deeper south. Movement stopped just before the Caucasus—he had caught a dangerous intestinal infection; Anna received letters written by his comrades. She did not allow herself to be misled by their blatant attempts to disguise the seriousness of his condition with anecdotes and pleasantries; anxiety made her throw herself into her work with monomaniac industry. Then one day his writing appeared on the envelope again. The crisis had been averted with a diet of milk and tomatoes; they were crossing the Ponto-Caspian Plain towards Tagarog. Anna received several letters in close succession, defects in the lorry were dictating the pace, the vehicle was weary of traveling, Russia was too large. Eight days too late they reached the town on the Black Sea from where they would have to fly to Stalingrad for the grand finale. They had not been expected, had been given up for lost, so the lorry's crew remained outside the Grand Plan—they were officially sent on leave. One year after the dress rehearsal, Martin got permission to get married.

'Anna, Anna, come here, there's a telegram for you.' Frau von Garlitz's voice resounded through the passages. One of the cleaning
women from the village, who had been keeping a fattened goose at
the ready for the postponed marriage, hastily slaughtered the main
course of the wedding feast. A pigskin suitcase was packed full of
provisions, another with the wedding dress, necessary papers and
other bits of the trousseau. 'You don't really think it'll happen now?'
Herr von Garlitz smirked. Ottchen, the old butler, took her to the station with the last remaining horse.

The crowded train was about to depart. Ottchen grabbed the cases
from the cart and shoved them inside over the bellies of the soldiers
who lay asleep on the platform. 'Go to the devil with a capital D!'
they protested. Anna exhausted herself apologizing, stepping carefully between them. After a trek along crowded corridors she found a
space in a first-class compartment. The train roared through the night
like a maniac; they halted in the protectorate of Bohemia-Moravia,
orders were yelled, and then they continued to just before Vienna,
where the train had to wait four hours for an air raid alarm to end.

On arrival the pigskin suitcase seemed to have disappeared. A soldier remembered that someone with a suitcase had got off in
Bohemia, perhaps he had scented the goose. In the commotion about
the lost item Anna did not realize that it was Martin touching her discreetly, accompanied by his father. She shrank back. Thousands of
kilometres lay between them; for weeks he had only existed in his
comrades' handwriting, he had been a concentric point drawing all
her feelings to it, a magnet for anxiety and longing. Now that he was
standing there, it was somewhat banal. They greeted each other formally—not here, in front of everyone. In the tram on the way to his
father's house, his clean-shaven neck fascinated her, a vulnerable,
timid neck, so complete despite snow, illness, inhospitability—despite
the war.

They were married in the Karlskirche. The bridegroom had made a
final attempt to get his mother's approval and to persuade her to be
present. 'The day of my life!' he cried, giving her a good shaking. 'It
is the day of my life!' She pressed the tips of her fingers to her temples
and screwed her eyes shut tight. So he left her behind forever in her

domain, where now she only had herself as victim of her domination. Overwhelmed by the scale and excess of the interior of the domed church, Anna let herself be led to the altar. Pillars, wall panels and galleries of pink, brown, sandy and black marble. Behind one of the pillars, she assumed, her future mother-in-law had positioned herself under cover to wait with a great sense of timing for the critical moment to spring out and perform a tragic drama that would make the bedroom scene of a year ago pale in comparison. But the paintings on the ceiling in the dome distracted her, as did the golden rays that came out of a triangle with a Hebrew inscription and angels floating between them above the altar, a window with golden glass through which a bronze glow shone, enveloping the small bridal procession—somewhere in the heavenly spheres there had to be a higher organization, a secret plan laid out in detail, delineating their lives from moment to moment, with a deeper, unfathomable purpose. She looked sideways at the bridegroom's profile—his Adam's apple went up and down as the organ, much ornamented with gold, began a hymn.

After the ceremony was over they floated down the steps between Greek columns, obelisks and two white marble angels holding crosses up to the sky. Anna looked around mechanically. The right one was staring at the horizon full of inner calm, the left one looked more stern—and a snake was entwined around its cross. A feeling she had presumed dead, but that was suddenly brought to life by the ceremony, went right through her. Lotte. Not the stranger who had visited her in Cologne, but Lotte as she was then . . . there she was . . . if anyone must not be absent from the wedding it was she . . . and why shouldn't she be there in the form of an angel, in which case she herself was the other one, with the snake . . . They were looking at the world with marble eyes as though they understood something of it. . . . The bridal gathering had crossed to the other side opposite the Karlskirche; the wind caught hold of her veil—for a moment tangible reality was something hazy and vague to her, through the fine mesh of tulle.

They moved into the apartment of Martin's dead grandmother; the

woman's hairs were still in a comb left behind on the chest of drawers. A house of one's own . . . they turned to each other with an insa-
tiable hunger as though the thousands of lost hours had to be made
up. The city and surroundings were a fitting backdrop for their honeymoon except for one small flaw, when they came across a small
group of people with yellow stars on their coats strolling slowly
down the worn steps in the Mölker Bastei in the old city. Martin went
rigid. With a strange sort of piety he took his arm out of Anna's and
stared at them, much affected, as they passed in silence. She shrunk
more from Martin's involvement than the procession, which was
silently manifesting something that was new and yet immediately
obvious to her. 'Come,' she pleaded, pulling at his sleeve, 'don't look,
please, come on.' He allowed himself to be led away with difficulty.
The whole day she reproached the procession for having appeared in
their way, like a somber admonition.

She wanted to live, to live intensively, in the three weeks that they
were allowed—enough for a whole lifetime.

When she was packing her suitcase listlessly the evening before the
departure, the voices of Martin and his father could be heard faintly
from the next-door room. 'Here, my son, I've bought long under-
trousers for you because it is so cold there, take them.' 'No,' Martin
protested, 'that's not necessary.' 'Why not, Anna won't be around
there.' A short wry laugh. 'It's not that . . .' 'What then?' 'Ach, father,
that cold doesn't mean anything compared to the other dangers we
are exposed to.' 'But surely signal corpsmen run less of a risk. You
don't fight at the front?' Incomprehensible mumbling. Anna brought
her head close to the door-frame. There were partisans everywhere,
she heard Martin saying, especially where you least expected them.
The signal corps was also vulnerable when they were working in a
small group behind the advancing front, placing poles, laying cables,
hauling wires. One day a technician high up a pole couldn't find his
pliers. 'Hang on,' cried Martin, who was supervising the work, 'I'll
just go and get them.' He walked to the lorry, which was hidden
behind pine trees. As he was looking for them he heard short, staccato screaming in the distance, followed by an abrupt silence. He

sneaked back cautiously, seeking cover behind the trees. Where just a moment before his comrades had been busy with hammers and pliers twelve bodies lay with their throats cut between motionless stems of tall grass. The perpetrators had dissolved into air, a hasty, soundless hit-and-run operation beneath a cloudless sky.

Her father-in-law's comment escaped her. Anna sank down on the edge of the bed next to the half-full suitcase. This then was the other side of the blossoming fields of sunflowers, of an untuned grand piano in a farmhouse, of a case of books in a flea market. It happened like that, from one second to the next, at the edge of a soft green pine wood amid blossoming grass. It did not matter whether the landscape was idyllic.

There was no convention for saying goodbye. They stood awkwardly on the platform. Whenever their eyes met they smiled encouragingly. 'We'll see each other soon,' he said with forced lightness. 'My guardian angel never leaves my side, even at forty degrees below zero.' I must imprint his face on my memory, she thought, his face as it is now. I'll take it home with me and make it appear whenever I want, whatever happens. It was painful, all the more so as they lacked the art of separating; no tears, no suitable words, at the most a certain impatience, on both sides, to be released from something that was too large for ordinary mortals. The delayed sorrow only burst out in the train going north. 'My husband . . .'—she apologized to a surprised fellow passenger—'my husband has gone back to Russia.' It was the first time she had designated him with that term. It filled her with a melancholy pride, which was immediately shouted down by the association 'widow, war widow.'

When she got back, the park around the castle was strewn with chestnut leaves. There was a frost at night. Thousands of stars glittered in the blackness; they were keeping out of the war, whether you saw them from Brandenburg or from the tundra. Martin was there; a hundred Russians were here and sleeping like pigs, propped up against each other in the stables. On one particular day two of them managed to escape the permanent guard. At an observation post in the forest, a simple wooden construction with steps and a plank to sit on, they discovered an aged forester intending to shoot a hare for

Christmas. Before he could defend himself with his hunting rifle he had been shot dead. The escapees took the rifle and ammunition. The body was found the same day and the starvation rations of ninety-eight Russians were halved. Two thousand troops from a nearby air-field combed the cordoned-off wood. The two Russians had buried themselves beneath a covering of leaves; the closing circle passed them without seeing them. They had almost made it when one of the soldiers, who kept his pores wide open as well as his eyes, sensed that two eyes were piercing his back and he turned around.

By this time the news had also reached Herr von Garlitz. He hurried to the hunting room, took down a horsewhip and raced through the corridors, hitting out wildly about him with the leather straps, cursing all Slavs. 'Murdering an old man, that scum, I'll beat them to pulp—they are going to suffer!' Anna went into the courtyard, nauseated by the sham masculine courage. The procession arrived there, the two prisoners stumbling at the front. Von Garlitz flew at them with his whip, roaring, two officers held him in check and urged him to calm down. Primitive revenge was not acceptable; officially they had to stick to the rules that applied to prisoners of war. One of them gave the order for the escapees to be freed—hesitantly, in disbelief, they began to walk towards the stables. At that moment he shot them in the back. They fell down silently onto the stones. He turned to von Garlitz: 'Shot dead while escaping.'

The incident caused resentment among the Russian prisoners. From then on Frau von Garlitz assigned personal escorts for Anna and the other members of staff whenever they went for walks in the woods. Anna brushed aside the surveillance; she was not afraid. In her view there was merely a dreadful misunderstanding; through an absurd, senseless exchange, Russian men had ended up in Germany and Germans in Russia. While Russian prisoners waited in frustration and resignation, somewhere in the heart of their native country their fellow countrymen were engaged in a bitter struggle against a backdrop of snow-covered ruins with icicles in the burnt-out windows—there were deaths on a huge scale in order to take one house, one barn, one wall. The fate of the whole world seemed to hang on the outcome of this icy battle in a slowly capsizing town.

The news that Stalingrad had held firm got through to the stables faster than the castle, where the raw facts were camouflaged in euphemism: we are returning home. The significant turning point had arrived. The castle, restored from the rafters to the cellars, prepared itself to receive guests on its shining polished parquet floors, between its white-painted walls in the comfortable warmth of the ever-burning stoves: old Prussian nobility who were also going to make a contribution to history. Anna, averse to interest in strategic developments, averse to political opinions, had but one burning desire: that he emerge unscathed from the gunsmoke.

LOTTE STARED OUTSIDE, her gaze glanced off one of the granite church walls. 'We were putting our lives at risk for those whom you yourself did not even wish to look at . . .' she said incredulously.

'Now you see it.' Anna nodded. 'That's how it was. I am not a bit better or worse than most people. For a whole year I had anxiously expected news of his death, now he was there in a living body for three whole weeks. Then it was back to the beginning again. All I had was that little bit of life we had been allowed. But if I had gone to the Mölker Bastei alone I certainly would have seen them, believe me. I had probably asked myself painful questions, but that bit of luck, you understand, dominated everything at that moment.'

'That's the way you always have an excuse for yourself,' said Lotte bitterly. 'But all of you were without pity for the Jews.'

'Hold on with that "all of you" . . . that little bit of luck was all I had, I had the right to it, I think, I had to make do with it for the rest of my life.'

The sun broke through, a wintry white ray shone on their hands— on a spreading network of blue veins. Skin, blood vessels, muscles— fragile and mortal.

'Here I believe we have the kernel of our disunity' said Anna pensively, 'and we have arrived at the cause of your rage.'

'Will you leave off "my rage" as something to be regarded as constructive, which will transform itself into forgiveness if I air it sufficiently.'

'Forgiveness doesn't concern me,' Anna said sharply. 'I haven't done anything wrong.'

'Let's drop it, shall we,' Lotte sighed, overwhelmed by a feeling of predictability, 'things are simply as they are now. You mentioned Stalingrad. I still well remember how relieved we were . . . our euphoria . . . and yet afterwards it became really difficult'

PAPA STALIN WAS not going to let himself be pushed aside just like that. The Allies had swept North Africa clean and marched off to Italy. For a short time they lived under the illusion that it was merely a question of waiting and persevering. The Frinkel family had returned in a overwrought state, having narrowly escaped two raids and forty-eight cats. At each meal the animals ate with them as full companions at table; the Noteboom ladies placed pieces of raw heart between their teeth so that the cats, decoratively standing on their hind legs, could tug them away. Excessive maternal love and spoiling had turned them into selfish nest-soilers who began to miaow *en masse* when Max and his son did their daily finger exercises.

Since Lotte had refused to register with the Nazi Department of Culture as a member of the radio choir, singing had officially ended too, and she became an essential cog in the fourteen-person giant household. Life became increasingly complicated not only in a practical sense but also in the abstract. From then on anxiety was permanently present, slumbering, subcutaneous. A sudden silence, a strange noise, hugely swaying treetops, rumbling in the distance, a vague rumour—a trifle was sufficient to inflame it. It could happen at any minute, no particular moment was in principle unsuitable. No one could imagine it yet they imagined it, their powers of imagination forcing them to confront the unthinkable, the unbearable. Anxiety drove the Meyers and the Frinkels into the woods on a false alarm, winter coats hastily thrown over their pyjamas. They lay for hours in a wet ditch beneath layers of overhanging spruce branches; in the distance there were voices and dogs barking. Mrs. Meyer chewed the soggy tails of her fox stole, Max Frinkel massaged his finger joints to keep the moisture from affecting them. Eventually the master of the house constructed a more refined hiding place in a deep built-in cupboard in his bedroom. He reduced the cupboard to a hole in the wall and hung a full-length mirror in front of it. Via a cable, the door clicked open and closed from the inside after the hatch was shut. Everyone could fit in, they dived through their own mirror image into the hole—an ambiguous form of existence and non-existence. Lotte's mother shoved her dressing table in front of it, purple and dark red perfume bottles sparkled attractively on it. From then on Mrs. Meyer would only sleep in the cupboard; from their bed they could hear her crying and praying in a strange key.

It was not easy to call a halt to the constant expansion of the household. For example, the doorbell rang; Lotte was alone at home—except for five invisible, inaudible personages who were playing whist upstairs. A young man with short red hair was at the door, his right hand on the shoulder of a small, very old man wearing a black hat, who raised his wrinkled face expectantly to Lotte. 'I've come to bring the father-in-law of Mr. Bohjul of the gramophone record shop,' the young man declared. Mr. Bohjul had been arrested, he explained, while his wife and daughter were in Amsterdam. Someone had caught up with them at the station and warned them not to go home. Bohjul had managed to smuggle the message out of the police station that his father-in-law was still in the attic and undiscovered. He advised the old man to go to a good client of his, more a friend actually, who would certainly be able to find accommodation: Lotte's father.

'He's not in,' she said, 'I can't decide on my own initiative.' She stood holding the door. No one said more; they looked at each other shyly. It seemed as though the old man, in his total dependency, was the only survivor of a catastrophe, as though he had been deemed too small and too light to go under with the others. Suddenly she was ashamed of her reticence. 'You can wait for him inside,' she said, opening the door wider. She led them to the dining room. The old man waited meekly, his hat on his knees, his white eyebrows curling downwards over his deep set eyes. His companion took in the surroundings as though he were sitting in a waiting room. When her father got home he scowled at them with a frown until the name Bohjul was mentioned—ah, the owner of the record business where he was one of the family, how many heated discussions they had had about specific recordings. Indeed he had certainly once seen his father-in-law—Grandfather Tak—shuffling through the shop. Of course he would do his best to find him a good address. 'A propos . . .' he said, turning to the old man in surprise, 'I don't understand, your son-in-law is a Persian Jew, isn't he? I have nothing to fear, he said to me last time, because Germany is not at war with Persia; we can go about freely.' 'Don't ask me,' sighed the other. 'Until 1914 the world could still be understood by an ordinary person . . . Since then it has gone over my head . . .' 'Hat,' his guide teased him, pointing wryly to the black hat that lay in his lap, now suddenly like a *corpus delicti* that had brought about the loss of the former world.

The TB house was patched up provisionally. Because his stay was temporary he could not know that he was not the only one in hiding. When the sun shone he sat dreaming on a rickety folding chair, an amber pipe in the corner of his mouth. Lotte brought him his meals. He told her about the diamond-cutting business, long ago, when the world was still worth living in. His white hair, in which the sun spun an aura of better times, his defeatism, his transparent skin—she felt despondently as if he had just popped over from death to cast a surprised glance at chaos, in the safe knowledge that he could go back whenever he wished. There was no success at finding him another address; new categories were going into hiding: students, soldiers at risk of becoming prisoners of war, men who wanted to avoid forced labour in German industry. Theo de Zwaan joined the people in hiding—as did Ernst Goudriaan soon afterwards, who was so endearing in his heroic efforts to hide his anxiety that Lotte's mother empathized with him. He was put up with Grandfather Tak; the more frivolous than solid TB house that squeaked in the wind was enlarged with a stylish extension, and there he got on with his violin making, with a view onto a field of blooming tobacco plants. Koen had to hide, too, because he had reached the age for military service. His temperament did not let him wait quietly at home until the war ended. He slipped out of the house onto the road, got picked up and taken to Amersfoort. At the end of a column of randomly captured fellow victims who had been picked up off the street, he was walking in the twilight towards an unknown destiny. The road was narrow; unseen he slid sideways into a porch and pushed backwards against the door, knocking on the wood with his knuckles. 'Open up, open up,' he pleaded. 'Are you a Catholic?' 'No,' he moaned. 'Pass on then,' said the voice.

They were taken to a barracks near Assen, where a plague of lice was in charge. Disgusted by the millions of crawling insects, he could not get any sleep. He slipped outside and gently dozed off, sitting against a wall. At the crack of dawn he was awakened by a wood-fuelled post-van driving in through the barrack gates. The postman climbed out and slowly emptied the letter box, then reversed and turned, the chimney smoking. The following day, the instant the man climbed back behind the wheel, Koen opened the back doors and hoisted himself in among the mailbags. He emerged at the ferry over the IJssel. The postman blanched. Although he was impressed with Koen's ability to improvise, he was not inclined to take this unortho-dox postal parcel further with him across the Ijssel. 'Boy, I absolutely cannot do that,' he complained, 'it is much too dangerous.' 'Hide me under the pile of wood,' Koen suggested. The official had to give in in the face of so much ingenuity. 'I must be absolutely mad,' he growled, carefully covering over the stowaway with sawn fruit-tree logs. Koen returned home with undiminished self-confidence. His mother took him in her arms after two sleepless nights, trembling with fatigue and relief. He freed himself from her embrace to make a sudden clothes inspection, for fear that he in turn had brought a stowaway with him from the barracks.

While Grandfather Tak took root between the apple trees and the tobacco plants and dreamed of his dead wife, beneath her photo-graph pinned up on the wall with a rusty drawing pin, his daughter and granddaughter were adrift. After rambling from address to address the latter had joined her fiancé, who was in hiding some-where in the Beemster, and the former arrived in a provocative tailor-made suit one summer evening—from no one knew where—looking for her father. Lotte's mother smelled trouble instantly. Her husband was defenseless from the first glance. He yielded to Mrs. Bohjul's request to be allowed to stay, no match for the transparent tempting manoeuvres, of which a pouting mouth painted red was the strongest card. She was given a bed in Jet and Lotte's room; from then on they slept in an atmosphere saturated with cigarette smoke and exotic perfumes. Many different dresses with low-cut decolletages were draped over the beds and on chairs, many different necklaces were conjured out of a jewel case inlaid with mother of pearl. If she was deprived of attention she collapsed; she flourished on admiration—everyone was exhausted from having to provide her with more of what she needed for peace and quiet. No one type of pastime could occupy her for longer than five minutes. She walked back and forth like a caged panther, the click of her nail scissors disturbed the others reading, playing cards, doing crossword puzzles. It was unbelievable that she was the daughter of the man in the orchard, who smoked his pipe in meditative tranquillity and grew cress in a narrow strip along the sagging terrace.

In the evenings when the horsehair curtains had been closed they all came downstairs to eat at two long tables. Lotte's mother did her best within the restrictions to put kosher meals on the table. Afterwards Max Frinkel sometime played a virtuoso piece by Paganini; his son took revenge with a melting gypsy song. Flora Bohjul sang a popular American song, in an exaggeratedly jazzy way. Finally all eyes as usual turned to Lotte who bit her lip and shook her head. To compensate, Mrs. Meyer recited a poem. The favorite was an iambic elegy about a mother who had to sell everything she possessed in order to fill her childrens' stomachs. The only thing left to pawn was the youngest daughter's doll, which she had with her day and night. The children were crazy about this drama, the adults hoped it would not prove prophetic.

They listened to Radio Orange and the BBC. Since May, when all radio sets had had to be handed in, they managed with a receiver improvised by Lotte's father; it had no case but it had very clear reception. They could hear the queen breathing during her broadcasts in London. There was a constant hunger for reliable information. Illegal newspapers and pamphlets went from hand to hand, someone read a bit out of an article now and then. 'What's this . . .' said Koen in amazement. 'Listen . . .' Without thinking he read out a piece from

Het Parool that mentioned the existence of gas chambers where 'captive opponents' were driven inside naked and gassed under the impression that they were entering a bathroom. The capacity of those gas chambers would soon be increased from two hundred to a thousand persons. Mrs. Meyer burst out in desperate sobbing; Ruben leaned over her and squeezed her hands fiercely in a clumsy attempt to comfort her. Lotte's mother cast a devastated look at Koen, who slowly realized what he had done. The news was immediately made light of. Of course it was no more than a sensational story from the overactive journalists' distorted fantasies. Bram Frinkel threw his napkin on the table and went to the door, his head lowered between his shoulders. With the handle in his hand he turned round and said to Koen with a grin, 'Perhaps you'll want to be the chosen people for the next two thousand years.'

6

THE BENEFICIAL EFFECTS of the peat treatments, carbonated baths and underwater massages were gradually becoming apparent. During the first week of the cure guests usually had to struggle with an unfathomable weariness bordering on depression, caused by the release of obstructions in the joints and poisonous materials stored up in the adipose tissues. For the two sisters there were in addition the toxins released during their talks, along with the obstructions in their relationship and their memories, which were being put to severe test. But usually a turning point was reached halfway through the treatment. As each movement was no longer plagued by pain, patients moved more easily, their blood flowed more freely, breathing became deeper. Anna and Lotte experienced some of this effect, too. They were both reviving physically, only their spirits were lagging behind, but then they were undergoing a quite different cure, the therapeutic effect of which was much less certain. They left the Thermal Institute after a morning of intensive bathing; before commencing the risky descent of the steps, they looked at the sky, which was sheer blue over the green dome of the Heures Claires hotel. The snow had melted to a grey slush. The two stone female figures that had guarded the entrance to the Institute since its construction in 1864—one with a staff in her hand and a fish at her feet, the other holding a small harp with a fallen pitcher at her feet, with water flowing out of it—jumped off their plinths, strolled nimbly down the steps and crossed the road to the Place Royal. They stood with amusement next to a *fin de siècle* style square kiosk. One raised her staff and pointed it at one of the four sides, on which was written:

Quand il est midi à Spa il est:

> 13 heures à Berlin, Rome, Kinshasa
> 14 heures à Moscou, Ankara, Lumumbashi
> 15 heures à Bagdad
> 19 heures à Singapore
> 7 heures à New York

The other played a few chords on her harp and sang in a hoarse voice '... the mystery of simultaneity, when one lunches in Rome, one dines in Singapore ... while bombs rain on Berlin, breakfast is being prepared in New York ...' The words became soap bubbles that drifted over the Place Royale. Spring water flowed out of the pitcher, or was it melted snow—it flowed away over the Rue Royale and Avenue Reine Astrid. Lotte and Anna took each other's arm as they crossed the wet road, the water lapping inside their shoes. They passed a simple restaurant and decided to go in—when one break- fasted in New York, one lunched in Spa.

MARTIN'S COMPANY HAD been recalled from Russia to construct the air defences around Berlin. From then on he spent the weekends with Anna—something like married life was under way at last. She watched longingly for the first signs of pregnancy. In early autumn she had had an operation; it now remained to be seen whether they had succeeded in correcting the damage done at an earlier stage by hauling muck carts and pig feed. A child seemed the only thing, the most important thing she had been missing up to now. She herself would be born again with the birth of a child, the youth of her child would wash away her own youth. Her child would lack nothing. A child would also replace her lost sister, a child would reconcile her with everything that had gone wrong.

There was an extensive lake in the wood. On the banks were rowing boats in bright Viking colours with which to go over to an oval island. Hidden there, behind the willows and grey birches, was a wooden house with a pitched roof that had belonged to the castle for centuries, just like the lake and wood. Frau von Garlitz gave Anna the key. In sunny weather she strolled to the lake with Martin, they tied the boats together and rowed to the island towing the whole fleet so that they would not be disturbed by unexpected visits. They swam, lay in the sun in the tall grass, slept in the house that smelled of sun-baked wood and marsh spirits who, when the wind rose at night, moaned and creaked between the planks. The war was far away and unreal. Wind, the gabbling of geese, croaking frogs, instead of air raid sirens and the *Volksempfänger* blaring. At night as she listened to his breathing, it seemed miraculous that he was lying beside her. An invisible hand had led him through Russia to safety three times and had guarded him from stealthy murderers, freezing, fatal illness, because he had to be preserved for her. Their being together on this island in space and time seemed something sacrosanct to her, a form of being chosen. Through the window she saw the moon reflected in the water behind swaying willow branches—the island was drifting in the lake and time stood still. On Sunday afternoons the fleet returned in the opposite direction again. The walk back through the wood was the last thing they shared; Martin went to the barracks, Anna stepped through the gate into her old life.

At the castle, on behalf of the state, they took in five housekeeping students who had to be trained. They were placed in Anna's charge. Since the castle and housekeeping had undergone a metamorphosis under her direction Frau von Garlitz had had unbounded faith in her. And again Martin was to everyone's taste—when he stayed at the castle the trainees put on their best aprons. Anna was beside herself when she realized that their preening coincided with his visits. 'Those aprons,' she cried, 'are only for serving in. We haven't got enough soap powder to wash them if you wear them meanwhile.' Sniggering—with their female instinct they had correctly seen through her motive—they changed out of the aprons. From the kitchen window one Sunday Anna saw Martin give one of the girls a present in the garden before he left. 'What was it,' she asked, after she had waved him goodbye, 'that you received from my husband?' The girl gave her a brief guilty look. 'Well?' Anna insisted, grabbing her by the shoulder. 'I can't let on.' 'Tell me.' 'It is a present for you for Christmas.' 'Now? In August?' She nodded. 'In case your husband is stationed somewhere else at Christmas and can't come here to you. . . .' Anna looked at her in disbelief. In the girl's eyes she saw indignation and contempt because she had forced her to divulge the secret and because of the insinuation that lay behind it. Piqued, she walked away leaving Anna alone with her authority—at the mercy of shame and emotion, which the shame magnified, that Martin, now, in the middle of summer, was already attending to how he could comfort her in six months, at Christmas.

Activity picked up at the castle. The refurbished rooms were continuously filled with guests—highly placed officers came there to have a breathing space between missions. After dinner they retired to the library, leaving the ladies behind in the salon in the care of Frau von Garlitz, who was friendly, as always, elegant and entertaining, as though the war and her husband's promiscuity had nothing to do with her. In the corridors it was whispered that he had had an affair with Petra von Willersleben, the daughter of an industrialist who had had a meteoric career in the army. Since he had dislocated his knee in the Polish campaign, von Garlitz performed a vague staff function, for which he regularly had to go to Brussels. Anna could not imagine that this society figure could be trusted in the army with an important task since he ran his factory in Cologne by galloping round it like a hussar—this smart aleck who could not actually do anything and was no good for anything but constantly gave the impression that he was terrific. Mysteriously he seemed to succeed in maintaining high-level contacts. Lineage and money, she muttered to herself, that's how you get on in the world instead of by working hard.

Recklessly, von Garlitz officially invited his lover to a dinner. She infiltrated herself into his house under the camouflage of her weighty father. She wore a provocative dress to intimidate his wife. Anna served at table with her trainees. Among the guests she only knew Frau Ketteler, an aunt of Herr von Garlitz, who lived in the district and visited regularly. A woman of indefinite age, never married, she lived with a handful of staff in a villa that was hidden from view by tall spruces. Before the war she had had a stable full of sleek thoroughbreds, the cleaning women related; she loved to make the woods unsafe by riding a black stallion through there at a gallop, a hunting rifle on a leather strap on her back. Since the horses had been requisitioned, she indulged in long walks with her dog, a sturdy sheepdog who obeyed her alone. It seemed that she had given her fallow maternal instinct full vent with respect to her nephew since his birth—she adored him, blind to his shortcomings, and still tried to mother him from afar.

Anna followed the developments at table in snatches as she went to and fro with crockery and glasses. Herr von Garlitz, as Fräulein von Willersleben's host, concerned himself courteously with her. The conversation dealt with painting: nudes by Adolph Ziegler and Ivo Saliger. She seemed to have studied art history in Berlin; he feigned surprise and amazement, asking her innumerable questions, to give his wife on the other side of the table the impression that his table companion was a perfect stranger to him. The latter nimbly played along with the game—she got them both excited, it was almost as though they were making love, via painting, in front of Frau von Garlitz's eyes. She observed the performance coolly for a while, having known about the affair for a long time, as everyone did, until she had had enough of the role of naive, deceived wife and spectator that had been imposed on her in the presence of a tableful of guests. With control she stood up, raised the glass of red wine that Anna had just refilled, as though she were going to make a speech, and flung the contents in her husband's face. Fräulein von Willersleben jumped up with shocked cries, worried that some had splashed onto her dress. At the same time Frau Ketteler rushed round from the other side of the table to dab her nephew's face with her napkin in order to wipe away the scandal as quickly as possible. Anna breathed again. The exasperated tension she had felt, because von Garlitz apparently did not find it sufficient to cheat on his wife, but also took further perverse pleasure in belittling and provoking her, flowed away. She slipped out of the dining room with an empty dish, laughing at the grotesque helpfulness of his aunt.

The same evening Frau von Garlitz had herself taken to the station by horse and carriage. She disappeared without ceremony, leaving the company behind in bewilderment. Von Garlitz was filled with unspoken reproaches. He had to call his spouse, their hostess, the mother of his children, to order—a man at his level, with his background, status, he had to bring his wife to heel. After all, they weren't gypsies, or Slavs, who dissolutely let themselves be carried away by their emotions. A few days later he fell ill. Hurt pride, remorse, shame? At night the fever crept up high; he lay between the soaking sheets, sweating and delirious. Anna sat by his bed, eager to adopt the guise of avenging goddess. She moistened his forehead and temples with wet facecloths; she gave him drinks and whispered him to sleep with soothing words. But when the fever began to subside she told him what a *Schwein* he was. 'You can count yourself lucky to have a wife like that,' she said contemptuously. He had no strength to retort; like a dying front-line soldier he lay on the pillows, with swollen eyelids and a stubble beard. Mercilessly she continued. 'A woman with so much style, charm, character! Get it into your head once and for all, you've got the time to do so now.' He stared at her with the feverish eyes of a sick child being told a cruel fairy tale, with the difference that he was being accused of identifying with the monster, the dragon, instead of the hero.

After two weeks Frau von Garlitz returned home, a model of aristocratic self-control through which a touch of cynicism shimmered. A sigh of relief was breathed; this was no time for marital conflicts that, however passionate, paled next to that single gigantic conflict in which the whole population was involved. Martin tried all month to get long leave to take Anna to Vienna, even if it was only for two weeks, to be able to live as husband and wife in their own home, which they only knew from their honeymoon. But his ardent attempts came to nothing. There seemed to be only one possibility for getting long leave: to declare himself prepared to go on a short offi- cers' training course. Although the thought of promotion in the army disgusted him, he finally succumbed out of longing for Vienna and for a little shred of freedom, just to be able to escape from the mili- tary treadmill of total availability and self-denial that had already been going on relentlessly for four years, in the interests of a war that he could do without. He was stationed at a junior officers' school in Berlin-Spandau. During the course he lived shut off from the outside world. On the day he was to be discharged, Anna waited for him at the gate, suitcase in hand. 'Who are you?' The sentry stepped forward quickly, 'May I see your papers?' 'I've come to fetch my husband, Martin Grosalie,' said Anna, offended at so much suspicion. 'He goes on leave today.' The sentry blanched. 'Oh, God, please don't go in.' She put her suitcase down and looked at him affably. 'They are being punished,' the soldier whispered, shyly scratching behind his ear. After some hesitation he explained what had happened. The group was already standing in the courtyard, ready to depart, with one foot already outside the gate, as it were. They had to take their leave with an enthusiastic 'Heil Hitler!' in unison. In the commandant's opinion it sounded too weak. 'Louder!' he cried. The company repeated the obligatory salute once more without conviction but with more vol- ume. 'Louder!' roared the commandant as though his honour was at stake, next to that of his Führer. 'Heil Hitler' . . . It was still too low, they were exactly like a gramophone record that will not spin at full speed. 'We'll just see once more whether you are going to go home today!' They had to change, pack the clothes in their lockers, turn the key. Then they were chased outside, left, right, bend knees, crawl on the ground in the mud. One lesson in humiliation and humility that they would remember as long as the war lasted. 'Please,' whispered the sentry, 'come back in an hour and make out as though you don't know anything about it. They are ashamed, all of them.' Anna glanced at the emphatically closed gate behind which Martin was crawling in the Berlin mud, mud of the Thousand-Year Reich, for which he had to be prepared to sacrifice his life, which was also her life. She picked up the suitcase and went into a street at random and then other random streets, which were neither friendly nor hostile but indifferent. When she got back to the barracks he was already waiting for her, immaculate, glistening, alert—a wonderful *tabula rasa*. 'You're late,' he said, surprised. He made no mention of the punishment session. They had become well-versed in denying the war in each other's presence, like superior outsiders, deaf to the drum roll, blind to the lightning.

After their stay in Vienna he was posted to Dresden. It was autumn. Anna, who had already sewn and knitted a suitcase full of baby clothes, was still not pregnant—Hannelore was. She had got married in the spring and since then had been living in Ludwigslust in Mecklenburg, from where she kept up a nostalgic correspondence with Anna. Frau von Garlitz, who sympathized with the ups and downs of her staff, prepared a parcel of fortifying foods for the welfare of the mother-to-be, and sent Anna with it to Ludwigslust. Once again she was sitting in a train to Berlin with a suitcase. Involuntarily she thought back to the day she had travelled to Cologne in a trench coat with a hunting hat on, her possessions in a cardboard box. She felt slightly ashamed as she thought back to her provincial naiveté, the long way she still had to go then, from pig muck to table silver on damask. She jerked out of her reverie as the train slowed down abruptly and stopped. Then it continued wearily on until they were riding into Berlin with jolts and blasts. A grey steel wall rose up outside the windows of the compartments, without beginning or end, like the precursor of a tunnel. But the wall was moving . . . it seemed to be made of smoke, grit, thick smoke. The train rolled backwards, then it drove hesitatingly into the station. Anna got out, still used to the unblemished neutral atmosphere inside the compartment.

It happened to her at that moment, just as it did to hundreds of fellow passengers: as soon as they set foot on the platform their reflexes took control of their sense of direction, they scattered, everything around them was on fire, the roof was cracking as though it would give way at any moment. Someone pulled her away from collapsing wood or steel, the smoke stung her eyes, her throat, she walked blindly away from the fire . . . air raid warning, someone pushed her into a shelter. There she became part of a trembling, sweating tangle that was listening, huddled together, to the screaming and rumbling; the ground shook, the tangle shuddered with it, buildings, trains, people, everything would perish into dust, a ridiculous, communal downfall without meaning. For a suitcase of sausage and salt pork.

It took three days and nights to reach Spandau in the west from the eastern part of the city where she had arrived. Three days and nights in an inferno, sometimes dragged into shelters at the very last moment by someone whose face she never got to see. Someone gave her something to drink, she stumbled onwards, tripped over an electricity cable, a wall collapsed somewhere, she cowered, too tired to be afraid. Then it was night again, wailing sirens, a shelter, dozing off with exhaustion, going on further through the stage set of a horror opera, somebody gave her something to eat. Berlin-Spandau? Always the same question in the chaos—she was standing on a disintegrating map whose edges were being incinerated. Did Spandau still exist or was she on the way to a smoking heap of rubble? Why did the bombing go on day and night—did Berlin, did Germany have to be removed from the face of the earth?

Suddenly she seemed to find herself at Spandau station with her scorched suitcase. It was still there; a bulging train was on the point of departing for Mecklenburg. Someone lifted her up and shoved her inside through the window, followed by the suitcase. The train started off immediately. Dazed, she sat down on her suitcase. She seemed to have survived; it left her feeling indifferent. She made the journey in a state of semi-consciousness—she could not fall over, propped up as she was between other overtired bodies. They reached Ludwigslust in the middle of the night; she was the only one who got off. She wobbled towards the vague silhouette of a house in the pitch dark. Her trembling hand found the bell with difficulty. A light went on in the passage, the door was opened, someone appeared on the threshold, saw what was standing on the step and closed the door in shock. And she was in the dark again, collapsing from exhaustion. It was cold. A primitive fear crept over her, stronger than during the bombing, direct and overwhelming—the anxiety of being refused, shut out forever like a piece of dirt, like a creature that (an orphan who) did not deserve to live. She began to beat on the door in agitation. 'I come from Berlin, please . . .' she moaned. 'Open the door. I only want to sleep, please . . .' But nothing happened, the house shunned her. 'This is a person, a decent person, who only wants to sleep!' Beneath her hammering fist the door opened slowly. A blanket lay on the tiled floor in the passage. She stumbled in, fell down onto it and slept without a glance at her slow-witted benefactor. The following day she had just enough strength to complete her mission. Unrecognisable in a disguise of soot, scratches and tears, she handed over the suitcase to Hannelore, who was oblivious to bombing raids, floating on her pink cloud of blissful waiting. In her spotless home, organized for the coming event, the sausages, pork and hams were a perverse, animal element, emerging unviolated from the suitcase—in honour of the new life, stained by death. Anna looked at it and burst out in a joyless, overwrought laugh.

'ACH, BERLIN . . .' ANNA sighed. 'I happened to be there a couple of years ago with a friend. We rode through the city on a bus, she suddenly cried, "Look, the Anhalter Station!" I saw a splendidly restored station, but a second later it was on fire. It was burning before my eyes—just like then—and everything caved in. "Is anything the matter?" my friend asked. I had a light-headed feeling, hissing in my ears. "It's on fire!" I cried in a panic. It was the first time that I'd remembered it—I hadn't thought about it ever again, it was so awful. I had suppressed it for forty-five years.'

'How is it possible,' said Lotte, pointing at Anna with a piece of Ardennes ham on the end of her fork, 'that they could send you into a burning city with a suitcase of meat?'

'Frau von Garlitz didn't know; none of us knew. It was the first big bombing raid on Berlin, at the end of November. Your liberators lit up their Christmas trees above the city and threw their carpet bombs down below. Systematically, no square metre was to be spared. But something always remains standing . . . I, for example.'

Lotte stopped chewing at the cynical 'your liberators.' However hard she tried to imagine a burning Berlin, Rotterdam always appeared, or London. Berlin remained abstract, a point on a map.

'Martin wrote a letter to Frau von Garlitz: "I forbid you to send my wife out in such circumstances."' Anna laughed. 'But those were different times. The longer the war lasted the more important food became.'

Lotte endorsed this with a full mouth, in front of a salad so richly garnished that someone could have lived off it for a whole week in the hunger winter.

LOTTE HAD NOT yet got down to guilty feelings, swallowed up by the Moloch of housekeeping. Endless stirring of buttermilk porridge in gargantuan pans; next to them stood buckets steaming with washing; two meters farther on the iron was glowing ready. The linchpin of the constantly expanding family was ill; a tumour had been discovered in her uterus, which had to be removed immediately. Before the operation she took her three daughters—Marie, Jet, Lotte—to one side. 'You must promise me something—if anything goes wrong with the operation. . . . and I should suddenly not be there any more . . . then you will take over the care of the people in hiding. I'm worried that Pa is in a state where he could put them all out on the street in a bad mood. He threatened it again last time . . . it's getting too much for him . . .' She looked pointedly at them one by one, almost solemnly. 'I have calmed him down again . . . managed to conceal his attacks from everyone . . . They shouldn't have to put up with that extra strain . . .'

They stared at her in shock. The thought alone took their breath away. All three immediately understood that their mother's anxiety was far from unwarranted. They had known him a long time. At certain times he needed rows, preferably at the expense of his greatest competitors, the children. Why not one day at the expense of the people in hiding? Of course they were his, too, but his position was ambivalent in relation to them. When an appeal had been made to him on their arrival, he could not permit himself to refuse. Didn't he have a name to keep up? As a music lover—the Frinkels, Grandfather Tak, Ernst Goudriaan? As a Communist—Leon Stein? A pure impulse from the heart, which couldn't be helped—as with their

mother—was out of the question for him, although he had his sentimental moods, of course, provided he had the exact background
music to help him.

When the patient came round from the anaesthesia, Jet, Lotte and
their father were standing on either side of the bed. She lay between the
sheets, pale and worryingly delicate, the chestnut brown hair with grey
streaks in it, dull on the pillow. Her gaze was muzzy, as though she still
dwelt in hazy spheres of non-existence. She grasped her husband's
hand with unexpected strength. 'Take good care of . . . of everyone,'
she whispered. It was something between a plea and a command. Lotte
walked round the bed and stood next to her father and nodded on his
behalf, her eyes shut tightly, as though presenting a guarantee of everyone's safety from the notorious mood swings of the master of the
house. He stood in anguish beside the bed, waiting until he could hon-
ourably escape from the hospital, the death palace stinking of ether,
where he had only turned up in an act of exceptional self-sacrifice.

When she came home she was a shadow of her former self. She had
lost a great deal of weight. Nothing seemed to remain of her original
vitality, that mysterious primeval strength. With a forced laugh she
made her way through the room, seeking support from the edges of
the table and the arms of the chairs. Her husband put on Gluck's
Orfeo for her, thrilled that his Eurydice had indeed returned from the
underworld, but that was his only contribution to her recovery.

Eefje had received a piece of blue velvet on her birthday, to make
dolls' clothes. She had hidden the valuable gift deep in a secret
drawer in her bedroom. One day she opened the drawer and grasped
thin air. She looked in the other drawers with a thudding heart, the
whole bedroom, the house. She did the rounds of all the residents,
crying in disbelief and disappointment. 'Have you seen my material?' became a rhetorical question that seemed to symbolize everything about the lack of things because of the shortages. Eventually
she tossed back her plaits and pushed down the door handle of a
room she had not so far included in her search, because the prohibi-
tion on entering had been strictly maintained for years, even in the
war: her father's electro-technical sanctuary. From the threshold she
looked with bewilderment at the still-life on the workbench.

Between fittings, screws, lamps, flex and fuses, lay a packet of butter, like a pheasant by a seventeenth-century master, amid fresh bread, cheese and liver. He looked up, wiping the crumbs from his mouth, trapped. With his mouth full he shouted: 'How did you get it into your head to come in here just like that?' Hastily he began to pack the bread and cheese away. 'But I am looking for my velvet material,' she whimpered. Right opposite her on the wall hung a map of the world with little flags indicating the Allies' progress. The map was mounted on blue velvet fixed to the wall with tacks. 'My material, my material . . .' she pointed in astonishment. Her father followed her trembling finger with raised eyebrows. Was a more glorious purpose conceivable for a piece of material than to serve as the background for the Allied victories? She turned her back on him and ran down stairs sniffing. She told Jet and Lotte, busy in the kitchen, what she had seen, tripping over her words, not realizing that the greater crime was not pinching her material but the secret enjoyment of bread and butter and cheese while everyone else went hungry.

The origin of these delicacies was cleared up at the next hospital checkup when Lotte accompanied her mother, and the doctor took her aside to express his surprise and concern about the patient's extreme underweight—after all, her husband had taken away a stamped card authorizing extra food rations on the day he had fetched her. It was almost unbearable to know this; she confided to Jet but kept it a careful secret from everyone else. It had a paralysing effect on them both. It is true they had known that the boundaries of his egoism were flexible and reacted seismographically to his tempers and needs, but that there seemed to be no boundaries at all was so shocking that it went beyond their comprehension.

'I'll go and get the rest of the coupons,' said Lotte, 'at least if there are any left.' For the first time she felt a crack in her self-control. Calm thoughts, tactical strategies became impossible. She was not herself anymore, in a manner of speaking, or perhaps at last she was now herself. Grimly she set off upstairs, invaded his sanctuary without knocking. There he sat. . . . He was smoking a home-grown cigarette and looked up interrupted from reading an underground newspaper spread open on the workbench. It seemed as though two broken wires at the top of her skull made contact . . . as though twenty-one years had evaporated. She saw a dark figure standing in the doorway of a classroom, his black wings tightly folded. 'How dare you'—his voice intoned in the distance—'. . . to two children who are weaker than you. . . .' It was merely a glimpse, an echo that came and disappeared, but left a strong emotion behind it. 'How dare you . . .' she said with a trembling voice, 'to Mother, who is so weak. . . .'

'Just come in once again,' he said, 'and knock first.' There was a short circuit between the two wires. She took a step forward and held out her hand ostentatiously. 'Give me the rest of the coupons that were meant for Mother.' Raising her voice she added: 'Immediately!' He began to laugh in disbelief. 'Where in God's name did you . . .' he said stupidly. 'You know very well what I am talking about.' She wanted to injure him as he sat there and played the innocent—too cowardly to come out with it. But her contempt was even greater than her hate. This had to be settled quickly and efficiently; then she would have nothing more to do with it. The map hung behind him framed in blue velvet. Little flags everywhere, stubbornly stuck into it as though they concerned personal victories. Germany, flag-free, apparently had nothing to do with the war. Germany was a vacuum, an absorbent hole into which her gaze disappeared. How many ways were there for you to hate yourself?

He laughed in her face. 'Give those coupons back,' she said icily, 'otherwise I'll tell everyone what a scoundrel you are.' The grin disappeared from his face. He stared at her as though he was seeing her for the first time, overwhelmed, still not ready to believe it. Then the realization began to move up his neck in a red flush; angrily he pulled open a drawer beneath the workbench, rummaged about randomly in it and pulled out a mostly used sheet of coupons. He came at her with it threateningly. Lotte did not move a muscle and stood where she was—she felt no trace of fear; if he asked for it she would squash him like a flea. He pushed the sheet of paper into her hand angrily. 'A proper Kraut . . .' he hissed, 'as you see, after all those years . . . still a proper Kraut.' She had just enough strength to get to her bedroom, apparently composed. In a false scent of perfume and expensive soap she fell down onto her bed. Her pulse was throbbing in her temples. How did he know how to find her weakest spot so mercilessly . . . perhaps because he himself in effect was half . . . She was nauseated. With closed eyes she lay there until the knocking in her temples was less and the drone of English bombers flying to the east got through to her. How many ways were there for you to hate yourself?

When no one was expecting him any longer the barber turned up with the news that an address had been found for Grandfather Tak and his daughter, a miller who lived in a remote spot on the polder. If it had been for the old man alone they would not have accepted the offer, but everyone breathed a sigh of relief at the thought of being free of the daughter, who believed herself to be too beautiful for this planet and all imaginable worlds. Marie took her away late in the evening by bicycle. Lotte followed the next evening—the old man who weighed nothing sat behind and anxiously held onto her hips. It was freezing, the frosty meadows reflected the light of the moon. Bent, pollarded willows formed a guard of honour on either side of the narrow path, long dead greybeards who were welcoming Grandfather Tak into their ranks. But he was still alive and sighed nostalgically. 'Ach, Lotte, would you believe it. . . . If I were young I would kiss you here in the moonlight . . .' Lotte turned round laughing, the bicycle swerved dangerously. 'If you say any more naughty things,' she threatened cheerfully, 'we'll end up in the ditch.'

With regret she handed him over to the miller, who stood in the doorway like an apparition in his long white underwear. It was an unreal, disturbing transaction. Grandfather Tak leaned over and kissed the back of her chilled hand. The last she saw of him was his little bald pate shining in the moonlight, because he thought a *keppel*, such as his Persian son-in-law wore, humbug.

The news of what happened to him subsequently reached them indirectly and in crumbs. There was one constant: the rapid weakening of the thread of the old man's life. His daughter suffered from claustrophobia in the flat, frozen no-man's-land where her charms were wasted; she bit her manicured nails until they bled. When the miller was visited by his family she beseeched them to rescue her from dying of boredom and to take her with them to the inhabited world.

They yielded to her despair. That was how she landed in a village street. She took up a provocative pose by the window. At least ten times a day they asked her to move away from there because she brought not only herself into danger but also them and the chain of people who had taken care of her in the past. But for Flora Bohjul to be seen was an essential of life; she would rather give herself up and be interrogated in a risqué striped prisoner's uniform by a charming commandant than let her days slip through her fingers between pillar and post in a horrible anonymity smelling of cabbage. She slid out of the house and reported to the Ortskommandantur, confident that she was inviolable through her marriage to a Persian Jew. When this news reached the miller he threw the old man out of the house in the dead of night, fearing that she would squeal. Torn out of his deepest sleep he wandered displaced through the meadows. The guard of honour of pollarded willows offered him hospitality again, but he could neither see nor hear anything—the only thing his organism probably desired was a warm bed. No one knew how long his freedom that night had lasted. In the dawn light he seemed to have walked into the hands of the Germans, exhausted and numb with cold. To save themselves the formalities and the problems of transport, they put a permanent end to his weariness with a few bullets, in the back garden of the villa where they were billeted.

At Lotte's home dismay was everywhere. A very old person who scarcely took up space on this planet. Why? And if an old man's life was dealt with this carelessly so near home, what was the fate of those who were put on transports? The dismay had double foundations for Lotte. Who had neatly delivered him to the one who would send him on to his murderers? Who, in her so-called innocence, had once again become a willing tool in the hands of the occupier? Watch out for me! I am even worse than those who openly make war. I am friend and foe in one. I? There is no I, only an ambivalent treacherous we, who deceives itself in itself. . . . She immersed herself in housekeeping with an almost sardonic devotion, simply eliminating herself—her despicable self.

Spring got off to a hesitant start, as though crocuses and budding branches were out of tune with the phenomenon of war. Ed de Vries deserted his place of shelter to fetch the box; he needed a couple of things that were in it, he said vaguely. Lotte's father picked up a shovel and dug an immense hole, allowing for shifts in the earth and growth of tree roots, but the box did not surface. Perhaps they had made a mistake about the tree. Another spot was tried. The deeper the holes became, the greater the suspicion that fell upon him. He took it very seriously. His image in the outside world was at stake. He set the children to work on it. All day long they poked the ground in vain with long iron poles. Max Frinkel advised engaging a renowned clairvoyant; before the war there had been one in Curaçao Street in Amsterdam. Lotte's father dismissed the suggestion cynically, allergic to anything to do with religion or the supernatural. It was his wife, sufficiently recovered to contradict his prejudices, who sent Lotte forth—you never knew.

No crystal balls, tarot cards, Eastern trinkets. The psychic looked like a bookkeeper in a grey suit; his office was bare and businesslike. Sobered, Lotte took her seat by his desk. She looked at him expectantly, not knowing how to begin. 'You have come because something has been lost,' he said calmly, 'I will tell you: It is still there. There is a path with trees; parallel to it is another row of trees. . . .' She nodded in bewilderment. 'It is there . . . in the vicinity of the fifth tree . . . I would say.' It was as though he were walking around in the wood with her and in passing pointed out the spot to her with his walking stick. And that without evident display, without magic tricks or rituals. He spoke in a tone in which one discusses business matters. She did not know what she ought to think about it, a bit of hocus pocus might perhaps have made him more credible.

'Then I'd like to ask you something else,' she said shyly, fishing a photo out of her bag. 'Can you say anything about . . . him?' He took it. She watched with a calm that surprised her—she could always disregard his findings. He took the photo in, glanced at her, at the photo, at her—without seeing her. The photo began to tremble; it seemed as though the person who was depicted in it was coming to life of his own accord. But it was the hand holding it that was trembling. The whole man began to shudder. With eyes that were bulging from fear he looked at the photo, spellbound. He loosened

his tie, wiped his forehead randomly. 'I . . . I . . . can't tell you anything . . . ,' he uttered, breathing heavily, turning the photo over tormentedly as though he could no longer bear the image. Under his
hand he shoved it towards her. 'But can't you say . . . anything . . . at
all?' Lotte attempted. He shook his head, with tightly closed lips.
She put the photo back in her bag and stammered a polite phrase. As
she went down the stairs she felt slightly ashamed for leaving him in
that condition.

7

IT HAD BECOME a familiar pattern by now: tired of eating, talking, raking up the past, tired from listening, softened up from
conflicting sensations, they were leaving a restaurant. Anna put
her arm through Lotte's. She accepted it with a certain resignation.

They found themselves in the Place du Monument. Anna stopped
at the foot of the monument, bending forward to read the text on the
plinth.

'*Cette urne renferme des Cendres provenant de Crématoire du
Camp de Concentrations de Flossenburg et de ses commandos,
1940–1945.*' She exaggerated the pronunciation like all foreigners.

Lotte pulled her away, annoyed by so much perverse German
curiosity.

'*Mensch, Mensch*, are you still troubled by a guilty conscience?'

Now that was going too far. 'You twist things so beautifully,' she
said irritably. 'I have absolutely no guilty conscience. Why should I?
At the time I did take all the guilt onto myself. I was young and egocentric, thought I was the linchpin the world turned on, that I had
influence over the fate of another. The arrogance of youth . . .'

'You're saying something there.' Anna looked at her, touched. 'It
was like that with me, too, young and egocentric; you hit the nail on
the head. With heart and soul I only cared about that one person. . . .'

Lotte shook her head with annoyance. The egocentricity of her youth could not be put on a par with Anna's just like that—there was a chasm of difference between the two. Anna had a crafty habit of turning everything around. She sighed. She could not find the arguments fast enough to vanquish this presumptuous equal treatment. She walked off, offended.

'Wait . . . wait . . . Lottchen . . .' Anna pleaded after her.

That sounded like a very long time ago. As a child she had already been much faster than her plump sister. A whiff of nostalgia for her youth threatened to surface.

'Listen here, do wait a minute . . . I want to tell you something, something you'll be flabbergasted at . . . Wait. . . .' Anna was panting. 'Did you know that I could have changed the course of history? There was a moment when I. . . .'

Wearily Lotte turned. That tactic she recognized from long, long ago, too. Anna would try to tempt her by making her curious: I have discovered a jar of sweets somewhere, a jar of marbles. . . .'

Anna caught up with her. 'There was a moment,' she grinned, 'when the war turned on a stupid housekeeper in West Prussia, a certain . . .'

'Anna Bamberg,' said Lotte laconically.

'You don't believe me.'

IN THE TRAIN of a caravan of refugees from Berlin, which probably no longer existed, Anna returned to the estate. Frau von Garlitz had received a billeting order. The castle swarmed with homeless townspeople who had to be provided with everything in the way of food and clean clothes, and, on Anna's shining parquet floors, were trying to come to terms with the trauma of their burning, collapsing city.

When the castle was already thoroughly saturated, the wife of a senior officer arrived, with a baby and a whining toddler.

'My husband holds the Knight's Cross,' Frau von So-and-So introduced herself, reckoning that all doors would now be opened for her. Those who were awarded that cross had killed a lot of people, Anna knew. Whenever it was mentioned on the radio that someone had received this medal, Martin always said, 'Somebody will have a sore throat again,' because the order was worn hung tight around the neck. Anna had no idea where to accommodate the hero's wife. She crossed the courtyard brooding until her eye fell on the coachman's house above the stables. The coachman had disappeared at the same time as the horses. He had left an adequate dwelling behind, a large living room, two bedrooms, a bathroom and a kitchen. We could let the highborn lady live here without our needing to feel embarrassed, Anna decided. But three days later another young mother arrived with a baby and a toddler—the wife of a factory worker, without a 'von.' Anna reasoned: if the noble lady gave up one room, and they shared the bathroom and kitchen in a friendly manner, they could live together in the coachman's house. She buttonholed Frau von Garlitz half way up the stairs for her approval. 'What?' she cried, scandalized. 'You can't saddle a lady of status with a woman from who-knows-where.' 'She's just a mother,' said Anna calmly, 'with two children, nothing else, and that other one is also a mother with two children. She will still have two rooms to herself all the time.' Frau von Garlitz looked at her as though there were a dangerously mentally ill person opposite her. She shook her head. 'It is not on.' War or no war, she was not allowing a headstrong housekeeper to remove with one stroke her conviction that different sorts of people existed who, from their birth—each at their own level—had a different destiny and therefore lived in different worlds. 'Then I'll give her my own rooms,' cried Anna. 'Out of the question.' Their argument blared down the staircase; everyone could enjoy it. 'You are a bolshevik!' the countess accused her. 'Fine, then I'm a bolshevik.' Anna turned her back on her and left her standing there. At the foot of the stairs Ottchen—he who had licked his superiors' boots since childhood—was waiting with a stern expression. 'How dare you take such a tone with the *gnädige Frau*,' he hissed. Anna positioned herself right in front of him. 'Otto, I'll tell you something. What I have to say to her I say to her face. I'd give my life for her if need be. You bow low but with a knife in your boots. You say *"Jawohl, gnädige Frau"* slavishly but at the same time your eyes sparkle with hate. I've seen it, you don't fool me.'

For the mother, who was unaware of the storms raging over her head, Anna eventually found a draughty attic room without stove, without water, without window. The unsuitability of it deprived her of all the pleasure of continuing to have civilized contact with her employer. She had been accustomed to waking her in the mornings, drawing the curtains open and having a gentle morning conversation with her from the end of the bed. For Frau von Garlitz this was a precious ritual that reconciled her to the umpteenth day of war in the scarcely manageable chaos that had the estate in its grasp. Now Anna snapped her a contemptuous morning greeting, tore the curtains open and disappeared fast. After five days the countess could endure it no longer. 'Damned mule,' she cried unlike a lady from her four-poster bed, 'can't you say good morning at least?' 'I said good morning.' 'Yes, yes,'—she sat up against the embroidered pillows—'but how! Come . . .' She tapped her fingers on the edge of the bed. 'Don't be cross any more . . . sit down. Go and fetch that woman and take her to the coachman's house. . . . Do what you wish. . . . You understand so much more about that sort of thing than I do. . . .'

One Sunday in March a younger sister of the countess was getting married. Frau von Garlitz set off with her children before the crack of dawn for her parents' castle, where the wedding was to be celebrated: her husband would come by aeroplane from Brussels to Germany. *Deo gratias*, thought Anna, the empire alone at last. As she was turning over in bed once more, a popular song went through her head: 'This is my Sunday delight, in bed 'til ten o'clock, then nobody can get me out of it . . . .' But at nine o'clock there was a merciless knocking at her bedroom door. It was Ottchen, so agitated he could scarcely get his words out. The military aircraft that was to bring Herr von Garlitz to Berlin had crashed over Bohemia; none of the occupants had survived. Anna was quick to get over the shock. She did not delude herself into believing that she was sad. The only one she was anxious about was Frau von Garlitz, who reappeared at the gate halfway through the afternoon. The wedding had been postponed. She gave orders with the remarkable self-control required of her position—only her nostrils were trembling slightly. She kept a cool head about everything: A state funeral had to be prepared.

Anna was sent to Frau Ketteler at great speed to tell her in person of the tragic death of the apple of her eye. In a horse and carriage she rushed to the remote villa. Through a dark tunnel of spruces that exuded a damp, spicy smell she walked to the staff entrance. She pushed the door open. No one was there. The only thing that was sounding, with regular interruptions, was the electric bell with which the lady of the house summoned the maid to her room via a pedal next to her armchair. Surprised, Anna walked along the corridor. Where was the staff? Did they all have Sunday off? What was the point of calling them then? Although Anna did not know Frau Ketteler's villa, it was not difficult to find her room—she only needed to look for the source of the staccato sound. The door stood open a crack. She looked in on a dim room, spruce branches pushing up against the windows. On a Persian carpet in front of the hearth, where a professional fire was blazing, lay Herr von Garlitz's aunt—on her back. She was being mounted by her favorite sheepdog, both were at full gallop, which explained the continual on and off sound of the bell as she was lying on top of the pedal. Apparently she had not allowed herself enough time before the ride to pull this out from under her back. Anna held her breath. She had never suspected that what she saw here, illuminated from the side by the flames, could exist at all and even now, as she looked at it, she did not believe it. With fascinated horror she stared at the animal lover's flushed face— this was an unsuitable moment to trouble her. The sheepdog looked into the distance with glazed eyes. Suddenly Anna was afraid that he would get a scent of her presence. She fled down the passage, out of the house, between the antiseptic spruces to the ordinary world where the spectacle readily seemed like a bizarre dream.

Back at the castle she said she had not found Frau Ketteler at home. The truth could not cross her lips—it would be thought that she was imagining perverse fantasies. Moreover, everyone was preoccupied with the mystery of how the military aircraft had crashed over Bohemia. That was surely way off route from Brussels to Berlin? There had been no bombing raids that day that one would have had to avoid. Secretly it was suggested that a political reason had taken Herr von Garlitz out of the way; discredited individuals were increasingly having accidents. Anna remained level-headed. She could think of no single reason why the life of this clever dick would be worth the sacrifice of a military aircraft. Yet she also slowly realized that another truth might exist behind the generally accepted one. Just as beneath the exterior of Frau Ketteler something lurked that was completely, inconceivably different.

The coffin containing the material remains was delivered after a few days. It was entrusted to the gardener. He grabbed her behind the hedge and said, looking round with panic: 'Did you know there's absolutely . . . nothing in the coffin . . .' 'Oh no.' Anna swayed back. With a weathered hand, which had toiled in the earth for half a century, he led her by the elbow to an outbuilding where the coffin stood on trestles in the semi-darkness. It was too small to contain an adult man. When they lifted it up it seemed remarkably light, something rattled back and forth inside. 'I don't know what it is,' the gardener whispered, 'not a whole person in any case.' 'Frau von Garlitz mustn't notice,' Anna said hurriedly. 'Put stones into it before the funeral so that the coffin weighs as much as a person. That thing will have to be carried. Cover it with flags, decorate it with flowers and greenery . . .'

Until late into the night she sat at the sewing machine in her room making a mourning dress out of a black evening dress of Frau von Garlitz's for her daughter, fourteen-year-old Christa. 'What are you doing, Anna?' the countess's voice suddenly sounded through the noise of the machine, flat and robbed of any inflection. 'Christa doesn't have a dress for the funeral,' Anna mumbled with three pins between her lips. Frau von Garlitz dropped down into a chair in her nightdress. She followed Anna's actions with an empty gaze. 'What would I do without you,' she whispered. 'No one has done so much for me as you.' Anna, who had little experience of receiving compliments, blushed up to her hairline and cranked the sewing machine with double force. Her employer was seated on the upright chair, nodding off, as though Anna were her last remaining refuge. Her head sagged onto her chest—now and then she lifted it with a jerk as though the inner realization of early widowhood kept occurring to her. Anna's mind reverberated with worries about the funeral the following day: the state guests had to be offered a welcome befitting their status and function, no element must be missing from the military ceremonial . . . the whole farce in memory of a nonentity had to proceed faultlessly.

When the sun rose the dress was ready. There was no point in going to bed. She felt a strange lucidity that overcame her tiredness and would have prevented her sleeping. She took Frau von Garlitz, who leaned heavily on her, to bed, and hurried downstairs. It was a chilly, lustreless day. Everyone conformed to the scenario; the official guests played their parts with a practised, abstract dignity that led to the suspicion that funerals were just as much a commonly occurring and obvious aspect of their careers as thinking up strategies or inspecting troops. In the front rank, behind the coffin professionally draped with Nazi flags and flora, walked Goering's representative with clenched jaws, broad and massive as a tank; Frau von Garlitz, flanked by her children, floated behind like a black angel, pale and serene and not of this world. To the accompaniment of speeches, in which his services to the Fatherland were made much of, in rhetoric that vanished amidst the chestnut trees, the deceased was placed in the family grave on the estate where he had been born—not for long, as history would relate.

The undermining thing about the war, thought Anna, was that it continued as a matter of course and that you could not dwell on any single disaster or tragedy. Fresh problems immediately presented themselves anew and demanded immediate solution. Onwards, onwards, onwards, one cog slotted into the next. Work went on, plodding on, purely in order to keep everything turning in expectation of . . . of what?

There were also those who opposed the apparent inevitability. One evening, a month after her husband's death, Frau von Garlitz received a notable visit. From her window on the first floor Anna saw a group of gentlemen arriving—they walked towards the front door discreetly but purposefully, briefcases under their arms. She recognized some of them, officers in civilian dress, who had also been at the funeral. They were received in the great hall, immediately below her room. Murmuring voices ascended through the hot air duct that began in the fireplace and had an outlet in her room.

Anna put the inkwell on the table, dipped the nib of her pen, bent over a sheet of pale blue notepaper. But the words had difficulty forming themselves into sentences in her head, drowned as they

were by the fragments of conversation that entered her room from
downstairs—apparently they were sitting in a circle around the fireplace. There was repeated mention of the Wolfsnest and the Bendler
barracks. It sounded as though one of those present had to fulfil a
mission at both locations, the details of which were being compre-
hensively discussed, and the timing arranged to the second. Beneath
the controlled, rational tone in which they spoke she could hear a
subdued tension that sharpened her attentiveness. Frau von Garlitz's voice did not join in. Apparently her only female contribution,
typically, was to offer the place for this rendezvous. Although Anna
tried to regard what came to her as not intended for her, the more
the evening went on, the more her dry pen floated inactively over
the paper; the importance of all those words pressed upon her as
though they were specially meant for her. She felt cold. It started
with her feet and crept slowly up her legs to her middle. But in her
head she was dominated by the feverish awareness that she was the
only one in the world who knew about a breathtakingly bold plan.
A plan that would interfere profoundly in the order of things and
bring about changes too dizzying for her alone to grasp. Her head
felt top-heavy, the responsibility was too great. In sudden desolation she considered entrusting everything she had heard to the blue
paper, but her pen hesitated at the thought that it could be fatally
dangerous to entrust a letter with such contents to the post. So she
sat motionless until the visit had broken up and left an ominous
quiet behind in the castle where, within its walls, beside the unfortunate emperor's bed, there was now an explosive secret being kept
whose timing mechanism had been set.

As THOUGH GUIDED by an invisible hand, they ended up in the *patisserie* with the unrivalled *merveilleux*. At the other tables well-groomed
contemporaries spooned up their cakes in ladylike mouthfuls, chatting
pleasantly about everyday things. Why were Anna and Lotte doomed
to dig endlessly over that war, at this age, in a history that really would
not change for the better?

    They looked at each other expectantly over their empty plates.
'What I heard through the chimney then was precisely what took

place.' Anna interrupted the silence as was only to be expected. 'I read about it years later—except for that one unforeseen circumstance, of course. They had had enough of the Sunday painter. It began with the Stalingrad catastrophe. Then there was a turnaround in the disposition of the nationalistic nobility because their sons, too, were perishing there. It was the end of the great dream. The military experts among them realized that the war could not be won, their estates were in danger as the Russians approached, their whole status was in danger. Thus was the conspiracy created. Frau von Garlitz had offered her services, probably under her father's influence—that fierce Prussian of the old guard with his connections. And I in my maid's room heard them talking as though I were sitting there! All the conspirators were there and devised the plot to the minutest detail. It would have worked if they hadn't had such dreadfully bad luck. It was all fixed up in the Bendler barracks in Berlin—at a password the officers would revolt, take the government prisoner, form a coalition and offer peace immediately. The war over! If it had succeeded Martin would still have been alive as well as millions of others, many towns would have survived intact. I would have had a totally different life. Whether it would have been a better life I don't know; more interesting, certainly not—my God, as a housewife in Vienna! But I did not see that at all then. I was very badly shocked, did not know what I ought to do. I was law-abiding although I had not much faith in the Führer. I believed in the necessity of authority, still do for that matter. I was in charge myself . . . in that I am very German, I admit it. Martin came the following Sunday. I told him what I had heard. He went white round the gills. "Keep quiet about it," he said. "You've heard nothing. Absolutely nothing. God grant that it succeeds!"'

Lotte ordered another pot of tea. 'Yet, with hindsight, it would not have mattered much if you disclosed the plan or not.' She made light of Anna's secrecy. 'The plot would have failed anyway.'

Anna did not agree with her. 'If I had betrayed it at that stage, perhaps an alternative plan would have been devised that really would have succeeded. In that case it would have been better not to have kept quiet.'

After this speculation a senseless discussion followed, in which the

word *when* often appeared with the meaning of 'what if.' With their
invented variations, their hands still steered the course of history.
Their tone was argumentative because it fell to Lotte mainly to contradict Anna. Eventually they left the establishment squabbling
wearily: Anna provoked and exhausted—it seemed impossible ever to
convince her sister (ought she to approach with artillery?); Lotte
angered on account of the fact that Anna took upon herself a central
role in an event that had proceeded completely beyond her.

8

'IF YOU HAD a revolver in your hand at this moment and Hitler
came walking round the corner, would you shoot him?'
Leon Stein looked at her with an anguished laugh. They were
walking in the wood; he was a head shorter than Lotte. In broad daylight he was strolling cold-bloodedly along the beech path and had
taken her arm as though they were engaged. That coolness was part
of his survival strategy—up to now he had survived many daring
exploits. He did not worry about his own death; he dealt with that of
another more carefully. 'I think I would,' she said hesitantly, 'but I
don't know if I could really do it.' They passed the row of trees that
was still keeping the secret of the box despite the clairvoyant's proph-
esy. They had searched exhaustively following his advice but found
nothing; the earth there was loose and uneven as though colonies of
moles had contested the territory with each other. Moreover, 'In the
vicinity of the fifth tree' really was very vague.

'I have a problem,' said Leon. 'A month ago we took a Jewish family—husband, wife, children—to three separate addresses. Meanwhile the wife was betrayed and picked up but set free a short time
later. Since then she has been walking about unhindered and a number of us have been arrested, those who gave her coupons, identity
card, a hiding address. We have followed her, we can work it out.
You understand that we are not going to wait quietly to see who the

next victim is going to be.' He looked at her with partly closed eyes, as though speaking while half asleep. 'We have made a decision—she is going to be liquidated.' His arm held hers more tightly. 'Sometimes it is necessary to sacrifice one life to save other lives.' Lotte looked at him, shocked. 'To save my family I would also be capable of a lot, I think. . . .' 'Exactly so.' He nodded. 'Who has to do it?' she asked after a long silence. The little man, who could not permit himself to shirk answering the big question, poked at a tree root that crossed the path with the point of his shoe. 'That's exactly the problem.'

After a few day's absence he returned hurriedly; agitated dots of light shone in his glasses. There was no time to ask him anything. 'There's going to be a raid.' He waved his hands in a vague direction. 'They could be here at any moment.' There was the usual chaos in the house. Those who did not exist officially, who were not allowed to occupy a square centimetre of the surface of the earth, dissolved into nothing. The game of cards, still warm from their hands, the forbidden books that they read, their unmade beds—they had an astonishing routine for wiping out the life that should not exist. The ordinary Dutch family who lived there applied themselves to their daily activities with ostentatious industry, hoping that the deafening beating of their hearts would continue unnoticed.

They were mistaken in imagining that Ernst Goudriaan was, as usual, in the hiding place behind the mirror, until he appeared in the kitchen in a long leather coat with a kit bag on his back and misted-up glasses, where Lotte was doing the washing for the sake of form. 'I have come to say goodbye.' He held out a trembling hand. Lotte wiped her hands on her apron. 'Goodbye? Why?' 'I . . . I . . . can't take it anymore, . . .' he stammered, taking his glasses off and putting them back on. 'I . . . that tension . . . increasing again. . . . I . . . I am going away . . .' 'Away?' Lotte repeated, positioning herself in front of him. 'You'll walk straight into their arms! How do you get it into your head—you'll betray us all!' He shook his head nervously. 'I've got some arsenic . . . ,' he reassured her. Her mouth fell open. 'Arsenic . . .' She emphasized each syllable. 'You're crazy. . . . Give that coat and bag here . . .' She put her hand out authoritatively. He stood motionless opposite her. Was that the sound of voices in the dis-

tance? Barking dogs? Drone of an engine? Instead of his eyes all she
saw was his stupid steamed-up glasses, his narrow face behind them,
white and fixed in tension—by this time he had to be thoroughly rattled. They hypnotized each other, a silent test of strength with the
background sounds coming ever closer. 'Come,' ordered Lotte. She
began to tug at his bag, helped him out of his coat—suddenly he let
her do as she pleased, like a dog who submits to its master in blind
obedience, against its instincts. 'But I'm not going in the cupboard
any more,' he cried rebelliously. Without allowing himself to be
stopped he turned and rashly walked out of the kitchen into the garden, straight to his studio, leaving Lotte behind with his coat and bag.

A police van drew up in front of the house. A dozen soldiers
began to spread out according to ludicrously strict stage directions.
Some positioned themselves like macabre guards at strategic points
in order to close off possible escape routes, others searched through
the house and showed themselves at the windows to check whether
there were any camouflaged rooms. An officer strode through the
apple trees to the TB house. In the parental bedroom they allowed
themselves to be enticed by the lady of the house to the three-bay
window to admire the view of the meadows and edge of the wood.
The cloudless sky and sun shining through the branches seemed to
be ignoring the danger. Lotte, mesmerized by the quiet and stillness
around the studio, kept going to the window expecting to see Ernst
Goudriaan coming out with a rifle in his back and his hands raised.
Eventually she could not bear it any longer and went the same way
she had seen the officer go. She looked mock-casually inside through
the window at the back. Ernst, his glasses halfway down his nose,
was holding up a half-completed violin and pointing at something,
giving an enthusiastic explanation. The officer had put his cap on the
workbench and was listening in fascination, nodding now and then
and rubbing his chin. Lotte opened the door. Distracted, they both
looked over their shoulders. The German was stroking his middle
finger caressingly over the back plate of a violin hanging on the wall.
'*Ein sehr schöne Lacquer . . .*' 'I make it myself without pigments,'
said Ernst proudly. '*Wunderbar, wunderbar . . .*' the other cried

euphorically. He stood up and inhaled deeply with closed eyes. 'It smells good in here too,' he discovered, 'marvellous!'

Disconcerted, Lotte took long strides back to the kitchen, putting her feet down without thinking. But even before she reached the door she was overwhelmed by a feeling of triumph: At one moment he was prepared to take poison from fear of the occupier, the next moment he welcomed him in—enthusiastically—to the secrets of violin making. A wonderful alchemical transformation that enabled her to forget all danger. She was just going inside the house when violin music sounded behind her. An ardent, heartfelt passage from the Beethoven concerto arose from the studio and penetrated the pale blue planks. The soldiers, losing their interest in the insides of the house, assembled in the garden to listen to the officer's musical intermission. They listened in a controlled way, as though it were part of military discipline. The sun glittered on the buttons of their uniforms. Now that the raid was being graced with a famous concerto, Lotte's father also came outside to listen with his hands in his pockets. After the last notes had died away, it was more quiet than ever before, until a magpie flew off noisily from a branch and the officer dreamily left the studio. He swayed through the fruit trees, drunk from the music. Suddenly he saw his subordinates in view; he ran a hand through his dishevelled hair, put his cap on and adopted an expression suited to the war. 'Well then . . .' he said gruffly, 'what are you waiting for.'

The engine drone died away. Those who did not exist emerged sweating and smelly and gave vent to their surprise at Beethoven's wonderful intervention, which had even been heard behind the mirror. Max Frinkel had plenty to say about the power of music. Only Ernst Goudriaan stayed behind in his studio and went on planing the back plate of a violin. 'You seduced the commandant,' said Lotte delightedly; she sat down among the woodshavings. 'Thanks to you.' He grinned: 'She is doing the washing as usual, I said to myself as I walked to the studio. If the people in hiding are discovered, there's a huge chance that the whole family will be put against the wall, and yet she is doing the washing as usual. I thought, Why don't I get on with the plane then? Someone who is at work has something inviolable, something invulnerable . . . as though he is placing himself outside the war with it.' She was shyly silent. She did not feel indifferent to his singing her praises. It brought her into an enjoyable confusion that now for a change she had had a positive influence on the fate of another. 'And he even played a solo for you,' she sighed, as a diversionary tactic. Ernst nodded. 'An enthusiastic amateur. He said: If we weren't in the middle of a war I would buy this violin from you.' With a craftsman's pride he repeated, 'He wanted to buy a violin from me!'

The incident pepped her up and brought the credit-debit balance more or less into equilibrium. Chastened by the thought that this person in hiding actually belonged to her, since she had held him back from his ridiculous suicidal action, she offered no opposition to the feeling of being in love that flooded over her as an apparently natural result. In love with him and all the activities that are necessary to making a violin: sawing, planing, polishing, lacquering. That the front and back plates were of fine-grained Yugoslavian maple, the fingerboards of ebony on the other hand, that a bad lacquer affected the tone, that the sides were bent with steam, all of it moved her, even when she caught the stink of the bone glue that was used for sticking various components together. But the loveliest thing of all about him was that he seemed unlike her father in every respect.

IN A GUIDEBOOK promoting Spa's fame as a health resort it says: 'The resort guests at Spa should forget about everyday life. They are urged to live according to a slower, a more regular rhythm. They are gathered up into a caring and protective milieu, which is closely connected to the medical world, which is in itself a symbol of reliability and certainty.'

A fat lot the two sisters cared about these good intentions. None of the 'slow and regular rhythm' showed up. The more they confided to each other about their incompatible lives, the more the tension and the awareness of the irrevocability of the past grew. It was the last chance they were being offered for rapprochement and reconciliation. One wanted it, out of profound need, but was already too willing, the other was still bracing herself, because of a mistrust at least as deep. The war was overrunning their health cure. They summoned up ghosts, and the ghosts came with their frayed souls, into a deserted landscape, under leaden skies in a smell of gunpowder and phosphorous . . . one great lament against selling out the right to life, freedom, humanity, Christian charity . . . values that once had significance, words from an archaic language, an Esperanto of naiveté. The ghosts came past in columns and left deeply ingrained traces behind them.

It is true that Anna and Lotte were lying full length on their couches in the Salle de Repos, but they did not keep their eyes closed and they were not listening to the cooing of the doves. As there were no other patients there that morning, they continued as usual with the war, horizontally.

'The twentieth of July, the day Hitler was *not* killed,' said Anna. 'I remember it as though it were the day before yesterday. Frau von Garlitz had the radio on. She knew precisely when it would happen of course. There was a brief mention of the attempt, nothing more, she had been expecting it. "Thank God!" she cried, delirious with joy, 'The *Schwein* is dead!" It echoed through the corridors and staircases. I went rigid. Then Ottchen suddenly appeared and said: "The Führer is alive, he is talking on the radio now." Oh my God, I thought, let no one have heard Frau von Garlitz. The house was full of strangers! We only found out later what had gone wrong. The Führer, who never left his seat at meetings, had walked round the table to the other side—just before the bomb went off. The conspirators were arrested immediately, Von Stauffenberg was shot that same day. The gentlemen I had seen on the front steps with their briefcases, including a nephew of Frau von Garlitz, not one of them survived. All those senior officers from good families whom the *Schweinerei* did not want anymore . . . most of them were hung at Plötzensee, on meat hooks.'

'An exhibition . . .'

Anna nodded. 'As a terrifying example. Their wives and children were taken off to camps. They had a great purge right away, and absolutely everything with a bad smell was picked up and sent off.'

'And Frau von Garlitz?'
'No one knew that she had been involved in it.'

'I AM LYING on my back and watching the aircraft fly over,' Martin
wrote from Normandy. He had enclosed two photographs. In one he
was sitting in a military coat on the rocks of Mont St. Michel, looking out over the sea to England—the other showed him sitting on the
wing of a shot-down English aircraft with a star on its side. One week
later he telephoned unexpectedly: 'I'm nearby, I'm here, in Stettin.'
His signals unit had been disbanded, they had to go for brief infantry
training at a Wehrmacht barracks on the Baltic Sea. The inventive
company commander, who had once rustled up the illegal leave from
the Ukraine, had thought up a new trick. All spouses received a
telegram with the news that their husbands were seriously ill. With
this official document in her pocket, which authorized a journey
north, Anna got on the train. Again, at the end of this journey, a steep
grey wall rose up as the train tipped over sharply to one side. What
were they hiding behind that one? Anna thought. The miracle
weapon that had been highly praised on the radio occurred to her, the
weapon with which Germany was going to win the war. Perhaps V-2s
were indeed being deployed behind that wall! But wrinkles appeared
in the enormous wall, it was moving—simultaneously, the train
swayed, it toppled back, and for the first time in her life she suddenly
saw an unending grey water surface with a boat drifting on it.

The train stopped at a seaside resort. A conspicuously large number of young women with two suitcases got off. You could be for-
given for assuming that one suitcase contained clothes and the other
was stuffed full of comestibles. Hesitantly they trudged to the square
in front of the station, to and fro, until they discovered that they had
a common problem: How could they get to the hotel with their heavy
suitcases? Two tanned women with a handcart smelling of fish
approached Anna, after having looked around searchingly, holding
up one of her wedding photographs. 'Are you Frau Grosalie?' 'Yes,'
said Anna in astonishment. 'Your husband has sent us; we have to
fetch you and bring the suitcases.' Without waiting for her reaction
they took her suitcases and put them in the cart. The other women

burst out in a torrent of abuse. Why had their husbands not made arrangements for them? 'Dear heaven,' cried Anna, 'what's the matter? We'll load the cart full and all push it together.' A bunch of women in summer dresses of wartime floral prints pushed the top-heavy cart over the bumpy cobbles to the beach hotel. Martin had apparently explained the problem to a fisherman the previous evening and had arranged with him that Anna would be fetched in exchange for cigarettes.

The hotel stood resolutely on top of a dune and seemed to challenge the sea: Rise up, then! The barracks were three kilometres further on. Every evening the company went swimming with the commandant's permission. They left their uniforms behind on the beach, walked three kilometres in their wet bathing trunks, and spent the night with their wives in their hotel rooms. One warm evening Martin and Anna went swimming as they had done in the lake. The smooth water reflected the light of the moon. They swam out next to each other at a calm, even pace, the element of water gave a sense of freedom, as though the war's rules only counted on land. 'I've just heard on the radio,' said Martin with unrestrained joy in his voice, 'that the Russians are in East Prussia.' 'Then it can't go on for much longer.' Anna spat out a mouthful of sea water. He dived under and came up a bit farther on. 'When that stupid war is over,' he cried, sneezing, 'we can go to Vienna at last for good.' They swam on in an excited state until Martin turned and said with surprise: 'We really are rather far from the shore.' Anna looked round mechanically. An unreal white strip on the horizon was all that was left of the coast. They turned round and began to swim back in equanimity. But when the strip did not seem to come a millimetre closer, their strokes took on a grimmer character. The moon accompanied them impassively, Martin looked around frequently, encouraging her to keep going. The sea water was heavy, it seemed as though litres had to be displaced with each stroke. She became breathless. The more fiercely she tried to keep calm, the more forcefully panic struck. The strip of land continued to distinguish itself by keeping its distance. 'Martin . . .' she cried weakly—she disappeared beneath the water, came up again, 'Let me . . .' 'I'll help you . . .' Although his voice was coming from far away she felt his arm around her shoulders, '. . . right at the end of the war we surely can't dr—.' Suddenly, he sounded much nearer. She surrendered to him. Her sense of time was distorted. She did not know if hours or minutes stretched out before he no longer had enough strength to keep them both above the water. His cry for help, which skimmed over the surface of the water, vaguely got through to her. She was resigned to disappearing with him, to being sucked into the mother sea and never more needing anything. Unnoticed, without resistance, she allowed herself to float into a silent no-man's-land.

An eternity later she was lying on her back on the still warm sand, and someone was blowing his breath into her. A nauseated disgust flowed though her arteries along with her returning life. She was being rubbed dry and warm with a rough towel. Why hadn't they left her where she was, it suited her there. But Martin was sitting next to her, blue-white in the moonlight and watching anxiously for the return of signs of life at the hands of their skillful rescuer, a sergeant from his company who had the shoulders and biceps of a gladiator— Martin was even allowing him to give her the kiss of life. She could not yet know that a few months later, looking back on this evening, she would once again become consumed with regret that the arrival of the industrious sergeant had prevented her from dissolving into nothingness with Martin.

The following day the illegal holiday came to an abrupt end: the Waffen SS had permitted its eye to fall upon the group doing infantry training. Upset, they ran to the hotel that evening. They had had more than enough of the war. The approaching peace was already singing in their heads; they refused to join the corps of fanatics. Martin drummed his fists into the pillow. What could these orthodox officers, these war horses in whose vocabulary the word *surrender* did not exist, be planning, other than to prepare themselves for collective suicide? Hemmed in by the English and Americans on the one side and the Russians on the other, would they stop at nothing to bring about the sacrifice of young warriors to old Germanic custom in order to placate the gods once more? It was the first and last time he rebelled. Anna rocked him to and fro, without conviction trying to calm him. 'We have no say,' he capitulated finally, whispering, 'none.'

The company was moving to Nuremberg, from the Baltic Sea all the way through the Third Reich, in wagons used for transporting goods or cattle. The wives travelled with them to Berlin—except Anna. Martin would not permit his wife to travel in this way. 'No question of it,' he said proudly, 'there is no toilet, no sink. My wife is not going to travel in a cattle truck like an animal.' He climbed in irritably. She would wait for the next passenger train. Anna shoved the suitcase with provisions in after him. 'What's that for?' His glance grazed the suitcase. 'Provisions,' Anna said. He put it back on the platform. Anna lifted it up and put it in the train again. 'Take it with you—I get enough to eat.' He heaved the thing out again with pursed lips. Does this have to be our parting? Anna thought. The departure signal sounded. Martin held her face in his hands and kissed her urgently. Wringing her hands she was left on the platform, hemmed in by the two suitcases.

The news that the Russians were in East Prussia blistered into the summer heat, causing anxiety on the one hand and secret joy on the other. In and around the castle everything was as before, farming and housekeeping were turning at full speed—a perpetual motion machine cranked up by the war. But the Russian prisoners of war and Polish forced labourers, Wilhelm whispered, found themselves in a state of permanent excitement that they only managed to hide from their guards with extreme collective self-control. Anna nodded; it could not go on for much longer now. They were in the kitchen garden, behind a tall rhubarb plant. He took her hands and brought his furrowed face close to her ear; she thought he was going to kiss her. 'Warn the *gnädige Frau*—the day the Russians come to liberate us the Poles will kill everything German here. They are patriots, they will take revenge for what has been done to their country. Everyone will be murdered, except you. A finger won't be lifted against you, they have promised us that. The Russians are protecting you.' 'But, Wilhelm,' Anna stammered, 'you can't mean that . . . Frau von Garlitz . . . and the children . . . surely they haven't done anything . . .' He lowered his eyes, let go of her hands and walked away with drooping shoulders as though a lead ball hung from each arm. Anna stared at the powerful stems of the rhubarb; the word *barbarians* occurred to her. The well-tended kitchen garden, the

smoothly cut lawns, the glistening castle, the washing white as snow
hanging out motionless on the line . . . She could not imagine the possibility of this self-evident order being disturbed. The human linchpin of
this order, the inhabitants of the castle, the family whose name had been
associated with this spot since the seventeenth century, Ottchen, Mamselle, the cleaning women and chambermaids, even the refugees—all
these people with whom she had been involved day in, day out, had to
pay the penalty? What had they done? For the first time she began to
sense that the liberation that they had yearningly looked forward to
would perhaps be no liberation at all, that the war would continue as
usual—wearing a different mask. She began to move, walked straight in
to Frau von Garlitz, who reacted with neither surprise nor shock. She
had long understood that the hordes from the east would not bring liberation; her evacuation plan was ready.

A letter came from Martin, an SS letter from an SS barracks. The
Russians were approaching West Prussia, he wrote, resign and go to
Vienna—that will be safer, you will be at home there. A sensible,
understandable message. Martin, who had already travelled though
Europe for six years like a gypsy, spoke about her departure from the
estate as though it concerned a random change of posting. As though
she did not have ties to cut, for the first time in her life. The tie with
her employer, the two children, the staff—her surrogate family, that
unwieldy, tried and tested, capricious ragbag that she had been
involved with so profoundly over the years. The renovated castle, her
own creation, how could it function for a day without her? Did she
have to leave all that behind, prey to . . . ?

She left it all behind; goodbyes were said with tears and promises.
Frau von Garlitz was touched and hurt as though her own mother
were abandoning her. The children clung to her like monkeys; the
cleaning women blew their noses; Ottchen sniffed loudly to proclaim
his contempt for members of staff who did not regard their function
as a lifelong calling—he climbed up onto the box sullenly. A period
was coming to an end with her departure; everyone felt that and no
one knew what would take its place.

Anna heaved herself up with her eternal suitcases and rode down
the castle drive with red eyes, out of the gate, waving one more time.

They drove along the Frederickian village road, the emaciated Russian prisoners of war formed a row on either side, in their worn-out clothes, waving their blue checked handkerchiefs. Their guards looked on from the sidelines. Wilhelm was standing at the front, with a tortured grin from ear to ear. They stood there like the last faithful followers of a queen who was being taken to the scaffold. The queen of the handkerchiefs, the toothpaste, the combs with a few teeth missing, burst into tears. Wilhelm stepped forward to give her his handkerchief. It was her last sight of the village, through a veil, the sentries on either side with their sadly waving rags, their drawn faces—who was disappearing out of whose life? The village ended and the fields began and there was only desolation—apart from Ottchen, who stared unfathomably at the horse's hindquarters swinging to and fro.

'YES, THEY LOVED me,' Anna concluded.

Lotte did not react. She could not reconcile all that adulation with her own less flattering picture of Anna. Anna was romanticizing the past. 'And . . .' she said rancorously, 'was Wilhelm right?'

'It happened just as he had predicted. The castle was ransacked; many did not survive it. Frau von Garlitz fled at night to the west across the frozen Oder with the children and a few trusted ones. I heard it years later from Mamselle, whose tracks I came across by chance.'

'And the castle, have you ever been back to see it again?' Lotte, with her weakness for old houses, was curious despite herself.

'Don't talk to me about it!' Anna sat up in pure indignation. 'The Poles have the same mentality as those fat washerwomen when I came to the estate. They don't know what work is. They never will, I'm telling you.'

The bed, not intended for guests who sit up and talk emphatically, protested with strenuous creaking.

'I went to Poland by car with a friend last autumn. Warsaw, Kraków, Auschwitz, Zakopane, Poznán. I had an inspiration. "Let's go to the village where I worked during the war." "But surely that doesn't exist any more," my friend spluttered. "Of course it's still

there," I said, "only it's called something different." We went in
search, without a map, in an area with Polish place names that gave
you nothing to hold on to. I drove purely from memory: a gnarled
tree, an old barn, a three-forked road that struck me as familiar,
were my only points of orientation in this empty country. All of a
sudden we were driving along a straight road with chestnut trees:
ramshackle farms, chickens in the road, tipsy chaps round the door
of the post office that was also the village café. I got out and asked
about the village, calling it by its old name. They looked at me indifferently without answering. A drizzly rain was falling, which made
everything seem even more impoverished. I walked along the village
street a bit, stopped in front of a colossal neglected house of . . . a
landowner, I thought. Grass was growing in the gutters, which were
hanging loose, the unpainted shutters were coming off their hinges,
some windows were boarded up, the porch over the front door was
shored up crookedly, cracked plaster everywhere—geese were
scratching about on a stubbly patch of grass, further on a pig was
rooting in the mud, a mangy guard dog bared his teeth. I thought of
our immaculate farms in Germany. See, I said to myself, this is how
the Polish farmers go about their business. They simply haven't a
clue. An old man walked past. I buttonholed him, used the old name
of the village again. He stared at me through pebble-thick lenses as
though I were an apparition. Then he began to nod slowly.
"Stockow now . . ." he said in broken German. I nodded with him,
suddenly excited. "Familie von Garlitz?" He said nothing. "The castle, where is the castle?" He smiled, he had a broken denture, the
poor man. "*Das Schloss*?" he repeated in surprise. "But it's here . . .
right in front of you." I was standing in front of it and looking at it
and did not recognize it. Can you imagine!'

Anna's face had become flushed. The walls of the Salle de Repos
looked as though they were bulging out from the indignation that she
exuded. She opened her plump arms. 'There used to be a wall round
it, and the grounds with old trees. All gone. There was the castle,
threadbare, pitiful, between the mud and the exhausted grass. I can't
tell you what was going on inside me there. It was as though my last
remaining trust in humanity—and there is not much left of it now—

was being disposed of. As though everything, everything had been for nothing. "Can I see the house from the inside?" I asked, "I used to work there during the war." He nodded, but I don't know if he understood. Twelve Polish families had been living there since the end of the war, he explained, the farm had become a cooperative.'

She turned up her nose. 'One of those *kolkhozes*. We got permission to see a part of the castle from inside. My God, what an ordeal. We started in the hall, that same hall of the conspiracy. Washing lines were strung across it, with some yellowed sheets and shirts hanging up. The walls were grey, the tiles cracked. We opened the door to the dining room. I put a hand over my mouth. "Look at that, my parquet floor!" I cried. There was my pride and joy, my best floor that had endlessly been rubbed with wax—dried out and cracked, whole pieces were missing. A couple of rusty bicycles leaned against the wall, a thin, pale ginger cat slunk off with its tail between its legs. I was staggered, as you can imagine. "Let's go outside, please," I pleaded. We walked to the back door along an empty, ominous passage—without runner, unpainted walls without hunting scenes—I almost stumbled over a bucket of dirty suds. Outside I took a deep breath. "The cemetery," I suggested, "there must be something there from earlier times." The old man shook his head. *"Alles kaputt,"* he mumbled. I walked to the place where we had buried Herr von Garlitz in the earth, or what had had to pass for him. The old paths were still intact but dark holes gaped instead of the graves, overgrown with creepers and ground ivy. Here and there a fragment of marble. The branches of mature shrubs bent overhead as though they wanted to cover up the shame. "They have not even left the dead in peace," I cried. "Everything ruined," said my guide resignedly. So it was. They had been so vengeful they could not even leave undisturbed the graves that went back to the seventeenth century.'

'But that's easy to understand really,' said Lotte over the edge of her sheets. 'they certainly had enough reason to.'

'Yes, yes,' said Anna impatiently, 'but as I stood there looking into those gaping holes I didn't understand any of it.'

It was quiet for a moment. Then she said, in a voice suggesting that she was entrusting Lotte with an intimate secret: 'I picked up a

conker. A large shiny conker. I always have it with me, as a memory
of those days . . . when I was very happy, without realizing it.'

VIENNA. YOU WILL be safe in Vienna, Martin wrote. When Anna
arrived her father-in-law was just packing his suitcases. 'I am going to
Nuremberg,' he declared. 'The SS is inviting the parents to come and
have a look.' He came back content after a few days: 'You need have
no worries about Martin—he is having an excellent time. Order prevails, comradeship prevails, they've got brand new kit. Everyone is
friendly and polite.' 'You're telling me stories,' said Anna suspiciously. 'I swear to you, he is like a fish in water.' 'But he hates them,
those Nazis.' 'You'll see for yourself, the wives will be invited soon.'

She received a travel permit; she set off in the last week of August
for a fortnight. Bombing had not left much of Nuremberg, but the
press hotel, taken over by the SS, was still standing and undamaged.
Luxury suites had been reserved for the married couples—in the
mornings the officers had gentle training, the rest of the day they
could do what they wanted. The barracks, too, were an island of
peace amid the chaos. Everything shone and glittered—respect prevailed, for people as well as things. Her father-in-law had not exaggerated: Martin, who put so much store by good manners, neatness
and courtesy, had thoroughly come into his own there. They took
advantage of the unexpected reunion, it was just like a honeymoon—
the army leadership pampered its youngest scions. A bomb fell now
and then, a small aberration that had long since ceased to surprise
them. There was a mania for photographing each other: Martin,
good-humoured, in his uniform—Anna in a cream suit constructed
out of what had been a tennis outfit belonging to Frau von Garlitz.

The wives from the Baltic Sea adventure were all there. They
enjoyed each day, each night that had been given to them, with fatalistic eagerness—except for one of them, who confided to Anna in a desperate fit of crying that her parents had forbidden her to become
pregnant by someone who might soon be dead. 'Every night I have to
turn my back on him,' she sniffed. Anna, still fervently on the lookout
for signs of pregnancy, spoke from her heart, 'If he were to die, it
would still be a tremendous comfort if you had a child of his at

least . . . but what are we talking about, the war really is almost over! Then they'll come home and we'll live together under one roof and . . .' She raised a finger laughingly: 'Then it really will be war, *Liebchen.*'

Martin's concern for her welfare sometimes took grotesque forms. One morning the women met in the swimming pool. One of them came rushing over while Anna was floating on her back. 'Get out, get out, a column of officers is coming.' They heaved their wet bodies hastily out of the pool and fled to the lockers. Anna looked round with astonishment and drifted on, relaxed, without paying attention to the distant singing that was fast getting louder. Only when the officers were on the point of diving in did she sense that perhaps her presence in the water might be unwelcome. She swam to the side with languid strokes. In a decent black swimsuit that definitely covered her ample figure but did not conceal it, she walked between the officers to the lockers. As she passed she saw the pursed lips and furious expression on Martin's face. That afternoon he erupted. How did she happen to be the only woman in a swimsuit on show to all those men? She shrugged her shoulders. 'Simple. I was swimming.' He shook his head, deeply offended. 'My wife . . . among all those chaps.' 'But the swimming pool is for everyone.' She laughed innocently. 'My wife doesn't do such a thing.' 'Seemingly she does.' Their ideas about decency were irreconcilable. 'I won't have them making jokes about you—I know them.' She was oppressed by it. 'If you go on like that I'll leave you,' she blurted out to shut him up. He was so badly shocked and in such an endearing way that she flew to hug him, from regret and empathy. It was stupid to squabble about inanities. Time was pressing.

She awoke trembling, her teeth chattering, on the last night. Martin, who responded to her utterances in his sleep, too, opened his eyes and held her. 'You're frightened . . .' His voice was dark from sleep. She laid her head on his chest. 'I don't know what's the matter.' He pulled her tightly to him. 'We must talk about it,' he said calmly, 'I think this is the moment. Listen. Millions are dying in this rotten war—up to now I have had a lucky escape. Who can guarantee that will work until the end? Why, so many have died, why not I? For me it will not be bad to die; it happens very quickly, don't you worry. The only thing that will be bad for me is that then I won't be able to help you anymore. I know what will happen to you, I know exactly. You are as delicate as porcelain, but no one knows it. You always play the strong one and the sturdy one, but in reality you are emotional and vulnerable and you need me. But you must live even if I am not there. Promise me one thing: Don't put an end to it. I won't look at you anymore if you commit suicide! I won't greet you in the hereafter!'

There was silence in the room apart from the beating of his heart in her ear. It was out of the question that this beating could stop from one moment to the next—that a connection could exist between the things he alluded to and the precious beating of this heart and this warm, breathing body which belonged not only to the army but to her and him, too. The well-being of that body was so closely tied to that of her own that she did not want to hear what he was saying and yet it was engraved on her memory, word by word.

'Nor do I want you to stay in sackcloth and ashes for the rest of your life. Even if I am dead I want to have a beautiful wife. Will you promise me that? I'll tell you what you should do. You will only bear it by helping others who are worse off than yourself. Go and work in a military hospital or something like that, only then will you survive, I know you . . .' Instead of seeking comfort and courage from her for the possibility that he might die just before the peace, he was giving her a manual for the rest of her life, with serenity. Ease replaced her anxiety and eventually an immense calm—he had spun a cocoon of safety and invulnerability around her where there was a peaceful, reliable tranquility—where life and death flowed naturally into each other. They fell asleep entwined; entwined they woke in the morning.

IT WAS BRILLIANT weather. Martin had never looked so well. Tanned, alert, full of good spirits. Anna leaned out of the window of the train that was about to move. He ran alongside the train and waved. '*Auf Wiedersehen* until Vienna, this bloody hell will soon end anyway!' he cried cheerfully. She stiffened—such words in a tone of optimism were unforgivable from the mouth of an SS officer. And they resonated along the platform, too! Anna narrowed her eyes, anxiously expecting that they would arrest him. But he was still standing there and waving and no one bothered him.

Vienna was not that safe. In order to cut off the German troops' retreat from the Balkans the Americans were dropping a wide swathe of bombs that ran right through Vienna. Because they did not dare fly over the Alps at night, they only flew during the day. The windows of the new apartment were shattered. Anna fixed them with cardboard. The alarm sounded; she ran to the nearest shelter; on the way she saw an old woman hiding on a porch. 'What are you doing here?' Anna yelled, dragging her along with one arm. 'Come, hurry into the shelter.' It was a crush inside. 'Get up,' she said to a boy, 'I've got an old lady here.' The warden of the block, responsible for citizens' safety during attacks, rushed over to her, 'What possessed you?' 'How do you mean?' asked Anna. 'What have I done?' 'Do you know who you've got with you?' She looked at the woman who was sitting huddled up, like a bird in winter. 'It makes no difference to me, an old woman obviously.' 'A half-Jew!' he barked. 'Well and . . .' She shrugged her shoulders. 'There's a dog over there, can't a poor old woman be allowed in?' She was stared at with anxious eyes from all around, what recklessness to challenge the warden of the block. He tensed his jaw muscles. She looked at him defiantly. He lowered his eyes and slunk off to another corner of the shelter, as though his presence were urgently required there.

The whole month she waited in vain for a letter from Martin. She wrote to him at the beginning of October. 'I am sitting here with a pen in my hand, but I have the feeling I am speaking into the emptiness.' She bought a bunch of asters to comfort herself. She was climbing the stairs to her apartment with the flowers in hand when she met the neighbour halfway who usually greeted her noisily with a rolling Viennese 'r' but now he shyly quickened his pace. She opened the door. To her surprise her father-in-law was waiting for her in the living room. 'No post again,' she sighed with a glance at the empty table. 'Yes,' he said, pointing to the sideboard with his head, 'there is post.'

A parcel. She leaned over it and read: *Nachlass-sache*—estate matters. Wildly she tore it open. On top there was an envelope, she ripped the letter out. 'Dear Frau Grosalie . . . As Company Commander it is my duty to inform you of the heroic death of your husband . . .' Feverishly she read on. '. . . In the Eifel . . . grenade explosion . . .' The letter ended with 'In the belief that there will be ultimate victory and that this war is justified, I remain . . . Heil Hitler! SS-Hauptsturmführer, Company Commander . . .' The asters fell to the ground. 'It's not true,' she contradicted the contents of the letter in a quiet voice. She began to walk about, around the table, around her father-in-law, faster and more rebelliously, calling out, 'not true, not true . . .' as though a ritualistic denial of reality could undo the facts. Catatonically she kept repeating the same words until her father-in-law managed to force her onto the sofa. Above her hung a framed portrait of Martin; she lifted it off the wall. With the photograph in her lap she rocked back and forth. What a tasteless paradox—the unbearable would have to be borne in some way or other. She glided about the apartment, wanted to put on something dark, saw a repellent stranger in the mirror—the curls of her perm had disappeared instantly. Look at that, her hair was already dying, the rest would from now on.

She hadn't promised him that she would eat! For days she did not eat, drink, sleep or cry. At night she wandered about the shattered apartment blocks as though she were looking for something among them. All she wanted was to be there where he was, nothing else. Her restrained father-in-law, who was staying at the apartment with her on his wife's instructions, tried to see her behaviour as a normal phase in the mourning process. He brought her a long widow's veil for the requiem mass at the Karlskirche. Where she had advanced down the aisle in a long white veil two years before she now walked vacantly in a black one. 'The German woman doesn't shed a tear . . .' she heard being whispered in the pews. She allowed the sounds of the requiem to surround her as if she was a deaf mute.

After a week her father-in-law gave up his chaperonage. Because he alone had not been able to end the hunger strike he made her promise to come over to his home that Sunday, in the hope that his wife could persuade her to eat something. Hesitantly she went outside. The world was unmoved by Martin's death; there was no shadow of him even in his own city. She was alone, in a strange city, it was war—those were the facts. In that constellation there was no place for her, just as there was no place for the facts in her life. She sleepwalked into the centre, along the Ring, the glittering Ring, past the theatre, the Hofburg, the Opera. She followed her own footsteps towards the Karlskirche in a vague need for religious support, but mainly in the desperate hope that He would give her a sign, an affirmation of His ubiquity—a proof of His existence. She could barely push the heavy door open. The Sunday mass had just started. The voice of the pastor reverberated in the dome. The baroque gold trembled with it. At first she was in no state to let the content mean anything to her. Weakened by her fast, she slid down in a pew somewhere. Eventually, within the walls of the mother church, trusted since her youth, she was almost dozing, a result of the persistent lack of sleep. But suddenly she jerked out of her slumber. 'Every death at the front . . .' warned the voice, 'and every devastated home here is a punishment for our sins . . .' A punishment? How did he get that into his head, the idiot! This was the most insincere, the cruellest message she had ever received from the Church. In protest she stood up. She managed to walk past the rows to the back. Despite her weakness she had just enough strength to close the heavy door with an ostentatious bang. Still shaking with rage she descended the steps. In a reflex she looked round: on either side there was still an angel, each was carrying its own cross and staring ignorantly ahead over the world.

And she went on. The Hitler Youth was marching enthusiastically across the Ring with brand-new flags. Anna shuffled past in her black veil. One of the boys barred her way. 'Heil Hitler!' She stared ahead silently. 'Can't you salute the flag?' he snarled. He was at least a head taller than she; she tapped him on his chest. 'I'll say one thing to you. My husband has just died for that very same flag.' She brushed him aside and continued on her way. Exhausting himself with apologies he came after her. Anna did not look up or around; she had reached a state of collapse that made her immune to someone else's shame.

She did not know how she got to her parents-in-laws' house. As the door opened she slumped onto the threshold. All that time she had been on the point of fainting but her body had waited decently for a suitable moment. They laid her on the divan. In her muzzy, twi-light state she could hear arguing in the room next door. 'You haven't taken enough care of her . . .' sounded her mother-in-law's voice. 'You promised Martin you would take care of her and now she col-lapses in our hands.' Anna threatened to faint again. A pot of strong coffee was made. A cup with real coffee made from coffee beans was moved back and forth under her nose. Anna herself did not react. It was the primitive life spirit that forced her to open her mouth and take a swallow, provoked by the irresistible stimulus. Similarly, she ate a piece of cake mechanically. In this way, her suicidal urge was driven away very prosaically with coffee and cake, in order to make room for being merely unhappy. That feeling she was still familiar with, she had lived with it for many years.

Then the second part of the promise had to be kept. A black Mer-cedes with the SS emblem on it drew up in front of the cardboard-patched apartment where she continued her marriage on her own. The SS took good care of its people. The Head of the SS sent the chief of the Danube region welfare board to give the widow his con-dolences. He was friendly, knew faultlessly how to find the right words of comfort for which she had gone to the Karlskirche in vain, asked if there was anything he could do. 'I would very much like to work in a military hospital,' said Anna in a flat tone of voice. 'I promised him. But in my employment papers it says "Housekeeper" so I'll never be able to get a nursing position.' 'Come to the office and we'll give you an official testimonial,' he promised, shaking her hand sympathetically.

After the visit by the higher up, which had been observed by all those living around Anna, she was no longer "that German" but "the SS aunt." The more the bombing increased in severity and Hitler lost further ground, the more openly she was stigmatized. That's how it is, she consoled herself, as long as it's going well they cry Hosanna. When it goes the other way: crucify him. She reported to the employ-ment office. The necessary document was already waiting for her. 'Frau Grosalie is an orphan and childless and now that her husband has been killed she would like to be taken on as a sister in the Red Cross. I request you to issue a dispensation and to put nothing in the

way of her commencing work with the German Red Cross. Ober-
scharführer Fleitmann.'

AT THE CHALET du Parc, where they had walked from the Thermal
Institute, a woman made of stone stood ringed by soldiers, trying to
fend off a bayonet. There was no inscription, not even a list of names.
Anna and Lotte stopped, each sheltering inside their upturned collars.

'Where was . . . Martin buried in fact?'

'In Gerolstein in a military cemetery. But first in . . .'

'But didn't they bring him home?'

'Are you crazy? He was ripped to pieces by an artillery grenade in
the Eifel. They gathered him up and put him in the ground. Did you
think they brought the dead home? In 1944 there were far too many
of them! In Russia, France, the Ardennes, they lay all over the place,
the torsos here, the legs there. Come off it, it's a wonder they even
mentioned where he was.'

Lotte was hurt and silent. Anna adopted a tone towards her as
though she were stupid, as though she, Anna, had exclusive rights
over the war because her husband had been killed.

'He had seen it all coming,' said Anna thoughtfully, 'that night in
Nuremberg. Instead of being frightened of death, because he was the
one that was going to die—he was concerned about me. A boy of
twenty-six, so mature and well balanced, as though he had achieved
the inner development of a whole life at an accelerated pace. He
knew it all, that night.'

9

THE YOUNGER CHILDREN, a risk factor, had been well tutored;
as well as the four times table they had learned never to speak
about it under any circumstances whatsoever. If they brought
a school friend home unexpectedly then they always called out from
the wood: 'Mum, isn't it nice, Pete is with me!' In other words: Get

them all upstairs. The war had made them suspicious and inventive. Bart had been accosted in the wood by the gardener's wife from the next-door property. 'Tell me, who is that woman at your place who sits at the sewing machine? ' He understood immediately that she must have seen Mrs. Meyer, who did sewing and mending from time to time. 'I went to borrow sugar from your mother but there was no one there, only that woman in the dining room.' 'Oh,' he improvised casually, 'that is one of my aunts, a sister of my mother, who sometimes does some sewing for us.'

Lotte's mother was back in charge. She baked potato cakes and enormous loaves. The people in hiding took it in turns to grind grain in the coffee mill. Meanwhile she rushed upstairs to settle a dispute that had arisen about whist. Her husband, who played it fanatically, was not a good loser. Mrs. Meyer cheated if she was driven to it. The Frinkels were immersed in an English correspondence course in preparation for their emigration to America as soon as the war was over. As soon as the war was over! A lofty phrase, a toast, a hopeful expectation, now that the Allies were in France and no one any longer looked up at the English bombers daily flying east in formation—everyone was agreed that the peace, alas, could only be achieved by means of destruction. Meanwhile two more people arrived to go into hiding. A saboteur who worked at the post office and read all the letters for the Security Service had discovered that Sammy Goldschmidt, and his wife's address in hiding, had been betrayed. They had to be taken somewhere else at once. Without wasting words, two beds were added and everyone shoved up a bit.

Two large brooms were slowly coming closer, one from the east, one from the south. Brooms with long bristles that were sweeping the Germans up into a heap, like dust. It was awaited impatiently all around. On Monday evening, the fourth of September, Radio Orange reported: 'According to Dutch government sources, the Allied armies have reached Breda.' The people in hiding hugged each other, laughing and crying, the master of the house fetched a bottle of gin out of his war supplies. But some days later the report was partially withdrawn. The Allies had only liberated a vulnerable corridor crossing through Brabant. They were marching north through this groove. A number of bridges over the rivers had been taken in a lightning raid, but at the bridge over the Rhine outside Arnhem it had failed. The onward march had been brought to a standstill. Lotte's father had to take down a couple of premature flags.

In the pale blue studio Lotte allowed herself to interpret everything in terms of millimetres of thickness; Ernst Goudriaan took off his glasses and brought his face close to the wood—he seemed to be involved in a secret conspiracy with the emerging violin. He forgot to put his glasses back on as he embraced her clumsily amid the shavings and a pot of bone glue, which fell on the floor and immediately began to spread a sickly rotting smell. Perhaps it was love, perhaps they used each other as an antidote to the war that put his nervous system and her conscience too much to the test. Unconsciously he was banishing her tarnished origins, releasing her from her earliest memories that had to do with a previous life. *Tabula rasa*—with him, through him, she was becoming undilutedly Dutch.

They were walking in the wood in broad daylight; with her at his side he was coolly tempting fate. They rested on a fallen oak. Over his shoulder he discovered a beefsteak fungus on one of the heavy branches, a tongue-shaped red-brown piece attached to the bark. He loosened it carefully. That evening Lotte fried it quickly on both sides watching that the blood did not run out. The fungus appeared at table like a *pièce de résistance*, everyone was served a portion of this gift from the gods, because everyone was always hungry.

The food shortages were becoming dire. They took it in turns to walk to the soup kitchen in the village, lugging back a churn of watery cabbage and potato stew. In response to the rumour that geese could be bought in Barneveld, Lotte and Koen, who still couldn't stay at home, went over on their bicycles. Just before Amersfoort they came across a caravan of evacuees from Arnhem including two little girls who were stumbling along with a cat on a rope. Further on they swerved onto the verge, ahead of a bus full of Blitzmädel dashing past at full speed. 'Bats,' said Koen scornfully, 'to hell with those bitches.' They cycled on in the stink left behind by the bus. It began to rain. An aeroplane skimmed so low over the road that the birds flew out of the

trees in terror. A second later they were startled by an enormous
bang—right in front of their eyes, in the distance, the bus exploded. A
column of fire shot up, the smoke evaporated into the rain clouds.
Koen, astonished that his wish had been fulfilled so rapidly, stared at
the scene open-mouthed, hesitating whether to think it was great or
terrifying. Lotte, on impulse, in a dumb reflex that she was not
responsible for, thought of Anna. They had still been there a minute
ago, they had whizzed past like birds in flight in their spotless grey
uniforms—now the war had become oddly visible here, between the
meadows in the drizzle. Imagine that Anna had been in that bus, then
she would have just lost a sister. The thought did not arouse a single
feeling in her. Anna had already become so blurred into a shadow figure that it was all the same to her whether she went up in smoke right
in front of her nose or not. Yet she cycled on with a slight reluctance,
until an evacuee stopped them and told them breathlessly that the station at Amersfoort had been bombed and all the transport trains were
ablaze. It was no place to cycle through, for a goose. They heaved
their bicycles over the ditch into the meadow and went around the
town in a semi-circle; the wind carried apocalyptic sounds to them.
They found their goose. With the goose and a bag of woodshavings,
in which fresh eggs were packed a safe distance from each other, they
returned home via a short cut.

There was a shortage of flour. Sara Frinkel remembered a gentleman farmer in the vicinity of Deventer, before the war a vigorous
admirer of Max's performance on the violin. She volunteered to make
the journey herself: nothing could happen to her, she had an impeccable identity card in the name of an Aryan seamstress from Arnhem.
She dismissed Lotte's mother's objections, 'He won't give you anything without me.' On a wet autumn day Sara and Jet set off for
Deventer by train armed with two empty sacks and Bart's old pram.
Max Frinkel's fame had not yet faded: they left the farm with full
stomachs and an overflowing pram. On the way back they found
shelter for the night in a stately manor house on the IJsselkade in
Deventer. The next day another address flashed into Sara's mind. She
was becoming ambitious: the one time she had left her hiding place
she wanted to come back laden with provisions—there was still room

in the bags. They left the pram behind under supervision and walked out of the town. There had been a storm in the night; the road was strewn with broken branches. Autumn rain assaulted their faces. A German police van stopped halfway—the window was wound down. 'Where are you going?' Daringly Sara named the village. 'Get in,' invited the driver jovially. 'Two lovely women in this beastly weather, that's not right.' They got in the front between the driver and an officer with a tight, tense face. They drove on in silence. Although the driver needed all his attention to keep the van on the road as it was being buffeted by the wind, he smiled roguishly at them in between. The other cast furtive looks to the side and discovered one of the famous noses of the Rockanje family, the hallmark of authenticity. 'You are a Jewess,' he cried shocked. 'Stop . . . stop! . . .' The driver braked. Trembling, Jet took her identity card out of an inner pocket to show it. He was not at all satisfied with its innocent contents. 'Nevertheless you are a Jewess,' he said stubbornly. 'Come now,' said Sara in High German, 'if she is a Jewess then I certainly must be one.' 'Let them be,' said the driver. The rain beating on the roof created an intimate, oppressive atmosphere in the cab. 'But she is a Jew,' droned the other. 'A child can see that.' He threw the door open in anger because he could not prove anything: 'Get out, both.' 'You'd better get out,' said the driver, giving them a defeated look. They did not know how to get out of the van fast enough. When it had disappeared behind a mist of raindrops they fell into each other's arms. The rain streamed down, but they did not feel it, wet as they were with anxious sweat. The desire to fill the bags had passed. They now had to conserve their strength for the journey home the next day with a laden pram. But it did not turn out like that. That night the town was bombed; they fell into a shelter and waited, crammed together in the semi-humid darkness. At the moment when the attack seemed to become more intense and the floor and walls were shuddering so violently that they no longer knew what was up or down, left or right, Jet began to scream incredulously, indignantly. 'The whole shambles is coming down like this all at once . . .' She went on ranting and raving, slumped, her hands over her ears. Fear gave her voice a volume that exceeded the din of the air raid. Sara tried to calm her in vain.

Hours later she was still on the verge of a breakdown—rigid and unapproachable, she crouched on the floor, only prepared to leave the shelter if she could go home on the first train. 'And what about the pram then,' said Sara. Jet looked at her witheringly.

They could only think in terms of food. A pram full of flour, that was so many loaves, which so many people could eat for so many days. This simple logic drove Lotte to Deventer, where Sara had left the pram behind with a sore heart. She went on a man's bicycle without tyres but with panniers, wearing oversized lace-up shoes from Ernst Goudriaan on her feet over a pair of worn-out socks held together by Mrs. Meyer's home efforts. In Deventer she loaded the contents of the pram into the panniers. The big barrier was the bridge over the IJssel; first she went without the bicycle to reconnoiter. There was a wooden building at the entrance where WA men were inspecting the traffic; halfway along was a shelter where a German sentry checked once more. He noticed her and winked. 'You want to bring food across the bridge?' he said softly. 'If possible,' she whispered. She would not be the first he had helped, he told her. He had thought up a system to lead people unseen past the Hollanders who stole everything edible. The bridge consisted of two parts, one for motorized vehicles and one for pedestrians. Between the two was a high wall, interrupted halfway along by his sentry box. If she navigated through the ruins of the Sperr district with the laden bicycle and ducked as she walked via the pedestrian part, towards the back of his sentry box, he would take the sacks of flour from her. Then she would have to walk back with the empty panniers and go past the Hollanders on the official road. Finally he would load the bags up again. She took his advice. They ordered her to go inside the Dutch post with the bicycle and all—a promised land of confiscated potatoes, bread, butter, cheese, bacon. The sentry peeked into her empty panniers, saw from her passport that she was far from home and said cheerfully: 'We'll give you some bread to take with you.' He took a loaf from an enormous pile and shoved it in her pannier. She could continue. Wheeling the bicycle she approached the German sentry. A squadron of Spitfires swerved over the bridge like a storm out of nowhere. 'To the wall, quick!' she heard someone shout in German.

She threw down her bicycle and pressed herself against the dividing wall. The bridge came under heavy fire, its groan was audible even in the infernal racket. From the corner of her eye she saw that one of her sacks had been hit. Her grain was beginning to flow out like a column of ants. Her breath caught: as the shells flew all about the German crawled towards it to stop up the hole with a rag, as carefully as though he were bandaging a wounded soldier. The Spitfires circled over the bridge once more then disappeared, leaving a gloomy silence behind. Beneath the bridge the IJssel flowed on impassively. Crumpled, Lotte struggled to her feet. She was still alive and everything was going on as usual. The German heaved the grain over into the panniers. His generosity so confused her that she thanked him in his own language. 'You remind me of my wife,' he said melancholically, 'we have two little children. I am looking forward to the end of the war with longing and fear. Hamburg has been bombed heavily. I don't know if they are still alive.'

The grain, the grain . . . only the grain mattered. She set off on her journey. On the road from Apeldoorn to Amersfoort the broad-leafed trees flamed orange and yellow between the permanent green of the pines. The sun was low and cast a sharp, uncompromising light on the colourless pedestrians wrapped up in old coats who were trudging along the road with anything that could be ridden, exhausted, hungry and continuously on their guard, fearing that at the very last moment they could still be deprived of the meagre supplies they had obtained in exchange for a ring or a brooch that had been their great grandmother's. Lotte walked among them and lugged her spoils of war with her. Two men were stumbling just in front of her; the contrast between them and the autumn colours on either side of the road was striking— they looked as though they had come out of damp dungeons and had not seen daylight in years. Their coats seemed mouldy, their hands and feet were wrapped in filthy bandages. The moment she caught up with them a deafening tumult broke out. The shadows of bombers slid over them, explosions sounded behind the copse. German soldiers appeared out of the crêpe paper shrubs. The two men looked around bewildered. 'Come, help me push,' yelled Lotte to give them an alibi in case there was a sudden checkpoint. 'Push!' They seized the handlebars, the luggage rack. Something exploded nearby, the three of them fled into the ditch, dived into a manhole. Gradually they realized that the railway line parallel to the road and soldiers' transports were the targets. Hidden in the earth, a grey film over their thin faces, in fits and starts the men told the story of their flight from Germany in the pandemonium around them. Prisoners of war, sent to work in a steel factory, at morning roll call like circus artistes they had to jump up high because the guards whipped them under their feet, for amusement. The feet ulcerated and did not heal. When the factory was bombed they fled in the chaos through the woods at night to the west—sleeping during the day. Their families lived in The Hague; they doubted whether they would get to them, the soles of their feet were festering away, their strength was exhausted by persistent delirium from hunger.

It grew quieter around them, except for the soft crackling and hissing of burning trains. The rumble of bombers died away; they disappeared over the horizon like angry insects and left an empty road behind, which soon became populated again with those who had to continue. In a village Lotte exchanged some grain for rye bread in the hope of bolstering the escapees' fortitude a little. Although they were slowing her down, she did not dare leave them to their fate. 'Let's sit down,' wailed one of them. Lotte was unrelenting, afraid that he would never get up again. 'Keep going . . . keep going.' 'It's finished,' he said, three kilometres further on. 'I can't anymore.' 'Just a bit . . . just a bit . . . you're almost there.' It was already dark; they were approaching Amersfoort. Lotte showed them the way to the hospital—it was known that the gates were always open, for everyone. 'They will certainly take you in there.' But they held on tight to their talisman. 'Don't leave us alone,' they pleaded. 'We will be picked up without you.' She shook her head. 'I can't go with you, with all that grain.' The grain, the grain . . . she had lost so much time already, she had to get out of the town with the grain before curfew.

Hastily she disappeared out of their sight with her top-heavy bicycle. She quickened her pace. It was one of those evenings, without moon, without clouds, ruled by an absolute blackness made even stronger by the window blackouts. The suspicion that she was becoming lost crept up on her. A man passed her with a cart behind his bicycle. She spoke to him. Yes, she was on the right road, but why didn't she put her things in his cart; then she wouldn't have to push so hard. He had a lamp. He could accompany her for a bit. She went along with his offer gratefully. He cycled at walking pace with her; nothing was said. What was there to talk about after curfew to an invisible stranger? All of a sudden, next to him, she became aware of an acceleration in his movements—her guide gained speed, cold-bloodedly he cycled away out of the silent bond. He disappeared into the darkness, swerving like a will o'the wisp in a marsh. All she heard was the dumb mechanism of her heart pumping. An emphatic absence of sound prevailed outside. And now anxiety got to her. On the bridge over the IJssel it had not succeeded, nor in the bombing of the railway—it had bided its time quietly. She began to scream. In the pitch blackness, intended for no one, she screamed straight through the curfew. Her volume had once rocked the water tower to its foundations, her voice had an exceptional carrying power. A police surveillance car arrived; a policeman gripped her by the upper arms to calm her; she gave her account in fragments. He pushed her into the car and began the pursuit. The headlights bored a tunnel into the darkness. Beyond emotion, a strange apathy came over her; she did not care whether they caught him, the once clearly delineated concept of friend or foe had become blurred, the undertaking had got out of hand, it was no longer her affair, others seemed to have taken it over. He was caught, forced to stop, scolded. Perhaps he had twelve starving children waiting for him at home for the proceeds of the nocturnal raid. She looked uninterestedly at the figures in the light of the headlamps. The grain was handed over for the umpteenth time—it would get worn away.

THEY HAD SETTLED on the Chalet du Parc. Once again they ducked behind a menu card; they did themselves proud. Their arthritis cure was mainly happening within the privacy of the bath house, the restaurants, *patisseries* and cafés, because it was January and they wanted the heat of the peat baths to last the whole day—but chiefly because it was easier to talk over a meal, a pastry, a cup of coffee as lightning conductor.

'Well,' Lotte considered, 'if you hadn't ransacked our country such scenes would not have happened.'

'We had our rationing, too,' said Anna weakly.

Lotte raised her eyebrows. 'You were the storehouse of Europe.'

Affronted, Anna let the menu drop. 'The French took revenge after the war. They starved us in the French zone.'

'*Ach.*' Lotte sighed. Always that *explaining away*. Always that: But we didn't have it easy either.

'What are you having?' said Anna. She had got an appetite from all those stories about shortages.

'I think . . .' Lotte hesitated, 'an *entrecôte marchand du vin* . . . or shall I have a *truite à la Meunière*?'

ANNA GOT HER military hospital. It was run by nuns; she learned fast, in her eagerness not to disappoint Martin. She was given responsibility for two wards, one for soldiers and one for officers—all had lost limbs at the ever-shrinking front. The alarm went at ten o'clock every morning: enemy aircraft on the way! The wounded had to be rushed to the shelters on special stretchers with wheels on one side and two handles on the other. Wooden rails had been fixed to the stairs. 'Sister Anna, hurry up!' cried one of the nuns. Needless to say, Anna was already running halfway down the stairs to the hairpin bend, a precarious moment for the amputees. Whipped on by the sirens, she hurried back and forth until the last patient had been taken to safety; as the first bombs fell she rushed back up to fetch their prostheses. No assistance could be expected from the nuns, they were completely preoccupied with getting the monstrance to safety. They prayed and sang and carried the Blessed Lord to a small improvised chapel so that he would not be hit by the bombs. Anna had no time to take a breather; the daily programme continued with energetic relentlessness despite the bombing: washing, distributing medicines, cleaning bandages. High and dry in the sky her beloved puppet-master could see his suspicions confirmed. The wounded were concerned—clearly seeing that Anna, driven by a motivation that was not of this earth, scarcely managed to eat or sleep. One day those who could move a little with the aid of their prostheses knocked together a regal couch for her made of coats, jumpers and pillows in a corner of the shelter. She allowed herself to be driven there under protest, thermometer still in hand—to fall instantly into a bottomless sleep, after they had put a blanket over her with brotherly tenderness.

In another ward there was a patient with an inoperable piece of shrapnel close to his heart. He could not move or be moved. He simply had to wait for the bombing raids in his hospital bed, in complete tranquility—excitement was a greater threat to his life than a bomb. The sisters took it in turns to watch over him together with his doctor. So Anna regularly sat there by his bed next to the window like a living target and chatted gently about innocent subjects. Opposite her on the other side of the bed the overworked doctor sat wearing an anti-aircraft helmet. Her idle chatter did not often misfire on him either. She saw his eyelids, his head, slowly droop. Before he dozed off he was still sufficiently conscious to remove the helmet from his head and put it in his lap. If a bomb fell close by them he sat up and put the helmet on in a reflex, and then it began all over again. Not unaware of this slapstick effect, Anna suppressed her laughter with difficulty, in the interests of the shrapnel.

While looking for one of the nuns, she lost her way in the hospital's building complex. She opened a random door that seemed to be the way into a large room, and froze on the threshold. She could barely control the impulse to run away again immediately, through the labyrinth of corridors outside. It was a ward without beds—soldiers missing all their limbs were lying on the floor. Their wounds had healed. Their bodies had been wrapped in leather so that they could roll over the floor like babies. The skimming autumn sunlight slid over what was left of them. All they could do was talk and roll. Anna shut the door abruptly. This was forbidden territory. She had seen something that did not exist. The other side of military grandeur, of

sabre rattling and insignias, of heroic words. Which soldier going off
to war was warned that this, too, could be his hinterland, as well as
the hero's death?

In the evenings she walked home through darkened streets, a journey full of surprises. The damage done during the day continually
altered the familiar look of the city. With difficulty she pushed her
front door open—two windowpanes had come out again, an icy
autumnal wind had blown the Feldpost letters she had been rereading
the previous evening around the apartment. She felt her way to the
chest of drawers to light a candle, she reached into a hole and almost
lost her balance. The chest of drawers was lying down below on the
street. A day later a woman collapsed before her eyes at the entrance
to the staircase. Anna recognized the pale face. After Martin's death
the woman had given her condolences on the staircase. 'I think it is so
hard for you,' she had whispered with a bowed head, 'you probably
think that the worst thing of all has happened to you, but there is
something worse.' She had run up to the top apartment in tears, leaving Anna behind with her cryptic, riddling prediction. Anna brought
her around with a wet cloth. 'I'll murder them!' cried the woman, getting up. 'Gently, gently . . .' soothed Anna. 'I'll know how to find
them when the war is over, I shall drink their blood, I swear it,' the
woman raved. The outburst brought some colour to her cheeks.
Anna held her by the shoulders: 'What's the matter then?' Immediately slumping into a position of resignation, the woman shared with
Anna in a dull voice her husband's unexpected arrest some months
ago. He had been picked up while leaving his daughter's watch for
repair with an old acquaintance who had a watch shop. The daughter
was a nurse and what is more she wore the brown uniform with sin-
cere conviction. Unaware that the watchmaker was suspected of
communist activities, her husband had been wrongly taken to be one
of them. Since then he had been in prison under sentence of death,
chained up, unable to move. Water was dripped on to his head every
minute, day and night. The thought of it was driving her mad. 'But
they have really made a terrible mistake!' Anna cried indignantly.
That an innocent had been convicted, that they had acted so unfairly;
with her sense of justice and her orderly efficient approach, she could

not understand, but on top of it all she immediately felt the urge to take action because it was so unacceptable that they could let the poor devil die an endlessly slow martyr's death in a cunning way that could only have been conceived by a madman. She put an arm around the woman. 'Leave it to me,' she said grimly.

The Gauleiter resided in the old parliament building of the former Habsburg monarchy, which had become the administrative headquarters of the Ostmark under the Third Reich. Anna was in one of her tempers; she marched there, up the stairs, into the historic buildings that bore evidence of superabundant riches, through a long columned corridor with motionless SS soldiers like stuffed corpses with rifles every ten metres. Although no one ever came into this sanctuary uninvited they were too dumbfounded by the appearance of a hurtling Red Cross sister to intervene. Anna was not troubled by anxiety or modesty; the ring of her footsteps on the marble floor sounded like a confirmation of her righteousness. At a crossing in the corridors she became confused for a moment. Eventually a sentry barred her way. 'Where do you wish to go?' 'To the Gauleiter.' 'Why?' 'I want to see the Gauleiter!' Two others came over, they looked at each other quizzically. What was a hysterical hospital sister doing here? 'My husband has just been killed serving with the Waffen-SS.' Haughtily she held the letter of condolence from the Obersturmführer under their noses. They had no reply to that. They escorted her to the required place as though she were a diplomat.

In her fantasy the Gauleiter had acquired monstrous proportions. In reality he sat in a gaudy room that must once have been the emperor's study behind an immense desk: a kind-hearted old man with a long beard—a sort of Santa Claus. Surprised, he gave her an encouraging nod. After taking a deep breath she cast the scandalous error at his feet. 'I know those people, they are Nazis, their daughter is a Brown Sister! The Führer would not stand for such a thing! He does not know that an error has been made here, someone must inform him!' The Gauleiter nodded like a weary grandfather who can refuse his granddaughter nothing. 'Do me a favour,' he said slowly. 'Go home and see that the wife writes a letter requesting mercy. And bring the letter to me personally.'

The fruit of Anna's efforts was the return home, fourteen days later, of a man who could only whisper about the forms of entertainment they had thought up for him in advance of his execution. He had lost the knack of eating, each movement was painful and exhausting. He slid into his bed with the last of his strength and stayed there, too weak to live or die. His wife had to go to work during the day. That was why she was not there at the end of March when a bomb fell on the block and blasted a hole ten metres wide. When Anna came home all she could see, instead of her flat, was the flats behind it. There was a heap of rubble up to the former first floor—beneath it they had found the one sentenced to death, a neighbour explained. 'God, you are a sadist,' cried Anna. The wind whispered in her ear: Do you still believe in justice, idiot? She clenched her teeth. She could not complain to the Gauleiter about this . . . she had to look for a higher authority . . . in a more rarefied district . . .

That same wind also carried the smell of dried mud—the Russians were advancing. During a staff meeting the sisters heard that the hospital would have to be evacuated in two hours. A hospital ship was ready on the Danube; all the wounded had to be transported there. Anna crept out unseen to say goodbye to her father-in-law. She pressed the packet of Feldpost letters into his hand hastily; since the apartment had been bombed she had kept them in the air raid shelter at the military hospital, stuffed into two suitcases with her other paraphernalia. 'Please burn these,' she said hurriedly, 'otherwise they might yet be published in *Izvestia*.'

When she got back there was a line of buses at the entrance to the hospital. She had just finished helping in the patients from her wards and was going to sit at the front, flanked by her suitcases, when she was pulled out again by her apron. 'Wait a moment, Sister, you can't do that!' Before she knew what was happening, the medicaments and medical history notes of all the wounded, numbering a hundred and sixty, were handed over to her, Anna, an improvised Red Cross Sister, by the nuns who were staying behind. She was pushed with these into a bus containing seriously wounded men she did not know; it set off immediately. Hopefully her suitcases were travelling behind her in the other bus. The bus moved off at a rapid pace as though it wanted to cast off the imminent deaths of its passengers—unfortunately it was forced to stop halfway at a tunnel whose ceiling was too low. Another bus was ordered. Meanwhile Anna and the driver unloaded the wounded and laid them on stretchers on the verge. It was getting dark—the Russians were coming—they stood there and waited and looked at the tunnel as though that was their last connection with the world of the living. Another bus, of more suitable dimensions, appeared in the darkness. The patients, chilled to the bone, were shoved inside and it proceeded to the banks of the Danube. There one hundred and sixty wounded were laid in the damp grass. Hastily rustled-up orderlies carried them into the ship one by one over a narrow gangplank. Anna was buttonholed by a couple drenched by the rain. 'The boy being carried in now is our son. He has a pistol on him. We are frightened he is going to do something to himself. He can't bear it that we are losing the war.' She promised them she would keep an eye on him and went to look for her suitcases. In the distance she heard her name being called in unison: 'Sister Anna from 3-C, here we are!' In her ears it sounded like a *Missa Solemnis* whose passages were being borne on the wind in fragments—she ran towards the sound, criss-crossed between the wounded, and found her own wounded, who had refused to board the ship without her. They were sitting in a large circle with their prostheses on the grass, guarding her suitcases. Their Sister, her patients—during the previous months a mutual craving for possessiveness had come into existence; they were a big family that would only board the ship together.

After completing their task the orderlies vanished, leaving Anna behind in an overloaded ship. To assist her in the care of the wounded, who lay around about in no particular system, she had five hastily recruited middle-class women, without training or nursing experience. They wore aprons and caps and were regarded as being endowed with a natural talent for the business of caring purely on account of being female. It became clear all too soon that their talents resided at another level, and that they had a completely different idea of their duties. Whenever she needed them to hand out the urine bottles, medicines, meals, Anna found them after a long search in the arms of soldiers. They had been grass widows throughout the whole

war. Now they were making up for their loss under the charitable
pretext that they were providing a divine medicine for the poor devils
who had been wounded in the battle for the Fatherland—perhaps
even fatally: an extra *frisson*.

From sheer necessity Anna split herself into one hundred and sixty
parts: one changed bandages, the next assisted the emptying of the
bowels, a third mopped the fevered brows—all at the accelerated pace
of a silent film. At night those fragments could not all get back together
again, they continued as usual with their own activities. After two days
she was stumbling about with red eyes from tiredness. No one noticed
it except Herr Töpfer, a high-ranking SS officer from her own ward
who had lost a leg on the Hungarian front. 'You will fall over,' he
observed, pushing her into a chair, 'sit down.' Leaning on his crutch he
looked around like a general; he raised his voice to address his officers:
'I say the following to you. Sister Anna cannot cope anymore. She must
have sleep. We need a couple of walking volunteers who can take over
the duties from her; she has a list and she can tell you where the people
are—it's a question of organization.' His audience nodded in agreement. 'Secondly,' continued Töpfer, 'there is a spare bed in my cabin. I
am offering it to Sister Anna. If any one of you has any reservations I
will gladly hear them now. Woe betide anyone who I only get to hear
from tomorrow morning. I'll shoot him dead. Do you understand?'

He took her to the cabin and tucked her in tenderly. Anna slept
instantly; when she woke the caring Töpfer was lying next to her, he
had retreated to a corner and held on to the edge of the bed even as
he slept, so that he would not roll onto her. He had given his own bed
to a dying man who was gasping incomprehensible swear words.

They moored at Linz the following evening. The seminary stood
like an impenetrable fortress in the rain, a colossal dark building,
which was to be set up as an emergency hospital. When Herr Töpfer,
who had limped up to it, supported by Anna, used the weapon of his
voice, the door opened a crack. A fat sleepy man appeared in the
doorway in silk pyjamas over which he had slipped a uniform tunic
and looked at them with bad grace. Oh yes, the ship with the
wounded . . . he scratched his head . . . but they would have to be
deloused first of course? '*Verdammtes Schwein!*' cried Töpfer, beside

himself at such ignorance and incompetence, 'watch out that you don't have lice. We don't have them, we come from a tidy hospital. Find us beds immediately!' The man opened the double doors trembling.

Everything had been prepared inside: there were wooden platforms with sacks of straw in the former classrooms, large cavernous rooms. At least the wounded would get beds again. The ship departed immediately after unloading. The surrogate Sisters went back with it, satisfied from overwork. Anna was left alone as Mother Superior of the wounded. Everyone tried to sleep, including her, seated at a large table in the centre of the room with her head on her folded arms. Töpfer woke in the middle of the night. 'What are you doing here? You can leave us alone peacefully, everyone is sleeping! Go to bed!' 'But where is that bed?' Anna yawned. 'What?' His blanket moved, he grasped his crutch and limped out of the room indignantly. Silk pyjamas was bawled out of bed: 'If you don't immediately . . .' 'Yes, yes, yes . . .' he cried nervously. He found a bed for her somewhere; it was still warm from whoever had to make room for her, but Anna did not ask herself any more questions of conscience.

THEY HAD BOTH chosen trout—easily digested—with boiled potatoes. Lotte thought of 'The Trout,' Schubert's song she had once studied, and of the tragic ending: '. . . The little fish wriggled on it . . .' She associated the image of a powerless fish, floundering on the line, that only had a body and a head, with the fourfold amputees in the Viennese hospital. 'It had never occurred to me,' she said, 'that anyone could lose all his limbs . . . gruesome.'

Anna put her fork down. 'They were young men. I have asked myself what became of them. I've never read a word about them in a paper, a periodical, a book. Yet they were still alive! Where have they gone?'

They ate on in silence, each at the mercy of her own speculations.

'Your husband's letters from Poland, Russia, Normandy,' Lotte remarked. 'Were they actually burnt?'

Anna sprang up. 'I could still kick myself . . . they would have been a lovely memento now, a document. Unfortunately my father-in-law bravely did what I asked him. Burned everything. It was the effect of the propaganda: When the Russians come they will take everything they fancy. If they find my letters, largely written from Russia, I reasoned, they would find them very interesting and print them in their communist newspaper. That's how we thought then.'

Lotte laughed ironically. 'As if they would have been interested in them! One soldier's life meant nothing to the Russians. At any rate, a human life represented nothing under Stalin.'

'Nevertheless we were still being brainwashed! Up to the end of the war. "The Führer would not stand for such a thing," I said to the Gauleiter. Imagine it! In all sincerity. Although I had never marched behind him and just like everyone else I knew that he could not win the war, I was still so naive I could not imagine that the innocent were being sentenced to death and martyred under his authority. End of 1944! God, how naive I was . . .'

From pure anger she forgot to eat anymore.

THIS WAS THE second atheist-Jewish Christmas they celebrated together. Everyone had lost weight; the stew from the soup kitchen had become so thin you could drink it. Lotte's father, who secretly supplied electricity to the doctor and the liquor merchant, and befriended farmers, had come home with a perversely large piece of pork and a bottle of gin. His wife disappeared to the kitchen with it and basted the meat, simmering it gently in a casserole. Lotte fetched the dinner set from the cupboard. Mrs. Meyer came downstairs, alarmed by the distinctive smell of *fricandeau* with ground cloves. 'Er . . . we're not allowed to eat that,' she said, looking peevishly into the pot. 'What would you rather be,' inquired the cook sensibly, 'a dead orthodox Jewess or a sinner, alive and kicking?' Mrs. Meyer capitulated, no match for such healthy opportunism.

The table was laid, the candles were lit, everyone drew up a chair. Lotte and Ernst were still in the kitchen peeling a second batch of potatoes boiled in their skins, when they heard the distant rumble of an aircraft that was approaching fast. They stiffened with the potato knives in their hands. A bang, as strong as a lightning strike, took the ground from under their feet and made the windows rattle in their frames. A bizarre change of air pressure beat them to the ground amid the scattered potatoes. 'We're going to die,' squealed Mrs. Meyer's voice. The whole gathering fled from the dining room with the fragile bay window into the walled-in-kitchen. They crouched there—Mrs. Meyer, in the idle hope that youth was immortal, hung round Eefje's neck; she bravely remained upright. Then it became absurdly quiet and they straightened up suspiciously one by one. In the dining room they found Sara Frinkel, who had meanwhile gone on with the dislocated Christmas meal on her own. She was eating with gusto. 'I didn't want my potatoes to get cold,' she uttered with her mouth full. All the windows had cracked, the glass hung like fine lace curtains. Sara pointed to the meadows with a piece of meat on her fork. 'I saw an enormous flash.' 'It sounded like a crashing aircraft,' said Bram. 'If the pilot has ejected . . . we can expect a large scale operation here,' suggested Ernst Goudriaan, with increasing panic in his eyes. He was still holding the potato knife in his hand as though he thought he could defend himself with it. He looked around in terror. 'The Jews . . . the Jews . . . must go upstairs . . . !' 'What "Jews,"' cried Sammy Goldschmidt, offended. 'That's how it all started, they swept us all into one heap.' 'You're right, you're right . . .' Ernst raised his hands guiltily. 'But what ought I to say?' 'Person in hiding,' said Sara carefully, 'after all, you yourself are person in hiding, too.'

While they were disappearing behind the mirror upstairs—those who coincided with their mirror image neutralized themselves and ceased to exist—Lotte's father went to reconnoiter, as his job permitted him to leave the house after curfew. On going out he discovered the front door had vanished; he retrieved it undamaged in the meadows. The other members of the family had to create the illusion of an ordinary Christmas celebration in case there was going to be a house search. The plates of the people in hiding were taken away—they were sitting crestfallen behind the cold turnips; the candles flickered and dripped in the draught. A chilly wind blew through the curtains, now and then a piece of glass fell to the floor. They sat around the table like actors waiting for the curtain to rise. Lotte was aware that it was a long time since they had been by themselves—it seemed that

they had forgotten how to be like that. Covertly she looked at her
mother, who was still the linchpin. She was sitting bolt upright . . .
she still puffed her chest out against the wolf and kept her cubs from
his jaws. But the chestnut glow had disappeared from her pinned-up
hair, even the tortoiseshell comb had dulled. Somewhere during the
war she had begun to go grey and to abandon some of her invincibil-
ity. A strong gust of wind blew all the candles out. The door was
thrown open, her father came in. 'They can all come down,' he said.
'It was a bomb. Where's the gin?' After he had knocked back the contents of his glass in one gulp he told them that a stray bomb had
blown a deep crater in the lawn of a nearby eighteenth-century
manor house. The neoclassical entrance porch had been rammed into
the salon, pillars and all; the lady of the house, who had gone to
stand by the window to see where the racket was coming from, had
been taken away screaming with her eyes full of glass.

Life narrowed down to survival—the increasingly frequent poach-
ing expeditions inclined more and more to the demonic. Lotte and
Jet, Marie and Lotte, foraged about the tip of the province of North
Holland from farm to farm like peddlers with linen, rings, strings of
pearls, watches, brooches, light-headed with hunger. On the gate a
placard said 'We don't give out water.' Dogs were set on them. Somewhere people were threshing—uninvited onlookers waited patiently
until a few grains fell by the wayside. A nasty polar wind raced across
the frozen fields, the ice groaned in the ditches and canals. Near the
Afsluitsdijk the road passed a German outpost. To comfort the hungry hordes who were stumbling by with the promise of a better
world, a world of plenty, the officers had put the dining table outside—ostentatiously they sat at their steaming plates piled high with
vegetables and sausage, the buttons burst off their uniforms from
guzzling. Lotte looked at this tableau with a dry mouth. By means of
an intricate psychological manoeuvre she forged her inflamed feelings
of hate into contempt, which was more bearable on an empty stomach.

There were generous farmers, too, who gave food and drink to
passers-by and laid out straw sacks in the stables. The most cynical
stayed awake at night to rob their dozing companions; as a matter of

course Lotte slept with her head on the jumper in which the jewels were wrapped. When they had already given up all hope on the way back, in the Beemster their sacks were filled with potatoes by a farmer's wife who refused to accept anything in exchange. To return home with full bags was the only triumph on earth still worth achieving. In Amsterdam they crossed the IJ by the ferry—a thick, chilly mist was hanging over the water. WA men turned up to search through the passengers' bags. Jet and Lotte made themselves small—depriving them of the potatoes would rob them of their souls as well. A boy of about eight was standing by the handrail, his worn-out trousers flapped round his legs; there was a a resigned expression on the sharp old man's face beneath his cap. He had a cart, its load covered by a piece of sailcloth, yet the approaching inspection seemed to leave him cold. He was staring out over the IJ into the mist, screeching seagulls were emerging out of it; he saw no reason to turn as the two uniforms came up to him decisively. 'Young man,' said one of them ironically, 'would you be so kind as to lift up that sail so that we can look at the cargo.' The boy looked ahead impassively, motionless. 'Looks like he's a bit deaf.' They became impatient. 'Lift that sail up!' Lotte's throat went thick with rage. He is a child, leave him in peace, she wanted to shout, but the potatoes disabled her tongue. 'Get a move on, lout, do what I say!' The boy leaned over stiffly, a thin wrist came out of the frayed sleeve as he gripped a corner of the sail and dutifully pulled it back. Beneath it lay a dead man, with bent legs—emaciated, with hollow eye sockets and ears sticking out from his bony skull. His body was strangely twisted midway, as though it had snapped. 'Who is that?' said the guard, vainly trying to make his question sound like an order. 'My father,' said the boy flatly. He drew the sail back and stared across the water again. Fragments from *Der Erlkönig* came back to Lotte. The boy was the representation of the opposite: '. . . it is the child with his father . . . in his arms the father was dead . . .'

A week later, it began to snow. Misery hid beneath unspoilt whiteness; from the air the occupied north seemed to be united with the liberated south, thanks to the snow. The iron stove in the studio, fed with damp kindling, gave out more black smoke than heat. Ernst tried to keep the plane under control in his numbed fingers, forced to squint through his sooted-up glasses. 'And meanwhile at home in Utrecht I still have sacks of coal,' he grumbled. Lotte volunteered to fetch them; he did not refuse her offer, convinced as he was of her indestructibility. She set off—she made her way through the snow with the bicycle, pausing now and then to take a sip from the beet-root stew her mother had given her to carry in a small pan. It snowed again from time to time; she made slow progress, the little flakes stung her face. Bent forward she pushed the heavy bicycle onwards, her consciousness solely on that one radiant point of coal glowing on the horizon, which was already spreading heat into her spirit. Outside of that there was only the white void, absolute deso-lation. Her hands and feet froze; the cold spread inward from those extremities and settled itself within, in a not unpleasant heaviness. She had no idea how long she had already been on the road, how far she still had to go. Every notion of time dissolved in the abstraction of all-encompassing whiteness—a benevolent peace descended upon her. Clods of snow stuck to her laced-up shoes; the contours of a lumpy fort were vaguely revealed in a snowy expanse of white, through a fine network of crystals that had settled on her eyelashes. An irresistible temptation emanated from a tree with white branches like a photographic negative: a brief repose. She leaned the bicycle against the trunk and let herself sink into the snow, a soft blanket beneath her that soon covered her. She could not finish a single thought anymore—like white butterflies they fluttered through her heaviness. All contradictions and paradoxes dissolved in a woolly nothing; she vaguely remembered a corresponding perception from long ago, when she sank through the ice and a few seconds stretched into an eternity. She forgot that she had a body. The sound of falling snow . . . was her last thought before she sank away into a carefree, delightful oblivion.

'Come . . . if you lie there you'll die.' Someone was pulling her roughly by the arm back to reality. The snow slid off her. She was too far gone to resist. The bicycle was pushed into her hands. 'I'll walk with you.' She walked like a wound-up, mechanical doll, accompa-nied by a man in a long, black coat with a snowy hat. He was breathing heavily—the only sound to be heard as they trudged onwards. He asked nothing, said nothing, but confined himself to brief exhortations when the pace slackened. 'Keep walking . . .' She had the sense of being on the threshold of an important memory, but one that could not break through the screen of her dullness. It was already dark when the town loomed up and they trudged along empty streets to the centre. At the fish market he suddenly took his leave of her by removing his hat, piles of snow falling from it . . . it seemed again as though the shadow of a memory was catching her unawares as a dark street swallowed him up.

Only then did she realize that the person she was staring after had saved her life. He had turned up out of nowhere like a *deus ex machina*—he had disappeared again as though he were no more than a hallucination. It had stopped snowing. The town was deserted, the snow lay on a few corpses in the shelter of a wall, hunger had left clear traces behind on their upturned faces. An astonished landlady let her in. His rooms were still intact; his possessions, mainly books about violin-making, and family portraits, were waiting stoically for his return—she looked at them as she slowly returned to normal temperature. The only thing missing from the interior was the coal. The landlady, who cleaned the rooms, gave herself away in the exaggeration of her denial. Coal? No, if there had been any coal she would have known about it. Lotte could not prove anything. She spooned the last remains of beetroot stew out of the pan and crept into his narrow, chilly bed.

10

O EUFS À LA *neige* is the poetic name of a dessert that was a means of conquering hunger with air during the war. At that time Lotte got cramps in her wrists by whisking up the miracle of the age from the whites of two eggs into an ever-expanding foam.

'I made that for the children in the hunger winter,' said Lotte, spooning one of the islands out of the vanilla sauce, 'to chase away the empty feeling in their stomachs.'

Anna sighed. 'I did not know that you had endured so much hunger.'

'It was a better weapon than the V-1,' said Lotte curtly.

Anna switched tactically to another subject. 'And you were almost snowed under. . . . I recognize the feeling of absolute desolation in the midst of nature, which is essentially indifferent . . . and the longing for death that can assail you against the background of the war.'

THE DOCTORS AND nurses turned up the day after they had arrived at the seminary, and it was business as usual with normal equipment. Herr Töpfer, who was already in the convalescent phase, asked official permission for Sister Anna to accompany him on his practice walks in the garden. They walked very slowly between the snowdrops and budding hazels. There was a watery sun; they rested on a mossy bench. 'Sister, it's over with us,' Töpfer stated mercilessly. 'Up to now the pendulum still swung back and forth to the east, to the west, but now it has come to a halt in the middle—they are advancing from all sides and will crush us.' 'We still have the V-2,' Anna interposed. 'You don't really believe that, Sister. It simply is finished. My parents, my wife, my children—they are all hoping for my return, but when the Russians come they will shoot all the SS here.' Anna nodded mechanically—the Russians' revenge was proverbial. The SS were recognizable, even naked, by the tattooed blood group on their arms. She looked around, soon the snowdrops would be trampled under Russian boots. A sense of fear came over her for the first time, not for herself but for the wounded whom she was trying to patch up, and for whom she sacrificed her night's sleep. '*Ach*, Sister' the sombre Töpfer held her by the chin and looked at her dolefully. 'We had such beautiful dreams.'

The feeling of approaching calamity no longer left her alone; it was difficult to wait calmly and yet not to wait. At any rate, waiting calmly for the collapse of the Third Reich was not on for the boy with the pistol. Anna kept her eye on him, waiting for the opportunity to filch it from him. She went to sit on the edge of his bed in between her duties and listened to his feverish plans that concealed his inability to face up to the loss of his ideals. He had been active in the Hitler Youth even when it was illegal; he had lost an eye in a street fight with communist youths. He had reached officer rank in the Wehr-macht—even though he was in the military hospital with a shattered knee he was not contemplating capitulation! One night as he slept, Anna carefully removed the pistol from beneath his pillow. She threw it into the Danube with relief. The next day she went to sit with him with an innocent expression. He grasped her hand, his eye shone. 'Sister,' he said conspiratorially, 'come with me to the Werewolf!' She shook her head. He aroused her pity with his naive fantasies about the Werewolf movement, a group of desperadoes who were with-drawing to the Alps to continue the fight to the death. 'You're crazy, *Junge*, it's over,' she said softly. 'If you are right I will shoot myself in the head,' he cried vigorously. 'They won't get their hands on me alive.' To demonstrate that he meant it he rummaged under his pil-low. The emptiness he found there enraged him—where was the thief who had stolen from him the right to decide on his own life? He twisted himself out of his bed and limped through the ward with a flushed face and clenched jaw, dragging the leg with the shattered knee behind him. Anna barred his way. 'Stop screaming! The pistol is in the Danube. I took it, no one else did. Your father and mother asked me to. I promised them I would.' The one eye stared at her in bewilderment. He stiffened and clenched his fists—she should not see the shuddering tension suppressed in his body—then he burst into tears, his lust for battle collapsed; he crumpled up as though she had given him a beating—leaning heavily on her he allowed himself to be led willingly back to his bed.

The war quickened. The front was just twenty-five kilometres away from Linz; a night-time transport to Germany was improvised for all the patients who could move at all or who could somehow be carried. All reported except twelve patients with serious back injuries—they could only lie prone. Anna was given the task of watching over them that night. Moved, she went to say goodbye to her old patients from Vienna. 'Open that box a moment,' ordered

Herr Töpfer, pointing with his crutch. Anna fiddled with the lock; inside there was a packet on top. 'Take it out and lock the box again please.' She obeyed his instructions carefully. Her heart was thudding; it was as though he had been watching over her all that time, and now he was going away. 'Come,' he beckoned. 'Come with me.' In a recess in the long, cold corridor he opened the packet. His hands were trembling. 'Listen carefully, I am giving this to you, it is chocolate. I had been keeping it for my wife but I think you can make better use of it now. We are all leaving, tonight you will be all alone; eat the chocolate then, you will need it.'

He had prescience. That night as the seminary emptied silently, Anna sat by the light of a candle near the twelve wounded whom she recognized by the nature of their injuries, not by their faces. She sat there and obeyed Töpfer's last order; she ate herself into a delirium with his chocolate so that it would not strike her that they had all absconded. By morning she emerged from her stupor. Wobbling from tiredness and nausea she stumbled out of the ward. The seminary seemed just as deserted as on the night they had arrived; the doctors had disappeared, the nurses with their bandages and the medicines, even the caretaker in his silk pyjamas, had fled the sinking ship. A solemn, almost pious, silence prevailed—was this the silence that preceded the ultimate slaughter, like the squalls that presaged thunderstorms, an oppressive, charged silence? What was she doing in this godforsaken spot, far from home. Far from home? She had no home, there was nothing to long for, no fireside, no apple orchard . . . no one waiting for her with yearning. She heard the echo of her footsteps on the tiles as though she were chasing herself. Each cavernous room that she went in to emphasized her solitude . . . a house with empty rooms from a dream, every room led on to yet another empty room. 'Sister . . .' the wail of the patients who had been entrusted to her like terminally ill babies drove her back to the ward. But she could neither relieve their pain nor cleanse their wounds—she had nothing but some pieces of paper at her disposal to wipe away the pus, as she calmed them with hollow words. Thoughts, ideas, perceptions went through her without touching any other emotional thread but morose long-suffering. The day slipped by her, gradually changing into evening, and still no one came to take her place. Had they been forgotten by everyone; did they not appear in any plan, no single scheme, had they already been crossed out? The electricity had stopped a week earlier, they had managed with candles—these, too, had been taken away. She sat at her post in the dark; you could have thought they were already dead. Although there were thirteen of them, each one of them was alone and fighting against despair in his own way. It was clear that she had come to the end of her peregrinations. This was the point all lines had been leading to. Her soap bubble burst and left an emptiness behind, where only the smell of dying soldiers hung.

But she was not alone. A familiar companion of old emerged; he was trustworthy; a precise allure emanated from him that suited the circumstances. He did not burden you with an unreliable strategy for living, he laughed at all the senseless striving, he asked nothing, demanded nothing . . . the only thing he desired from her was that she not resist him. She left the ward without looking around; she picked up one of the suitcases, which contained baby clothes. Hypnotized, she walked outside, went down to the river. The Danube was black; she hesitated: if she went in from the bank she would not be able to prevent herself swimming. She walked up onto the middle of the baroque bridge. I promised you that I would not do it, she murmured, forgive me. The words dissolved into the sound of the rain. The bridge was there, and the water beneath it, and the promise of peace that lay enclosed there. She lifted the suitcase up onto the balustrade, which came up to her shoulders, and tried to pull herself up. But the mossy stone ledge was wet and slippery; she could not get a grip and suddenly lacked the strength in her arms, which used to be so tough in the old days. Once again she tried, and again . . . she scrabbled up and slid back again. She refused to resign herself to failure . . . how could something as banal as a balustrade of a bridge stand in the way of a matter of life and death. In frustration she seized the suitcase and flung it over into the depths below. What worked for the suitcase would work for her too. But the balustrade was just a bit too high and slippery everywhere. Up there, there was laughter at her ludicrous efforts: Anna, always so resolute and efficient, going about her suicide so pitifully and clumsily!

She gave up and trudged off the bridge up the slope back to the seminary. It was all over; she had left her life behind, tossed it into the Danube, it was floating away in the suitcase—only her body was still there; there was nothing else to do but let it move the way it usually did. She went back into the room and waited with resignation until the waiting would come to an end. But only the rain ceased; she stared outside indifferently and saw, without actually taking it in, that the sky was slowly clearing. She had no sense of time; somewhere in that endless night there was a knocking on the door. Half asleep she shuffled down the corridor. They seemed to be in a hurry; the doors were flung open. 'Where is the military hospital?' cried impatient SS orderlies. 'What hospital?' said Anna, 'Surely this is a military hospital!' 'I don't know if this is still a hospital . . .' She hesitated. 'I should have been relieved, but no one . . .' They had no time to listen to her, the front was very close, they had to unload and get back. The wounded were laid on each side of the corridor in a great hurry; the stretchers were taken away for the subsequent victims, the blankets, too. Before she had realized it they had gone away, and she paced to and fro between rows of badly wounded—at least a hundred. Boys who had been taking part energetically in the battle a couple of hours before lay naked on the chessboard motif of the stone floor, reduced to a memo that stated where they had been operated on. Moonlight came through the high, Gothic windows onto their unconscious, pathetically young bodies. The romantic moon, patron saint of lovers, shone without compassion upon their nakedness, in a perverse aesthetic. Anna walked up and down, taunted; she could do nothing except witness their deaths. Her disgust at the phenomenon of war became greater with every soldier who died. This was how it was, everything that she had gone along with up to now had been merely a prelude. This was it—all care, fostering, sacrifices of anonymous mothers, all dreams and expectations, everything was felled by an obtuse, premature death. The son, fiancé, father, no more than a naked, numb, redundant thing, a name on a card.

A soldier came to. '*Schwester . . .*' he rattled. Anna bent down over him. He seized her arm, his eyes glittered. '*Schwester,* we're still holding out!' 'Yes, my boy,' Anna nodded. He wanted to add something else, opened his mouth with elation, but at the same moment something invisible happened in his body. The unspoken word died on his lips, his body went rigid—the frozen expression of stubborn passion was so unbearable that she quickly closed his eyes.

Somehow or other the dawn broke; the dead were grey in the dull morning light. Once again the doors were flung open, doctors and orderlies swarmed inside the building. They looked around fleetingly; what they saw seemed not to surprise them, except for Anna's presence. She was stared at as though she were a ghostly apparition. 'What are you doing here,' cried one of the doctors in astonishment, stroking his ginger moustache. 'Have you gone mad, the Russians are coming!' 'And so . . . ?' she said indifferently.

A day later it was teeming with industrious Red Cross Sisters. Anna did not know where they had come from; she had long ago given up wanting to understand anything about it: suddenly there was talk of organization again, everyone got on with their own duties—but she was not taken in by it, it was no more than a cover for the chaos that could gain the upper hand at any moment. A meeting was called, too. The adjutant summoned all the doctors, orderlies and sisters together to receive the Gauleiter's instructions. 'The Upper Danube region is holding fast,' he announced. 'We will remain here at our posts under all circumstances. The Sisters, too. They have no reason whatever to be anxious about the Russians. Their safety in this hospital is assured.' Anna, sceptically letting his soothing words bounce off her, stepped forward from the middle of a group of nurses and shouted, 'But you have already sent your own wives and daughters away, eh?' The Sisters pulled her back into the group in a reflex so that she became a uniform among uniforms again. 'Who was that?' said the Gauleiter sharply. He sent his adjutant over; the Sisters were asked in turn who had called out but no one answered—they closed ranks.

After the meeting the doctor with the moustache took Anna aside. 'Listen, Sister,' he said confidentially, 'I have four wounded patients

here and only their arms are bandaged—they can walk. Now I am
going to give you and two other Sisters a marching order to accompany them to Munich.' Anna nodded mechanically. Naturally, she
still did what she was told, even if it was something rather pleasant
like leaving the seminary. 'Incidentally,'—he scratched behind his ear
with his pen—'did you hear that yesterday, that woman who called,
"But have you already sent your wives and daughters away?" ' He
looked at her with such a shrewd but at the same time faithful dog's
expression that Anna replied in a tone that implied a confession, 'Yes,
I heard it.' At once she realized why he had thought of the marching
order to Munich. Because she could not thank him openly she let him
know with her eyes that she knew that he knew that she knew.

'IT SEEMS LIKE something from a former life,' Anna murmured.

Lotte was staring at her. For the first time behind the face opposite
her she could see the young woman Anna must have been—on a
stone bridge in the rain, in a corridor with dying soldiers. It touched
her more than she could concede to herself. Making an effort to get
her voice to sound matter-of-fact she said, 'How could all those badly
wounded soldiers possibly be left behind?'

'You have to imagine it: The front is close by . . .'—Anna gesticulated—'Orderlies carry the wounded out of the battle and take them
to the field hospital. The most severe cases are dressed there, something is scribbled on paper—such and such was done—then they are
chucked into a vehicle and ordered to a military hospital behind the
lines. Then they dump them and have to go back straight away. They
were SS, the Waffen-SS were the ones fighting to the last, the
youngest, healthiest boys. One after the other died before my eyes
that night. There was no one to nurse them. That long, dreadful corridor. I was alone and I could do nothing. I have repressed that night
for years, I could not talk about it. There's a song, "A moonlit night
in April," that always makes me think of it.'

SEVEN INSIGNIFICANT LITTLE figures progressed with difficulty
beneath a heavy sky. Anna was lugging her possessions in a fat

leather suitcase. They slept in schools or churches on the way—villages were obliged to provide shelter for them on presentation of the collective marching order. One of the soldiers discovered a cart somewhere into which they could put all their baggage and they trudged on, day and night, even further, until they came to a railway junction that professional bombing had turned into a moribund moonscape with craters where shining pieces of twisted rails protruded. They manoeuvred through with their cart; the wheels were creaking dreadfully. Suddenly Anna saw that her suitcase was no longer on it. She ran back, stumbling, one foot tripped in a hole. Was that her case, that shiny black thing floating in a crater's inland lake? She fished it out. Now it really was heavy. When they put it back on the cart a wheel broke—they left the cart behind in the company of capsized railway carriages.

Anna stopped to empty her shoe. Her soles were full of holes—her feet were sliding about in the worn-out leather. One of the soldiers gave her the extra pair of boots he had with him, and his helmet as protection from the rain. Still not satisfied, with his one arm he took her suitcase from her and she carried his rifle instead. During the evening it cleared up; the moon peeped out onto the plodding travellers between scurrying clouds. Two guards sprang up from nowhere and barred their way. 'Mensch, Meyer, look,' one of them called in amazement, 'That soldier here is a female!'

From now on reality consisted wholly of having to put one foot in front of the other; every metre was a metre closer to Munich, a metre farther from the Russians. One evening, when every metre had become a metre too much, someone took them to an old school. There were wooden bunk beds. Anna was shown to a bed, apathetic from tiredness. She lifted herself up with a last effort—still wearing her helmet she collapsed onto the bed then and there. But the bed could not bear so much tiredness, she fell though the middle and onto the person sleeping below, straw sack and all. He rolled the weight off him without waking up, she landed on the floor with a bump and went to sleep immediately. Early in the morning she opened one eye—a dwarf-like old man with a knobbly face above a narrow,

sunken chest was looking at her from the bed with shock. 'Jesus
Maria Joseph, what a dragoon fell on me during the night. I thank
God I am still alive!'

Every kilometre on the other side of the border had to be conquered on foot, too. Stabbing pains in her knee warned her that it
could not go on much longer, the joint was swollen up to the top of
the boot. Defeated army units were hurrying to the middle of Germany; cars and freight lorries whizzed by, loaded with women, soldiers, officers. They tried to get a lift but nobody stopped—the ghost
of the defeat was breathing down the military neck. The pain became
intolerable—her body now refused for the first time, too. Anna
dragged her suitcase into the middle of the road; she took off her helmet with a bow, as though greeting the traffic, and sat astride on it.
'Have you gone mad?' cried her companions indignantly, 'you'll be
killed.' Anna laughed disparagingly. 'I couldn't care less whether they
take me with them or run me over!'

A freight lorry approached. There was something comforting
about the dumb mechanical strength that took no notice of living
creatures—she waited for it with an inviting smile: do it quickly. The
screams of panic from the others sounded like a choir singing in the
distance. The justice of a primitive fairy tale was being invoked in the
middle of a main road: if the maiden completely surrendered to the
monster it would turn into a prince. The lorry came to a stop at a
polite distance. A young officer got out; he invited her to get in with
military respect for her cold-bloodedness. Stoically she stood up. She
beckoned to the others over her shoulder and got in.

The reception at the hospital was not what they had expected after
their brutal journey. 'What do you want here?' the Sisters were
snarled at, 'we don't need you here at all!' Only the wounded soldiers
were allowed to stay. The three Red Cross Sisters got a new marching
order: back to the Bavarian Alps, to a military hospital on the Chiemsee. They were back on the road again, and everything began anew.
They took it in turns to hold a hand out, listlessly, at the kerb. 'We
don't need you,' echoed in Anna's head. Now I understand, she
thought bitterly, how it is possible that a hundred soldiers could die

in a cold corridor while there were no Sisters to care for them: there are too many here.

A military lorry stopped. The driver stuck his head out. 'Who knows the way to Traunstein?' 'I do,' cried Anna. They had been past it on the way there, it was not far from the Chiemsee. Anna had to go and sit at the front; the driver drove on slowly and watchfully. A soldier on the bonnet was scanning the sky with a telescope. 'What's he looking for?' Anna asked. 'Fighter bombers,' her neighbour grimaced. The corners of his mouth were still twisted when the cry came from outside 'Get out! Bombers!' They jumped out blindly, threatening circles were being described above their heads. They dived into a deep trench; Anna was buried under her own suitcase. At that same moment the lorry bringing them nearer to the Chiemsee exploded. It was as though it was being hit repeatedly—one explosion set off the next in a chain reaction, debris rained on her suitcase. Only when nothing more could be heard did they creep out from their hiding place. They stepped timidly into the silence that followed the bomb—everyone was still intact. There was a smell of ammunition in the air. 'It is—' the driver began, 'it was a munitions lorry.' The scorched remains were smouldering; looking at it was not helping to get them farther so on they all went, silently ruminating on the thought of death narrowly escaped. A freight lorry from Hitler's construction organization, TODT, stopped. They signalled. 'Only the Sisters,' cried the driver sternly. As though he thought he would be tempting the irate gods above if he spoke, without saying a word he took them straight to the military hospital by the Chiemsee, which had been set up in a former hotel. It proclaimed itself from afar because—with an eye to the same gods—big white circles with red crosses had been painted on the road.

Two men without lower limbs were sitting in wheelchairs at the side of the road. They watched as the TODT lorry unloaded Sisters instead of building materials; they saw Anna with her impossible suitcase twist her knee and land on the asphalt. They were not unmoved. One of them wheeled over smartly, gathered her up and put her on his lap; the other took her suitcase. At a brisk pace they traversed the two hundred metres to the chief doctor's office, where they left her on a bench in the passage, proud of the compensatory strength in their arms. A passing soldier reported their arrival. 'Don't drop them in here just like that,' they heard the doctor storming on the other side of the door. 'We don't need anyone! The war will be over the day after tomorrow. We have nothing to eat, they'll have to manage for themselves.' Anna let her head sink onto her chest. She looked at her nails with great attention; they were black as though she had been digging up potatoes. All her emotions had been used up, the doctor's roaring did not move her. One thing was certain: she was not taking another step. If need be she would take root on that bench, opposite his door, to remind him of her existence. 'Those poor women,' she heard the soldier complain. 'There are still some beds—why can't they sleep there? And they could get that ration of three potatoes, too.' The doctor changed his tack, hearing out the soldier's plea was more exhausting than consenting. That night she lay in a real bed between smooth white sheets. Anna vaguely remembered the perception of unfamiliar luxury from long long ago, when she had arrived at her uncle's house in Cologne.

Although the chief doctor did not need anyone, on her rambles around the hospital the next day she had discovered a room with mattresses strewn on the floor. Young children were lying on them with a large bandage where an arm or leg had been lost, or with a bandaged head, eyes staring straight at the ceiling. Anna, who thought she had experienced the very worst with the dying soldiers in the night, who had intended to get rid of everything to do with children with her suitcase of baby clothes, walked in a daze between the mattresses, now and then kneeling down by a motionless child who looked at her with dejected resignation. No child was playing or laughing; an oppressive silence ruled as though they were all in a permanent state of shock and were waiting passively until their mother or father came to take the shock away with a kiss. But there were no mothers or fathers, no tellers of fairy tales to distract them. They lay there, but overwhelmed by a collective resignation as though they were doing penance for something they had not done. An associated absurdity also struck Anna: they were light blond without exception, they all had blue eyes. Well fed as they were, they looked like plump little cherubs who had been shot down from the fluffy clouds by a misanthrope whose hate extended to heaven. Although the chief doctor did not need anyone, Anna got down to work as usual.

'WHAT HAD HAPPENED to the children?' Lotte looked at her nervously. The speck of foam on her upper lip made her look a bit ridiculous—and so Anna found it easier to distance herself from the oppressive images that she had been recalling.

'They were living in a children's home on the Obersalzberg,' she said soberly, 'that had been bombed by the Americans. They were the Lebensbornkinder, children of the Nazi breeding farm. Specially selected blond men and women were brought together—for insemination, as it were. A child then arrived and they donated it to the Führer.'

'And what did he want to do with it?'

'After he had tidily exterminated the Jews and the gypsies, the noble Master Race had to be created instead, to rule the world. These children were being brought up on the Obersalzberg, well hidden from the outside world. After the bombing they were fetched down and taken to the emergency hospital on the Chiemsee—and then the chief doctor said he didn't need any Sisters.'

It baffled Lotte. It was too much, too complex, too macabre. She disengaged. 'I think I'll ask for the bill, I'm so tired all of a sudden. It must be from all that eating, and the alcohol.' She pushed her half-full wineglass aside deliberately.

'At our age you can't take as much,' said Anna ambiguously, 'you are reminded of it over and over again in a painful way.'

Back at the hotel Lotte received a telephone call from her eldest daughter, who inquired expectantly 'on behalf of the others, too' about the progress of the cure. Lotte gave a flattering picture, full of false enthusiasm. I must tell her about it, hammered simultaneously in her head. But what should she say? I have found my sister, your aunt. And then? The incomprehensible, unbelievable, unsavory drama in X acts? How could she ever explain it? She let her daughter's counsels wash over her—take it quietly, enjoy it, relax, don't worry, have you already met nice people—and said goodbye. I must stop all that talking, she said to herself angrily, the receiver still in her hand. It exhausts me—the children are expecting me to come home rejuvenated; they have a right to, it is their present, it has cost them plenty of money.

Nevertheless she left the bath house with Anna again the next day—at last the liberation was in view. Their whole meeting was a film she had failed to walk out of in time; now she wanted to know how it ended. The sun was shining, the world looked deceptively amiable. They dawdled around a little until they arrived at the Parc de Sept Heures and their nostrils were tickled by the aroma of *frites*. Anna sniffed with closed eyes. 'That's what I want!' she said from the bottom of her heart. Although Lotte had an aversion to doughnut and *frites* stalls and snack bars 'because they makes your clothes stink so,' she walked behind her automatically. A little later they were sitting with paper cones on a bench in the park, surrounded by intrusive pigeons. The war, the vicissitudes of humanity, painful matters of conscience—all paled into insignificance compared with the adolescent enjoyment of a portion of *frites* in the winter cold—long, firm, crisp, golden yellow fried potatoes. Greasy, salty fingers. But the idea that life was actually very simple only lasted as long as the bag of *frites*. Then they wiped their mouths and their hands and the war resumed its rights.

LOTTE'S FATHER RAN out of flags to mark the Allied victories; his wife, who had read too many war novels in her time, shivered at the thought of the strategic and moral vacuum usually associated with the handover of power—a period in which the enemy reacted blindly to the frustrations of its defeat with arson, rage, devastation, murder. What would happen to them if by chance they were in the line of fire? This was the first fear she had admitted out loud since the start of the war. The situation had became increasingly distressing. Tension was mounting, and for Ernst it was released in a clumsy proposal of marriage. Moved by his awkwardness, Lotte did not play hard to get. Not only did she love him for his frank vulnerability, his unmasculine weakness, she also nurtured a secret fear that life after the war would resume its normal course again, even though it could never really be the same as it had been before the war. Marriage would save her from having to be involved in the disintegration of the enormous clan of family and people in hiding—a priceless microcosm in a certain sense, although one could become addicted to anxiety—she hoped to escape via marriage from the emptiness that they would be leaving behind, and the excess of time, suddenly, in which to pose yourself difficult questions. She would also escape from her father, whose proximity would no longer be tolerable in peacetime.

They could not afford a wedding. Everything they possessed had been turned into provisions. They decided to marry before the war was over—a good excuse to let the ceremony take place quietly. Nevertheless that quiet was tactlessly disturbed at the critical moment by a squadron of low-flying Spitfires. On the way to the town hall the discreet company—the betrothed couple, her parents and two improvised witnesses—continually had to dive into the bracken. On account of the bridegroom's status as a person in hiding they had chosen an inconspicuous route through the wood; for the same reason the ceremony was performed by the deputy mayor, who was reliable: Lotte's father, always so charming outside the house, had his contacts. The formalities were managed without a glimmer of festive spirit, the deputy mayor's words were lost in the roar of aircraft. As she picked sprigs of bracken here and there from her brown suit, Lotte thought that never in the history of the world had such a joyless wedding taken place. After it was over they rushed back to the house taking the same route, where the lifetime contract acquired a little lustre from a dish of rye cakes and a bottle of gin—the very last one.

As THEY CROSSED the Avenue Reine Astrid, their patience was tested by a military procession—the very one they had seen riding to the west a few days earlier was now returning to the east. Tanks with soldiers in battle dress, jeeps, Red Cross lorries, all the colour of mustard.

Anna observed the procession with a stern expression. 'There you see, it all goes on as usual,' she mused. 'As long as the economy is dependent on the arms industry there will continue to be new flashpoints, and we will all stay armed to the teeth.'

Lotte did not rise to the bait. It was such a generalization again, bending the question of guilt into a safe direction. If re-arming was a worldwide pattern, then that saved Germany from responsibility for the economic revival in the 1930s—based on the arms industry—and everything that had flowed from it. But she was tired of refuting Anna's theories, so she held her tongue and watched the mud-spattered column with mixed feelings. That was how the occupier, that was how the liberators, had entered the country.

PART 3

PEACE

Après le déluge encore nous

1

THE FÜHRER WAS dead; it was a matter of days. The night before the capitulation evaporated in general drunkenness. There were pre-war stocks of alcohol under shrouds of cobwebs in the cellars of the former hotel. Fearing that the Americans would start an orgy there and rape the Sisters to the rhythm of their perverse jazz music, the hospital management divided up the bottles among the staff. Anna sat on the floor in one of the Sisters' rooms, and it gave her bitter satisfaction to undermine her sense of reality with red Martini. Humming, she took her tight nurse's cap from her head and combed her blond hair. 'Take a look at this'—the others stared at her in surprise—'actually you look really sweet! Why stuff your hair under that cap, show yourself as you are!' Anna brought the bottle to her mouth again. She had no inclination to explain that 'to look lovely' was the last thing she aspired to. Everything to do with feminine coquetry and seductiveness—how perverse in relation to the dead—could count on her contempt. At the end of the evening she was led, laughing and giggling, past Reception to her dormitory.

The next day the brand-new peace made itself known right through her piercing headache: An endless procession of emaciated, exhausted soldiers dragging themselves along the Autobahn, chased by well-fed Americans who burned with conceitedness and disdain. Anna clambered up the slope and saw a disillusioned mass trudging past her on the sunny liberation day—grey faces, lips cracked from dryness. She also became acquainted with the phenomenon of the black American. Chewing gum, he turned to her on his thick rubber soles. 'Hello, baby.' He grinned casually. She turned around, offended, and ran down the slope straight to the kitchen. She entered breathlessly. 'Our soldiers are coming down from the alpine fortifications . . . my God . . . they can't go on anymore!'

All who could free themselves filled a jug with lemonade and hurried to the road with it. But as soon as three, four soldiers had drunk some, a Wild West type appeared, pushed, knocked the Sisters down off the slope. They quickly scrambled to their feet and climbed up once more to give out lemonade. The boys drank eagerly and stuffed letters into the pockets of their starched nurses' overalls. 'Please, please . . . write to my wife that I am still alive,' they pleaded as they passed by, 'tell my mother that you have seen me . . .' Inside the hospital the Sisters emptied their pockets and filled the jugs; tirelessly they held their positions. They were flung down, threatened with rifle butts, but obstinately kept coming back until the last soldier had passed. Back in the hospital they sorted out the post. Someone had thrown Anna a small parcel, without an address, without a letter. She opened it, inside was dark blue woollen material for an officer's uniform—a gift? When the postal service was working again she wrote dozens of letters: 'From Heinz, for my dear Hertha . . . For Mutti from Gerold . . . via Anna Grosalie.'

That same day the guard was changed. Jeeps arrived and the Americans quietly took over the military hospital. Soldiers who had recovered were taken prisoner and removed; doctors, orderlies and Sisters had to continue their duties under guard. Huge revolving searchlights were installed in the grounds around the hospital to discourage daredevil dreams of escape. Among the wounded there were dedicated Nazis who had photographs of Hitler and other Nazi things on them. Just in time the sisters had collected these paraphernalia and, fearful of provoking the Americans, thrown them in the Chiemsee. One soldier, who could not be separated from his decorations, his Iron Cross and his photograph of Hitler, had withheld everything unnoticed. He buttonholed Anna a few days later. 'Would you do me a favour, Sister, and hide these things for me?' 'But where?' she said sceptically. 'In the wood behind here. Bury them, mark the spot and draw a map with it indicated precisely. I'll retrieve them when it's all over.'

Anna could not refuse him. In the evening, as soon as the light beam had passed, she ducked as she sneaked along the ground—continually looking around. She dug a hole between two birches, laughing quietly to herself: she saw herself rooting in the ground like a dog hiding a bone. After she had made a quick sketch of the location in the moonlight, with a cross on the spot where the Führer had been buried, she went back the way she had come, cursing the Americans for the ridiculous show of strength of their searchlights, as a result of which you could not move anywhere freely in your own country in peacetime.

It did not take long for the Americans to discover the charms of the original hotel: You could swim and sail in the Chiemsee. They requisitioned it for their general staff. The military hospital was disbanded; the SS were sorted out and transported; the Red Cross Sisters were taken as prisoners to a Wehrmacht barracks in neighbouring Traunstein, where little remained of the celebrated German orderliness. When the Americans were so close they could smell their fried bacon, the High Command had chosen to seal the Third Reich's downfall by carousing—the Sisters were ordered to clean out the pigsty they had left behind. They felt degraded by their captivity, which conflicted with the neutrality of the Red Cross, and by the filthy work that was so remote from their calling. But all that very soon paled into insignificance in the light of the daily ration of one cup of black surrogate coffee, a slice of dry bread and a plate of watery soup. Light-headed from hunger, they scrubbed floors. After a week Anna could only carry buckets that were a quarter full.

One day one of the Sisters broke the solidarity of the collective empty stomach and bartered herself to the Americans for a plate of food. Full of self-hate she returned; she wrung out her mop, crying about the irretrievable. They took turns trying to comfort her, but she stubbornly refused to accept charity from those whose self-respect was still intact. Sister Ilse, who was friendly with her, knew that it was her birthday that week. 'We should do something for her,' she said to Anna, 'something nice.' Anna nodded gently—excessive movements of her head made her dizzy. 'There are daisies growing on the other side of the road,' she suggested cautiously, 'but how could we ever get past the sentry by the gate?' 'Leave that to me,' said Ilse, 'I speak a little English.'

After lengthy dealings in a charming gibberish mixing English and German Ilse succeeded in softening the sentries. The gate opened— they had to restrain themselves from running into the meadows like

liberated calves, but rather to pace with the absentminded detachment of privileged prisoners. Walking in blossoming grass, daisies,
buttercups, sorrel . . . lying down in it and ceasing to exist! As Anna
picked flowers the stalks of the grass on the banks of the Lippe
scratched her legs again and she smelled once more that prickly green
smell that was like nothing else. It did not bother her that there were
American army tents further on, just as, long ago, she had ignored
the proximity of the farm in which her step-aunt concocted new tor-
ments. From the constant bending she fell into a dizzy state, a dazed
sensation of almost fainting in the Arcadian meadow and forgetting
everything.

All of a sudden a piece of chocolate landed at her feet and another
and a piece of bread and something else and something else. She came
back to the here and now with a bump. 'Verdammte Schweine,' she
snapped. She wouldn't even think of touching it. Ilse was also carrying on as though she hadn't noticed that anonymous delicacies were
flying at them from the tents. One of the sentries cried from the other
side: 'Jesus, pick it up, they're only giving it to you!' Ilse wavered. 'If
we take it with us,' she whispered, 'then we could all enjoy it . . . .
Then it will be a proper birthday party.' Anna had not seen it like that
before. She picked her Red Cross apron up by the corners, bent down
and began to fill it. Eventually she stood up with a bulging apron and
called haughtily, 'Danke schön!' The birthday girl would never in her
life receive a bouquet to equal the exuberant bunch of wild daisies.
The Sisters sat down in a circle; each had a little heap of American
benevolence in front of her; the birthday girl got the most and naturally shared it out again.

On the other side of Traunstein there was a military hospital. Since
the Brown Sisters had been arrested and taken away there was a
shortage of nurses there. One of the SS doctors, who worked under
guard, drew the Americans' attention to the Red Cross Sisters at the
barracks—under an escort of two soldiers they were fetched and
taken to the hospital. Anna was not in condition to carry her suitcase—someone put it in a cart. All she carried was the parcel of blue
officer's material under her arm. Thus they walked in procession
through Traunstein, stared at by the inhabitants. They were relieved:

not only could they get on with their normal work in a hygienic environment where the reliable SS orderliness still prevailed, but they could also eat again. The head of bookkeeping, an SS sergeant-major born and brought up in Traunstein, had his connections in the hinterland. While the Americans stood at the gate out front, the farmers shoved smoked pork, sausage and potatoes through the rear windows and the Traunsteiners dug a tunnel to the cellar to bring the stocks up to the required standard. Anna stuffed herself for three days.

Even so, they still had prisoner status. It was high summer. The landscape of the alpine foothills spread out seductively, but they were not allowed beyond the gate. Anna leaned out of the window of her room with claustrophobic longing and stared at the Garden of Eden. Free citizens were walking on a country road that wound around a hill until it was swallowed up in a wood. Two anachronistic soldiers were patrolling on the same road and saying 'Hello, baby' to each dress that passed by—did they do that on the prairie, too? She decided to take the law into her own hands. She took off her Red Cross uniform and fished a crumpled suit out of the suitcase that had been through so much. Disguised as a citizen, she wormed her way out of the window; under cover of scattered bushes she managed to get to the wood unseen. It was an ordinary wood, in the simplicity of its multifaceted appearances. An oak was an oak, no more, no less— she greeted the beech, hugged the oak, ran from one tree to the next, inhaled the smell of humus, clambered onto a fallen pine tree and started a distracted song that turned into a fit of crying halfway through. The trunk bounced beneath her in time with the sobs—it was a fit of crying like a natural phenomenon, a cloudbreak that cleansed the dust from the leaves. It was not so much a question of heartache; her whole body was crying to the roots of her hair, everything contracted together and opened wide—the crying sang itself free from its origin until it became a free-standing form of more rarefied crying that slowly dissolved. When she came to herself dusk was falling; she picked sprigs out of her hair and went in search of the path. The way back was barred by two soldiers involved in conversation. She waited, crouching behind a tree. Eventually they strolled off together in the evening twilight and Anna could walk some way along the public road as a free citizen. She passed a farm—look at that, she thought in amazement, people are sitting there eating, no bombs are falling, the light is on! She realised that since 1939 she had not had an evening without blackout; she had got so used to the abnormal that she regarded the normal with astonishment.

From one day to the next the hospital at Traunstein, too, was disbanded. The patients were taken away, the guards disappeared, the doctors and nurses were left to their own devices—not one of them thought of quitting. After two days a goods lorry drove up with an American at the wheel. They climbed into the back all together and sang at the top of their voices, 'I am a prisoner of war . . .' A surgeon conducted the chorus with his sensitive hands. The sun was shining, apples were hanging on the trees, there was no shooting, no vehicles jumped in the air, there were no swollen knee joints. Surprise and uncertainty were modified into fatalism, transformed into collective wantonness. The war was over, no matter how—slowly slowly this awareness was trickling into them.

Singing, they entered captivity once more, this time at Aibling near Munich, a massive prisoner of war camp on a former airfield. The women, nurses and Blitzmädchen had been accommodated in hangars; the leaders of the Wehrmacht in the other buildings. Further on, under the open sky, separated from the rest, were thousands of SS soldiers, on the ground, in sun and rain, anxiously guarded by soldiers with machine guns. Anna and Ilse walked to the washroom to clean off the dirt from the journey. Women were jostling each other in front of the mirrors over the wash basins. They were painting their lips and making themselves pretty. In the background popular music echoed through the hangar. Between two numbers a disc jockey sent greetings from Wolfgang to Sabine in a horrible accent, and congratulated Hans on his birthday on behalf of Uschi. 'What is this, in God's name,' Anna said. 'Have they gone mad?'

The purpose of the finery soon became clear. Outside, past the hangars, the heavyweights of the Wehrmacht mooched about in their uniforms with medals, decorations and badges—the tarted-up women at their sides, one lovelier than the next. The Americans,

crazy about a show even thousands of miles from home, took care of
the music and played the records they had played at home. Each day,
from five to seven, there was a great courtship display for the top
Wehrmacht, for those who had sent thousands and yet more thousands to their deaths, while beyond the reach of loudspeakers and
pretty women, the SS soldiers who had survived lay down in the fields
like cattle. Anna and Ilse looked at the grotesque show with open
mouths. The generals, the senior officers who had stayed out of range
of the war, were parading around like honoured prisoners in time to
the music of their conquerors. Anna stood there and watched and listened with clenched jaws to the inane American music and did not
know what to do with the rage that flared up in her. Rage against all
those self-important fops without whose orders the war would not
have been waged, without whose cooperation Hitler's wings would
have been broken. Rage against the conceited cowboy-stupidity of the
Americans. Rage against her own powerlessness—all that was needed
was for her to join in the applause or go and paint her lips, too.

A week later the daily parade suddenly ended. No more music, no
greetings, no generals, no more tarting up. The women lay on their
beds sighing. For a time there was almost nothing to eat, until the
Bishop of Munich visited and, as an intermediary between God and
his sinners, negotiated an improvement in the daily ration. Meanwhile the women were examined for venereal diseases and, irrespective of the outcome, gradually released from captivity. Ilse also left, in
search of the authorities who could plead for the release of her fiancé,
an SS soldier who was lying outside in the field. Anna was still
detained on account of an inflammation which created confusion in
the Americans' laboratories. When it appeared that she was mainly
suffering from greatly reduced resistance, she, too, was put outside
the gate.

A PEDESTRIAN IN the centre of Spa moves from health, via capital
and faith, to the war—back and forth, depending on the buildings
and memorials he passes: the bath house, casino, church, the monu-
ments to the fallen. It is difficult to be there in the final decade of the
twentieth century; everything breathes of the past.

The sisters landed in front of a shop window with a tempting display of items from the Second World War. Soldiers' jackets, helmets, kitbags, decoratively embroidered handkerchiefs of the American marines, tins of Emergency Drinking Water, an English parachutist's folding bicycle, an advertisement of a girl with a doll in her arms and the slogan, 'That she may never know the horrors of Dictatorship, let's all pull together for a victorious, prosperous America.'

'I hate that language,' said Anna from the bottom of her heart, 'I never wanted to learn it. That silly people, the one more stupid than the next. Hello, baby. . . . And they came to us with their fat backsides and behaved as though they were bringing us culture. They felt they were the rulers of the world.'

'They were our liberators,' Lotte said drily.

Anna laughed huskily and pointed to the window with a gloved finger. 'Those idiots are still being honoured as heroes. Yes, you see it, so many years after the war, all American and English things, no German of course. My feet hurt, can't we go and sit somewhere?'

They descended on the nearby café with the view onto the Pouhon Pierre-le-Grand. Lotte felt uneasy.

'I don't understand,' she said hesitantly, 'why you bear the Americans such a grudge. They didn't do anything to you.'

Anna sighed impatiently. 'Because they were mean dogs. Because they impressed us. You mustn't forget what we had behind us. Then those boys came over. . . . In many ways they weren't worth a shot of gunpowder, we could have blown them to bits if we had wanted to. . . . each one of us, every wounded soldier was worth more than them. . . . It was dreadful for us . . .'

'I don't understand that,' maintained Lotte. 'They did bring the war to an end.'

'Come off it, those chewing-gum boys, straight out of the middle of Texas!'

'They could have been in Normandy,' said Lotte sharply.

'Oh them? Those two or three Americans who had to perform there. They helped to win the war at the end. The English, the French, the Russians—just think what they have done.'

'But a lot of Americans were killed.'

'*Ach*, God,' Anna leaned back sarcastically in her chair, 'here come the tears now. What do a couple of thousand Americans signify when millions have died?'

'It is not about numbers.'

'You Dutch have a different conception. We had this one. You have to accept that. They utterly disgusted us. We had six years of the war behind us, twelve years of dictatorship. Then those scallywags arrived, who knew nothing about it, those illiterates straight off their farms. Those arrogant, inflated, Wild West boys, puffed up with gold. What sort of people were they really? They have been there for three hundred years—after they had evicted the Indians. That's all, isn't it? Am I mistaken?'

'One people is no better or worse than another people,' Lotte said in a trembling voice. 'As a German you ought to know that by now.'

'But they simply are more stupid,' cried Anna. 'They are uncivilized!'

'There are intellectuals as well.'

'Only a thin veneer. Look at the masses.'

'That goes for our masses and yours, too. Originally they were all English, Germans, Dutch, Italians.'

'But it was the real dregs who went over there. Look how they've turned out!'

'They were poor emigrants who had no future in Europe.'

'Fine, fine, you're right.' Anna raised her hands in resignation. 'That puts my mind at ease. . . .'

They were sitting opposite each other like badgered dogs at a pause in the fight. Lotte looked outside past Anna—suddenly she could not bear the sight of her face anymore. A furious, intolerant feeling of enmity inflamed her tongue. Her own criticism of the Americans, the communist witch hunts by McCarthy, the Ku Klux Klan, the Vietnam adventure, the way they chose their presidents—changed chameleon-like into an absolute, sacred need to defend them by fire and sword. But she did not say another word. Weariness overcame her. Two different planets, she said to herself, two different planets.

Anna was aware that her ferocity had had an off-putting effect. She loathed herself for her ardour. In an attempt at mitigation she said, 'You are a Dutchwoman—that is quite different. I didn't want to have anything to do with the ones who were stuffed full of food. Our soldiers were emaciated, ill; they had no nation anymore, nothing anymore; they were my comrades. You don't understand that, you weren't in the military hospital with the German soldiers, in the squalor. If you had experienced it you would see it exactly like that.'

That was the *coup de grâce*—preemptively gagged, even Lotte could not protest anymore. And it went on, Anna continued irrepressibly in the way that a teacher repeatedly explains the same thing with infinite patience to a backward pupil.

'But they did nevertheless liberate you from the Nazi dictatorship,' Lotte tossed in with a supreme effort.

'Ha,' Anna leaned across the table with a cynical laugh, 'You don't really think they came over to rescue us? They grabbed our scientists and took them back to America: chemists, biologists, atomic researchers, military professionals. Gestapo people like Barbie were brought in by the CIA. And then you say I must look on them as liberators. They made Adolf Hitler and his SS army the scapegoat—the Wehrmacht generals with their stripes, who have the deaths of millions of soldiers on their conscience, have never been punished. They were regarded as gentlemen. Whoever declares war decently and leads an army is a gentleman. And think about the judges who signed the death sentences, who sent the people to concentration camps—most of them have never been punished.'

'And what about Eichmann?'

'Wiesenthal did that. And the judge at the Nuremberg trials, he was an idealist, an exception.'

Lotte was listening and not listening. These arguments were familiar to her. A peculiar feeling of *déjà vu* distracted her. Where had she heard all that before, the same and yet different? She tried to hear that other voice behind Anna's voice. Suddenly she knew. Her father had blustered on about the Americans with the same heat. For years. It began immediately after the war, initially inspired by the charisma of Papa Stalin, entirely under its own steam after his demasking. The Yankees!

LIBERATION: NOT ONLY from enemy armies but also from anxiety. The contrast made the continuous anxiety, day and night, almost tangible the moment it disappeared. In its place was a general euphoria that did not last long because anxiety still had a last fling from time to time.

A crowd had gathered in the centre of Hilversum to welcome the marching Canadian and English troops who were probably going to the radio station, where the Dutch tricolour waved with abandon. Although everyone had kept a close track of the Allies' advances and setbacks since the Normandy landings, their heroism had remained abstract—now people wanted to see them, embrace them, hug them for joy. Lotte and Ernst stood on the edge of this force-field, waiting for the first tanks to appear around the corner. But shots sounded from a building on the other side instead, cutting right through the exuberance. The crowd scattered; Ernst pulled Lotte by the arm into a side street. The surrender was definitely a fact, but had everyone capitulated? To be shot during the war would have been sad, but it would be a ridiculous, senseless tragedy to become the victim of a frustrated soldier after the war. They decided to go home and so missed out on the spectacle, shown in all the bioscopes, of the jubilantly welcomed liberators amid hordes of women and lanky boys clambering onto the tanks—symbolized by cigarettes and bars of chocolate.

A few days later Lotte saw a column of disarmed Germans filing past—her excitement was tempered by the dull sight they presented, the stuffing beaten out of them. They were jeered from the pavements; abuse exploded like grenades among the soldiers; five years of anxiety and hate were unloaded on the heads of the defeated. A vague feeling of sympathy flared up in her, but she caught herself immediately and censured herself.

The Jews in hiding could not be restrained anymore. They wanted
to go home, they wanted to look for their families. Pent-up impatience and anxious premonitions drove them outside into the freedom
that would never be as it had been before the war for anyone and certainly not for them. They had been warned: Not all Germans have
been disarmed yet, not all Dutch Nazis have been picked up. They
stayed inside for ten long days of extreme self-restraint. Only Ruben
could not stick it out. He wanted to see his parents' house, surprise
the neighbours. 'How glad they'll be to see me!' He set off despite all
admonitions, ill at ease on a rickety bicycle, stared after anxiously.

Seemingly unharmed he returned. He sagged into a chair silently
and sat still, only his eyes moved back and forth in bewilderment
behind his glasses. Finally his head sank onto his chest and they realized that he was crying. That was unusual, alarming, after being
strong and without shedding a tear for years. Without lifting his head
he recounted how the reunion had gone. When the neighbour opened
the door at his ring she recoiled with horror and dislike in her eyes.
Her first reflex was to shut the door again, but he had already stepped
inside. He walked into the room as of old, his eye immediately fell on
the chair where he had so often drunk a glass of lemonade or warm
chocolate milk as a boy. But she did not invite him to sit; she paced
up and down with agitation, flinging in his face that all that time she
had been convinced the whole family had been taken off to Germany.
'Mother is still alive,' he told her. 'She will be delighted that you have
looked after her things so well all those years.' He pointed absentmindedly around at the Persian carpets and paintings that his parents
had given to her for safekeeping. 'Your father gave them to me,' she
corrected sharply, 'I can still hear him saying: Liesbeth, have these
things, we have no use for them anymore, they are nothing but bal-
last to us.' Ruben stared at the portrait in oils of his grandfather, who
looked at him disparagingly through a monocle. 'You had better discuss that with my mother,' he whispered diplomatically. 'I have nothing to discuss with your mother,' she said haughtily. The knuckles of
her hands were white, gripping the edge of the table. 'Listen,' she
blurted out, 'other people have already been living in your house for

years. The world has changed and we have all had to adapt, and now you come here out of the blue thinking that everything will be the same as it was. . . .' 'You're right . . .' Ruben went to the door as though in a dream. 'You're right . . . excuse me for disturbing you.'

Little by little the community that had been founded on provisional strategies was being disbanded—one after the other they left Lotte's mother's Ark. When the machinery for keeping everything going stopped and it had become silent all around her, her body began to cramp. She lay on her bed writhing—first she screwed her eyes closed in pain, then she opened them wide in astonishment. A bitter odour hung in the bedroom. Her soaking sheets had to be washed all the time. The family doctor called an ambulance after he had desperately sought a diagnosis. What irony: Those whom she had managed to keep alive all those years had simply walked out into the lane by the meadows on both feet, while she had to be carried away by orderlies. The cause was found at the neurology ward: an abrupt relaxation in the nerves, which had been giving out the 'danger' signal for years but had not been able to produce the associated 'flight' reflex.

For her husband the stresses were different. He grumbled about the English, the Canadians, the Americans; he lashed out against the new government; he opposed the rejoicing and glorification of the Western Allies while nothing was said about the grandiose exertions in the east. 'The western front would not have stood a chance,' he argued, 'without Stalingrad, without the eastern front, without the millions of losses in the Soviet army, without Stalin's indomitability and slyness,' he argued. 'The serious danger came from the east, Hitler knew that very well, all Germans knew that—why is everyone silent about it, why is it deliberately covered up in the press?' During his tirades he was generous enough to give himself the answer: 'From fear of the bolsheviks! Ha! Because their actual enemy is communism, not fascism.' He added a further prediction without obligation 'That fear will unite them all.' Shaking with indignation, he put a record on the turntable. Only the greatest composers could calm him—apart from Wagner, who had to spend the rest of his life at the bottom of a deep drawer.

2

LONG AGO THEY used to sit in a bathtub together, now they were lying in separate baths in pastel-coloured bathrooms and thinking about the bizarre, painful relationship that attracted and repelled them. Every day they met in the deserted corridors on the way from the peat bath to the underwater massage or the carbonated bath. Overlooking the water flowing tirelessly from the fountains, they were driven together at the end of the morning by the longing for a cup of coffee in the Salle de Repos. At least they had their penchant for coffee in common; could such a thing be in the genes? They met beneath Leda and the Swan and drank their coffee in little gulps. Usually it was Anna who dispelled the heaviness and languor of the *après bain* by bringing 'it' up again.

ANNA WAS OUTSIDE the gate with her suitcase. It was the end of September, it was raining, it was peace. She had no one to go to. There was only one person she longed for; having decided to go and look for him, she had thought up a plan of campaign for getting as close as she could to his vicinity.

The first phase of it was Bad Neuheim in Hessen, where she would meet Ilse. She was allowed to ride in the back of an open freight lorry, crammed in with sixty released Wehrmacht soldiers. The wind went right through her wet nurse's uniform. Shivering and with teeth chattering, she clung to the side of the lorry. 'Go and sit inside, next to the driver, Sister,' urged one of the soldiers. 'If he gets fresh, call us and we'll make quick work of him.' One of them knocked on the cab, the lorry stopped—he explained the reason in broken English. 'Of course,' nodded the black American, opening the door courteously for Anna. Inside it was warm and comfortable. He shared his lunch fraternally with her. Each communicated in their own halting words on an unfamiliar wavelength. 'Where are you going to?' he asked. 'I have no one,' she explained. 'My husband is dead, my home has been bombed. I have a meeting in Bad Neuheim with someone who can perhaps help me find work.' Shocked by her own frankness, she looked at his supple brown fingers that held the steering wheel loosely. Who was he? Who was she herself? Where did they originate? Where were they going? A former slave from Africa come to Germany via America. A former maid from Cologne back in Germany via Austria, as an ex-prisoner, in the company of an ex-slave from Africa who had been regarded as a potential rapist until a few moments ago. As though he sensed her confusion he laughed with her in an amiable way.

At Bad Neuheim she went in search of the address Ilse had given her, lugging her suitcase. Dawdling Americans spoke to her. They looked at her, surprised to be ignored; most women put up no resistance to their lures, only too glad to saunter through the village on their arms and smoke their cigarettes. Anna was so focused on her unapproachability that it took a long time before she discovered that the street she was looking for was right there under her feet. The woman of the house let her in and pushed a letter from Ilse into her hand as though it concerned a state secret. She had already gone to her parents in Saarburg and requested that Anna follow her at her own convenience. 'How do I get there?' Anna asked. Saarburg was in the French zone, only the original inhabitants in possession of the correct papers had the right to return there. Anna, as a Viennese, had no ghost of a chance. 'We'll think of something,' whispered the woman, leaving her in a neat bedroom.

An American officer was billeted in the same house, a lawyer from Chicago. She was introduced to him the next morning and discovered that the enormous empire reaching from one ocean to the other, conquered by covered wagon, lasso and rifle, had for once brought forth a civilized citizen by chance who, above all, spoke her own language. 'I find it so awful, what the Nazis have done to the German people.' 'They haven't done anything to me,' said Anna dourly. 'American artillery shot my husband, American bombs destroyed my apartment, Americans took me prisoner.' But he would not be put off, patiently he laid out his arguments so as to bring her another perspective. At the same time his lessons in politics and war studies were a form of subtle seduction—Anna, not deaf to the erotic undertone, managed to keep her distance with polite objections during the days of enforced waiting. Bad Neuheim teemed with German soldiers who had lost an arm or a leg; they sat wearily on benches next to each other and stared silently at the passing Americans who had conquered their women as well as their country. Anna recognized Martin in their midst—it cut her to the quick to see them sitting there.

One evening the American invited her to a party. 'What's that?' she asked. 'Well . . .' he felt his clean-shaven jaw, 'there's a bit to eat, a bit to drink, a bit of being happy.' 'And then?' she asked suspiciously. 'Well, and then? It would be good for you, you are young, you can't be sad forever.' '*Danke, nein,*' she shook her head, 'the end of the party is quite clear to me.' 'I can't help being a man,' he apologized. 'Nor I a woman,' she added, 'and my husband died a year ago. Excuse me, but you didn't seriously think I would go to a "party" with you.' She uttered the word as though she had a bitter taste in her mouth. He bowed his head in acquiescence. He was no match for such intransigence, whether as a soldier or a man or a wordsmith. He was being re-posted the following day. An enormous bunch of red roses was delivered for Anna; it was proof of a frivolous extravagance in this time of shortages. A card was hanging among the leaves. 'For the first German woman to say No.'

Arrangements had meanwhile been made for her. A carter from Bad Neuheim who had permission to cross the zone boundary was prepared to smuggle her to Koblenz. He drove up with his horse and wagon, she had to lie down with her suitcase on the floor covered by a tarpaulin. Sacks with unknown contents were piled up over her, leaving an air hole. The relaxed Americans let them through but the French made spot checks, poking their bayonets into the sacks—just missing Anna, who was inhaling the smell of tarpaulin and waiting fearlessly. Perhaps she was only spared because secretly she longed for death and preferred it to the fate of struggling victims. The man on the box said his prayers, sweating, he admitted afterwards to her as he helped her out at Koblenz station.

No more trains were running that night. A herd of stranded travellers was sleeping in the station. Anna installed herself on the ground next to an old man in a patched army coat who put a bottle of wine to his lips and then generously allowed it to circulate in his immediate vicinity while he spread butter on chunks of white bread and distributed them at random. Anna declined his offer, but he pushed his bottle into her hands with a gesture that would brook no opposition. 'I've got lots more.' He grinned, unconcerned, pointing to his bag with a shaking finger. She hesitated no longer; the ebullient atmosphere around the generous old man was infectious. The vineyards on the slopes of the Mosel were praised unanimously, the bottle went pragmatically from mouth to mouth. Anna stretched out on the floor, the suitcase beneath her head, and slowly dozed off. In the morning she was woken with wine—breakfast had the same ingredients as the previous evening's supper. They forgot their cares, there was singing, the autumn sun shone, even the train to Trier puffed into the station. Festivities continued in the compartment, the ragged host at its beaming centre.

The train stopped halfway, the rails were missing for a distance of a few kilometres. They continued on foot, singing travelling songs, drinking; the sun glistened on the profuse tinsel of wild hops along the railway line. Another train was waiting farther on. Nothing could suppress the jollity. 'What sort of company is this,' growled a priest sitting by the window, 'that boozing, that drunken talk.' Irritated, he took up his breviary and began to pray, to compensate for the immorality surrounding him. 'Will you have some?' Anna offered him the bottle, laughing. He shook his head with pursed lips. Everyone got out at Bernkastel, leaving her alone in the priest's company. She leaned out of the window to wave to the creased philanthropist who had spread so much happiness around him. He tottered along the platform, awaited by his wife who, with hawk eyes at a distance, had already put together the diagnosis of an empty bag. 'Where is the bread,' she let fly, 'where is the butter, where is . . . !' The shrivelled-up little man raised his arms to heaven. 'In paradise,' he moaned.

The train set off again. The feeling of happiness caused by the wine turned to sadness. Sentimental tears dribbled down the lowered window as she stared at his ever-diminishing figure. She flopped back into her seat. The priest looked up flabbergasted from his breviary. Remembering his Christian duty he inquired haughtily why she was crying. She explained why the number of times she had been happy since October 1944 could be counted on the fingers of one hand. Moreover it was not an insouciant happiness as before but one that was rooted in despair. Familiar with this sort of paradox—suffering for the sake of salvation was another one—he nodded.

It was already dark and they were not yet in Trier. 'Have you got an address for the night?' he asked matter-of-factly. 'The station,' said Anna laconically. He looked disapprovingly at her. 'Why do you think I look like this?' she pointed to her dirty uniform. He was silent, pensive. 'If I took you to the nuns, in the convent? Would you come with me?' 'Good heavens!' she cried, 'does such a thing still exist?' 'Yes of course.' 'In these times?' 'Yes,' he said, ruffled. 'Of course I'll go with you.'

When they arrived at Trier, Anna was in the middle of the hang-over-thirst phase. She got out, dead beat. 'Follow me,' said the priest sternly. He walked rapidly into the dark town. She dragged the heavy suitcase behind her like a dog on a lead over the bumpy cobbles. He walked ten paces ahead of her without looking around, for fear of compromising himself. Her thought about it was that he was not so much driven by Christian charity as by concern for his own place in heaven. 'Inasmuch as ye have done it unto one of the least of my brethren, ye have done it unto me.' She followed the black habit past the dark façades, panting. Every step was a step back in time, up to the Romans in the form of the Porta Nigra that towered threateningly above her in its sombre massiveness. The representative of the church turned right and stopped at a heavy wooden door with iron studs. He knocked, muttered three words and was gone, without shaking hands, without saying goodbye, no sign of humanity whatsoever escaped from this servant of God.

God's female servants had quite a different attitude to their status as the chosen. They raised a hand to their mouths when they saw her and immediately began to put things in order. A bathtub was filled with warm water, her dirty clothes were received; while she lay in the bath the convent filled with nocturnal activity. She was wrapped in a chaste towel and taken to a guest room where she slid between clean, smooth sheets and fell asleep with the picture of a heavenly smiling nun before her eyes. When she woke her light grey striped nurse's uniform was on the table, shining in the morning sun—washed, starched and ironed.

She arrived at Saarburg as an impeccable Red Cross Sister. History repeated itself. Ilse had already departed again, as advocate for her fiancé who was still in captivity, prompted to hurry by the disturbing prospect of the approaching winter. But there was work for Anna. A particularly unsavory chore had waited patiently for her all that time. In revenge for five years of war the Luxembourgers had crossed over the border and had given full vent to their feelings of displeasure in a hit-and-run raid on the villagers' property. The walls and windows of Ilse's parents' half-timbered house had been smeared with excrement. Linen had been pulled out of the cupboards and dirtied—they had sprawled on it, said the woman with a mouth taut from suppressed rage, and had manufactured the material of their revenge before her eyes. 'The tit-for-tat answer, you understand, a disgusting people those Luxembourgers.' She was too sickly to take on the great cleaning herself, while her husband spent long days in his sawmill.

Anna rolled her sleeves up and began. She had left a pigsty ten years ago, now she was back in it. What difference did it make? But when a lorry from the sawmill was able to take her some way in the right direction, she threw the mop and brush in a corner—she had done enough. Ilse's mother, who knew what had brought her diligent cleaning woman to these parts, had to let her go. The lorry drove out of the town in a thick drizzle, to Daun in the Eifel. She continued on foot, through immense pine forests that dissolved in a mist of fine droplets. It was chilly, the damp penetrated through her soles, but the knowledge that she was getting closer all the time made her indifferent to discomfort. This deserted road, sauntering uphill, downhill between melancholy pines, was precisely what you could expect of a pilgrim's route to the underworld. She was not afraid, the end of the journey was coming into view; afterwards there would be nothing more to wish for, afterwards . . . there was no afterwards. The cold crept up to her middle, she progressed more slowly, her soles were worn out, the patches hung loose and flapped with each step. All she could see was shining black tree trunks and dripping branches. Although her body was showing increasing signs of unwillingness, her spirit stubbornly insisted. At a given moment he could not bear to look any longer and began to interfere. Listen, dearest, he said compassionately, do go home. What do you want? I'm not there at all. . . . Thus he chatted to her; initially she ignored him but when he—carefully as always—arranged for an approaching driver who loomed up out of the mist, she capitulated. Today you win, she admitted, but come I shall . . . at a more suitable moment. . . .

Back in Saarburg she continued the cleaning. The grousing about the Luxembourgers did not cease. It pursued her into all the rooms like a revenge-driven drill which was also heard by an old lady who lived in some rooms at the rear of the house. 'How can you stand it here?' she said, observing Anna cleaning. 'You're surely not going to stay on here doing that forever.' 'What should I be doing then,' said Anna defensively, 'I'm waiting for Ilse.' 'My God, then you could be in for a long wait—who knows when she'll find help. But listen, I've got a suggestion for you. I have an acquaintance in Trier, a retired teacher from the grammar school. She is looking for someone to do the housekeeping . . . not just anyone, you understand. Perhaps it's something for you.' Anna nodded slowly—her life ultimately hung together on improvisations.

She recognized Kaiserstrasse in Trier from her nocturnal journey in the priest's wake, and there she got to know a fascinating type of person full of incomprehensible contradictions: Thérèse Schmidt, a narrow, bony woman with thin grey hair held together by a clip, stingy in terms of material things but generous and helpful where the intellect was concerned. It was not apparent that she went to her brother's farm every day just outside the town, to stuff herself with bread, meat and dairy foods. Without shame she expatiated upon it. It never occurred to her to bring something back for Anna, who was trying to stay alive on two slices of bread a day, some potatoes and a cup of black coffee dregs—the rationing imposed by the French in retaliation for the hunger they themselves had had to suffer. Frau Schmidt's rare stinginess was much harder to reconcile with her daily visits to

church, Bible study and fervent praying—never had Anna encountered close-up so much bigoted religious zeal. There were a lot of
books in the house; her earlier appetite for reading returned between
the housekeeping tasks. Surprised, the teacher drew up a chair when
she returned from her daily visit and found her reading. 'You are not
destined to spend your whole life between the stove and the kitchen
sink, I could see that right away. What do you really want to do?' 'I
have no idea,' Anna stammered, overwhelmed by the sudden interest.
Her plans for the future extended no further than completing that
one mission. 'Isn't there something you have always really wanted to
do?' Anna frowned. Dante slid from her lap but was intercepted in its
fall by Frau Schmidt's narrow hand. The idea of having the freedom
to choose a career for oneself was so revolutionary that it paralyzed
her thinking. She had to let go of her picture of the world in which
women were clearly divided into three categories: a broad lower layer
containing farming women and servants, a small upper layer of privileged women who had the decorative function of being civilized, elegant wives, and the remaining category of unmarried women in
teaching, nursing or convents. No one chose for herself, it was something she went straight into—through birth or circumstances. Frau
Schmidt repeated her innocent question. 'Well,' Anna sighed. Her
head was light, she did not know if it was from hunger or the thorny
questioning. Her thoughts flitted criss-cross back in time, in search of
examples for possible candidates to identify with, for someone who
could say the word for her—thus she landed up in a dark, stuffy small
room that smelled of sweating feet and a dead soldier hung on the
wall who had been born to die for the Fatherland (such an inevitable,
obvious destination again). Opposite her stood a woman resolutely
closing the door with her backside and lovingly opening her arms:
come here . . .

'Child welfare,' Anna blurted out. 'I believe I have always wanted
to do that.' 'I see . . . but why aren't you then?' 'It would be quite
impossible,' Anna said brusquely, 'I would have to matriculate first.'
Frau Schmidt laughed at her: 'Is that all!' From her past in the education system she ferreted out a teacher who was prepared to help Anna
cram for the state examination. Another woman was taking lessons;

Anna could join her. From then on, every afternoon she walked to his
house through the centuries-old streets between piles of debris and
people collapsing from hunger, worn-out rubber overshoes over her
worn-out shoes. 'Listen, you don't need to understand,' the teacher
impressed upon her, 'all you have to do in the exam is be able to give
the correct answers. Read it out of your head.' Everyone had already
been astounded by her memory when Anna recited 'The Song of the
Bell' next to her proud father. Now it was the teacher who was breathless at the speed with which she acted on his advice. He rushed her
through grammar, the foundations of mathematics, through history,
geography, German literature. After fourteen days he said: 'I am working with two dissimilar racehorses here. You race ahead like a runaway, the other woman can't keep up. I shall have to separate you.'

Her head was entirely empty—she had hidden the war deeply
away, deliberately lost the key. There was plenty of space for the
dizzying quantities of information, so agreeably neutral in their
capacity as cultural wares. She crammed and crammed, almost fainting away sometimes under the high pressure. 'Are you dizzy?' the
teacher inquired. 'Yes,' she said hazily. 'What have you eaten?' 'Two
potatoes.' 'Good heavens, you should have said so earlier!' He made
her a plate of porridge. 'Don't be concerned, I get food parcels from
the English zone.' Each day the lessons began with a plate of porridge: first the body, then the mind, was his view. He also pointed out
that her overshoes had had it. It did not occur to her employer, who
had at least ten pairs of shoes in the same size, to hand over one pair
to her. The teacher bartered two bottles of gin for sound leather
shoes. At home Anna showed them to her, elated. Frau Schmidt
raised her eyebrows without interest: 'So?'

On Christmas Eve she went to her brother as usual for an advance
on the Christmas meal. She had said before her departure that she
wanted a bath when she returned—to cleanse the body before she
dealt with the soul during midnight mass. Anna had to get everything
ready and heat a large cauldron of water on the coal stove in the
kitchen. It was already dark when the bell rang unexpectedly. A
woman was standing at the door, clasping a crying baby wrapped in
rags to her, threatening to collapse from exhaustion. Anna caught her,

brought her to the kitchen and took the child from her, which smelled
as though it had not been changed in weeks. She could see the steaming cauldron and the tub from the corner of her eye—everything was
ready for the *gnädige Frau*. Without thinking about it she filled the
bath, unwrapped the child and threw the stinking rags in the passage.
After she had washed the baby she wrapped him in a flannel towel.
She gave the mother a piece of bread and butter, a boiled potato and
a cup of black coffee. Not a word was said, everything happened in a
hurried sequence of self-evident actions—under the constant threat of
the phantom Frau Schmidt, who might come home at any moment.
What now, Anna asked herself feverishly, where should they go? The
convent! The nuns, those angels of mercy! She slipped a coat on and
took the mother and child to the Ursulines, who eagerly took pity on
them. A comfortable feeling of synchronicity came over her on the
way back: It was the eve of Christmas and there was no room at the
inn! Above Trier's piles of rubble the sky was strewn with stars, she
was walking beneath it in her new shoes. Everything was in equilibrium—for a little while.

She came home at the same time as her employer. When a tubful of
dirty water was awaiting her there instead of a warm bath, the
teacher was outraged. She raised her arms in a grotesque gesture; a
torrent of accusations descended on Anna. 'Just a moment,' she
squeezed past, 'I'll put a new cauldron on the fire, I'll clean everything up, it will be done in a moment.' Frau Schmidt only calmed
down when order had been restored and the picture of the kitchen
corresponded with the one she had in her mind as she walked home
flushed and satisfied from the meal.

During the midnight mass she sat in the pew, smelling of soap and
starch, singing, rejoicing, praying with a passion. She ranted and
raved like an angel of Our Lord with the same voice that was so good
at torrents of abuse. Anna watched stoically. On the way home Frau
Schmidt said, 'It escapes me how you could let such a dirty woman
and dirty child into my house.' Anna stopped, looked her in the eye
and quoted serenely what the pastor had said shortly before: ' ...
because there was no room for them in the inn ... and Mary gave
birth to her firstborn son in a stable ... she wrapped him in swad-

dling clothes and laid him in the manger. . . .' 'You are trying to get out of it by making a pun,' said the teacher, walking on gruffly. Nevertheless Anna received a Christmas present. No warm stockings, no vest, no milk or meat, but a Latin missal: the *Sacramentaria*, the *Lectionarum* and the *Graduale*—a silent hint that Anna still had a lot to learn when it came to Christianity.

Frau Schmidt's altruism lay more in the didactic sphere. Her search for an academy of social work had not been made easy. All training colleges indoctrinated by the Nazis had been shut down; what survived was a reliable Catholic institute in North Rhine Westphalia. The director responded immediately to her impeccable letter: She would be visiting the seminary at Trier in March, she would take that opportunity to assess Frau Schmidt's protégé herself.

As protection from the dust that blew out of the rubble heaps, Anna wore a headscarf that flapped in the breeze. The closer she got to the seminary the more exam nerves took hold of her. The director, haughty and short spoken, did nothing to put her at her ease, but subjected her to a cross-examination. 'Why do you want to be a social worker?' she asked in a cynical tone, as though a plan so arrogant, so brazen had never come to her notice before. 'I want to help people,' sounded weak. 'Why?' 'Because I want to help people!' Anna repeated, raising her voice, forgetting all ceremony and polite phrases. An uneasy silence fell. I've blown it, she thought, I saw that in no time. But why does she treat me like a dog? But you stroke a dog's head, you say: You're a good dog. Finally she broke the silence penitently: 'I myself was a child who needed help.' Again that silence and the scornful, piercing look of the authority who was going to decide her fate. 'You can go,' said the woman curtly. Anna came home dejected. Frau Schmidt dashed towards her. 'And how did it go?' 'I can forget it; it was nothing.' The teacher sniffed in disbelief. She had her own channels for getting objective information; some days later she reported with triumphant victory: 'You made a deep impression on her. That one at least knows what she wants, she said to the abbot.' Wearily Anna looked up. She did not want to hear any more about it, the teacher was concocting it. But the mail proved her right. A well-thumbed, damaged telegram was delivered: 'First semester starts: 1 September.'

Farewell Frau Schmidt, teacher! But before travelling to North Rhine Westphalia she had to make a second attempt. This time she had solid shoes, the sun was shining, she got a lift in a post office van up to the village itself. She got out in the centre; villagers told her where it was. With an armful of flowers plucked on the way she pushed open the squeaky wrought-iron gate. There was an aisle, as in the church, with rows of graves on either side. The oldest at the front: names from the district, mossy, worn away by rain and frost, on crooked headstones and cracked tombstones. Clipped yews and conifers in between and an impressive absence of noise, only interrupted by birdsong. Further behind were the more recent graves. One stood out immediately because it was square instead of rectangular, and three amateurish wooden crosses stood on it next to each other, as though seeking support from one another. As she began to walk intuitively towards it, a sudden irrational anxiety crept over her: the anxiety that he would still be proved right and would be all about there except in this one spot . . . that he would laugh at her from all points of the compass for her naiveté. But there was no escape: She had been en route to this pathetic two square metres since her release from the American camp. So, inch by inch, she approached her disillusionment with diffidence. Each cross bore a name carved out in cuneiform-like letters—the middle one bore his. The earth underneath had been covered with evergreen sprigs with white roses on top. From whom, who were the flowers from? She knelt down, laid her bunch of wildflowers there and stared at his name in the hope that something of his presence would manifest itself, but the only thing she could see before her was the tanned soldier who waved to her in the tidy station at Nuremberg: ' . . . this bloody hell will soon end anyway . . .' If he was living anywhere it was within her, there was no place on earth where that was as certain as here.

'What are you doing at my grave?' sounded behind her, straight through the silence, a female voice. Anna stiffened. She said carefully, not turning around, 'If there is anyone in the world whose grave this is then I am that person. My husband lies here, as it happens.' The cheery song of a blackbird came from a conifer; there were muffled sobs in between. Anna turned around. A young woman with swollen eyes was staring at her. Although the grave displayed the unpopular attribute of graves all over the world, by remaining proverbially silent, a suspicion arose in Anna that was too awful to be contemplated. There are two others, she reassured herself. 'Are you Frau Grosalie?' said the girl in a slurred voice. 'Yes, yes' said Anna curtly, 'I am Frau Grosalie, but what have you got to do with my husband?' The other looked up to the sky as though she were expecting a sign. Anna could not think of anything to say to put it all into perspective. Their gazes crossed fleetingly.

'I will explain,' said the girl. She scratched her chin. 'He was billeted with our neighbours. We got to know him over the fence, my mother and I. Right away we found him sympathetic . . . both of us . . .' In this way she shyly introduced her story. Martin was making contact with Anna in an unorthodox manner via the last female being he had seen before his death—via her he was telling his wife the details. Only now did his abstract death—'the heroic death of your husband'—become something that had happened to him at a specific moment in a specific place. At one moment he had still been alive and could see, hear, smell, talk, laugh—a moment later his mortal remains were being gathered up. In a dull voice the girl recalled the day it happened in September 1944. The office where she worked in Prüm had been closed because the whole district had become the front zone and all traffic was shut down. She was obliged to stay at home. She was sitting on the bench in the garden when the officer waved hello to her and called out that he had received an order to go to the Westwall with his men to take possession of a bunker full of signals equipment. She sprang up from the bench: 'Could I have a lift with you to Prüm,' she asked on spontaneous impulse. 'I've left a bag of things at the office.' He shook his head: 'The roads are not safe, the Americans are shooting at us from all sides.' But when she urged him and pleaded with him to take her along he gave in. 'Well, if you absolutely insist.'

They set off; the lorry navigated a woodland path. Something exploded in the distance now and then, leaves and berries trembled in the air, then everything went quiet again. 'My goodness,' she cried suddenly in a panic, 'I've forgotten the key!' Martin made light of the mistake: 'You don't really need a key, you'll see, there are no windows left in that house, you'll be able to climb in.' 'That may very well be,' she said stubbornly, 'but I would rather fetch the key.' She prepared to get out, he stopped her: 'It's perilous to walk back alone.' But she would not be dissuaded. An immovable belief in the indispensability of the key obliged her to go straight back. She said goodbye, got out and walked back the way they had come.

Halfway through the afternoon the signals technicians returned to the village. Three of them wrapped in canvas like mummies, six others unhurt. The villagers thronged together, the girl stood there among them in confused desperation and asked the survivors in an apologetic tone for an explanation, not suspecting that they were already weighed down by heavy feelings of guilt. One of them gave the account, with a hanging head. The lorry was approaching a village. Martin was sitting up front—as she knew—between the driver and a soldier. The others called from behind, 'Stop for a moment, we want to pick a few apples.' There was an orchard on a slope, red apples glistening defiantly in the sun. 'We can't stop,' Martin had said. 'If we stop we will be an easy target for the Americans.' But the men whined 'Just for a minute' and Martin, good natured as he was, did not persist. 'Hurry then!' he capitulated. Six soldiers jumped out of the lorry and ran into the orchard like six rascals. They forgot the war, they shook the branches and collected apples until they were startled by an explosion below. The cab with the three who stayed behind blew up before their eyes, hit by shell fire.

The girl listened to him speechless, staring at the three prosaic parcels, and saw before her the men she had sat with fraternally a few hours earlier. Meanwhile the men's baggage had been assembled; in Martin's suitcase there were a pair of pale blue children's shoes and a silver evening purse among the books. Only the sight of his personal possessions now conveyed the full magnitude of the disaster to her. She turned her back on the scene in a flood of tears. Meanwhile someone took his chance in the commotion—when she had come to herself and turned around again the shoes and evening purse had disappeared.

Anna nodded slowly. 'The hero's death of your husband.' Killed for a handful of apples. It connected to that one apple that had brought

TESSA DE LOO

disaster to mankind. Martin had trudged through the steppes of Russia and the fields of the Ukraine, he had survived the cold, an attack by partisans, a fatal illness, he had been spared throughout the whole war so that he could die on the outskirts of a farming village in the Eifel for a handful of apples. However absurd and senseless this death seemed, it was one that nevertheless suited him: He had died while giving others pleasure. She could recognize him as he had been in this. He had suddenly come close to her in the story of his death. 'Are the flowers from you?' she said gently. 'My mother and me,' the girl assented. 'We bartered butter and eggs in Trier for those roses.' Anna turned around. The other graves were neglected, the square one with the three crosses was a lovingly maintained island amid overgrown tombstones.

The girl insisted on introducing Anna to her mother, who shook her hand emotionally. 'Your husband was such a good man,' she sighed, dabbing her nose. Then she prepared a reception for the widow as though she were a long-lost member of the family from America. Everything edible that could be found in the house and garden was put on the table, prepared with fragrant herbs. Anna understood that it was a celebration meal as well as a memorial meal. He was dead but the girl was alive—thanks to her paranormal obsession with the key. 'The thing that I don't understand,' said the mother at the departure, 'is that the SS buried them and put the crosses on top, but our pastor has refused to bless them because they are SS. Now is that Christian?'

'AT LEAST YOU had a grave you could go to,' said Lotte coolly. She was disinclined to get carried away by the story of Anna's pilgrimage to the grave of her SS officer.

Lost in thought, Anna looked at her. 'How do you mean?'

'There was no cemetery at Mauthausen.'

Anna stroked her painful legs. For some days she had believed that the pain had been diminishing through the soothing influence of the baths, but now it suddenly returned in all its ferocity. 'I went to Auschwitz a couple of years ago,' she said. 'Six thousand people were gassed there each day. I stood there, where all of them had gone, and remembered the beautiful summer of 1943. Martin came, we went swimming in the lake, we went over to the island, wonderful weekends for us alone. I did not know that it was my Last Supper. That millions of people had gone this way at that time when I had been experiencing a bit of good fortune in my life . . . I could not cope with it, it was so dreadful. . . . She massaged her knees. 'But whether or not I was fortunate, they had not been helped.'

That was a truism. Lotte was silent.

'I did not believe it at first,' Anna continued. 'I saw the pictures on television for the first time in the fifties. Do you know what I thought? The Americans have collected the corpses out of the towns they themselves bombed and thrown them on a heap in a concentration camp. I could not believe it.'

'When did it finally get through?' said Lotte sharply.

'It began with a big exhibition, "The Jews in Cologne from Roman Times." The truth slowly trickled inside there. You must understand—politics did not interest me. I was completely obsessed with my work, there was nothing else.'

'We did not know, we had other things to do,' Lotte railed scornfully in German.

'Yes . . . no . . .' said Anna irritated. 'You didn't hear anything about the Jews in everyday life. I don't recall anyone ever saying anything about it.'

Lotte stood up, overcome by a dull sense of futility. A nurse came in and asked them to get dressed. Closing time was approaching, the staff wanted to go home.

The inescapable family connection was continuing to claim its rights whether they wanted it to or not. Something was still forcing them to go on rowing against the current, towards each other—the one in active pursuit of conquest, the other as a passive victim of a maddening sort of affinity to which she could offer no resistance.

That evening they dined together in a small restaurant on the Avenue Astrid. It was Saturday, they did not have to be at the bath house at the crack of dawn the following morning. They went on to the Relais de la Poste in search of a little bit of Saturday-night ambience and made themselves comfortable on the leather settees from the thirties, a time when they had still been young and did not know what was hanging over them. They drank coffee with Grand Marnier; the jukebox filled the space with velvety perennials from the fifties.

'Life goes on, they always say,'—Anna sipped from her glass— 'when we have suffered a great loss, the other person gives us a clap on the back and says, "Chin up, life goes on." A cliché and at the same time a bitter universal truth. Our towns lay in rubble, our soldiers were dead, crippled, stripped of illusions. As a people we acquired the collective guilt for the greatest mass murder in the history of mankind. We were economically and morally bankrupt... and yet, somehow or other, life went on. I threw myself into studying, my work. Everyone went to work, my God.' She emptied her glass in one gulp and laughed to herself. 'The whole reconstruction was one big occupational therapy!'

Lotte stared absently into her glass. Memories of the dreary peace drifted past. She did not want to think about it, and precisely because of that she thought about it.

ERNST WAS WORKING, too. He was taken on by a violin-maker in The Hague who had rheumatism of the hands that obliged him increasingly to leave the work to him. They had moved into a small flat behind the workshop—Ernst earned a post-war pittance, like many others. Obsessed with his new responsibilities as husband and future head of a family, he stirred himself to ever greater productivity: five days a week he repaired violins, on the other two he made new ones that he sold. Seven days a week Lotte was alone with the thoughts marriage was supposed to have released her from. She paced about the room, wrenched from her family—a painful déjà-vu. Where had she come to, had she wished for this? She dreamed of a large old house with high ceilings, a house that would reconcile her to the loneliness of the marriage, a house that she would re-create as a home. The dream drove her through a criss-cross of streets and canals. Autumn came, winter, the dark façades warded her off, the lit-up rooms shut her out—only the Little Match Girl was missing. It was as though she were still doing penance, in the form of an eternal roaming, homeless, without relatives, the just deserts of someone who was neither one thing nor the other, a hybrid, treacherous on both sides.

Perhaps it was music that was missing. What had happened to Amelita Galli-Curci? The *Exultate jubilate*? The *St. Matthew Passion*? She found a singing teacher, but already at the first lesson it seemed that not much was left of her voice. She wore herself out apologizing to the teacher—with great nostalgia she mentioned everything she had sung before, but when she saw the doubt in the other's eye she began to doubt it herself. What had happened to her voice, that had once effortlessly filled the water tower from top to bottom? Her vocal chords were like dried-out rubber bands that crumbled between your fingers.

If she wanted to hear music she had to visit her parents. But their displacement had altered the façade of normal family life. Her mother, who had held everything together with an artificial cheerfulness, had developed an obsession with eating, to forget the hunger and everything else. She had lost almost all her children at the same time the people in hiding left. Something seemed to have developed secretly between Jet and Ruben since she had lain in bed with concussion and he had read aloud to her for hours to kill time. Theo de Zwaan had long ago known how to melt Marie's Cinderella-heart. Mies had gone to live above the hat shop shortly before the war. They had all married and were living independently. Koen, invited by Bram, had gone to America, which had enjoyed almost mythical popularity since D-Day as a country of unlimited possibilities. The two youngest who were still at home could not concentrate at school and were boisterous and unruly.

Lotte also could not bear to watch her father being so cheerful, now that he had his wife almost to himself. He had been stopped in the street by an older gentleman who stared at him flabbergasted. 'You're still alive! Are you really Rockanje?' He nodded suspiciously. 'Once upon a time I gave you an injection,' cried the other enthusiastically, 'straight into the heart—a desperate act because I had already given you up!' Lotte's father, who remembered nothing about it and had heard everything about his sickbed secondhand, thanked him in bewilderment for his brave intervention and went home with a spring in his step. He felt as though life had been given to him for a second time and this time he decided he wasn't going to let anyone hold him back from really enjoying it. (The great disillusion was still awaiting him: Father Stalin was still a man of irreproachable behavior.)

The war was regurgitated somewhat poisonously, for a moment, and an ugly crack would have appeared in his reputation if Sara Frinkel had not made a forceful appearance. A Jewish dinner had been organized. The Frinkel family, not yet departed for America, was also invited. Ed de Vries said during the meal, in that loud manner with which he had always known how to attract attention as a singer-entertainer, that the Rockanje family had swindled him out of a box he had given to them for safekeeping containing valuables worth half a million. Indignantly Sara Frinkel had cried, 'How dare you!' across the table. 'You take those words back immediately, old rat. How do you get that into your head? You didn't have a sou! Don't make me laugh, you with your half a million in a box about which you said: 'I'm coming to bury a few knickknacks.' I've got your measure: You're trying to claim the insurance. That's your business, but don't think of dragging the Rockanje family through the mud!'

Lotte sometimes looked at the film star photos Theo de Zwaan had taken of her and Jet before the war. With what self-assurance and defiance they looked into the lens, as though the world lay at their feet. What recklessness, what ignorance! She thought back to how life had been before the war with a sense of bitterness and nostalgia. Although they had been opposed to God and Colijn, under their mother's lead they had had a romantic belief in Justice, Humanity, Beauty. While Beethoven flowed out of the open window on summer evenings and she looked at the stars and the dark edge of the wood with the others from their wicker chairs, they thought: If such splendid music can exist, life must be splendid, too, in the most profound ways. Now she was ashamed of those grand feelings. Beethoven was a German, Bach too, Mendelsohn was a Jew; the Nazis paraded with their German composers and prohibited the Jewish ones—never again would they be able to listen to music free from associations. To have to be silent about the *Kindertotenlieder*. Everything had been defiled.

THEY HAD NOT noticed it becoming busy around them. Older couples had settled at the tables, the men in suits with starched shirts and ties, their ladies—fresh from the coiffeur—in dresses with pleated skirts and patent belts. The age of jeans and T-shirts had not yet penetrated here. A popular song began to play; a few couples dared to make their way to the middle, now rearranged as a dance floor. A sweet-voiced Louis Prima led them on; they turned with snappy steps proficiently . . . '*Buona sera signorina . . . buona sera. . . .*'

'How lovely,' Anna sighed, 'that they still have so much fun at their age.'

Lotte followed the greyheads with a disapproving expression. 'Don't you find it a bit embarrassing,' she said demurely, 'that sentimental fuss—for such oldies.'

'*Mensch,* don't be so harsh . . . for yourself. Did you never go dancing with your violin-maker?'

That 'with your violin-maker' offended Lotte, and the idea that they would have danced together like these dolled-up old people was simply revolting. 'My violin-maker has been dead for years,' she said sharply, hoping that Anna would be ashamed.

But it did not trouble her at all. A burly old man presented himself. He was buttoning up his jacket and bowing slightly ironically towards Anna. She stood up with an amused laugh, wormed past two tables and disappeared from view for a short while. '*Oh mein papa . . .*' warbled the jukebox.

Anna circled over the dance floor as though she had never been doing anything else since the nuns had taught her to dance in the shadow of the Von Zitsewitz castle. Chuckling, she thought back to the bother about '*Was machst du mit dem Knie, lieber Hans,*' but the Casanova in Spa behaved himself impeccably. He led her self-confidently, without suspecting that he was holding someone in his arms who had not allowed herself to be led for a long time, by no matter whom. Yes, he even made so bold as to dance his own version of the tango with her, with one arm stuck out straight and abrupt one-hundred-and-eighty-degree turns. Afterwards he brought her back to her seat chivalrously.

Anna was out of breath. 'Who would have thought it,' she laughed hoarsely, 'a peat bath followed by dancing.'

They left the café late in the evening, after Anna had been tempted onto the dance floor twice more by her silent partner. The bath house cast its shadow over the road like a mastodon. They turned right, dizzy from the Grand Marnier.

'Those who dance keep death at a distance.' Anna giggled, bumping into Lotte. 'Just look what a clear sky! Tomorrow it will definitely be fine weather; we can go for a lovely walk. What do you say to that, *Schwesterlein?* The pain has gone, I'm telling you, disappeared . . . *ffft* . . .' She put her arm through Lotte's.

She, too, had lost some of her reserve as a result of the alcohol and the unreal scenes that she had been absorbing all that time. 'Listen, Anna,' she said, 'just then, when I saw you whirling around on the dance floor, I remembered something from earlier, in a flash.'

'You mean from a very long time ago?'

'Yes . . . you were dancing in the hall, wild, unruly, ungainly—or perhaps you weren't dancing but playing tag with. . . . There was a boy there . . . .

'The caretaker's son,' Anna completed, intuitively.

'It could have been. . . . You were romping about up the stairs, your excited screaming echoed through the corridor. Suddenly you were lying at the bottom of the stairs shrieking . . . there was something wrong with your arm. . . . I was frightened and shrieking with you. I don't know what happened then . . . although yes, wait a minute. . . .' She spoke louder from the excitement. The memory was unstoppable once it had got going. 'You were taken to the hospital and came back with your arm in plaster in a sling. I was jealous. . . . I wanted everything that you had . . . Your pain, and also your bandage. They put my arm in a tea towel or something . . . as consolation.'

'Now that you say that'—Anna stopped—'now that you say it . . . yes . . . I had completely forgotten. It was broken, in two places even, I believe. You still remember it! Now you see!'

She wanted to say something else, but instead she embraced Lotte.

The alcohol and their emotions were beginning to ferment dangerously. Their bodies swayed back and forth alarmingly above the
asphalt, as though they were clinging tightly to each other on a ship
in a storm. Before Anna's eyes the *Athenae* sailed, with them in the
background; before Lotte's the oranges and lemons in a greengrocer's
window. They walked on inch by inch, the town of springs, Spa,
came and went pleasantly, as though it had overindulged itself in
Grand Marnier. Anna stopped in the middle of the bridge over the
railway; leaning heavily on the balustrade, she made a grand gesture
towards the stars, which were sparkling above the silhouette of roofs
and surrounding hills, and recited in a pompous voice:

> 'For seeing begotten,
> My sight my employ,
> And sworn to the watch-tower,
> The world gives me joy.
>
> I gaze in the distance,
> I mark in the nearness,
> The moon and the planets,
> The woods and the deer . . .

'Er . . . how does it go on . . .' she cried plaintively. 'My God, I
can't remember it anymore.' Her arms were still raised to the stars, in
an empty gesture now.

'Come,' said Lotte, tugging at her arm.

3

LOTTE HAD CHOSEN a route with the idyllic name Promenade
des Artistes with the help of a walking map. She regretted
her sentimentality of the previous evening. A shared memory was no reason for fraternizing—strange that the word *sisteriz-*

ing did not exist. She maintained a careful distance and placed her hands firmly in the pockets of her winter coat. A watery sun shimmered between the branches. A narrow brook meandered like silver beside the path.

With each step Anna rejoiced at the suppleness of her joints—the peat was beginning to take effect. She inhaled the tingling forest air and thought she could feel the oxygen penetrating deep into her lungs. Very soon her cheerfulness translated into communicativeness. She chuckled to herself. 'You'll never guess, Lotte, who came looking for me in Salzkotten.'

THE INSTITUTE FOR Social Work was located on the top floor of a Franciscan convent. Successful studying depended a good deal on the talent to improvise. There were no textbooks or exercise books. Those who managed to get hold of a roll of wallpaper or a sheet of wrapping paper could take notes. The lecturers, who had been scraped together from all over the country, arrived at the Institute from their ruined towns after an adventurous journey over a devastated railway network. They stayed at the convent and drove the students into the ground non-stop for fourteen days with psychology or sociology. Mindful of the Gospel of the Nazarene, the nuns shared their scarce provisions with the pupils, and when winter came they willingly sat in the cold so that the classroom could be warm.

There was an ironic coincidence—the village on the Lippe where her father had been born and her grandfather had died was within walking distance of Salzkotten, the village in the fairy tale about the swineherd—but without the prince. She preferred not to assume that her peregrinations and destiny had combined to contrive that she should end up here in the inescapable course of nature. She ignored the fact that that spot of calamities was so nearby, even the finest weather could not entice her to walk in that direction. But Salzkotten with its weekly market was the hub of the surrounding villages. One day she ran into someone from her village who had once sat next to her in school. They exchanged information, surprised at the reunion.

This chance meeting provoked one that was far less coincidental.

Some days later there was a knock at her door. 'You have a visitor,' said a fellow student bashfully. 'If you would come to the parlour.' 'Visiting me,' Anna exclaimed. 'That can't be so, I have no one in the whole world. Who is it, then?' 'Well, it's not a lady. It is some woman or other who claims she is your family.' Anna walked downstairs unsuspecting. At the doorway she stiffened. The soberly furnished room was completely taken over by the figure awaiting her; the mere fact of her presence was itself a form of sacrilege. She was hefty and flabby; her skin gleamed, her eyes and hair were darker than ever; her vulgar self-importance contrasted stridently with the modest biblical subjects on the walls. '*Mein Gott,*' she said in a whining, small voice adapted to the surroundings, 'what are you doing here, are you becoming a nun?'

Anna kept a suitable distance; extreme self-control was required to resist the tortures and humiliations that emanated from Aunt Martha like a dark devil's aura. No . . . oh no . . . she thought, warding it off . . . not this. In a flat, impersonal manner she explained what the purpose of her stay at the convent was. 'Ah, is that so,' sighed the visitor, still insatiably curious. 'Listen, whatever you need—butter, cheese, eggs—you just have to say.' Anna was forced into a dilemma by this reckless offer of hers. The threats of ten years ago buzzed in her head: 'You will come crawling to me begging for bread.' On the other hand there plainly was hunger, for everyone in the convent, and there was the settling of old scores: She was entitled to all that this aunt owed her. 'Terrific,' she heard herself saying haughtily. 'We would all be glad of that, it can be left at the gate.' Her aunt nodded, not completely satisfied, and Anna thought that it was not something evil in her demeanour but a primitiveness to which every form of morality, of self-doubt, of intelligence, was alien. When there was no more to say, Aunt Martha left with her great breadth, having entirely fulfilled her role as the amiable aunt who, concerned, had searched for her hungry niece with the nuns. Flabbergasted, Anna remained behind. What drove her to the convent? It could not be charity. Was she trying to bring inside the fence the sheep that had escaped from her influence ten years ago? Did she still need a cheap source of labour, someone on whom she could indulge her destructive tendencies?

Nothing was delivered to the gate. Rather, Anna met people from the village more often, who brought her up to date, in fragments, with how her aunt had led her sordid, unpalatable life. While Uncle Heinrich had been fighting on the Russian front, his wife, it seems, had turned out to be the most disreputable black marketeer in the area. Unhampered by sympathy, she had taken everything the refugees from the towns possessed—a jewel, table silver, a tobacco box, a portrait in a gilded frame—for an egg, a piece of bread. She made every piece of bread pay four times over. She was respected and admired in the wider district; hunger was stronger than fear. And the only one who could have put the brakes on her was now a prisoner of war in Russia.

The latest item of news that reached Anna was so bizarre that initially she burst out jeering. But her laughing very soon turned into an un-Christian anger that contrasted painfully with the tranquillity within the convent walls. Aunt Martha was broadcasting that she was financing her niece's studies at the Institute for Social Work. If you thought you had seen everything after a fashion and had coped with it, you were immediately punished for your naiveté. The convolutions of a perfidious spirit—again it was succeeding in upsetting Anna's barely regained peace of mind; it was proceeding as usual, as though she had never been away.

But the influence of the intervening years did make itself felt. Anna crossed the meadow landscape of her youth at a brisk walking pace—no hills or mountains but fields as far as the eye could see. She was not burdened by melancholy or nostalgia—her resolution shut out all other feelings. She avoided the elder tree and the Lady Chapel by the bridge over the river; encountering the farm again and the grown-up children did not disturb her equilibrium. She burst into the kitchen unannounced and seized her bewildered aunt by the blouse with both hands, at the height of her bosom: 'So, you are paying for my studies!'

'Please, please, what's the matter?' Aunt Martha's eyes narrowed with fear, like a vicious cat grabbed by the scruff of its neck. 'What are you paying, how much, since when? Well?' Her aunt's greedy mouth dropped open, closed and open again. No words emerged, only incoherent protesting. Anna continued unperturbed, without sympathy, without triumph. 'Do you really know how much you owe me? You owe me my youth, you owe me everything! I'll turn you in! I'm telling you. If you don't retract the lies you have been spreading all over the place, officially in the newspaper, I will set the police on you!' 'Please . . . please . . .' She wriggled free, nervously looking for a way out. 'Paper!' Anna commanded. 'Bring me a pen and paper.' With revolting servility, Aunt Martha brought her what she had asked for. Anna smoothed the paper flat on the kitchen table, pushed the pen into her hand and dictated in forceful High German: 'I, Martha Bamberg, withdraw the remarks made by me about the studies of my niece, Anna Grosalie-Bamberg, in Salzkotten. When I made out that I was paying for her studies I was not speaking the truth.' Anna checked the text, altered some writing mistakes and ordered her aunt to place the retraction in the local paper. Although in the corner of her eye she could see the draining board and the stove, two of the fixed reference points from her youth, from a time of serfdom, she did not deign to look over the whole mess. She closed the door behind her and walked across the yard without turning around.

With her hands clenched into fists she marched back across the fields. She would let nobody trifle with her anymore, Anna Grosalie, war widow, Red Cross Sister, training to be a social worker in child welfare. The pathetic creature that should have succumbed to tuberculosis, cancer or a bombing raid a long time ago would let nobody trifle with her anymore—she was studying subjects the names of which Aunt Martha would not even have been able to pronounce.

But the fanfare of triumph became blurred, because above her head in the rustle of the poplars she could hear the hoarse lament of herself as a girl of twelve. She slowed down. She realized that, irrespective of the sweetness of revenge, irrespective of the number of children she would help in the future, she could not protect with retrospective strength the child she herself had been. That child had permanently, irrevocably been handed over to Aunt Martha's will, she would have free disposal of her until eternity. The idea of repayment was ridiculous in relation to a rudimentary soul that would never be able to think in terms of good and evil—the most she was capable of was to recognize that Anna was the stronger one now. A pyrrhic victory.

New teachers braved the obstacles of public transport to bring the group of chosen ones at the Institute into contact with such unfamiliar disciplines as the law of guardianship. Anna's thoughts went back involuntarily to the peddlers of the sterilization order and the guardianship declaration in which for years Uncle Heinrich had written that she was a bit simple-minded and frail. What kind of judge had he been in fact, if it had never occurred to him to send an inspector to the farm? To find that out she presented herself at the district court. The judge from that period seemed to have been replaced by a new one immediately after the war, a young man who presided there dejectedly as though he had been locked up in the heart of a pyramid with the job of finding the exit.

'How is it possible,' he sighed, when Anna had explained the story to him. 'That's what I am asking you,' she said. 'How is it possible? And why, please?' The judge played with his fountain pen for a moment. 'The law that you allude to,' he said thoughtfully, 'had at that time to prevent congenital disorders being passed on, by seeing to it that affected persons were sterilized. A judge in the Nazi period, sitting in this chair . . .'—he faltered—'had to prove that he was a Nazi by actively cooperating. If he said there were no simple-minded cases in his district, then he put himself under suspicion. Whereas if he offered such a case, a poor child, moreover an orphan—there, thank God, he had something in black and white.' He laughed shamefacedly. 'Might I see that declaration?' said Anna. 'Of course,' he said. 'It must be somewhere in the archives. We will find it and send you a copy.'

But the declaration seemed to have disappeared without trace. She received a letter a fortnight later: the declaration preceding hers was still there, properly preserved, the declaration following it, too—but hers was missing. Who had allowed her declaration to disappear, when, why, could not be found out. If Uncle Heinrich survived Russia she would not be able to go to him and push the declaration under his nose. The truth about her youth, including the lies, could only be found in the archive of her own parrot-memory now, where for inexplicable reasons nothing ever disappeared.

Aunt Martha's retraction did indeed appear, clearly legible in the newspaper. Anna's satisfaction about it quickly ebbed away in the middle of the metre-long roll of lining paper, the Dead Sea Scroll of social work, that had to be studied for the examination. She became acquainted with Freud and with the significance of the first six years of life. She thought about her father for the first time in a long while, in that context, about his cough, the tapping of his stick on the cobblestones, his black coat, his hat, his pride when his daughters succeeded at something, his suppressed sadness when he could no longer take them onto his lap. The memories came in waves, that all-recording memory of hers did not spare her. She had to remember Lotte now, too. Together in the bed, together in the bath. Their self-evident inseparability, as though it would remain so in the years to come. Whispering in bed in the evenings, competing for their father's attention during the day—he could not simultaneously give both of them affection or reprimands. They had each developed their own talents and characteristic attributes in the competition for their father. Anna, her legendary memory in the art of recitation, her empathy with a poor girl (a good exercise for later) on the stage in the casino, and her irrepressible vitality: running, jumping, falling, groaning, screaming. In contrast to all that commotion, Lotte presented her singing. With childlike veneration for her own voice she directed her songs up high to the round dome in the hall and listened to the reverberation with amazement. When she was not singing she was silent and compliant—her way of gaining her father's special protection, so that Anna, in her jealousy, ran, jumped, fell even harder. The more Anna remembered, the more her interest grew. These two people who had been her

closest and most intimate family aroused an academic curiosity in
her—or was it a longing, a profound, rash longing, now that she
had been left alone more emphatically than ever before.

Old acquaintances spoke to her in the street to tell her that
Uncle Heinrich was back and to describe, each in their own rhetoric, what sort of effect Russia had had on him. He was back, he
was alive! An irrational, ambivalent excitement came over her. She
did not want to see him. She wanted to see him. The image of
Uncle Heinrich back from the event at Bückeberg came to mind:
shocked, speechless, full of fear and loathing. He had seen visions
of what was to come, in the perfectly recorded Great Germanic
harvest festival, in the enthusiasm of the crowd, in the inflamma-
tory, hypnotic language of the Führer. He knew it but could not
prevent himself being sent to Russia as part of the same performance. It was so poignant that her heart would have winced, if all
the other things had not already existed in contrast. She did not
want to see him; she wanted to see him. She wanted to ask him for
clarification about the guardianship declaration. She wanted to say
to him: My husband was in Russia, too. She wanted Lotte's
address, which she had lost, and her father's books, a row of bound
German classics—the only thing he had bequeathed to her. She
wanted to show him: look, the simple-minded, frail child is still
alive, she is a tough one—surely we did have a bond, once, or have
I imagined that?

When she realized she would never be able to manage not to go,
she borrowed a bicycle and went. She had carefully chosen a Sunday morning. Her aunt, who ignored God's commandments, never
missed a high mass. Anna had gambled well, the house was empty
except for the small living room, where she found her uncle by the
stove in the chair where his father had slowly died, a little more
each day, beneath the print of the dead soldier. She had prepared
herself for this, that he would be thinner, but what she encountered in that history-laden, genetically determined spot was an
emaciated old man who looked at her without seeing her, with a
hollow, faded gaze. A thin neck poked out of his shirt collar, narrow wrists emerged from the sleeves of his jacket, his fingers hung

down from the arm rests. His stiff blond hair had gone grey, a bony skull shone through it. Nowhere was the young uncle recognizable, the muscular farmer's son who parodied Christmas carols in Cologne. She greeted him shyly. Did she detect a reply in a very slight nodding of the top-heavy wrinkled face? The next obvious step would have been to ask him how he was—a question, she now understood, that would demonstrate obtuse lack of feeling. Sour air hung in the stuffy room, just as before she had sensed she could not breathe in there. But he sat in silence; it even looked as though he rather blamed her for something. The things she had wanted to say died in her mouth. She moistened her lips. 'Uncle Heinrich,' she began. He did not react, how should she continue? To start with the declaration was impossible in these circumstances; Russia was a painful subject, Lotte taboo. The only one to occur to her as tangible, not dangerous, was the row of classics. 'My father's books,' she said hurriedly, 'you remember: Schiller, Goethe, Hoffmannstahl . . . I would like to take them with me.' A miracle happened: the head moved from one imaginary end of the horizon to the other. 'Why not?' whispered Anna, but no further enlightenment followed. He looked at her, froze her out; she was suffocating beneath the low ceiling, between the oppressive walls, between two corpses and another apparent corpse. She turned to the door and fled.

At a furious pace she cycled back, oscillating between indignation and sympathy. You really would have thought that Russia had been an exercise in detachment—what did possessions matter if you were hungry, thirsty, in pain. But she corrected herself: Don't you see that he is broken, a piece of ice from the tundra? Don't you see that all he can still say is a big flat no to everyone and everything? This man, this shadow of a man, she would never be able to call him to account, let alone ever be able to make peace with him.

A day later she was thinking differently about it. If everyone eluded her, all that remained was the material. She decidedly wanted to have the books, her father's only tangible memorial. Once again she went to the district court. She got an official order, a written order to release the books. She made the pilgrimage to the farm for the last

time. Nothing had changed inside. Although he did not speak he
could still read. Respect for authority had been ingrained in him, first
by his tyrannical wife, then by the army and after that by camp regi-
men. He understood very well what the official document that he
held between his fragile fingers contained. This time the top-heavy
wrinkled head moved from the low beamed ceiling to the wooden
floor and back. Anna lifted the books off the shelf above the sideboard. Clutching the pile to her chest she looked at him one more
time, over the classics. *Faust* was on top. She looked at the desolate
figure next to the stove and swallowed. Why was the Faust figure
always masculine? Their Faust was in church with hands clasped in
prayer.

THEY LOST TRACK of time and distance while Anna was doing the
talking. They had already twice passed a crease in the map when
Anna stopped in mid-sentence, clutched her heart with an almost
pathetic gesture, and gasped for breath. Lotte stood next to her,
resigned. She recognized it. First running and jumping, then a broken
arm or a tooth through the lip—first overwhelm the other under a
torrent of words, then breathlessness.
   'Let's . . . go back . . .' Anna uttered.
   Lotte nodded. She actually gave her sister an arm; inch by inch
they walked back on the winding paths to the rhythm of Anna's
lumbering body and rasping breath. It occurred to Lotte that the
return journey had taken an eternity, as she unloaded Anna in the
lounge of her hotel. Coffee . . . Anna gesticulated, strong coffee.
Coffee had brought her back to life before in the past. With a
forced laugh she dropped into a chair, fanning herself with a waving hand. Her pale face was shining with sweat; she waited with
closed eyes until her breathing calmed. Lotte sat there sheepishly
without worrying: Anna emerged from her own life story as indestructible, as someone who would make even death flee by telling it
the frank truth, straight to its face. And sure enough, Anna slowly
came to, her eyes opened again, she was already looking at Lotte
cheerfully and perceptively again.
   '*Entschuldigung*, my body is a spoilsport from time to time . . .

We're so comfortable here. . . . Please, order something yourself. Do you remember . . .' She made an effort to move closer to Lotte and lay a hand on hers. Rising airily over her own body, which came to a halt now and then, as though over a fallen tree lying across the road, she said, 'Do you still remember, Lotte, when I came to look for you in The Hague?'

Lotte froze. But Anna waltzed on; it seemed as though she genuinely was in a hurry.

'But first I went to Cologne . . . hoping that Uncle Franz was still alive, the only one who had your address.'

Anna ordered a second cup of coffee. Two hotel guests went past looking at the noisy old lady with surprise. Lotte thought she could see aversion, yes, hostility in their gaze.

'Cologne,' Anna said dreamily, 'I shall never forget being on the east bank of the Rhine and looking right through the city to the west where the lignite factory chimneys stood out against the horizon. You could tell it was Cologne from the two spires of the cathedral, which had miraculously been spared. There were still walls here and there, nothing in between. I was on the bank with some others—we looked at it but did not believe what we were seeing, because the city had always been there between the Rhine and the lignite factory. All the bridges had been destroyed. We were standing there and wanted to get over to the other side; a canoe paddled up to take us across as though it were a thousand years ago. Someone was waiting on the other bank with a cart for our suitcases, and we began a journey along winding paths between the heaps of rubble and around the heaps of rubble, and people were living somewhere in a shelter or beneath the remains of a wall.'

Lotte listened uneasily. She felt a strong urge to go to her hotel. Not to have to hear, just for once, not to have to react to anything—to succumb to a languid Sunday afternoon feeling, no more.

'I wanted to see you, it had all begun there. Of course I also wanted to know whether my uncle and aunt were still alive. They had been lucky, the hospital had been spared—they were not suffering from hunger, the English supplied the hospital plentifully with food.

The only thing I could utter after the surprise of seeing them again was "I'm hungry." They made me a saucepan of rice pudding, I ate until I could eat no more. I got Aunt Elisabeth's address from them and thus eventually I came to you. . . . God in heaven, I'll never forget that!'

WHILE ANNA WAS waiting for news from her great aunt in Amsterdam, of whom all she remembered was that she had separated Lotte from their symbiotic duality with surgical precision long ago, the fear that Lotte was no longer alive either suddenly crept into her. She remembered the successful bombing of Rotterdam at the start of the war—beyond that she had no idea what the war had brought about in Holland.

Some weeks later it looked a little more rosy. Lotte was expecting her; in a cryptic letter she had assented to Anna's coming. From the train the destruction of The Netherlands turned out not to be as bad as expected. The meadows lay smooth and mown, the cattle stood, well-fed, in a picture postcard with bridges and church spires. The situation was less panoramic in the tram in The Hague. All seats were taken; the passengers were pushed against each other in the central gangway on each bend. A middle-aged man politely stood up for Anna. She flopped down with her inseparable stage prop, the leather suitcase, whispering 'Dankeschön'. 'What!' cried the man in shock. 'You are a German! Stand up immediately!' Anna stood up, only half understanding what he was saying but understanding quite well what he meant. All faces turned accusingly in her direction. 'I understand you very well,' she apologized clumsily. 'I understand very well that you don't want to have anything to do with us. But I was not a Nazi, whether you want to believe me or not, I am an ordinary woman, my husband died in the war, I have no one else. I cannot say anything else to you . . .' There was a very telling silence around her; people turned away from her disapprovingly. Anna hung on tightly to the strap and sensed for the first time what it would mean to be a German from now on. To be found guilty by people who knew nothing about you. Not to be seen as an individual but as a specimen of a type, because you said *dankeschön* instead of *dank u wel*.

But an unshakeable solidarity with her own history and the lack of political awareness temporarily preserved her from the schizophrenia of collective guilt and individual innocence. For her, Anna Grosalie, this was a historic day. She was not so much a German as someone who, left alone in the world, was in search of the security of her first years of childhood. The ties of blood that were taken for granted by most people, that you could always fall back on, were for her something that had to be forged. She got out, stopped a passer-by and showed him the letter with the address, without saying a word. She would not let her own language cross her lips—perhaps he would send her in the wrong direction on purpose.

'THOSE ARE THE things you never forget in your whole life,' said Anna.

'You don't forget anything,' suggested Lotte sombrely.

'What a disillusionment that was, my visit to you. . . . You refused to speak German, I could only communicate with you via your husband—insofar as there was contact at all. He translated everything I said, the brave soul, and the rare answers you gave.'

'No further word of German passed my lips until now. I had no more to do with that language; you might as well have spoken in Russian.'

'But surely that couldn't be so, your mother tongue! Even now you still speak it fluently.'

'Yet it was so.'

'It was psychological of course. You did not want to have to deal with me, and you entrenched yourself behind Dutch.' Now Anna became fierce. 'You have no idea how difficult it was for me. You were the only one I still had; I wanted to get to know you, I wanted to apologize for my behaviour when you came looking for me. I wanted to show that I had changed. But you were busy with your baby. A baby—that made it all the worse! You bathed the baby, fed the baby, combed the baby's hair. . . . You ignored me. I did everything to awaken your interest: I was thin air to you. Your husband was embarrassed by the situation, he tried to take care of it as well as possible. Why didn't you rant and rave at me, call me everything under the sun, so I could have defended myself? But that evasiveness . . . I did not exist to you.'

Lotte looked around with agitation to see if anyone was walking about whom she could pay for her coffee. She wanted to get away as fast as possible. The longer it went on, the crazier it got; she was even being called upon to justify herself now. The world stood on its head. 'I hadn't asked for you to come, you didn't interest me.'

'That's true, I didn't interest you . . . you had your baby.'

'That child was my rescue,' she snapped at Anna. 'It reconciled me to my life . . . my children are everything to me.'

Anna sighed despondently. Her sister was still unreachable behind the fortification of her progeny; she herself was still alone and child-less, notwithstanding the hundreds of children she had helped in her life. She sensed a vague pain in her chest . . . from the excitement . . . stupid, stupid, stupid. Silly to have thought that she could still have put anything right.

'Lotte, don't walk away,' she said remorsefully. 'It's all so long ago. Let's . . . let's eat together, I'll treat you. It really is a miracle that we have found each other again, here in Spa—let's enjoy it as long as we can.'

Lotte allowed herself to be persuaded. What was she making a fuss about actually; it was Sunday evening, there was nothing she had to do. They transferred to the dining room and ordered an aperitif.

'I've brought my sister with me,' Anna cried proudly. The waiter laughed formally. Lotte felt irritation creeping up like an itch.

'When did your husband die in fact?' Anna asked, 'I liked him. He was serious, civilized . . . refined, I would almost . . .'

'Ten years ago,' Lotte interrupted her curtly.

'From what?'

'A heart attack . . . overwork, all those years.'

'Do you ever go to his grave? Or was he—'

'Sometimes. . . .' Lotte refused any form of companionship here. She was not inclined to compete on this point—with an SS officer killed in action.

'I go twice a year, on All Saints Day and in the spring, with a wreath and a candle,' Anna told her.

TWICE A YEAR she was warmly welcomed by the mother and her daughter to commemorate the tragic death and the miracle of the survival. It gnawed away at her that the grave had not been blessed. She decided to speak to the unyielding pastor. She waited for him, straight after the mass, at which the holy commandment 'Love your enemies' had been the theme. He was still in full regalia. 'Father,' she buttonholed him, 'one of the three soldiers in the cemetery was my husband. We are Catholics, my husband and I, that is why I ask you to bless the grave.' He laughed scornfully. 'I do not care whether you are Catholics or not, they were in the SS.' 'But,' Anna reminded him, 'you have just been preaching: "Love your enemies."' He raised one of his heavy black eyebrows, which made him look rather Mephistophilean himself, and sneered, 'I do not bless the grave of a member of the SS.' 'He had only been in the SS for a fortnight,' she cried. 'He had absolutely no choice!' In response to her emotional outburst the pastor cast her a dismissive look before leaving her where she stood and walking away down a dim aisle.

Blessed or not, she saved up for a headstone with a sandstone cross with all three names chiselled on it from the first money she earned as an employee of the Cologne local authority. It stood in place between the yews and conifers for a decade, well tended by the three women, until the end of the fifties, when the rumour went around that the three soldiers were going to a newly laid-out military cemetery in a nearby village. In that case, thought Anna, I would rather take him to Cologne. She succeeded in getting a permit from the city council to have him interred in the soldiers' cemetery in Cologne. Thus armed she went to visit the pastor once again—the graveyard came under the church's jurisdiction. After she had informed him, formally and neutrally, of her intentions, and had shown him the permit, she left her address with him with the request to warn her when the grave was being emptied.

All Souls came around again and Anna made her ritual journey. A thick mist hung low over the earth; it smelled of wet leaves and chrysanthemums. Experienced, she pushed the squeaking gate open. She walked between graves with burning candles; the flames were motionless in the damp air. At the spot where her journey usually ended in wreath-laying and a prayer she found an impersonal square piece of grass with dry autumn leaves on it. Puzzled, she looked around. Had she walked the wrong way? My grave, she thought in panic, where is my grave? A procession was approaching along the mossy central path, enshrouded in the mist. The pastor was at the front in his chasuble followed by the villagers with their candles. It dawned on her. There he strode, the unbending representative of the Mother Church, in his solemn robes that were a harlequin costume on him. There went the uncharitable, sanctimonious one, under whose direction people were going to pray for the salvation of the favored dead. Perhaps he would be called to account one day, but she was not inclined to wait quietly for that. With long vengeful strides she walked up to him and stationed herself halfway along the path with her hands on her hips. The heavy eyebrows rose. 'Where is my grave,' she flung in his face. 'Where is my husband? Where is my headstone? After all, I gave you my address, you should have warned me!' The villagers stared at her in amazement. They knew precisely what Anna was talking about: She was their war widow. The pastor said nothing; he shifted his weight from one foot to the other and observed her disapprovingly, as though he had a hysteric in front of him. 'There's nothing there anymore,' she cried, 'nothing.' She heard a ringing in her ears, the sound of her own voice disappeared into the background. She wobbled out of the way, overcome with dizziness, sinking down disrespectfully onto a slanting tombstone, her head in her hands, the wreath lost in the grass beside her. As the procession moved on an old woman knelt down by her and whispered; 'They were exhumed and taken to Gerolstein, to the memorial cemetery.'

Having come to her senses again, hours later, in Gerolstein she found no idyllic cemetery with mossy tombstones and crosses overgrown with ivy but a brand new field divided into geometric squares. Parallel strips of white sand between vertical planks with numbers on them. She laid her wreath in the middle of the field of the dead. I am sorry, Martin, she apologized, the wreath is for all of you now.

'CROSSES WERE ERECTED later on there. The three soldiers are still next to each other.' Anna laughed. 'The fact that the three of them stayed behind instead of pinching apples has bound them to each other for eternity. It says "Unknown soldier" on many crosses. I still go there sometimes, mostly in the spring. The cemetery is high up on a hill, on the edge of the world, forgotten. It is quiet there. Sometimes mothers walk there with small children, because it is a peaceful spot. I sit on a little wall, right by the grave; they chat to me, ask me where I come from; why. Then I say: I am visiting my husband here. That terrifies them; they cannot place it anymore, it was so long ago. Actually, neither can I. In recent years I have asked myself, What am I doing here?'

Lotte nodded drowsily. She was drinking more wine than was good for her; the subject did not please her. And Anna still went on with it, bringing yet more facts to light. That the death of a hero could have such consequences.

'Now I ask you,' Anna was imperturbable, 'why do we really believe that the spiritual existence of the deceased should still be connected to that one spot? Why do we go back there? Out of nostalgia? And whom does it benefit? The flower sellers, the groundskeepers, the people who make headstones—there's a whole industry connected with it. It's their livelihood, and that's why we still come. Do you want to be buried?'

'I?' Lotte started. 'Of . . . of course,' she stuttered. With an inappropriate frivolity provoked by resentment she said: 'I want a grave full of wildflowers. . . . I have five children and eight grandchildren to care for them.'

'When I die there will be nothing left of me,' said Anna, being contrary. 'Then there won't be any public garden you can go to, where anyone has to spend money to put flowers there. Who would do that for me? Who would interest themselves in it? After all, I myself won't even be there.'

Lotte pushed her empty coffee cup aside and stood up slowly. 'I really must go now,' she murmured. It seemed as though the alcohol had shifted all her weight to her head. She left the dining room with a top-heavy feeling, Anna busy talking behind her.

She grabbed her by one shoulder, breathing heavily; 'Do you remember the day that . . . mother . . . was buried?'

'No, absolutely not.' Lotte hazarded a grab for her coat. No more cemeteries, she implored silently.

'They had placed her coffin on the sofa. We had climbed up onto it, to look out from the bay window, to see if she was coming yet. Our feet were resting on the windowsill. We drummed loudly on the window with our patent-leather shoes because the waiting went on so long, hoping she would hear it and hurry up. Indignant members of the family lifted us off the coffin. Only now do I understand that we were sitting on top of her.'

'Well . . .' said Lotte, unmoved. For her there was only one mother: the other one. She buttoned her coat and looked around wearily.

'I'll see you out,' said Anna. Beneath the harsh ceiling light she could see an expression midway between resignation and irritation on her sister's face. She remembered her father had looked exactly like that in the latter days of his illness. That facial expressions could be inherited! She did not dare state her discovery out loud. Lotte pushed off so swiftly that there could only be one reason for it—she had been too boisterous again.

Lotte pulled the heavy front door open with all the tipsy strength of an old lady. She hesitated on the doorstep. 'Sleep well,' she said weakly to the round figure who filled the doorway and still radiated an uncurbed vehemence.

'I am sorry I talked nineteen-to-the-dozen today.' Anna put her arms around Lotte guiltily. 'Tomorrow, I promise, I will let my quieter side show. Sleep well, *meine Liebe, schlaf gut und träum süss . . .*'

That night Anna lacked the light-heartedness to fall asleep just like that. Images of funerals and cemeteries jostled each other. Her life had been punctuated by the dead, when she looked back over it, in the way that a cross-section of a glacier recalls the ice ages—how often it had given her life a brusque, harsh turn. She was full of a wonderful elation, as though something celebratory was going to happen. What else could it be but the apotheosis of the approaches she had been making for two weeks now? It was time for a proper reconciliation with her stubborn, squirming sister, discussed out loud. If the two of them, born simultaneously from the same mother, loved by the same father, could not succeed in stepping over the silly obstacles tossed up by history, who on earth could do so? What was the prospect for the world if even the two of them, who were supposed to become milder in their old age, could not?

She was oppressed, threw the blankets off and turned on her side. When it was almost morning she fell asleep despite herself. Her dream was populated with angels of diverse plumage. She recognized most of them at once, some only after thinking it over a little. With one exception they were acting in unison. The angels on either side of the steps to the Karlskirche left their plinths and flew, with strong beats of their wings and rustling robes, over the green dome into the clouds, grasping the crosses to their breasts. The graceful female guards at the Thermal Institute stepped off the porch and flew after them. Up above, on a gold-fringed cloud, lay the two naked women who normally reclined on a shell-like decoration in the hall; one strenuously tried to catch the eye of the other who was (deliberately?) looking past her pensively. The pink reflection of the setting sun touched all the faces. In back, where the night announced itself in deep purple, a figure suddenly dived from a great height, gliding down in a broad, black coat. He held his hat down on his head with one hand, he clutched a walking stick in the other. Two plump children followed astride a fish, making use of the slipstream behind his wide flapping coat. Anna thought she vaguely remembered coming across them in passing on a

monument to the famous people who had visited Spa over the centuries. On either side of a stone frame bearing the names, a cherub
with a malevolent expression sat on a fish.

After that it was night. Nothing flew by offering a distraction
except an unexpected angel in the light of the moon, no, an eagle,
which cleaved like a thunderbolt through the blackness that was
exactly as deep and absolute as the blackout nights had been in the
war. Anna tossed onto her other side—which abruptly deprived her,
released her, from her dreams.

4

A CORD HUNG above the decorative curved copper bathtub
with a handle that said 'Pull' in four languages. When the
alarm clock gave the signal that the prescribed time was up,
a short tug by the bath guest summoned a woman in a white overall,
who helped with the getting out and drying off.

Lotte's final week had begun with a peat bath and a carbonated
bath. She was resting, swathed in a towel; glasses of Queen-Spa were
also cleansing her within. Silence reigned as in a padded cell. No
sound whatsoever penetrated from the outside world, as though the
complex of bathrooms lay in caves deep beneath the Hoge Venen,
right at the source of the springs.

But the silence was rudely interrupted. Somewhere nearby somebody cursed: 'Mon Dieu!' Hurried footsteps in the corridor. A scream
immediately suppressed. Her door was thrown open; the woman in
the white overall stood on the threshold wringing her hands.
'Madame, Madame . . . since you were always together . . . venez . . .
votre amie . . .'

Lotte slid into her slippers and followed the woman to one of the
adjoining bathrooms where the door was wide open. Inside, the doctor
was being summoned; someone ran out blindly and almost bumped
into Lotte. She took two steps on the tiled floor. At first she could only

see the broad back of the woman in front of her, who then stepped aside ostentatiously to allow her to see what had not passed her lips.

Anna was staring at her with glazed eyes out of a peat bath—it looked as though she had been decapitated, or her body had sunk forever into the deep brown morass while her head had remained, forced up by the muddy mass. She was staring at Lotte with a gaze that lacked any emotion: excitement, irritation, scorn, rage, sorrow . . . a total absence of all those feelings that had alternated kaleidoscopically with each other for two weeks long and had formed the complexity called Anna. The most oppressive thing was that she was so obviously silent . . . that she was not explaining what had happened to her, as usual, talking energetically and gesticulating. Lotte looked around, orphaned. It was a bathroom like all the others, warm and damp; had she become breathless? The light blue tiles ended at the top in a border with shell motifs—this was the last thing Anna had seen; had it reminded her of the Baltic Sea where she had almost drowned, together with her husband . . . where, subsequently, she would have preferred to have drowned. . . . This was the last thing Anna had seen—just before then she had been alive and had got into the bath as vital as always. A macabre, tasteless joke was being played on her. . . . Next thing she would start to move again: *Mein Gott,* what a ridiculous situation this is!

A doctor rushed in followed by a rescue team. 'What is *she* doing here . . .' one of them protested. 'This is no time to let a guest in.'

'But she is her friend . . .' stammered the nurse who had alerted Lotte.

Lotte moved back, away from that empty, hollow gaze where only a heartbreaking nothing still looked out, away from all that unexpected, ultimate intimacy that Anna had involved her in without asking.

The nurse came running after her. '*Excusez-moi, Madame* . . . I thought you ought to know immediately. . . . Perhaps . . . perhaps they can still help her. . . . Sometimes wonders are done with resuscitation. . . . We have to wait. . . . Where are you going now?'

'To the Salle de Repos,' said Lotte hoarsely, 'I . . . think I ought to lie down for a moment.'

'Of course . . . *je comprends* . . . I will keep you informed.'

There was no one in the rest room apart from the busts of two professors who had contributed much to the development of the healing baths, and a solitary female figure who walked through a deserted landscape in a large painting that dominated the whole room. Lotte flopped down on a bed at random. *Too late, too late* echoed in her head. She realized that she had constantly taken for granted the luxurious presumption that she still had all the time in the world. And now, all of a sudden, on a Monday morning, with one week still to go, Anna had taken herself out of that scenario. How was it possible. . . . Anna, indestructible Anna, who never ran out of talk and, not just because of that, always seemed to have eternal life. . . . Like Sam and Moos in the joke with which Max Frinkel kept morale up in the war: Sam and Moos, only survivors of a shipwreck, answered the question, 'How did you manage it?' gesticulating busily: 'We went on talking as usual.'

Outside the doves were cooing, as always. Everything was as it always was, only now something essential was missing. Fourteen days ago she did not exist for me, thought Lotte, and now I will miss her? Yes, roared the silence in the Salle de Repos, admit it! 'Tomorrow, I promise, I will let my quieter side show,' Anna had said. That airy promise was now coming true in ominous daylight. Whether she opened or closed her eyes, Lotte still saw that one frozen image before her. They had not been able to say goodbye. There was so much I still wanted to say to her, she thought, in a crescendoing feeling of remorse. Oh yes, what then, cried a cynical voice, what would you have said to her if you had known what was going to happen? Something nice, something that spoke of involvement, something consoling, perhaps? Would you ever have been able to say to her what she actually wanted to hear, which had come to mean everything to her? Would you ever have succeeded in squeezing out those two words: 'I understand.'

Those two words, apparently so simple, so revolutionary for Lotte, assembled in her throat as though she still wanted to project them out; now it was too late, too late, too late. Instead of that she began to cry, noiselessly and discreetly, entirely in keeping with the atmosphere in the Salle de Repos. Why had she remained stuck all that time in the resistant position she had adopted from the beginning? Although she had gradually acquired more and more understanding of Anna, and sympathy, she had remained fixed in unapproachability, intentionally obstinate. Out of misplaced revenge, not once intended for Anna? Out of solidarity with the dead, her dead? Or out of a deeply ingrained mistrust—beware the apology 'We did not know', beware of understanding—you could even understand a hangman if you knew his background.

Her powerlessness flowed down her cheeks—too late, too late. The cooing of the doves sounded increasingly like mockery to her ears. Irrevocably too late. To escape from herself she raised the blinds and looked at the grey courtyard hiding behind them, the doves' domain. As she stared outside from behind the glass she recalled the memory Anna had wanted to share with her the previous evening, right at the very end. She saw herself, as vividly as though it had happened the day before, sitting on a coffin on the sofa together with her sister and tapping on the window with her shoes—a *tam tam* to demand that their mother make haste. She saw two pairs of sturdy legs, white socks, shoes with bows. They pattered exactly in time, as though together they had one pair of legs— not only to warn their mother but also to drown out the din of the strange voices behind them and in order to keep an unbearable reality at a distance. She looked sideways at Anna's blond head, her tightly closed lips were pursed and fierce eyes cast her a conspiratorial look.

Too late! Lotte let go of the blind. The door opened at that moment and the woman in the white overall, her personal angel of death, tiptoed in.

'Alas . . .'— she clasped her hands together—'they could not do any more for her. The heart, ah. We knew. . . . It was in her dossier that she had a weak heart and that we should not make her bath too hot. Do you know if she had family? Someone must organize her transport to Cologne and the funeral. . . . We don't know. . . . After all, you were her friend.'

'No,' said Lotte, straightening up. Her gaze fell on the bottles of mineral water and the stack of plastic beakers. Again she heard Anna asking in school French 'C'est permis . . . for us . . . to drink this water?' And again she heard herself replying: 'Yes, *das Wassser kön-nen Sie trinken.*'

'No,' she repeated, looking at the woman defiantly. 'I am . . . she is my sister.'